Illustration entitled "Study for Maximum Mass Permitted by the 1916 New York Zoning Law, Stage 4, 1922" was by Hugh Macomber Ferriss, an American architect, illustrator, and poet associated with exploring the psychological condition of modern urban life. A preeminent architectural draftsman of his time who through his moody chiaroscuro renderings of skyscrapers virtually invented the image of Gotham visitors came to the city to see and residents identified with so fondly. The illustration is used by permission.

Ordering Information: For quantity sales details and orders by U.S. trade bookstores and wholesalers, please contact Novabook Publishing at info1@novabook.us or 323-871-0889.

First published in the United States by Novabook Publishing 2020.
10 9 8 7 6 5 4 3 2 1

NOVABOOK

Novabook Publishing
Los Angeles
www.novabook.us

ISBN 978-0-9894896-8-3

THE LABYRINTH IN WINTER

a novel by

Michael Jeffery Blair

by Michael Jeffery Blair

CONTENTS

Sometimes the only thing left to hang onto

is the blade of a knife.

Chapter 1

The crimson rowing shell sliced the harlem river like a stiletto. Reflections of the city on its glassine surface were barely disturbed as he drew his knees up tight, racing forward, feathering the oars that hovered millimeters above the water, then cut into it again with a ferocious rhythm. The air was pristine and still as breath steamed out into the icy January morning. It had snowed in the night and the river ran black through the white over which people struggled against darkness.

In the distance were sirens and car horns and longings, the rumble and hum of traffic, the tangle of voices. He glided under bridges reaching over to the Manhattan side where commuters were just beginning to crowd up. A flock of wild cranes suddenly took off in a blue blaze of white water and headed south. Alabaster light peered through cracks in the clouds stroking the waves like paintbrushes of Pre-Raphaelite saints. Devlin focused through the chaos, fleeing against waves, straining every fiber to win because if he let up for a moment he would roll over in his round bottomed racing shell—like him designed to keep moving and never stop.

Rowing was his emblem; a spiritual connection gliding past

Swindlers Cove where the now vanished Sherman Creek had once met the river. "Sculler's Row" they had called it, once home to the city's legendary rowing clubs manned by the privileged sons of East Coast Brahmins: Atlanta, Nassau, Nonpareil, Wyanoke, First Bohemian, Harlem Rowing, Lone Star, Metropolitan, Dauntless and Union. Their boathouses had lined the shore and thousands of spectators celebrated the great regattas at clubhouses festooned with twinkling lights filled to overflowing with cheers and laughter. All that ended abruptly when a mysterious inferno swept the row in 1911 devouring the wooden structures and hundreds of handmade boats like matchsticks—the fact it was coincident with an aggressive planning commission push for "waterfront improvements" somehow went unnoticed. The last boathouse disappeared in 1978, ironically consumed by fire. Devlin sculled in solidarity with the dispossessed in the same blood level intensity he pursued freewheeling global capitalists who were giving new meaning to the words "wealth management." He wanted to eat the rich.

It was the Zen of it, he and the boat, like a single moving part, striving for the illusion of motionlessness; no jerking of the shell as he powered the oars, no telltale spray from catching carbon fiber tips, nothing that would betray the truth of human frailty; still a barrier he had yet to work through on the job, in the office, surrounded by other attorneys dedicated to big game in the commanding heights. There he had serious issues. The problem was that in only seeing numbers and patterns the human dimension was forgotten; perhaps that's why he entered public service as a Federal Securities and Exchange Commission Investigator and not the private sector. A necessary outlet for his rage. Because when the dust cleared, it was all about money and this was the only way he could seek retribution for everything he felt was unjust and out of balance.

On the shore, a black kid was running along Harlem River Drive the hood from his sweats covering his face. Strong and agile he bounded forward like some rutting, muscular gazelle defying all odds against survival, every eight or ten strides glancing over his shoulder across the glimmer in silent challenge exuding an unwavering certainty he could best the man gripping the oars. Devlin grimaced trying to ignore him, but put his back into it gaining speed and pushing his body until the pain radiating from his solar plexus felt sweet as he raced at the top of his form, gasping for breath, icy air stinging his lungs, feathering the oars without a ripple. He loved to tell them at the office how he beat the twenty-somethings on his morning ritual. Still the runner moved off as if pursued, but he wasn't worried yet and kept up the pace working out strategies in his head, sure that the kid would grow tired after sprinting so hard, positive he could overtake him a little further along—if he could endure the agony just enough to demonstrate the triumph of superior tactics. But it wasn't in the cards this frosty morning.

He heard the sound before anything; then came the sudden jolt. It broke into the zone where he had retreated blind to distractions—a thick, dense thud against the bow of the ultralight, carbon fiber racing shell. Now the whole boat rolled violently to the left clambering over the deadly semi submerged obstacle and by instinct he flattened one oar skimming the waves to brace himself while he turned the other wildly in the air to keep the narrow, rounded shell upright desperate not to fall in the freezing water. The one oar slammed the craft sideways throwing up a sheet of spray while he managed to dig the other in deep and stabilize cross current. Still rocking precariously, he took a calm, deep breath and at the same time a long stroke. He had to move to keep from rolling over. The boat wasn't designed to stop.

It was then, when he came around alone in the middle of the river, that he saw it. A man's body floating on its back staring up at him with lifeless blue eyes and now a gash across its chest from where the boat had hit it, a distinguished looking man. The fine suit he was wearing that drifted with the current like the arms of a willowy sea anemone must have cost two thousand dollars.

After he made the call it took the police forty minutes to reach him. In the still of the waiting there were tiny breaths of wind on the water as if selkies were deciding whether to keep the man or release him back into the world of the living. Death was ethereal; he retreated from the finality of it. All around the city boiled yet he sensed the eerie divide between earth and sky and circled the weightless body resolving to keep it from going under as a last gesture of humanity. By the time New York's finest pulled up with their sullen faces in their blue and white launch he had imagined a hundred scenarios about who the well dressed man floating in the Harlem River was. He watched as they caught hold of him with a gaffer's pole and hauled him up. The body flopped across the deck. Then Devlin Winthrop Wolfe shoved his ID at them.

"Didn't see him before ya hit him?"

"That's right."

"How fast would you say?"

"Maybe 14-16 knots?"

"How do you know?"

"There was a runner. Over there — on the drive."

"Running away?"

"No. Just a runner."

"Anybody else out here?"

"No. No one…"

*   *   *   *

An amber glow across an icy Hudson River reflected sunset. People stopped where they were to watch it anxious for the future. Snow flurries brushed concrete precipices and beat silently against glass and steel as they tumbled forming frozen eddies on the pavement far below. Traffic snarled. Breath frosted. Tempers roiled. It was the coldest winter most people could remember. So cold that snowflakes scattered like dust and didn't even melt in the full light of day and the river was frozen all the way across in some places. The arctic front had pouted restlessly since November gathering its forces in the far northern stretches on the shores of the Great Slave Lake. It had become a cause célèbre among academic meteorologists who had been observing dramatic shifts in aurora borealis patterns since autumn, and was debated interminably in blogs and scholarly journals and across a hundred university campuses. Exactly what the trigger was that sent the weather cascading down across the Eastern Seaboard was a mystery, but doubtless there had been a signal just like the drumming of raindrops awaken blooms in the spring. All natural things are connected, but men have forgotten how.

Bixby Endicott settled back in the luxurious, butter colored leather and fastened his seatbelt. After the call, he had a driver hurriedly wind his way to the airport from his compound at Northeast Harbor, Maine— long a quiet enclave of the rich and famous and the Grand Duchess of Social Register summer homes. The snow had let up as he rolled to a stop on the tarmac and then embarked for New York City in his Citation X, a sleek little number that could cruise faster than the speed of sound.

He was from a seeming timeless world: a realm of debutantes, clashing leisure wear, huge summer lawns always smelling of freshly cut grass and sprawling houses whose doors were left unlocked at night— living a highly discreet and circumscribed life, except behind drawn curtains where anything was OK short of bloodshed. There he was an addict, a player in the financial markets and a man with the conviction he was set apart by destiny to guide the great American experiment by reason of his ability to amass wealth. Although he wasn't the type to watch his hairline slowly recede as a long succession of cocktails eroded his wits, he yet clung to his membership in The Brahmin caste of New England—the harmless, inoffensive, untitled aristocracy.

Lift off shoved him back into the seat as they soared away from the rarified wooded inlets, sawtooth rocks streaming with seafoam and faux gothic manses whose bay windows peered off into the Atlantic. They rose above the polar clouds and stars flamed white hot beyond which only imagination lingered. He felt lightheaded even before the one drink of single malt scotch, which was all he had time for on the flight that took less than an hour. This elusive moment was the reason he bought the fastest civilian jet in the world; it was so swift, the experience so fleeting he would never tire of it and that alone was worth the price that gave his accountants apoplexy—the ephemeral newness he sought in all things. Bixby Endicott was a stocky figure who mysteriously remained fit without exercise as he hovered in that season somewhere between thirty-five and fifty, unless a casual game of tennis punctuated with daiquiris could be construed as a workout. His plain yet symmetrical face was a chiseled piece of Americana invoking confidence from the uninitiated of both sexes, which he was quick to take advantage of, under the spell of his Ivy League grin. "Just call me Bix…" he was fond of saying to disarm opposition. The helicopter from the airport landed on the roof just above the 52nd floor where his office was, incandescent Manhattan glittering at his feet. He hurried through the cold.

The call that had brought him into the city transcended everything else. "We're hemorrhaging money," the voice proclaimed blowing cold into the pit of his stomach as blackness opened up threatening to swallow him. It had all been flawless until now and the sheer brilliance of his technology had buoyed the financial industry with innovations so unexpected they disrupted the flow of events demarking everything as before him and after him. Nothing would ever be the same. The idea grew that he had found the formula perfectly describing how the market moves—the philosopher's stone of quantitative analysts, the utterly impossible—quants called it "Alpha," the truth that would lead to incalculable market riches. But it wasn't the money. It was never about the money. It was about huge egos. Money was only the indicator of what people wanted and how much that desire controlled their lives. It was a symbol of having gotten it right and the power he had over others because of it—so essentially it was all about the money, that object of universal desire. Now he sat before the array of flat screens struggling to understand the crisis; if it could be understood, if indeed there was a single error in the millions of lines of code that comprised the total value of the company, it had to be found. While in the periphery, in the menacing blackness another thought lingered and it was that he might have been wrong in the first place and if he had, his whole existence would vanish as if he never had been.

The Chief Technology Officer glided through a lobby so sumptuous it was as if conceived for Borgia princes. High heels clicked on marble floors butted against dark sapele wood veneer and polished granite that ran up two stories into the skylights tinged with copper oxide, which gave daytime a slight aqua glow. The slender Indian woman, Sanja Singhal, walked past a bored receptionist, kept after hours, who was picking at a slice of cold pizza and past priceless paintings in succession so huge they would have dwarfed a museum; here they were only accessories against the cavernous entrance to ENTEC, the trading name of Endicott Technologies. She, like all the other principal employees, was a scientist.

As a child, she was feared and ridiculed for her brilliance at all things technical and the shunning left her emotionally isolated despite growing to be a subtle beauty pursued by men who would never know her sweetness. Her consolation for the wilderness years was twin PhDs; one in mathematics, the other in computer science with a specialty in artificial intelligence and hundreds of companies vying to recruit her.

"Somebody is getting inside information on our sell transactions," Sanja said coolly.

Bixby was agitated. "Isn't that why we're paying millions to be in dark pools so we can trade invisibly? If I wanted everyone to know what we're doing, I'd put it on the New York fucking Times website!"

"Bid price drops so fast we can't even execute orders without bleeding money," she replied numb to his emotional outburst. "Even if we refuse bids, securities we hang onto are losing over fifty percent of their value once the market reacts."

"Fuck…! Security breaches?"

"Possible…" she crossed her legs luxuriously letting the ultramarine wool crepe slide across her body until it drooled with sensuousness. "We don't know yet, but frankly I doubt it."

"Networks check out?"

"No latency issues reported; none in the logs. Whatever the algorithm, it's running like a bat out of hell on crystal meth with a caffeine chaser"

"Do you believe the logic of the trading system is still true?" he asked in hushed confidence during a rare moment of vacillation as his ego flickered.

"We don't know," she paused, "but the one thing you can't teach a computer is intuition. Could be anything. My guess, a robot algorithm is pinging the incipient sell order and triggering a selloff before we can fully execute depressing the market price. Then whoever it is buys cheap, sells high. They win, we lose."

"We can't continue like this. Christ…if it leaks to the media…" wringing his hands, frustrated by her chilly intellect, infuriated by her suppressed emotions—barriers he felt compelled to overcome. "Confidence is all we have; it's just a game of confidence!"

"Yes. Oh, there's another thing you should know," she interjected with the pained shadow of a smile, "Guillaume Marchand told me something about ten days ago. I didn't think it important…until now. Last week, before the accident…he said he'd found an anomaly, something in the system—"

"What…?"

"I was waiting for clarification when…but it was urgent enough to tell me…and then…I still can't believe he's dead…only last week we were speaking about it…" She looked emotionless.

He winced. Bixby's conviction that coincidence was mathematically impossible reinforced a sudden, shocking, cathartic realization: someone was targeting ENTEC for extinction! First his quant ends up dead and now…the mere idea filled him with panic and set in motion a whirlwind of possibilities that made his head spin because no matter how much he had, he never felt secure. The precise amount of disruption that could send him over the edge tumbling free fall was an unknown, but always present threat. The firm was his creation, a breathing token and everything he cherished pivoted around it—even if he had created a monster that had become so complex neither he nor any other single person understood it all. It wasn't just the phenomenal success; it was the things he couldn't give up just yet, things too precious to lose.

He had started his career as a theoretical mathematician and prominent in his resume were stints for the Department of Defense and as a quantitative analyst for several Wall Street icons before he founded his own hedge fund and trading firm. A business based totally on algorithms and computerized investing. ENTEC was a company that specialized in high frequency trading, an extremely secretive discipline that nobody outside the industry, and few inside, truly understood: as if an alien invasion were in progress with the underlying goal of planned obsolescence of the human race—at least in the markets where programmatic trading was considered safer than the meddling of mere men. It was very hard for anyone to find out how HFT firms operated and that mystery was precisely their safeguard—until now. His employees were almost all PhDs—in mathematics, computer science, artificial intelligence and other scientific disciplines—because computers made all trades automatically from software programs comprised of robot algorithms— "algobots" that cruised financial networks seeking profits. "Rent seeking viruses," his enemies had said describing high frequency trading as "basically evil." Now, absorbing the shock of what was happening, watching the money bleed, he mulled over their names compiling a mental list of suspects behind the opening salvos of the algobot war and began planning his counterattack. There could be only one at the top.

Alone in his corner office he started the interminable process of trial and error rifling through infinite snippets of code testing each line's workability one at a time. A single glow bathed his face as he floated above the endless shimmer of Gotham and through the floor to ceiling glass imagined he could see all the way to the Hamptons where flying fish darted out in front of mahogany sailing skiffs splashing through the blue chop. Beneath him lay the four-hundred-year old infrastructure now supporting optical transmission networks that executed millions of transactions within nanoseconds and an ever evolving skyline containing a voracious population with the same human needs and desires people have always had. Some things never change. Inconceivable fortunes wafted through the cyberspace among the buyers and the sellers and the homeless and the toiling masses all infected with greed; the impetuous of capitalism.

He frowned, picked up the phone and dialed a number. "I can't make it tonight. Something has come up." A great wave of anxiety washed over him because of all the things he cherished the one he just had to cancel was the most personal of all.

Chapter 2

Only diehards drove themselves as indiscriminate snowflakes fell making already slippery streets treacherous. Everyone else took public transport or a taxi, but he had hired a limo to deliver them from confusion—one of those big black American affairs that nobody ever bought anymore—and conspired how to get reimbursed for it. Devlin had obtained scarce invitations for the most coveted political event of the season through an unknown grapevine of "connections." All he knew was the passes were worth a cool twenty-five hundred dollars apiece and rumor had it some tickets were going for up to forty thousand. "More than I make in a week," he quipped. Nobody laughed. The limo was for show; the mission was for blood.

She was an East Coast patrician who, when younger, everybody thought was pretty, mistaking healthy blonde sunburnt youth and athletic prowess for beauty. Now a glacial lawyer with the Justice Department, Veronica Wynwode had the beginnings of lines around the corners of her mouth and crow's feet at the corners of her eyes and wore lipstick that was too red perhaps confusing days of teasing and longing for the present. But her hair was still blonde and flaming and Devlin liked the spur-of-the-moment sex they shared and the way she handled herself in court, which earned his admiration since the law ruled him most of the time. It was unclear in any remaining moments exactly what drove him, and this caused serious introspection because he had learned early in the legal profession that when there was conflicting data, one side was wrong. Contradictions explained nothing; they were barriers to logic and so he dove into the future with blind faith hoping he would clear the water's edge.

In the bleak static after a case closed, he imagined whatever his reasons had been, they were now without value because in every triumph was an emptiness he couldn't fathom. These emotional catalysts were rare, and he always rebounded with verve and energy in a day or so, but the hollow feeling lingered as if a portent of a shipwreck yet to be. He called these episodes *twilights* and it was in one of these states he had met Veronica; was drawn into her resolute legal reasonings mistaking admiration for love and fell into the compulsive physical relationship that eased so much of his anxiety. But he still felt hollow, even in the aftermath of passion where the faint glow of light painted sex soaked bodies sprawled across damp white sheets.

They moved from the chaos of the streets up snow covered steps through the monumental limestone Beaux-Arts façade and entered another world. Here heroic lighting embraced the three saucer-shaped domes and eight dramatic arches springing from enormous masonry piers of The Great Hall of the Metropolitan Museum. They rose hundreds of feet above the aristocratic crowd already swirling glasses of overpriced wine under their noses. Just beneath was a continuous balcony with its own vaulted ceiling all in polished limestone where a small orchestra played "Pictures at an Exhibition" by Mussorgsky. Floral arrangements dotted the floor, some as high as twelve feet in explosions of color and form like jungle tableaus.

The neoclassical palace of art was so overwhelming he hadn't noticed the extra security for all the celebrities, politicians and glitterati rubbing elbows. Devlin was yanked aside and polite but surly men pressed him to explain the concealed weapon he always carried—found by metal detectors in a small holster tucked into the back of his trousers. It took fifteen minutes, Federal ID inspected all around and a call to the NYPD to verify his carry license before they begrudgingly let him pass.

"What was that all about?" Veronica frowned.

"Nothing," Devlin replied indignantly, "my watch lit up the metal detector." It was a habit he'd gotten into when the stakes reached celestial proportions—a good investment banker was now worth more than many small countries and could not be expected to roll over quietly.

Encircling the throng along three sides of the hall, under massive arched alcoves with darkened passageways leading to other parts of the museum, was a special exhibition of sale paintings for the cause. They waltzed past this dazzling mélange of color on the way to the wine bar like water drops across a waxed surface while calloused art auction veterans loomed making mental calculations of each one's resell value.

Devlin wanted a drink: he didn't like crowds.

"What's this?" he asked taking a sip from the glass with an impossibly thin stem.

"Chateau L'Eglise-Clinet," the man behind the bar droned, "spicy oak emerges as the wine sits with a hint of raspberries."

Taking another sip and nodding glibly, "Where is it from?"

"Pomerol. A region in southwest France," then noting the blank stare added sardonically, "it's a Bordeaux."

"Of course…" Moving off with Veronica he confided, "I know what a Bordeaux is, just not one that costs $75 a glass."

"Think of it as a political contribution."

"I'm a Democrat."

The annual ritual of new money attracted an eclectic array of sycophants, high rollers and social climbers all thrown together in a Republican fundraising cauldron. At the far end of the hall streaming above a small stage was a banner emblazoned with "American Voices," a sobriquet for the conservative super PAC sponsoring the event.

The rarified atmosphere of the room was saturated with the musk of the crowd; hundreds of scents heady and divine mingled with the smell of humans and alcohol and everyone talking while looking for someone else; middle aged socialites in low cut evening gowns trawled for amusing conversation leaving vapor trails of perfume. People huddled together as if seeking warmth in igloo like gatherings laughing too loudly, as cocktails took their toll raising the decibels in the limestone cavern until no one could be heard without shouting. But it was the grand sweep of it that got him, the restless haut monde moving in waves across the floor to the strings of the effervescent orchestra hovering above like a scene from the Belle Époque; from a time when an intoxicating lure of the limitless infused everything with life greater than what it natively possessed and people careened breakneck into all they did. While women flitted about like starlings on fire men strode and traded salvos with each other smiling in that self-assured misogynous way.

"It is imposing!" he said. "Isn't it grand?"

Veronica was chattering: not listening, "…and then I told him, you can't expect people to just take responsibility *automatically*…" she emphasized with exuberant disdain, "you've got to manage them! What an asshole…" she continued, anxious to make her stress vanish. "Know what he said? 'I *am* responsible!' Can you believe it? The guy that never shows up for teleconferences, that makes me wait around all weekend until he wants to work…what an asshole!"

"It's part of the job, isn't it?" Devlin sighed.

"Not one I want," sweeping blonde hair back off her forehead with a glare. He could still see the blue-eyed dynamo winning at tennis against boys with names like *Scooter* or *Chip* on courts of the grand houses of East Cost aristocrats. She had to mix up that blue blood, he thought, to keep from degenerating. Unlike him, she was hampered by good breeding.

"There's always corporate counsel. Nice office. Reasonable hours. All you have to do is defend the interests of fast food franchises or intellectual property rights of software developers or…"

She took a drink of wine. "Maybe that's what I want…" staring into the glass.

Narrowing his eyes with a little shake of his head. "Don't think so."

"I could work for some fat financial firm and check compliance all day."

"Never happen."

"What makes you so sure?"

"You're like me…you've got juice."

"So what if I do? I'm not like you. You're obsessed."

"Look, lots of things you do like about your job."

"Didn't think there were any," she shot back in mock surprise.

"Burning down criminals, that's what does it for you isn't it? How many times have you been ecstatic about winning a case? You're hooked…like me."

"Yea…maybe…"

"You're the one that takes on that load. You want it. Nobody expects you to do it."

"Who else will? He doesn't know what I do...nobody knows what I do."

"I do," he said touching her hand. "You do."

"Yea..."

"Life's a river. Sweeps you into the current; pretty soon you've gone too far. We're all there...except these..." looking around with animosity, "...these people of course." A *twilight* passed over him. "They've bought exemption from the human condition."

"Too far...guess I like you alright." Smiling, giving him a slight hug. "In a pinch..."

An older man stepped from the crowd; red cheeks, gray hair that needed trimming and an English cut suit. "Veronica!" He barked. "What-a-surprise!"

"Judge...!"

"I always took you to be one of those weak-kneed liberals. You know, bleeding..."

"This is my friend Devlin Wolfe. A Democrat with the SEC."

"Ahhh... 'It is not the creation of wealth that is wrong, but the love of money for its own sake.' Margret Thatcher...am I right?"

Devlin shook hands, but after a few moments of social banality dropped out entirely having just spotted a man across the room, the one he had come for, a very ordinary looking man, mid-forties, dark worsted suit, just slightly overweight with the patina of someone who has eaten too well for too long and the look of someone who never had to worry about survival. He seemed innocent enough next to his tony wife and teenage princess daughter who they had brought with them for the first time as a sort of a millennial substitute for a debutante ball.

"Oh look…" said the wife. "there's George." She waved in frantic little circles. "George! George! I don't think he sees us…"

"He sees us…" The husband replied under his breath with a hunted look then reaching out to shake hands suddenly all smiles, "Hi George."

A large man appeared as if a ship from the fog, his coat open to an expansive stomach and a glass in his hand full of half melted ice cubes. "Guess I don't need to ask how's the wife and kids?"

"Well…" the man smiled looking at his daughter, "it's a special night…" She retreated with a red flush. "Just got back from Florida and thought…well, you know…"

"I've got kids…"

"How is Madge?" asked the wife.

He pointed across the room. "She's over there. You know how excited she gets with these things. Shopping all week just to wear that black dress…women!"

"Very sexy. The price you pay—"

"Well, she was miffed I'd been at the office so much and then the poker tournament—"

"I heard about that…" the husband perking up. "you made out OK…"

"I don't believe in luck."

"Are you going to let me in on this, or is it some private man thing?"

"George won over a hundred thousand—"

"Accidently…"

"…he bet on a hand he didn't even look at."

"George!" the wife said reprovingly. "No wonder Madge went shopping."

"I don't believe in luck. You have the knack or you don't…" he grinned taking a swig of scotch, his sixty-thousand-dollar wristwatch glinting in the light. "And you," he turned toward the daughter, "what are your plans now that you're a young woman?"

"She's going to Yale or Columbia," interjected the wife, "they've both accepted her."

"Yale." The husband stated; no room for discussion.

"I want to be a lawyer," said the daughter.

"You're Yale alumni, right?"

"Yes," replied the husband.

"A big donor too…" the wife added with a sidelong glance.

"How could they refuse!"

"I've got a 3.95 GPA," she shot back, "and got 174 on the SATs!"

"Remarkable…" he patronized.

"Really, didn't need any help—"

"…outshines both of us." The daughter flushed red again wishing she was anywhere else than dying at the hands of her parents.

The crowd had reached its zenith. Whoever was coming had arrived; all caught up in the slipstream as music from the orchestra high in the balcony pierced the hearts of even those not listening, even those whose haunted memories kept them from feeling anything at all. The night was dark and legendary. Snowfall deluged the city that lay beneath its dreaming hand, spellbound, afraid to move for fear skyscrapers would shatter like ice crystals in the wind. One after another politicians arose on the platform at the end of the hall to reveal their vision of a conservative agenda filled with homilies and anecdotes from their unremarkable lives hoping to reach a common chord. But the audience were evangelists of the American way. A cynical and savvy lot: a been-there, done-that, street-smart lot and only applauded at points they envisioned more unbridled profits.

Suddenly, the room dimmed, and a single spotlight came up on the stage. Everything grew silent. The orchestra's bleeding strings drew out an Andalusian anthem filled with heartbreak and desire. Mirella Elderia appeared in a mass of tangled auburn curls: haughty, prancing through the light, a shawl thrown low across bare shoulders, possessing, demanding, taunting. With seductive eyes lowered, she unleashed the power of a haunting mezzo-soprano voice capturing everyone within hearing, gripping them, mesmerizing them. *L'amour est un oiseau rebelle, she sang, love is a rebel bird*...from the great "Habanera" aria of Bizet's "Carmen."

The crowd soared snowblind, enchanted by the French Gypsy on loan from the Met. Devlin, however, was on edge. His eyes darted looking for a sign, unable to join in the spirit of things. Everyone he saw was transfixed except two figures elbowing their way through the sea of bodies with a single mindedness verging on brutal indifference; what was wrong with that picture triggered shockwaves of adrenaline; he touched Veronica's arm for an instant and whispered in her ear, "I'll be right back." She patted his hand absently listening to the aria as it wove its tale of unrequited lust thinking how insensitive he was to interrupt such a moment. *L'oiseau que tu croyais surprendre Battit de l'aile et s'envola... The bird you thought you'd caught by surprise beats its wings and flies...*

Footsteps. Now he'd lost sight of them and scanned the crowd frantically for movement, looking for one ripple in an ocean of people. Then he saw the man with his wife and daughter again. They were standing portrait like, surrounded by their tribe, unconcerned if lives elsewhere were crumbling because at that moment they felt the world couldn't get at them and everything would be just fine. But like sharks the two others were closing in, so he shoved his way through the throng, jostling drinks and stepping on toes to get there first—he had to, otherwise it would all be for nothing. Then the unsuspecting couple hovered before him just as the man gave his daughter an affectionate hug.

"Chase Ellison?"

Startled, he looked at Devlin. "Yes…?"

Flashing his Federal ID as he had done with security earlier in the evening; "In a moment two men are going to come over here and I want to ensure you understand what's going to happen."

"What do you mean…?"

"You're going to be arrested and arraigned on Federal charges."

"Charges? What charges…?" the man demanded still absently hugging his daughter. "Hey, who the hell are you…?"

"What is it?" the wife asked anxiously.

"That will all be explained…my name is Devlin Wolfe. I'm an investigator with the SEC and…do you have a lawyer Mr. Ellison?"

The man's eyes darted around the room, "A lawyer…?"

"That's right. Unlike the people you fleeced, you have a right to an attorney you son of a bitch. You can afford one…" looking at the wife, "didn't you know your husband was a crook?"

The man lit out across the floor like an athlete shot from the starting line, careening through people, struggling to keep as low a profile as possible under the circumstances, tearing up all the distance he could between him and incarceration. "He's running!" Devlin barked at the first of the two FBI agents to arrive. The three men leapt in pursuit leaving the shattered wife cradling a sobbing daughter while the crowd swayed and parted and then knit together again, as wheat in the wind, as if nothing could interrupt them.

The terrified man found the nearest staircase and bounded up two polished stone steps at a time, puffing and wheezing, three Feds close on his heels. He wove quickly through the orchestra that played on undisturbed—the musicians assuming he was just one of the guests who had lost his bearings after too many martinis—while Mirella Elderia bared her soul under the hot lights on the stage below getting the crowd to feel like they were alive for once. Looking back from the balcony's edge and seeing only relentless pursuers, he scrambled onto the limestone baluster railing and teetered there precariously his wits numbed by the chase uncertain where to, what next. It was then, exactly at that moment someone below spotted him; the lone, distressed silhouette of a man dancing on the edge of oblivion; skittering across the railing balanced on four enormous columns a hundred and fifty feet above the marble mosaic floor; directly under the apex of a huge stone arch soaring two stories above making it all seem heroic. There was a scream. The music stopped. Everything was silent and the diva looked up from below with fierce indignation scintillating in her eyes, breathless at the peak of her performance, furious at the interruption.

"Daddy!" cried the daughter next to the crumbling wife…and after a brief moment during which everything that mattered flashed before his eyes he melted into the pursuers' hands.

The French gypsy on loan from the Met for the night picked up the corner of her skirt and held it hands on hips, arching her back and lowering her head until she was peering out from under dark brooding brows and then with a fiery look of evil delight let loose her song again in full sounding fury as if there had been no intrusion. *Mais, si je t'aime Si je t'aime, prends garde à toi !* She belted out filling the entire hall with her sorceress voice…*but if I love you, if I love you, then beware!*

Later, after the man had been taken into custody and the restless mingling of the hall resumed, albeit now abuzz over the ignominy of the pinched guest, one of the agents spoke to him.

"You know that body you found floating in the Harlem?"

"Yea…?"

"He was one of you guys."

"What do you mean…?"

"A computer analyst. A French quant. Turns out he works for the Paris office of Endicott Technologies. I thought you should know…maybe something in it."

"What makes you think so?"

"Just that he was one of you guys…been here less than a year, just bought a place in Larchmont overlooking the harbor. Seven million and change. Wife's an artist…blonde, Dutch, body like a porn star…has an exhibition over in SoHo…he was stabbed. Too much money in that business not to be connected."

"Murdered huh…didn't think he got there by accident."

"We haven't decided if he was pushed or keeled over and fell, but that's not all… someone burned his house to the ground at the same time he was being disposed of on the Upper East Side. And his wife's missing. Vanished. Even her gallery hasn't heard from her."

All of a sudden, he was consumed with thoughts of conspiracy; what might be at stake, who stood to gain and why the Frenchman? When Devlin finally found Veronica, she was rushing out to the entrance.

"If I had known what you were up to…!"

"Whe're you going?"

"…how could you!"

"What? That rich fuck will be out on bail in an hour…!"

"The daughter…the wife…you destroyed them!"

"Where are you going? What does it matter, they're part…c'mon. I'll take you home."

"No." she stated coldly. "I'll take a taxi."

"Don't be that way…"

The last he saw of her was the long black coat sweeping across her bare white legs with the night gusts and her wild hair come undone that she pushed back with her hand as she hailed a cab. "I don't want to see you again!" she yelled back at him closing the door. "It's become all numbers and patterns…you've lost your humanity!"

Chapter 3

Eidolons travel in the night: they streak above the cirrus clouds between where humans walk and phantoms linger, where millions of voices are all talking all at once, where one misstep meant he would be lost. Asleep, the city became a place of illusion, became ephemeral losing its grimy bricks and crushing substance revealing a parallel world where poverty, brutality and defeat were overcome by thoughts and wishes alone, leaving a mystery as to why all things spiritual were portrayed as dark and fearsome because in his slumber they were not. Was there truth in the old tales that seemed instinctual at birth or was something being hidden, some exit point from the human condition no one was supposed to know about?

It left a sort of hunger in him when he awoke. But all Bixby Endecott knew was if he didn't get there first, someone else would and he hated the very idea of being under anybody's thumb.

From his townhouse against the sky he had a panoramic view of the full green stripe of Central Park. It was an investment he had been advised to make because the celebrated Finnish architect who designed it was on a meteoric rise since the buildings he spawned in Abu Dhabi had received critical acclaim. Now the man's every doodle was touted as genius and whole editorial sections in architectural folios were set aside to dissect his tossed-out sketches, urbane city magazines debating his inner meanings, clients paying through the nose for all this heightened brand awareness. The structure was organic and its shell was composed of concentric asymmetrical layers of translucent metal that reflected light like pearls with a faint rainbow hue. Never willing to pass up a killing, he had bought a whole floor and subleased all but his opulent apartments.

Weeks had passed since he missed the fundraiser for American Voices. There had been phone calls, inquiries; "Was he OK? Anything wrong?" Pandering phone calls, introverting questions, but he was used to it. When you've got money, you've got lots of …besides…he was the prime mover behind financing the super PAC, idealists depended on him to butter their bread; not that he didn't hold deep political convictions. If that were true, there would be no super PAC and they could just eat their reactionary brioche dry. He had other problems. Though he had managed to temporarily staunch the loss of money with new algorithms, he felt violated and under attack and he didn't like it. He didn't like it at all.

Sun danced through the wall of glass that cocooned his apartments. Outside the pearlescent metal sheath hung low and askew across one corner like a jaunty Finnish hat, frost just beginning to melt off its surface. It was a bone chill day with a clear sky deep blue far across the Atlantic. Traffic wrestled at all hours like muscular serpents undulating far below except for a brief interval just after 4am when the most suicides occurred and the most babies were born. Everything smelled new like leather and lacquer and furniture polish—the slight odors that had become his constant companions and followed him through the hive of environments he moved daily shielding him from the real. His ears popped as the elevator plunged thirty stories to the parking level below the street and even there the smell of new cars greeted him just like the showroom where he had purchased the Rolls Royce Drophead coupe at nearly half a million dollars. Inside he hardly felt the road, reclining on hand finished hides magically crafted into luxurious seats that cost more per square foot than the average family of four made in a month. Conditioned air drifted languorously from hidden ducts, its sweetness masking the stench of unclaimed garbage from the city's restaurants, closed only hours earlier, and noxious exhaust fumes from Transit Authority buses. Newness engulfed him. It defined him. Anything that showed wear was replaced.

He drove around the park past his favorite breakfast place, a lurking ground for writers and aspiring celebrities, with the tinge of excitement he always felt when he brushed the art world: like being inexorably wrenched inside a black hole by god-like gravity. Creation was that way, a gaping maw of unruly energy that did not obey the rules. His closest taste of it was programming robotic algorithms that cruised the financial networks with a set of hair triggers sending buy or sell orders. Art spoke of deeper unknown rivers. He pulled into a subterranean lot and was whisked up inside the complex to the general manager's office of the Metropolitan Opera where everything was black and white except the polished concrete floor and a huge eggplant carpet centered on it—all the art on the walls made him feel uneasy from the moment he walked into the room.

"You're the only one I would get up this early for," the tall elegant woman in a perfectly draped black suit gushed. "Mimosa? Bloody Mary?"

"Too early," he replied immune to servile flattery. Bixby had been a guest here many times, often when it was crowded with people under dimmed lights and wine was splashing in crystal goblets hobnobbing with others of his ilk, but not exactly of the same breed because while they were merely donors he was a financial impresario and the Met's greatest angel. Immense wealth had ingratiated him into the alien world of opera where he installed himself as a centerpiece propped up by fawning hands.

"I'll have one then if you don't mind…" a hint of a frown, "I was here 'till three…"

He watched Analetta move with studied grace as an actress upon a stage, private yet revealing, never overstepping the fourth wall. He perceived clues to her unspoken age from the lines on her face and the bones showing on her hands where the skin was beginning to grow thin and though at a distance she appeared timeless, he was somehow surprised it didn't hold up on close inspection. There was darkness just beneath the eyes that betrayed a crumbling infrastructure behind the public bon vivant that made him ponder whether a woman should be inspected too searchingly because it is in their genes to be ethereal and wild. She was a work of art, a dynamic spirit always on, who could change instantly from the chore of administration to the blinding visions of creation as she nurtured the repertoire the house was renowned for. Her flame burned bright.

"There must be some way."

"She will never come."

"I just can't accept that."

"Artists are mercurial beings. Frankly I don't understand it myself. I've extended every offer—"

"I've heard that she's…"

"Yes," her look became distant, "it's true. She's remarkable, truly a prodigy. Many say she surpasses La Divina, Callas herself and who knows…she is so young…a terrifying intensity, a burning sense of theater."

"We must have her!"

"I can't see it right now."

* * * *

He only knew her as Analetta and had never heard her called by any other name. Never seen any other reference in the volumes of press devoted to her as if her surname was a closely guarded secret adding to the mystery of Analetta, grand dame of the Met.

He made her acquaintance only by chance. It had been one of those coincidences that exposes the transparent nature of reality; an event that was not supposed to happen. One summer at Northeast Harbor when the fireflies were out in number, on a rare weekend far from the city just as his firm began to see real results after years of chasing theorems, he had decided to take some time to remember who he really was. Like rain swollen rivers, torrents of money had swept into accounts and the earnings from interest alone were too indecent to mention in public: the company reaping unprecedented profits all the while downsizing staff as automation reduced the need for anything human. It left Bixby Endicott in a fragile conflicted state, threatening to shatter at the core, struggling to be a calm observer of his life obliterating in the Jetstream.

When she swept across the summer lawn that day like *Our Lady of The Grasses,* he first noticed her blood red fingernails. He watched as people were drawn into her mysterious umbra mesmerized by some hidden attraction as she descended amongst them an enigma: seemingly at home in the banal social flurry yet with a tempest churning in her. She glided with grace among the elite and the common treating everyone as equals: they sloshing drinks, talking and laughing too loudly; she quickly ingratiating herself and enduring many unsolicited hugs and kisses. Compared to her, his social graces were reduced to being a target at fundraisers like a piñata stuffed with hundred dollar bills. In those instances, he was an all-star; but here it didn't seem to matter.

"What is your secret?" he had asked handing her a frosted strawberry mango daiquiri as she was composing herself between conversations.

"Secret?" she accepted the tall cool drink with her long gentle fingers and gracefully sipped it leaving a blood red lipstick mark on the glass.

"I can't see how anybody could endure so many hugs in one afternoon."

"Don't you like people Mr.…?"

"Bixby Endecott…just call me Bix."

"Is this a peace offering…Bix?"

"More tribute. You seem to have all the graces I lack."

"How do you embellish life then?"

"Finance. I run a hedge fund…couple of them actually. A small Wall Street firm."

"That means you have money I guess—" she said.

"Do you live on the island?"

"No…I live in Manhattan."

"You're lucky then."

"Why would you say that?"

"It's dangerous. Disastrous blaze once you know."

"Really…a fire. When was it?"

"Once," he said. "when it was a grand place. When families on the 'Social Register' built their mansions on Frenchman's bay, and when there were five great hotels—until '47 when fire swept the island.

They think it started in the cranberry bogs, took out sixty-seven majestic summer homes on millionaires' row, a couple hundred other houses plus leveled the five hotels to the ground. Two thousand people were evacuated through the burning forest—seven hundred cars pelted by sparks, flames roaring overhead and glancing off their hoods. Can you imagine? Burned for a month. Finally blew itself out in a gigantic fireball over the ocean; even after the rains and snow it still smoldered for weeks underground."

"I am lucky," she replied.

"Like I said."

After that first encounter, he did not see her again for a long time. Summer turned brittle and floated from the trees without him noticing, whitecaps secretly appeared on the sound and winter darkened the sky making it more translucent through which the greater universe could be perceived. Light retreated earlier and earlier from intense days spent inside. Only the hawk like chill of the wind touched him as he rushed between some building and a waiting car. Within this matrix only his smartphone kept him fully informed, and from its cue he pinpointed himself in time, located his position in the celestial whirlwind and relied on it heavily for voice navigation while driving to tell him where to turn and when to stop on streets where he had been at home since childhood. It all fit, somehow unquestioningly, into the new order of evolution as technology split his personality in two with half in real life and the other an avatar roaming cyberspace like a fish pressed against a glass aquarium wall desperately seeking an egress point that does not exist.

It was only by chance that he saw her picture. A feature in a magazine about "The acclaimed general manager…" of the Metropolitan Opera: there she stood austere and statuesque, possessed of an elegant beauty, accented by ethnic silver bracelets with a textured, gray, lamb's wool scarf wrapped over a simple black dress. It was then he realized how self-centered he had been never even asking about her life, assuming something about her that was in reality a figment and the thought festered, caused him to lose sleep and made him feel inadequate; disturbed by the fact he had not perceived the quality in her when she had been close enough to touch.

In penance, he walked into the darkened hall already filled with murmurs, hushed whispers and furtive glances, a lone voyager in a sea of people. The strangeness made it a supreme act of contrition as he made his way to a seat in the center of the tenth-row orchestra at the Metropolitan Opera on a sold-out Saturday night performance of "Tristan und Isolde," Wagner's great monument to love and death. Bixby Endicott was a blank canvas: he had never been to an opera; never listened to more than a few minutes of a performance; knew none of the names, none of the legends, none of the magnificent god-like works that transcended the human condition with immutable almost unendurable beauty, winnowing out the last exquisite emotion from anyone alive whether they had it in them or not. Lights dimmed. Darkness fell. Silence swept the audience.

Somewhere in the distances were children running: yelling, small and dirty, feet hitting the pavement raising miniature clouds of dust as they struggled through the sweating day; tears streaming down little cheeks, aching and learning to live; kicking and fighting and squirming, raising hell wherever they could, protesting for as long as they could until inevitably all were driven down into the depths of the mundane existence the multitudes were destined to, slipping year after year into a deeper apathy. He had run that gauntlet with all the rest; but how could he have missed it? The assumption had always been present that he was blessed, that he had made it and somehow had risen from the abyss that put a ceiling on other men's achievements; but how could he have missed it? Now he sat transfixed, weeping like some teenage girl at the impossible beauty, at the unattainable grasped, at the infinite realized. How could he have missed it?

In the darkness, he trembled: he the charismatic business icon, maker of fortunes, forger of deals, trembled at something profound enough to move him yet that could not be touched. As he listened to the lush orchestral "Liebestod" aria of the final act, he came to realize music had never laid bare inner life like this before, he had not imagined the extent to which it alone could embody the human condition and now it rose in his mind above all other arts. Transfixed, he watched love doomed from the beginning find its fulfillment in death; Isolde sinking down with the vast wave of the world's breath under luminous violins. The last ecstatic notes fading into an extraordinary chord finally resolved by oboes, bassoons and English horns and it left him haunted by the unexplainable, primal nature of love.

From that moment he began a double life. Whereas he was devoted to amassing wealth, he pledged a portion of that wealth to support this extraordinary universe he had discovered so late, that had shocked him into realizing something else shared a common space with the struggling multitude not as what they are, but as what they could be; something unseen, something wonderful. At first, the opera was bestowed with small endowments from an anonymous donor; finally becoming a benediction, then a consecration from the most prodigal angel the company had ever known. The lavish donations astonished even the most embattled fundraisers who had taken advanced degrees in nonprofit management from elite Ivy League schools and thought they had seen everything. When he finally went public, he became an instant celebrity. At last he met Analetta again in the austere office where they stood together now; it was an off evening when he entered her domain absolved of sin after true penance with a confident grin on his chiseled face and without a word she handed him a frosted strawberry mango daiquiri.

*   *   *   *

"Perhaps if I spoke to her—" Bixby stood in frustration. No was something he did not understand, just part of the programming process that eventually the proper algorithm, the smart snippet would resolve.

"Why is this so damned important? She suffers from artistic temperament!" With a deep breath Analetta calmed to her normal volcanic intensity. "We have the greatest talent in the world...artists vie for our attention; many are dying to work with us—"

"But not Revenia."

"Not Revenia. We don't need her! She's arrogant. Too young. Too spoiled. A diva in the worst sense." Walking to the window and staring absently at the Empire hotel across the street. "I have created one of the greatest companies on earth without her."

"Think fundamental economics; the law of diminishing returns. You cannot move into the future without innovation—it's the driver of everything—that means new blood, artists who aren't handicapped by fixed ideas and preconceptions of the 'how-it's-supposed-to-be,' those who can create something undiscovered. Otherwise, everything stagnates... it's inevitable...always a time when returns on investment are no longer viable: you just can't get out of it what you put into it no matter how good it is. We all have to give it up at some point and move on. Only the weak give up and stay. I think she's important, a Caravaggio like figure, a catalyst...I think people will flock to see her and I think it will put us on the leading edge of art—and be good box office."

"Ahhh…art! You should have told me sooner! I lack experience in these things!"

"Analetta…" he patronized, "you can do anything. I know you can."

"May be true…but someone has to be the gatekeeper and guard the criteria of what will and what will not be on the Metropolitan Opera stage—despite what the unions say."

"From what I know, opera has always needed patrons; never been able to support itself. Art needs an audience to exist—"

"I have offered her more money than our principal soprano and was dismissed! I was told she's not interested in money…told…by some god-dammed flesh peddling agent's secretary! Do they think this is a carnival? Midwest summer stock? Times Square buskers—?"

"I'll speak to her. You have a declining box office, rising labor costs, a growing reliance on donors and heavy spending from the endowment… didn't you open negotiations recently by asking the unions to accept pay cuts?"

"She won't see you. Won't even record in a studio; they have to bring all that damned equipment into…can you imagine dragging it through *le Grand Foyer* at the *Palais Garnier* and scratching those seventeenth century floors the French government pours so much damn money into: everything comes from the French state: huge permanent staff, an orchestra of a hundred and seventy, a chorus of a hundred and ten, a corps de ballet of— "

"You have me."

"She has the Opéra National de Paris. She will not leave it, perhaps because she is French—no one knows why—she has never performed anywhere else. No one can get her to leave Paris."

Folded in the theater's embrace, past the ancient wooden stairs that lay against a time blackened stone wall where generations of stagehands have scrawled their names in chalk, two figures struggled with their demons half hidden by darkness. Their music lifted up on wings above the saddened footlights; past the cluttered wall of spots and fills and colored gels running three stories up; to the stratospheric plank walks of the gantry a hundred and forty eight feet above the stage where ill-tempered stagehands jostled equipment, wires and ballast for curtains and scenery; then further still past rafters and a metal walkway to the majestic crowning dome, the secret beehives and the statue of Apollo with its golden lyre, to the night sky beneath which the Palais Garnier lay in splendor: a palace of mirrors, gilt and lush. Twelve Paris opera houses had come before it, eleven had gone up in flames, which is why the only audience this late night were the staff of melancholy firefighters employed full time just to keep watch.

She stood wraith like by the grand piano as she sang; an elegant, ethereal yet dark creature whose angelic voice was indescribable: somewhere between a true mezzo and a dramatic soprano embodying the finest qualities of both. Since a child, she had been a prodigy. Her singing was so resourceful and multi-dimensional that many, many great teachers had paled before the girl, collapsing into a self-abnegation, reevaluating their inner grasp of music and when fumbling for words to describe her finding them inexpressible. Breathtaking, marvelous, wonderful, staggering, amazing…the reviewers, too, struggled with language, but confirmed she was an impossibly singular phenomenon that occurs in art only at rare points winding through the centuries, points that no one questions, no one inspects too closely for fear they may vanish and never come again. Despite her youth, she was an eternal presence in the world of opera and the company who possessed her knew they were blessed beyond price, so nobody ever, ever questioned her past and she never, never spoke of it.

Rumors materialized though, in small jealous minds, that she was the product of a tryst between a reclusive French industrialist and a sensual cabaret dancer in Marseille—later found dead under mysterious circumstances. After a hush-hush inquest, so the story went, the child was quietly folded into the family and as soon as she was old enough sent away to private school in Austria. Everyone thought it sensible. Her father could trace his ancestry into antiquity—to the Cotentin Peninsula in Normandy—the Havilland family who derived its surname from a fortress situated on a river, three flights of an arrow above Saire Point at a very remote period. The family had been there even before the Norsemen overran Paris and stole all the tin roofs sailing away with them up the Seine. But whatever darkness swirled around her, the mystery of her voice enraptured all and that was enough. Aloof. Impenetrable. Unfathomable. No one really knew her; so, no one would have suspected she was possessed of a terrible secret.

Revenia de Havilland's eyes were filled with a desperate intensity as she struggled with the impossibly elusive melody and the unattainably deep emotions never meant for mere humans; eyes that frightened and thrilled the young Italian pianist to fits of brilliance making him sweat in the cool empty night theater. Though only practice, in the passion of the moment it was all or nothing. She trembled on the edge of the possible wringing an unendurable beauty out of the concluding aria of Verdi's "Requiem," the sparse crew of firemen stopping whatever they were doing wherever they were in the great hall frozen in time. Janitors and cleaning girls, stage hands who had worked there forty years and could remember Callas well, all bewitched, all listening to the sound of heaven.

She slipped out the huge metal door backstage unnoticed into the cold early hours. Footsteps etched in stillness. It had rained, but now a few snowflakes fell and in places the wet street had frozen over and her reflection danced across them in staccato shimmering flashes, but there was no shadow, no shadow anywhere. In the City of Light, named for the street lamps that had been continuously burning since 1667, under remnants of the Belle Epoch whose luminance had given safe passage all through the years, the lithe flitting figure cast no shadow whatsoever. It was that which gave her away, because a malevolent presence had been waiting in the darkness and took up pursuit as soon as she had appeared. Seemingly unaware, Revenia hurried along the deserted streets anxious for a taxi to deliver her from the night to her apartments, fearing it may not come and resigned to make her way on foot. Down the Rue Scribe her breath frosting the air with only a few cars passing, her pursuer biding time, slowly gaining ground, plotting points where light was weakest; but if circumstances demanded, he was prepared for the ultimate sacrifice.

The young diva disappeared into the Paris Le Grand Hotel brasserie—doors left ajar by the afterhours cleaning crew. He rushed into the shaded room like a waft of chilled dark smoke with violent eyes piercing shadows, seeking prey, but there was none. Nothing moved. All was still. One light shined from the kitchen where sounds of the brigade de cuisine preparing things for the next day echoed; but when he threw open the swinging door everyone fell silent, the graveyard staff looked up surprised, an aura of innocence and shock told him at once she had not passed through, told him she had vanished.

IV | Chapter 4

When he first walked out of the double doors marked "medical personnel only" with that dour look on his face, the doctor had offered up a hatful of Latin names, impenetrable explanations and opinions divined from academic learning; but Devlin knew his father had died of failure. The spirit had simply dissipated before his time with the atrophy of uselessness. After a long succession of jobs—none of which he held for long complaining that none suited his intellect and therefore never right from the start—he struggled in vain to find work forever blaming the lack of a university degree. It had all been fine until technology reared its maw and devoured whole segments of industry spewing obsolescence and unemployment in its aftermath. Then no one cared what his experience was or what he'd accomplished or what his potential might be. He never worked again. Afterwards, his mother struggled. Her pay was eaten away by attrition; a rising cost of living set against stagnant wages. The firm she had been with for 25-years went bankrupt from incompetent management and inflated executive compensation packages sending real estate prices plummeting and causing exodus en masse from the small Midwest town built around the one large factory.

People left in ruins. Her savings were quickly spent on living expenses. Her retirement vanished through scam investments and bad business at the commanding heights on Wall Street. Her house lost 85% of its value and was repossessed by an out of state bank that had bought the bad paper as a derivative. He was only ten.

From this bruised youth, he had one stable idea that had stuck with him; money is the root, the wellspring and the one thing he desired above everything else. So, he was not like other children: studied with a vengeance, had no friends, grew tired of being told he was mature for his age and believed implicitly in himself, which he camouflaged with a disarming Ivy League grin. He worked his way through school where he gravitated toward being an economist because it seemed only natural, as the study of money. First came his bachelor's from NYU in economics, but even before finishing he knew all real money was made with algorithms. It was the age of algorithms and "bots"—old-style economists and traders hated the "quants," as they called *Quantitive Analysts*, but they controlled all the markets. In some subliminal way, he came to view them as responsible for all the bad that had happened to his family, and in a broader sense everyone's family, so he changed course and earned a Juris Doctorate focusing on financial law, then a masters in computer science with his thesis on complex economic models—from the University of Chicago, ironically home of conservative Nobel laureate Milton Friedman; the poster child of self-reliance. By this time, he had serious issues and when he passed the bar, took a job with the Securities and Exchange Commission perhaps feeling there he could legally met out vengeance. It was the only way to vent his moral rage that seemed to grow with the scarcity of anything spiritual in his life—like now with Veronica refused him the relationship he had grown dependent on.

Her reaction was a mystery. He had left messages, sent notes and letters and emails without any response at all, and so drifted in flames now that she had cut him loose. The burning singed him, and the smoldering denied him sleep, those wakeful hours filled with bitter self-recriminations. It had all started out so differently, so full of emotion and brightness and promise with neither of them wanting anything of the other, until some elusive desire to fulfill a hunger entered in. It would never have occurred to him before, only on sleepless nights do people consider these things, these hidden meanings. They were like echoes that tainted his views on everything now, and caused him to feel hopeless, trying to make it alright, wishing he could just let it go, but couldn't. He missed the feel of her warm body loving his caress.

*   *   *   *

"Devlin," the voice on his cell announced.

"Yea... Thierry? You know it's only six a.m.?"

"I wake you?"

"No...I'm down at the docks, having coffee, couldn't sleep—can't sleep..."

"Pick you up in fifteen minutes—"

"Wait! I have to be at the—" but he had already hung up.

He justified getting in the car with the rationalization that the Zen of the open road would smooth out the tired ragged edges left over from not sleeping and be a good thing, make him more productive, make the darkness less pronounced. So, he just went with it, sat back in the unmarked police cruiser with the shotgun bolted to the center divider trying not to think about showing up hours late at the office with an as yet undecided alibi. Twenty minutes later he was heading north out of

Manhattan on Interstate 95, holding a tall steaming coffee in a thick paper cup with a corrugated band around it so his fingers wouldn't get burned, listening to the traffic horns and eighteen wheelers going way past the limit putting everyone's life at risk and starting to question the prediction of a "thirty-minute drive."

"In normal traffic…" Thierry Reynard was a cop, "normal, this is rush hour. No one can predict rush hour."

"What is it? What is it you want to show me so badly?"

An hour and twenty minutes of chitchat later they turned off heading toward Larchmont Harbor and soon were cruising down roads with no signs or sidewalks where the real estate was so exclusive houses couldn't even be seen, only walls of trees and hedges. Bastions of green through which winding drives, sometimes gated, offered an egress point from the real into the world of endless lawns and countrified Tudor mansions, butting up against the Long Island sound with sweeping breathless views of the harbor and beyond the Atlantic: immaculate historic properties that looked out across huge private yards bounded by hand hewn stone walls against which the sea and loam relentlessly mingled and over which private docks embraced sleek sailing vessels lightly secured against the tide as if tying them too tightly would break their spirit. An aura of carelessness mixed with perfection gave the neighborhood an insouciant prodigal feel, as if there was so much money any conceivable loss would go unnoticed and anything could be replaced because price was just not a consideration. It was that impression that had finally brought Devlin fully into the morning as if he had just awakened from a dreamless sleep. He took another sip of coffee, but it was cold.

Thierry stood on a charred mound of debris quietly gazing out over the acre of grass to the waterfront where a few empty sailboats bobbed and beyond which Long Island sound loomed with rolling gray thunderheads. Mist in the distance obscured the horizon line making one seamless vista from earth to sky.

"I could live like this," he said, "I could live like this real easily."

"What the hell...?" Devlin exclaimed.

"This house was designed by architect Walter Karl Pleuthner in the 1920's using salvaged historic materials," Thierry kicked up some burnt wood pieces. "I read it at the real estate office. It had six bedrooms and seven and a half baths; oak-paneled vestibule with original stained-glass windows; a grand reception foyer with sandstone fireplace and another in the living room made of polished granite; dining room separated from a sitting area by early 20th-century, Art Nouveau, wrought-iron gates and a master suite with marble bath...who wouldn't want to live here? 30-minutes from Manhattan...give or take during rush hour—"

"What happened?"

"It's the French quant's house. The one you found floating in the river face up."

He heard the trees rustle as wind gently ran its fingers through the leaves and a bird sounded with a nut like warble answered in kind from further off. The chill of the water knifed through his thin wool coat. That morning came back to him, the feel of the oars in his hands, the black kid running on Harlem River Drive and for some reason he thought of all the departed souls all swirling in a maelstrom of unfinished business, and the turmoil of mortality continually at war with the tranquility of death pulling him into the conflict.

"Cost him seven fucking million just two months ago—only been in the country for six. Makes me wonder about all that money: where does it come from, where does it all go...who's got it? How can anyone be that valuable...? So much wealth...I don't believe anyone can do it legally."

"It's a mystery, isn't it?" Devlin said.

"Something else going on here that I don't know about because I'm…just regular, normal, an outsider. I can't even think with seven million dollars; I'm stonewalled, and I don't like it!"

"Doesn't make sense, never has…nothing's based on…not the importance of something that determines price, not merit, not social good; it's what gets peoples' attention. They put their money where their attention is. People don't seem to have any moral, religious or ethical constraints on profit. It's the hidden law—guess that's why I exist, to find weaknesses, make them accountable to everyone else that's trying to survive."

"He was one of you guys."

"Yea—"

"I need help on this one."

"That's not how it works."

"Look around! Place was probably still burning when you found him in the Harlem!"

"Located the wife yet?"

"No," the cop frowned, looking down. "Vanished with the house. For all we know she's dead too. Has a show in SoHo opening in a couple days…probably make a killing…you know, 'deceased artist,'" he kicked at the charred wood again. "Her dealer was drooling at the idea."

"What is it you want?"

"Endecott Technologies," he said in a low cold voice. "Every time someone tries to explain what they do I get sleepy, but the Frenchman is the key, that I know. Too much fucking money for any of this to be coincidence. Something's dirty. I need someone that speaks the language."

"That's not how it works."

* * * *

The night gallery was an explosion of light and iridescent color on the cold, rain slick street with hundred-year-old bricks glistening in the moonlight. Shades of icy jazz drifted out of open doors. Sophisticates glided through the mélange of people making an appearance on their way somewhere else; to some hip, trendy, new restaurant only the initiated knew where they would end up spending six hundred dollars a plate for Japanese food the ingredients of which they couldn't identify. Eyes darted around trying for connections, following secret mating protocols innate to humans who can decipherer thousands of subtle signals in milliseconds like praying mantises. Devlin appeared uncomfortable at the entrance, an advance scout observing the social landscape as if for danger, a stranger afraid to reveal himself and seeking anonymity then settling for hiding in plain sight like an alien who had lost his way.

He joined the crowd meandering in groups, talking quietly as they scanned the room for diversions and staring at paintings with the look people get when they're computing the half-life of stars in distant galaxies. Snatching up a glass of Chablis from a long table covered with a white cloth he tossed it down like a shot and then grabbed another. Across a stark floor of polished concrete, he watched everyone move as fleeting impressions formed in his mind of who they might be.

"Are you a collector?" A young woman with a severe blond haircut and flawless ivory skin inquired. Her exquisite painted lips and tight black dress impressed him: the left side of which contrasted with a bold, white, geometric pattern on the right.

"No, a lawyer."

"Well, I won't hold it against you…the paintings are numbered," she smiled. "Please, look around…maybe we can make collector of

you—everyone can use a little padding to his nest egg. Lieke Marchand
is the artist to own right now."

"You're advising me they're good investments?"

"Good is relative—but if she really is….prices are set by the market
more than by desire; unfortunately you can only find out what they're
worth after you buy them…sometimes you win, sometimes… oh, guess
I shouldn't be telling you that…" She cracked a grin and relented, if only
slightly. "Work is valuated compared against other work…the art market
is funny, tends to be thought of as a material thing, but it's more a living
thing. I suppose it's a lot like a jury—can't ever tell what it will do—"

"I'm not trial law—"

"…the slightest thing can sway the outcome."

"Such as."

"Some mystery…when Warhol got shot prices skyrocketed."

"Did the artist get— "

"Neo Ex."

"What's that?"

"Neo Expressionism. It's her style, part of that movement, it all sort
of fits in when you consider what happened."

"What?"

"Lieke Marchand disappeared. Vanished. Yes, yes I know…it may
just be a publicity stunt to inflate prices for her work…but what if it isn't?
This may be her last show. Imagine…?"

"…good investment."

"A steal. Paintings are numbered. If you see something that strikes
you, let me know and I'll give you a good price," she said sashaying off
seeking more willing prey.

The paintings unnerved him, made him feel he had become too
fixed on the things in life he could not change and had mislaid his

dreams. The artist somehow knew they were missing. He wondered about this quant's wife as he looked at her art, the missing blonde, the enigmatic Dutch artist who had everything money could buy yet spoke this elusive language of spirits. Was she dead too? After a few moments, he returned to earth, tossed down another Chablis and noticed all the available women in gliding through the crowd. They looked at him with sad, excited eyes, but he could not return any emotion. Since Veronica had left him there was none. So, all the pretty things smiled in vain. Though his face betrayed no sign of pain nor of longing, only a slight hollow loss mixed with a deepening curiosity over the mystery of the murdered man and his misplaced wife.

In the weeks that followed he aggressively pursued that curiosity at the cost of his official case load. No mean feat considering life in the SEC was petrified like tree rings, especially in the Division of Enforcement where Devlin labored as a staff attorney lost in the center of the tree. Individual initiative was discouraged. Some mornings he could barely face the hierarchical confinement, which was not a dictatorship, but not a democracy either and brought out his antisocial tendencies. He wanted to be like Bob—Cornell alumni, all around even-tempered team player, on everyone's guest list, Ivy League to the core—but he couldn't because it wasn't in his genes. Among other things the issue ate at him that all cases were reviewed with extreme personal prejudice by higher ups to determine whether they could be pursued at all. Only if the evidence was guaranteed to stand up in court were specific teams assigned, only if winning was a forgone conclusion and only then could meticulously researched evidence be meticulously categorized and translated into legalese for trial lawyers, judges and court reporters. Assistant Directors in turn supervised by Associate Directors answerable to the Deputy Directors and finally the Director oversaw all cases and all staff attorneys—all watching their backs. He could barely breathe much of the time, but considered it a necessary evil to let loose his consuming purpose, even though the bulk of financial crime lie beneath the waterline impervious to the stratified system allowing the really big fish to flee the net.

Long days bled into long nights as he balanced an already full workload with his extracurricular inquiry into the mystery of the French quant. Not a formal investigation: he was just rummaging up some facts for a friend and making sense of an arcane financial technology, which just happened to touch millions of lives and on which mercilessly balanced the economic stability of global markets. It was intense. Most lawyers who had dealings with high-frequency computer trading missed the point entirely; the normally astute became stupefied when faced with nanoseconds, exabytes and algorithms; the not so astute were oblivious that anything was happening at all. It was still an unregulated wildcat business. The SEC was only beginning to grapple with it and only had a few staff that could fully decipher the implications. Fortunately, he understood what an algobot was, could even write one and expect it to function like proper code wrapped in the anonymity of a robust operating system, but he couldn't match the ephemeral heights, the ecstatic brilliance, the screaming genius of the robotic code warriors autonomously navigating the cyberspace of all financial markets where trillions of transactions occurred within the interval of a single heartbeat. That was a godlike realm, invisible to humans—silent robots that came and went without footprints determining the rise and fall of men's enterprises. But he could envision it, and the last vestiges of humanity being secretly drained away leaving no one any the wiser was a specter that terrified him.

Days were an energetic cycle of meetings, research and legwork as he chased down every clue, interrogated every interested party, pulled every string that might shed light on the dark financial dealings of upstart Endecott Technologies. Buoyed by a machismo facade and buried in work, he only vaguely missed Veronica when he came up for air, but fatigue soon spiraled him out of control. Then she consumed his every thought and only vanity kept him from running after her like a fool. There were other consequences: one of which was keeping extremely late hours until he could finally sleep uninterrupted if only from exhaustion. Then one morning after a long sleepless night he realized that she was no longer in his mind: there was no ache of loneliness, no compulsion to find her, no illusions, no mental images, no feeling at all just an equilibrium of forces as the reality settled in. It was at that point he decided to live again, and things began to return to normal. His *twilight* faded. Everything was satisfactory, but not especially good, until one night knocking woke him from a dreamless sleep. Veronica stood looking weary at the door with her too red lipstick and flaming blonde hair. They stared at one another for a long time, reaching and withdrawing—in her eyes was a burning cold wind, tides racing, moonlight fleeting—and then she smiled that queer little smirk only patricians have mastered that somehow disarmed everyone.

"It's too late," Devlin said, "you should have come yesterday," and closed the door.

Hands gripped the wheel following the ancient glimmering Hudson river, as he headed north towards Poughkeepsie where a boathouse waited along its banks. On top of his car sat the crimson rowing shell and long carbon fiber oars. It was on this shore where the hotly contested regattas were held that sparked illegal betting sometimes well into the six figures—a huge amount of money a century ago. Collegiate races on the Hudson started here in 1895 soon followed by magnificent professional ones and the tens of thousands of people who queued to watch them. Poughkeepsie then was famous for the regattas, and the violence that escalated with the heavy betting. Old timers tell stories of runaway corruption and wild out of control crowds: especially at one particular competition where Thomas DeMott accused William Stephens, the stroke of the Poughkeepsie boat, of throwing the race. DeMott was killed in the scuffle.

Thursday and he was on the road. His sculling gear was stowed neatly behind the back seat of his dark, late model, Swedish SUV, but everything else was a little out of whack. He wasn't used to taking time off midweek, so he had grabbed his boat and escaped the city seeking solace and enlightenment alone in the middle of the river, the ancient glimmering river where everything came into focus. Now he was on the cell venting with Thierry.

"Where the fuck are you?"

"Halfway to Poughkeepsie."

"Must be nice…midweek—"

"Pissed by the evidence I dug up that no one who knew acted on!"

"Such as?"

"Edicott Technologies has attracted a top tier sampling of Republican investors."

"Top tier…"

"…blue blood, family fortunes…into its high net worth management schemes."

"So?"

"It's a red flag. An anomaly. Those funds were all based on computer driven, high-frequency, algorithmic investing: edgy stuff that conservatives avoid like Ebola. Doesn't make sense."

"What else?"

"The fact that super PAC 'American Voices' and Bixby Endicott are somehow intimately connected. Makes me wonder if the high frequency trading firm is illegally funding political races with money laundered through the super PAC's tax-exempt status."

"That's right...he's hinting at a run for Governor."

"Connect the dots; where else is this tax-free money going? Clearly something is rotten."

"Stinks. I love it."

An event the preceding morning had catalyzed his fury resulting in this impromptu trip. Devlin had been summoned to the office of a Deputy Director—one Arthur J. Biggs, no one he knew, just some remote, opaque, authority whose command was to be obeyed by unwritten law—and he appeared as ordered. The overtones of the request added to his already jagged-from-lack-of-sleep state, fallout from the Veronica affair, information overload from too many cases to track and amplified by his rogue inquiry. His emotions ran high and he was a bit touchy.

"This is Associate Director Patterson," Biggs informed him the moment he walked into the uninspired office indicating a humorless, slightly overweight woman in her mid-40s wearing a slate gray suit whose skirt was too short revealing thick muscular legs jutting out like pilings. He stood, buttoned his coat and asked, "Coffee? Tea?"

"What can I do for you?"

"There are reports," he continued, "and we just wanted to look into it personally…out of concern for my staff. You mainly. Not just one, but several. We want to make sure we're tracking with your thinking."

"My thinking?"

"We want to make sure you have everything you need to succeed," Patterson replied, "winning is a team effort."

He was interrogated about his department, how he felt about his associates and cases in progress, nothing too specific, just vague, insidious trajectories.

"We want to get the gist of your process…how things are progressing."

Patterson got personal. We heard you had some critical thoughts about the Director. Is that true?"

"I always think about politics."

"Is it politics when the command line is in question?" She asked to see his cell phone history, and when he refused focused on his personal life; did he have any family, any significant other, outside relationships, and kept on that way skirting employment laws until he let slip his recent breakup with Victoria—then smugly relieved at the cut she let up. But the two continued to circle issues like sharks nosing for blood, diving deep to disturb the sediment, to see if anything was moving, shaking things up, all the while a hidden agenda gleaming in their eyes with an almost uncontrollable fury waiting to strike.

The room grew warmer and though the air conditioning hissed, nothing seemed to come out. He didn't want to be careful, he wanted to be his normal insouciant self, impervious to criticisms and what others might think, but kept slipping into a subordinate identity, as if there were some subliminal set of instructions below his consciousness awareness that goaded him into behaviors that were not at all the person inside. Finally, in a cathartic moment, laughter welled up as he got the picture of a ludicrous, Kafkaesque interrogation where no one ever got to the point. He bit his tongue to restrain himself and keep a straight face, but let out a snicker nonetheless and had to pretend he had sneezed as a cover.

"You've been doing some sort of inquiry on your own I see."

"No, not really."

"Computer logs show you've made access to databases not related to any ongoing investigations," Biggs finally getting down to the purpose of the meeting, "at least none I could find."

"Look, there are countless trade orders these algorithms send out and then quickly rescind. Millions. Even on the inside, nobody knows what these abortive trades might be. Some speculate they're new algorithms being tested or strategic feints, sonar pings probing the market for a response. Some of the fake trades could be aimed purely at gobbling up bandwidth to slow down competitors. There must be high frequency traders who could tell us. We should be seeking them out to try to learn what's going on."

"We'll have to look into those things," Patterson said "sometime. But for now...have you made full disclosure of your investments?"

"You think I'm trading on the inside?"

Arthur Biggs picked up a silver spoon from the Lomonosov bone china cup that was sitting on his desk and wrapped the string from a tea bag around it twice then pulled it taut squeezing out the last drop. "This is just a friendly chat; we don't think anything. We have no viewpoint at all. We're a team here and ...would you like some tea?"

"If you are off program..." Patterson began, then sighed with the burden of many lifetimes, "it's a strategy from the top down, a consensus of thought leadership...can't just go off program, the whole thing hangs in the balance."

"Meaning?"

"Confidence," said Biggs sipping at his tea. "It's a delicate thing this economy; a house of cards that needs looking after. Sure you don't want some tea? Special blend I get."

"No." Devlin hated being patronized.

"We overlook certain things that viewed on their own probably shouldn't be allowed, but viewed in context are just politics...the concentration of wealth that leaves those nasty inequities between the haves and have nots is just fodder for Pulitzer seeking journalists. Socialist claptrap. It's a self correcting machine. Someone has to watch over all that to ensure it's undisturbed for the public good, someone has to otherwise...chaos. Like a forest fire. Think of that forest as the economy: fire the creation that changes potential into returns and the trees fuel; if it slows, we have to rekindle it; if it burns too fast we have to suppress it; if it turns in the wrong direction threatening huge populations we have to change its course; all in different political climates, sometimes with regulation, sometimes without depending on who is in office. Democracy is not the most perfect form; we have to make adjustments. Our one tool is strategy, when to do something and when to do nothing. Comes from the top down. Violate that and we have nothing."

"Seems to me," said Devlin, "the tree of liberty must be refreshed from time to time with the blood of patriots and tyrants."

"Jefferson, right? Unfortunately, that's not the way it works," said Patterson.

"We can't always be so altruistic," Biggs continued. "Compromise is the price of freedom."

"I always thought it was constant vigilance, constant willingness to fight back."

"We think it's best you take a sabbatical. Three weeks in another town, someplace you can regain your perspective. We're a team here. We need team players. That's the way it works."

Out across the Hudson river trees were dusted white. Clouds streaked off into the distance with wispy contrails reflecting the curve of the earth. Lost clouds on their way to New Mexico and Colorado where the Navajo held out with the animal spirits waiting for the white men to pass so they could live again. Devlin looked at the clouds and the river. It was what they wanted from him that was hidden, he understood that now pulling the racing shell down from the rack on top of the car and assembling the gear he would need, anxious to be out on the river where everything was in flux and problems drifted away with the current.

The strong arm of the river picked him up and swept him from its bank like a fallen oak leaf. He settled into the sliding seat, his feet nestled into the stirrups and pressed the oars down into the cockpit raising all sixteen feet on each side as huge wings. He rode on the back of the water like a raptor sailing high out over the windy plains. Carbon fiber tips dipped silently into the inky current at exactly the right moment, thrusting forward, wresting control back from nature, feeling the connection with the primal power of the cosmos that was greater than any force he could throw back. But he used that energy to gain an advantage because it was intellect and reason alone that kept him from going under, which kept everyone afloat in this human life. Soon there was a freshening breeze against his face as he was plunged deep into the heart of the labyrinth, embracing aloneness where only thought and sinew mattered, and all other significances winnowed away into the sky like smoke.

Chapter 5

"History is just an unfinished dialog," his journalist friend had told him on a long distance call, "come, be a footnote in this ephemeral city...it's a good place to get lost."

He had arrived three days ago and had not touched ground since, but now the euphoria was making him giddy like any novice traveler unleashed on Paris—where the multidimensional present was defined by many centuries of life all existing side by side. His friend—a hard drinking TV journalist who he had met as a fellow rower on the Hudson when posted in Manhattan—had invited him to housesit "his place" in Paris while away on assignment. In a late night call, Devlin had revealed the fact he had been summarily banished from his job for three weeks. "His place" turned out to be a hundred-year-old barge converted to a modern houseboat moored in Port de l'Arsenal, just off the Seine on the Canal Saint-Martin in the heart of old Paris—complete with a single seat, rowing shell.

Devlin stroked the oars until he felt his solar plexus burning, until his legs screamed as he pushed the sliding seat and his back ached, until the shell knifed forward in fluid harmony with the flow of the river. Gusts of wind feathered the chop. Wild, cold spray dashed from the surface and soaked his jacket. Impossibly long riverboats sliced the gleaming waves, ferrying eager tourists with faces pressed against the tall curved glass that kept them from falling overboard in the mad frenzy of capturing photographs. Their eyes were filled with a naïve illusory Paris: one of food, style, romance and sex where the haut monde was born, where the elegant, charming and witty lived—unaware that "La Ville-Lumière," the *City of Light,* was a city of contradictions, that the rigid classes were born of poverty, struggle and hunger making the sobriquet "Parisienne" synonymous with agitator, and their distinct accent a mark of distrust in the countryside. Shrugging off sleep just after dawn for the last three days, fighting cold and the river's commercial traffic, he pushed himself progressively further up the ancient Seine desperate to seize the once-in-a-lifetime opportunity. But on the third of these journeys something inexplicable happened, and he wasn't entirely certain if it was the intense workout, over excitement at just being there or if it was real. Passing beneath the stone walls of the looming Notre Dame Cathedral, past the Île de la Cité where Romans had first staked their claim nearly two centuries ago, the memories first began to flood over him, haunting, careening down through time.

An overwhelming sense of familiarity filled him, a strange feeling as if he had lived through it all before. This Déjà vu electrified his senses over the next few days until finally the clarity of his surroundings, the textures, the colors, the ebullient sounds severed him from Manhattan completely. He felt a huge sense of relief and of belonging somewhere he had never been before; prescient about everyplace he went as if he had. In night dreams, rocking on the wake of passing boats, he was a duelist skewering opponents with savage energy, his skill honed to the limits of the possible, artistic virtuosity funneled through a cold steel rapier blade. He experienced all the exhilaration, and the astonishing killing: the slicing, the insouciant disregard with which he ferociously attacked his challengers leaving only blood on white lace, as it should be, all for honor, all to the victor. There could be only one; understood from the start. Then he slept soundly dreaming of a Paris where men fled down shadowy avenues with capes flying like black crows whistling down the wind.

The taxi inched through morning rush hour in fits and starts. Devlin held a hot coffee between his knees, sloshing in a cardboard cup the Sumatra Mandheling's aroma filled the cab, making him drink so much his hands shook, watching the passing scene, playing with the ring of corrugated paper that protected his fingers. He was heading to the European office of Endecott Technologies, home to the mysterious quant he had found floating in the Harlem, on the pretext he was a New York funds manager on vacation and wanted to meet with a senior executive while in town. It was the last thing he wanted when he first arrived full of resentment and anger, but after his catharsis on the river now believed fate had arranged the unexpected trip to Paris and who was he to question universal law. It was as if the City of Light was a catalyst igniting a change in him, as if an avatar trying to awaken him.

Bixby Endicott was late. As the car traversed the long private drive he could hear powdered snow crunching beneath the tires, puffs of steam escaped the twin tailpipes turning to crystals, high beams bathed the scarlet elders, oaks and staghorn sumacs lining the way, ice sparkled in the light. He struggled to collect himself, calming his agitated body that had been fueled by caffeine since dawn, heading towards the most important meeting in his life, a meeting upon which his future rested. The gables to his Northeast Harbor, Maine compound were just becoming visible against the sky beyond the trees. A shot spray of diamonds blasted nuclear fire across the heavens in a clarity only a cold arctic night could give and not even a wisp of cloud could be seen for a hundred miles in any direction. Yellow light streamed into the circular turnaround before the imposing entrance to the magniicent house, an estate designed by the celebrated Richard Howland Hunt of the long vanished firm Hunt & Hunt. The unexpected angles and stunning deco details stole the breath away from first time visitors as it rose majestically above the cars of men who had travelled here to see him tonight, men of power who treasured the personal time a rare automobile trip gave them. He cursed himself for being late, but it was unavoidable.

The trouble began the moment the market had opened. Within minutes, officials at the Securities and Exchange Commission were swamped by waves of urgent alerts. On Wall Street, other officials scrambled to isolate the source of bizarre trades that were collapsing values as much as seventy percent threatening to shut down the New York Stock Exchange. Meanwhile, overlooking the Hudson River, at Endicott Technologies, panic was setting in. An algorithm their IT security people had first thought was a simple virus, had thought was deactivated and quarantined, had instead gone rogue, blasting out erroneous trade orders that were costing Endicott millions—only in tiny increments every fifteen seconds, a slow, painful death by small cuts. And no one knew how to shut it down! At that rate, the firm would be insolvent within hours. Endicott's horrified employees agonized 78 minutes before they found the runaway code and neutralized it. The lingering metallic taste of fear that struck Bixby Endecott was not from the attack, but from why there weren't multiple layers of security already in place, bulletproof risk control after the first attempt to bring down the firm only a few months ago. Why there was no automated stop-loss in the system to shut it down as he had ordered? Good programming discipline alone required a last-ditch backstop mechanism to close down trading when too many orders are going out or orders weren't getting updated the way they should—and the brightest and best worked for him! There was only one answer and the thought of it chilled him to the bone; someone was on the inside!

The remainder of the day was spent in crisis mode: all systems and all code had to be inspected, lawyers had to be briefed, trades had to be accounted for, losses calculated, clients reassured, and he would have been there still if this meeting was not of such primal importance. He was running behind even before he started: a pot of coffee had substituted for lunch, a quick shower and fresh shirt in the office, a rush for the airport where his Citation X was running up overtime charges, and finally the flight to the Bar Harbor airport where they came soaring in over the night sea and dropped down just as the runway met the wild grasses at the edge of the sand.

"Frankly," the young State Senator said, "you scare us." Transient electricity bristled in the air. Of the eight people in the room, none were still. The meeting had gone on for hours with no consensus.

A man with a grayed crew cut, meticulously trimmed goatee and leathery face raised his concern. "CEOs of publicly traded companies, hired and fired based on stock prices, increasingly worry—"

"—*about* that somewhat disjointed realm between what a company does and what its stock does!" The only woman interrupted: thin, approaching fifty, ice cubes clattering in the tall highball glass she lifted as a toast with a sardonic smile on her lips.

"—*that* their shares could be sent into a free fall by an algorithmic feeding frenzy," the man continued, frowning.

"That's right," another man said. "Fears of god damned algorithmic terrorism!"

"Fears well-funded criminals or a terrorist organization could find a way to cause a market crisis are not unfounded," the elder statesman, and senior party official, said. "This type of scenario could cause chaos for civilization and profit for crooks and constitute a major national security crisis."

"It's just bad politics."

Everyone nodded, except Bixby who was vexed, who was spinning in turmoil, but smiled charmingly despite his nightmarish day, which thankfully no one in the room knew about. "It is a delight to have such bright minds…on such a cold night, after such a day…once again I apologize for being late," he moved over in front of the massive river stone fireplace. "Politics is all about the future, and nothing exemplifies that better than the transformation of Wall Street by high frequency trading."

"I'm not so sure. In our own state, the New York Attorney General is prosecuting those marketing enhanced data feed privileges to high-speed trading firms such as yours, while the FBI still believes you traders are breaking U.S. laws by acting on nonpublic information since you guys get it before anyone else. Not quite insider trading, but 'spread's' the next best thing."

"What the hell is "spread?"

"*Spread*," Bixby replied, "is the industry providing hyperspeed connections for financial firms. A faster trader can sell at a higher price and buy at a lower one because he gets there first. A connection that's just one millisecond faster than the competition's could boost a high-speed firm's earnings by as much as $100 million per year."

"Is that legal?"

"Not if the FBI have their way."

"I'd like to remind you; your money is invested in our funds," Bixby said, the effects of stress and two glasses of single malt scotch rearing their snarling faces. He was fighting to maintain control, desperate to manage his newly acquired fear, longing to come off as a political contender and not just the piñata full of money. "If you're not on the leading edge, you're behind. Wealth management means investment in innovation. I think 'American Voices' proves that. We all need money for what's important. I provide that for you and I can provide that for the country."

"Here! Here!"

"We all have our doubts," the senior party official said, "some of them voiced here tonight, some not. Having said that, however, you are quite an evangelist and that's a marketable commodity. A plan with imagination is what the party needs."

"Government is wealth management," Bixby rolled with the turning tide "the problem is that no leader has been able to create economy, just regulate what's already there. Innovation fuels economy; I fuel innovation!"

The fire cracked with white hot oak embers. The eight people were finally still, cocooned in the great room where just beyond the glass windows it was seven below, of one mind, secure in the thought that money was the universal solvent as well as the measure of a man. Then out of the silent night, someone spoke.

"What's our next step?"

* * * *

In flight its wings were like elegant twin sculptures searing the rarified air across the Atlantic. Then finally descending into the light and the mist, into the swirling noxious fumes of jet exhaust, the confusion of crowds in transit and the world of lonely night laborers they fell. It was after two AM when the Citation X touched down at Paris's Charles de Gaulle Airport. The overwhelming chaos of the landing buffeted off the sleek round fuselage, within which the embrace of sumptuous butter colored leather reassured Bixby. If he had been more perceptive, events might have been different. But he rode above the visceral connection between men and the world in which they live as a hundred people worked to make his sojourn from New York to Paris a seamless lullaby, people he would never know or see or meet as long as he was comfortable and all desires fulfilled. He never had to lift a finger for himself. A limo whisked him into the urban heart where a five-star hotel awaited to absorb his weariness with high loft down pillows, whispering climate control, sound and light proofing, insulating him from the sweat and blood upon which everything in the city rested: where popular revolution was born, where men like him once lost their heads at the Place de la Révolution—now called the Place de la Concorde. Though sheltered from the real, his rest was fitful.

The next day he had his meeting with the enigmatic and humorless agent; he had meant to be charming and bright, but burned out right there before her.

Steam from black coffee swirled above the brioche in the cold morning air, yellow light barely peaked over the mansard rooftops as noisy cars left vapor trails down narrow avenues. People hurried to work with the insensitivity required in a major urban center while Bixby tapped his fingers on a white linen tablecloth not having had enough sleep and annoyed he couldn't have met Revenia's agent at the hotel where everything worked in his favor. She had called just as he was about to leave to say there must be a change of plan, and to meet him at the terrace that extends across the cobbled pedestrian street at Chez Julien overlooking the Seine. He made calls to his office to tell them he would be late, to his lawyers checking on liabilities and to New York for an update on systems trading—he had lain awake all night nursing a hollow feeling in the pit of his stomach, wondering when the next attack would come. Anxiety still gripped him.

"Monsieur Endecott?" The chic, graceful woman arrived in a bluster of wind flurries, her hair and scarf flying, the cold spanking out a ruddy color in her pale cheeks, coattails flapping in the breeze like a dragon descending.

"Bix. Just call me Bix," he stood grinning in the certainty he could will things right with the force of his personality, and if that didn't work with money.

"Déborah Beauvois," she sang tossing her bag over the back of the chair. When the waiter appeared at her elbow she said, "*Le Kellogs. Café au lait*," without looking up.

"Corn flakes?"

"I find it just *pas possible* that *les Américains* could even think about eating eggs in the morning; I would most certainly *vomir* if I did the same."

"I'm eating brioche," pointing to the plate, "I only devour the living in private."

She threw her loose scarf around her neck and pulled the coat tight while regarding Bixby with detachment missing his attempt at humor entirely. "Very civilized. You had no trouble finding the café?"

"The concierge was fully informed, but it was Google Maps that led me here. I walked—to warm up," he frowned. "Only asked him anyway so he wouldn't feel inferior to my smartphone."

"You could have sat inside."

"Better view out here."

"I hope you didn't come to Paris just to try to entice Revinia to perform at the Met. It's quite impossible you know, as I told you on the phone."

"We have an office here; our European headquarters."

Her eyes were green, at least that was as close as he could estimate. Actually, they defied color: shimmering like iridescent whirlpools of interstellar medium, revealing suspicious reasoning. Black auburn hair tumbled in disarray, loose strands falling onto her face; pale flawless skin, angular cheekbones beneath catlike eyes that were slightly slanted, as if there was some oriental blood in her ancient history—or perhaps she belonged to a race of felines long thought extinct. She moved in fluid sensuous grace with an unconscious eroticism, yet there was something completely asexual about her, something otherworldly that eluded him.

"She is a true artist," the agent said after being served her coffee in a bowl. "Naturally we get offers—constantly, flamboyant offers, but it's not for the money she sings, it's not even for the art she creates; it's for what she preserves. She is very pure; I can neither explain nor expect you to understand," she said the whole time scanning their surroundings as if keeping watch. "I help protect her."

"Miss Beauvois…"

Her mysterious energy intruded with an uncomfortable intimacy. She brought her gaze to his eyes adding to the discomfort.

"…look, I come from the future," he said, "a world into which we are all inexorably headed. No one has asked our consent; it's mandatory.

I'm helping to make opera part of what lies ahead, because right now it's prospects are tenuous at best. I admit, I'm part of that future. Can I tell you what that world is like? Can I tell you that at first we programmers just tried to imitate thought patterns: organizing patterns, work patterns, anything that could replace a menial repetitive task? However, success beyond anyone's dreams fueled the fire and programmers grew restless with potential, reaching a point of no return. Nothing can stop them now. Progress is aimed at making all human experience a paid for commodity, something that can be synthesized, manufactured, digitized…experience itself is the goal of computer science: duplicating, enhancing, elevating, and reinventing life until there is little will left except the decision to change channels; because all human experience will be found on virtual channels and someone will hold the patents to everything, the copyrights; someone like me. Life will be a paid for experience. Progress in technologies will cause a runaway effect wherein artificial intelligence will exceed human intellectual capacity and control, thus radically changing civilization in an event we call the 'Singularity.' It is inevitable. It's economics. It has already begun."

A chill wind brushed them as they sat in the café, two disparate individuals caught up in the great convergence of cultures that threatened everything precious like a cataclysmic sirocco passing over all human civilization.

"I don't think I like your future Monsieur Bix, though you explain it so charmingly."

"But we can never make an artist—a true artist. That's uniquely human. It's why I'm here. Despite all I've accomplished, I'm humbled before art…and I truly love opera."

A few blocks away a demonstration was just turning ugly over the right to wear headscarves in schools and workplaces; words from

Algeria, Ethiopia, Ukraine, Somalia, Kosovo, Iran and points east were contaminating the official language by being gene-spliced into French inciting jingoistic natives to violence. The first mark of Parisian identity had always been fear of what was beyond the city walls, and now its secret languages were being passed outside as borders became obscure. Arabs, black Africans, Eastern Europeans and Asians have stamped their own brand onto Paris: the main language in the rue de Belleville is Mandarin Chinese; bars in this part were run by Southeast Asians; street prostitutes of Saint-Denis—long the burial place of French Kings—were from Albania, Kosovo or sub-Saharan Africa. The City of Light is a magnet for the greedy, the disaffected and the ambitious: those who need to make their mark in a world rotten with inequality.

"It won't change anything. And you're wrong, art is not human; it's of the spirit."

Bixby regarded her for a moment. "You must like the cold?"

"I do."

"Is that why you wanted to meet here?"

"It was necessary," she said as if looking through him. "Though I do think the wind is…one of the best things about Paris is its unpredictable weather.

"Too far from the ocean."

"The river is our sea; full of sudden storms. It's ancient. We call it 'Deuona,' Celtic for 'divine.'"

"Divine?"

"Because of 'Sequana,' the river goddess, where the name Seine came from. Paris is her kingdom and stories say the waters are haunted by divine beings—especially in the spring—if you believe that sort of thing. Many sacrifices have been thrown in, offerings…they dredge them up sometimes—"

"If Revenia was to perform in New York, it would be a great historical event. Talent like hers only comes every few generations."

"She is nonpareil; there will never be another!"

"Then help me understand, why do you keep her from the world stage?"

"Not I monsieur. She will never leave Paris."

"There must be a reason. Everything has a reason."

"Many things have no explanation. Let's just say it's safe for her here."

"Safe? We can provide the best security. No expense is too great. Nothing—"

"Au contraire, you can't fight what you can't see. No, I'm sorry Monsieur Endecott, but you are wasting your time."

The no nonsense, enigmatic woman gathered her things, coolly shook hands and was gone leaving a perplexed Bixby Endicott in the deserted outdoor café overlooking the Seine with a cold winter breeze chilling him to the bone. It was a disgruntled man who rode in the back of the taxi pulling up to the European headquarters of Endecott Technologies.

The office manager swept into the room before him; files in hand, taking notes as she walked. "There's a fund manager here from New York. He called yesterday. On vacation. Wanted to meet with someone while he was in town. I put him with Sanja."

"Why didn't he go to the office there?"

"Didn't say."

"Well," he said thoughtfully, wondering if the visit had any significance, considering recent events, remembering he didn't believe in coincidence, disregarding his inner warnings as being too paranoid, believing that the man was just a tourist who couldn't leave work alone much like himself. "I can't see him. Here," he handed the women an envelope from his coat pocket, "give him these tickets for the opera and make my apologies."

Bixby Endecott was furious. Trembling. He couldn't stand the thought of travelling thirty-four hundred miles without getting the prize. Nothing was going right; he wasn't used to not getting his way, to not getting everything he wanted. He wasn't used to being under attack and thought about what the agent had told him, "You can't fight what you can't see," because that was exactly how he felt.

Devlin was in the belly of the beast. Well dressed, anonymous people hurried about on seemingly important business. A small meeting was taking place in a glass enclosed conference room that could easily have accommodated fifty; subdued associates sitting in high backed leather task chairs, ringing the flamed maple tabletop that was balanced on polished granite cones. An elegant young woman, torn from the cover of Vogue, sat behind the reception cubicle answering constant calls in a voice too quiet to hear. Art was everywhere: from the walls where postmodern masterpieces dotted every available space to the floors where a few Turkish carpets were scattered in strategic arrangement to the furniture on which Devlin sat impatiently awaiting his appointment.

Light streamed through the floor to ceiling windows spreading warmth into the already toasty foyer—overcompensating for the cold blooded. He could see out across Paris, over the mansard rooflines, into the gray mass of nondescript buildings dotted with medieval cathedral domes, challenged by high-rises flying over the rest. He had never been to France; it wasn't like New York. The whole ambiance was different. Everywhere he went the roots of discontent were deeper. It was mongrelized and far different than the images of carefree gaiety that dominated last century's media, as if it had grown organically from the centuries long influx of crass, opportunistic, immigrants unlike Manhattan, the new colossus where global refugees flocked to the "Mother of exiles" singing: "Give me your tired, your poor, your huddled masses yearning to breathe free, the wretched refuse of your teeming shore. Send these, the homeless, tempest-tost to me."

His meeting was brief and it didn't shed much light on the mystery of the French quant. Sanja Singhal had curtly introduced herself, and they sat in a small conference space that looked as though it was some avant-garde architect's wet dream. She was a lucid, intelligent, terrifically good salesperson sliding prospectuses and literature for their funds across the fine leather couch like hockey pucks. But when it came to questions about high frequency trading, framed as concern for his client's money, the answers were obtuse.

"It's the future; the evolution of securities exchanges," she had said. "Where milliseconds can mean millions in profit for your funds; it all depends on your tolerance of risk. But we have had unprecedented success because we have taken unprecedented leaps forward."

However, the specter of dark pools; algobots that did buying and selling as surrogates for people; the cutthroat "spread" industry leasing more direct, faster, high-speed fiber optic routes to the stock exchanges to shave off nanoseconds against competitive traders—for a huge cut in unfathomable profits—made Devlin think of his mother: how she had lost it all after a life of hard work and doing everything she was supposed to. He hated the rich. Business, in his mind, was simply the pursuit of profit without the slightest hint of conscience, morality, religious conviction or any of the qualities that distinguished the civilized from the barbaric. He imagined those businesses as flesh eating viruses that would eventfully consume their hosts in avaricious greed despite the fact it would mean their own death as well.

Sanja Singhal had sensed this inner turmoil because of, in addition to her twin PhDs, the one quality above all others that had advanced her career: she was a terrific salesperson. She slid next to him on the smooth, Italian couch. Her already short skirt slid higher as she sat down revealing plump round thighs sheathed in sheer blue violet silk. There was an inaudible rustle of fabric and an invisible smile in her eyes: like a severed electrical wire dancing on the ground.

"Here," she said handing him an envelope, "tickets for the Paris Opera." Then after a moment added, "I come with them. Nobody should leave Paris without one grand night. Pick you up at six; compliments of Endecott Technologies."

Devlin descended in the elevator so fast it made his ears pop. All he knew was he had an engagement to attend an opera accompanied by a representative of the firm he had been put on forced leave for investigating. Not once on the way back to the renovated barge moored in the Port de l'Arsenal, just off the Seine on the Canal Saint-Martin, did he realize that some things defied explanation, only for an instant did he have any misgivings as the nexus between the past and the future shifted imperceptivity beneath him. He could not have known that his destiny had just been irrevocably changed.

When he reached the boat, he poured himself a glass of red wine and sat down on the deck, his coat in a crumpled pile beside him, not believing where he was, watching the river traffic, traveling through time. He suddenly missed Veronica beside him and longed for her touch as everything bad that had passed between them vanished.

"Hi," he said holding his smartphone close as if her cheek. "I had to talk to you." A breeze messed his hair and then moved on. "I'm sitting on the deck of a hundred-year-old riverboat on a canal off the Seine in the middle of the old city watching reflections of Paris on the water. It's cold and the sky is clear, and the blue goes on forever and I'm thinking of you."

There was a long pause. "It's too late," she said at last, "you should have called yesterday." He heard her halted breathing before she hung up, then the only sound was wind on the water.

VI | Chapter 6

Traffic caromed recklessly past the Palais Garnier—nineteenth century Beaux Arts masterpiece and beloved Parisian icon. Normally home to the ballet, it was staging a temperamental opera director's comeback after he'd threatened to quit—infuriating vested interests all around. He was so fragile that the stress caused the Opéra national de Paris verged on hysteria: jealousies flared, mistakes went viral, stagehands cowered under cost overruns fearing for their jobs, and management held its collective breath beneath the sway of an erratic director with a vision—one in which the limits of the possible were routinely shattered. "Opera must be relevant to new generations…" he justified all excesses. Pandora's box had been unleashed out of which came an avant-garde Italian set designer with holographic visions, and a costumer whose eccentric designs were pilfered by guerilla fashionistas ending up in nearby Faubourg Saint-Honoré shops before the production even opened. But despite everything, the production was taking on a miraculous life of its own.

For months Jean-Luc Vigo had struggled with his terrible vision before revealing it to anyone. He had forged ideas and images from an impenetrable darkness and held them close until the phantom began to take form. Then he guarded his illusions, so they would not scatter in the chaos of everyday life, and when he woke from sleep would still be there. The fleeting, the ephemeral—like trying to capture the wild. In the ruins of his life he clung to these intangible essences; the hidden destiny that had saved him now drove him to obsession.

Once a prodigal tenor he was peerless, acclaimed for his unearthly power and range, admired for his ease and lightness, envied for his depth of repertoire resurrecting music and roles long thought dead. Until stricken one summer with a mysterious ailment that robbed him of his upper registers. Afterwards he could no longer hit the money notes. His soaring voice faded into the tragic lore of the theater, his career expected to be one of the great lights in Opera collapsed overnight. In bitterness he turned to alcohol, then to heroin and was nearly lost.

As fortune would have it, the director of the Paris Opera was caught up in a contemptible sex scandal and was dismissed out of hand by the board to save their government funding. Desperate, Jean-Luc was called in to stage "Siegfried," a role he had won much acclaim for—hoping his star still fresh enough to draw crowds. The press was shocked at the risky move: his flame had flickered, his personality unstable. In a drug stupor, insulted and unable to grasp his own inability to perform, he at first flatly refused. But sobered, and ended up producing a hit with legs and startling rave reviews, saving the opera's funding, gathering acclaim and resurrecting his celebrity—on which he rode breathlessly as his salvation.

It was a tremendous relief after the threat of a union lockout. The opera company issued a press release stating rehearsals would continue and the season would open as scheduled with a reimagined production of Mozart's "Die Zauberflöte" after eking out a deal with its stagehands and expecting to secure agreements with the remaining unions shortly: fifteen of which representing chorus singers, musicians, carpenters and others who had been in the throes of crisis since their contracts expired. The general manager had demanded pay-cuts citing skyrocketing costs and, "…there isn't enough new audience to replace the old one dying off!" Union leaders shot back: "We've always been willing to contribute to a solution that will keep the world's best operas on stage," but not willing enough to take any financial hits.

Now musicians, stagehands, seamstresses, scene painters, lighting designers, technicians, computer artists followed by the luminous performers began to populate the theater like snow lightly falling across the landscape until the old became unrecognizable.

A vision began to emerge: simmering shadows in deep blue violet, crimson flames rising from a strange landscape; a languishing monument on the banks of some fantastic river, scintillating in the glow of twilight, silhouetted under the billion lights of an imagined sky somewhere between sun and moon. Day after day backdrops rose and fell both real and illusory, as the stage became a blending of the actual and virtual holographic images flickering across gossamer scrims. Set pieces were raised and lowered and flown into position by burly, tattooed men with sweating, muscled arms hauling the century old turntables in the flyloft, others by keystrokes and touchpads controlling the computer generated graphic effects and pulley systems that worked autonomous of union labor. Lights flared as the design was settled upon. Stagehands wrangled spots and floods from the catwalk, taking orders barked over wireless from the lighting designer at the dimming rack in the control booth below. Groups of performers came and went from the stage: running lines, blocking positions, hammering out scenes. Tempers boiled then subsided, voices soared, rehearsals intensified, emotions raged in anticipation of opening night. Soon the old theater was alive as hundreds of people worked with a common purpose in a magnificent symphony dedicated to staging the world's greatest theatrical art form.

Revenia, however, became mercurial and moody. She kept to herself except when in the wings brooding, watching rehearsals, more diva, more unapproachable than her usual enigmatic self. Now she descended the dark ladder into a labyrinth no one understood creating huge concern in the front office whether she was ill, or her genius was faltering, or the director too neurotic, or the role too much…portending a massive liability at the box office. The General Manager called her agent, Déborah Beauvois, who reassured she was just getting into character, which made him even more suspicious of a cover up. It was only Mozart, after all, not Wagner's "Ride of the Valkyries".

Storming through the dressing room door the young woman slammed it with such ferocity that it nearly broke the hand of the man who caught it just before it hit and who, after peering into the darkened hallway making sure no one was watching, shut it silently slipping in after her. She raised both arms; one hand outstretched in supplication to the vault of heaven and held it there as if still on stage.

"God I hate her! I hate her! I spit on her!" She cried and then cursing, dripping venom, swinging her hands down into fists, "Prima donna bitch!"

"Quiet," he said peeking through a crack in the door down the hall. "Someone will hear you."

"I don't care!" Her perspiration covered breasts heaved under the tight costume gasping with emotion.

"You will if it's the diva's agent."

"I spit on her too!"

"Sit down. Have a drink." Throwing up his hands, "You make me crazy—"

"Did you see her?! Did you see…?"

"Of course I saw. What do you expect? She is so…exceptional!"

"Maybe the set will fall on her next time, maybe she will catch fire—"

"That's only a holograph, it's a projection—"

"Maybe one of the flats, or a counterweight, or a batten from the flyspace—that should do it! I want to see her brains splattered like jelly!"

"Your ladylike qualities and demure restraint are always attractive—"

"She has no shadow! None! She is a wraith with no shadow!"

"I know. I know. But we have to wait. You mustn't do anything; the others will know what to do. Get a grip on yourself!"

Looking right through him, "She can't upstage me like that! Nobody does that to me! Nobody!"

It was earlier when the alleged crime occurred. When the entire cast filtered into the theater, filling the green rooms to overflowing, layering on makeup and wigs and tight bodices, dodging carpenters and scene pieces being flown in on old hemp lines, avoiding a full complement of orchestra musicians struggling with their instruments through the narrow passageways and then assembling fully costumed for dress rehearsal. Flymen yelled out warnings as they moved a lineset shifting scenery into position and nearby cast and crew called in response, even in between reading lines, ignoring the interruption because it had always been done that way in theater. Everyone put up with the chaos for the simple reason that sometimes, amazingly, a production broke free of its mortal chrysalis to reveal high art of the most ephemeral design and those were the moments that they all lived for. Art was everything.

Except in rare instances where darker intentions were present, where other forces were at work, where hatred simmered in beings that were constantly fighting off long dead enemies. There had been so much trouble between management and the unions, the soaring costs, the accidents and temperamental artists nobody knew for sure where the malignancy lay, but the foreboding was palpable. Jean-Luc Vigo paced, a lone figure in a black coat with the collar turned up and a scarf circling his neck twice: around whom everything that mattered in the production orbited, the orientation point for all creative decisions, the master of the stage, the last word. People tended to stay out of his way so as not to disturb the vision for fear it would dissipate because as real as it seemed, everyone knew it was only illusion.

Then out of the swirling whirlwind a magical landscape appeared over which glimmered a skyfall of diamonds casting faint blue shadows; players arose forged in character accompanied by transcendent music rising from the pit at the foot of the stage. Voices pierced the air, high emotions swept the house, chills visited all who listened. Under the ivory moon three attendants to the Queen of the Night, bantered back and forth in turmoil, in distress, in despair. Something inevitable was going to happen, something tragic, something fantastic. The sopranos and tenors intertwined like climbing flocks of birds soaring as one and their energy transformed the theater into another world: one of spirits and hidden powers, of legends and forgotten histories, of immortal love and death, of virtue and perdition, of resurrection and decay, a world resting on a higher plane.

Just when all the singers reached a godlike crescendo the beauty of which they were certain no one could surpass, and one soprano in particular gloated in her achievement, an impossibly beautiful presence appeared in a burst of thunder from the shadows so emblazoned, so dynamic and so utterly spiritual even the players had to shield their eyes. It was Ravenia, Queen of the Night descending. "Here in my heart," she sang, "hell's bitterness!" Until this moment, no one had heard her sing this role, no one had heard her sing like this at all; her practice had been in secret, her complete withdrawal had left everyone unprepared for this, as if she had channeled the Gods for this one moment sweeping away lesser beings with just her presence alone. Her sudden voice pierced the firmament with a mystic power and exquisiteness that could have resurrected the dead. It was music no mortal ever heard as a voice beyond the range of mere humans lifted all present on wings of the divine whether they were ready for it or not.

The whole theater became still in emotion's grip, stagehands struck dumb froze in their tasks, onlookers became spellbound, musicians caught up in such rapture that the passion of their playing about burst their hearts. No one would forget the performance that night. No one. It was etched indelibly in their collective memory. It was destined from the moment Revenia stepped on stage as Queen of the Night to be one of those rare treasured moments in the history of theater passed down through the inner circles, through cabals of dreamers from performer to performer, teacher to student, acolyte to acolyte causing hushed reverence, everyone wishing they could have been witness and only the bravest wishing they could achieve its equal.

To everyone, it was an immortal performance. Everyone except the upstaged soprano, the one who now festered in a dressing room offstage, the one who was blinded by the light of brilliance and in it saw only something to be destroyed.

Devlin had found her by accident under the intoxicating influence of Paris's two thousand years. He had spent three days following every piece of information he could dig up on Guillaume Marchand, the employee of Endecott Technologies ignominiously dumped in the Harlem River, and it was like chasing down the wind because whatever he found he discovered more that was unknown. And now the missing wife had turned up, elusive Dutch artist Lieke Marchand; at least that's what a gallery owner in the Saint-Germain-des-Prés district of the Rive Gauche had implied when he stumbled into the place by chance—or perhaps by fate. Whatever brought him to the gallery hidden on the side street was a mystery, but he immediately recognized some of the paintings because they were like the ones he had seen in SoHo just two weeks earlier. Yes, he was her French dealer; yes, she is quite "Expressionniste Néo, très sexy…" just like her work; yes, he just saw her here, in Paris—this week!

Brioche for breakfast with coffee in a bowl was a quick fix before hitting the streets to try and find the missing artist. Once outside, the kaleidoscope of Paris was deafening. Taxis with surly foreign drivers barreled through streets with names he couldn't pronounce. Silent music seemed to waft down narrow boulevards, carrying lost emotions from the past, mingling with the cacophony of the present, foretelling an inescapable future.

In this parfait metropolis the Muslim community was huge, but so was the Algerian, the North African, Bosnian, Russian—somehow they all fit in to the diorama hinting at what was to come while still reflecting the city's celebrated history. Nobody here was out of place as if all the seemingly random events were scripted roles in an evolution of *Lutetia Parisiorum*, the Roman moment—each leaving an enduring mark then moving on to make way because it was always about the new here and what was to come. Devlin knew that. The old rules didn't apply and he began to get the impression that life was malleable, like Alice's Wonderland—now you see it, now you don't. Except for one crucial detail: wherever he went was the feeling he had been there before, knew what was around the next corner, could find his way in the dark, was scanning faces for old friends, understood the significance of the long running play that was Paris.

Here too he was hoping to outrun her, but whenever he slowed down he thought of Veronica. Her face, her eyes, her scent intruded, made it real that nobody could live alone even if they tried like he had. It was his weakness that drew him to her. Like a camouflaged hole in his makeup it gave him a hunger that only she could fulfill, whether through the clinging nature of love or raw, craven desire. The one true thing was an irrational sense of fear growing inside with each new step he took in the investigation. Only now there was no Veronica to help him sort things out.

He knocked on the door of the ancient flat two flights up from a small gourmet food shop at street level. Yellow light streamed from windows into the misty blue haze that oozed from the river Seine across the road where an occasional car passed.

"Lieke, Lieke Marchand?" Devlin asked.

"Who are you?" She peered from behind the door with a piercing gaze as if through a microscope at some oblivious single celled creature.

"I'm the one who found your husband."

Suddenly, she had the look of a bird flying into glass; everything else was put on hold.

Inside firelight cast flickering shadows. The city danced in iridescent whirlpools on the night river and he could see boats go by from the window. Lamps were turned down casting moody shadows while bebop streamed from the stereo. The small apartment was crowded with modernist treasures: midcentury furniture, abstract paintings, drawings pinned to the walls helter-skelter, and a huge mobile in the corner dangling with brightly colored geometric shapes that moved mysteriously in the stillness.

"Would you like some tea?" She said handing him a cup that smelled of spice and oranges. "Red Zinger, hope you don't mind… it's a friend's apartment," and sat across from him sipping hers, one leg folded beneath in a white leather Barcelona chair. "Thought I'd be safe," she said pulling a long, gray, cashmere, sweater close, hunching her shoulders slightly, holding the cup with both hands, staring straight ahead, trying to cover a translucent top and skin tight leggings that only came half way down her shins. "I wasn't expecting anyone."

Her skin was the color of hazelnuts but appeared darker against the white leather chair in the glimmering light. Her limbs, long and athletic, folded into perfect symmetry when she sat down. The face, however, was a sketch; thick, spiked blonde hair; a broad flat plain across her cheekbones with large intense eyes; a narrow jaw with full lips—he could not get an impression of what she actually looked like because she seemed to emit momentary radiance, as if being struck by photons or other sub atomic particles invisible to the eye, and then fall back into the shadow of anonymity. He felt like he was facing a reflection in a pool.

"You have disappeared."

"I know. I like to live with a small footprint. How did you find me?"

"There are questions, lots of questions…" he began bucking the fear that had been dogging him, "…does anyone else know you're here?"

Elusive by nature they talked nearly an hour before he even began to get a hint of who she was. It was touch and go whether she would throw him out. The fact he worked for a government agency wasn't exactly an endorsement, and stirred up things she didn't want to tell anyone—money secrets he guessed, more important than regular secrets. But she seemed to need someone to talk to. He offered up implausible explanations as to why he was there: that it wasn't official business, he was just helping a friend who happened to be a homicide cop...who happened to be working on the case of her murdered husband...the body of whom he just happened to have discovered...and that he just happened to find her while vacationing in Paris. It was a hard sell until he let slip he had seen her paintings at the gallery opening in New York.

"You speak the language of spirits," he said

A slight smile. She softened and brought out a bottle of Beaujolais Juliénas. Trust was everything. "This wine comes from a village named after Julius Caesar. The growers believe it was the site of the first vineyards planted in Beaujolais by the Romans over two thousand years ago. You can only buy it after the harvest, in December." After a few glasses the conversation turned personal, as if she had just been waiting for the moment.

"I'm a gold digger," she said," I admit it. I never want to be without lots of money."

"You marry him for money?"

"You have to understand what it's like being poor," she leaned over and placed the glass on the coffee table. "When I was a kid...my father was a brute, a pig, never had any money...I think he drove her to madness—my mother...when I was sixteen she left and I begged to go with her, but she wouldn't let me. Just vanished. Went to Gothenburg, Sweden. Found her years later and I went to see her—broken, bitter, irrational. She told me never to come back, never. My own mother. I don't know how she took care of herself until I started sending money."

Devlin felt her raw creative energy, the physicality with which she expressed herself, the erotic aura that drew him in.

"What did you do when she left?"

"Got a scholarship. Ran away and became a lawyer...ended up at the Erasmus School of Law in Rotterdam," furling her brow, "can you believe it? Took a while, I worked...paid my own way. It was at the law firm I met my first husband...a venture capitalist, he had lots of money and it was faster than law...none of the lawyers I dated ever had enough. Now I can afford to be an artist. I have to laugh, poor guy, wouldn't let him have sex with me for the longest time...told him he'd have to marry me. Then one day he blew up, really, really mad and broke things in my apartment. Put his fist through the door. Then he wouldn't see me, started going out with other women—I couldn't deal with that, couldn't sleep, became obsessed with him. Finally, we talked and he told me I was just another girl he was dating, so I let him have me...once. Then I teased him; I mean I really teased him, made him crazy until he married me. But I had to sign a prenup, if I walked away I'd leave with only what I'd arrived with. Of course, over the next couple years I wore him down until he gave me my own money...he didn't like not having sex... it wasn't like he couldn't afford it. He was stingy. A greedy, cheeseparing man. Then he changed his will, then he changed the prenup, and then I started to feel secure. But love, that never entered my mind. Like I said... gold digger."

"So when did you meet Guillaume?"

"He used to market where I did. Ended up having sex in the parking lot. He was generous and wealthy, didn't care about the money, all he wanted was me. Gave me anything I wanted, my own bank account, credit cards...we moved in together and married when my divorce was final. He got what he wanted; I got what I wanted.

"How wealthy was he?"

"Endless. I don't know. Never anything we couldn't have."

"Didn't that seem strange? He was an employee."

"I never asked him about money. We never talked about it, except toward the end. Something was different, something had happened. He was tense all the time, secret phone calls, all-nighters…he wasn't eating right—"

"What happened?"

"Don't know. They began having some computer trouble, something that affected trading. Had to be about money; must have been losing money. He was always trying to figure it out, working long hours—I hardly ever saw him. He was a mathematician you know, a quant, created mathematical models with artificial intelligence—"

"What kind of trouble?"

"My feeling was that they were under attack. It's a new field, a competitive business, there's big money at stake…but he'd found something toward the end, he'd found something…and somebody knew he'd found something! I wasn't there when they discovered him… when you…I was away. Then, when I heard about Guillaume, I left the country—" Suddenly intense, eyes wide. "Can't tell anyone I'm here! You can't! Something's wrong, terribly wrong. I don't want to end up like him. Thank God I've got my own money."

They talked until the clouds had passed completely from the sky and the moon rose, into the small hours when only the forsaken were on the streets. It all seemed so hushed. He knew he should go, but after the third glass of Beaujolais and listening to her in the firelight, impassioned like an artist in a mad flurry of creation rushing to realize a vision before it vanished, he found it harder and harder to tear himself away. She had needed someone to listen. He needed to hear a human voice. Nobody could live alone. There was an animal chained inside and he understood how men with power and money could be ensnared by this woman, foolishly dropping like leaves to caress her flawless nut like skin and possess that lean, athletic body when all she wanted was a confessor with a bank account. He listened to her lost in private thoughts. Then Lieke was standing before him, her long legs sheathed in white, her sweater falling open revealing the outline of small, pointed breasts as she stretched languorously like a cat. The atmosphere became electric, had changed from that of the mind to earth rhythms older than civilization. He tried to suppress his sexual feelings, but in the end, that only made it worse. Between the alcohol and the moment his emotions circled around in an ever spinning spiral.

He awoke in the cool white bed dreaming of warm smooth flesh, longing for things to be different. Daylight streamed through bare windows. Every thought was of sex as he lay half-awake struggling back to full consciousness. Images from the night lingered in the periphery. He had wanted to press against her, to come together in one fluid motion and fall onto the sheets where they would devour each other: all mouths and kisses, hands and hidden places, undulating like sea anemones in the current that was stronger than either of them, an uncontrollable force that bent them to its will, threatening to sweep them away into the infinite ocean where they would be lost like all who violate the laws of nature. He felt her hot breath on him, but when he turned she was not there, only a phantasm of the night before. Throughout the day he felt remorse. He had fallen into the vast cauldron of confusion that lay just beneath the surface and hid the truths by which right and wrong could be deciphered and ended up reeling, thoughts of regret and pleasure stalking him, though instinctually he understood that if he allowed too many chance meetings to escape any hope of happiness would elude him in the end.

*   *   *   *

"Art is as important as air and water." Sanja Singhal said as they drove to the theater in the back of the long Maybach salon car in which she had called for Devlin at the river quay. "Going to the opera is to totally immerse yourself in the sounds and visions of a work of art. Opera is not a sort of extravaganza, it's just like an exhibition or a museum; it is art, and art is as important as air and water. It makes us better human beings."

From the moment he pierced the veil of the Palais Garnier that night, he entered a world lost in time. Out of nowhere he remembered that the Paris Opera dated back to the founding of the Académie d'Opéra in 1669 during the reign of Louis XIV, that the "Sun King" had been an accomplished dancer, had acquired his epithet the from his performance in the *Ballet de la Nuit* of 1653. He could have sworn there was a carriage waiting outside from the stable of pure white horses kept for the original opera troupe underneath the forecourt just as when it had first opened. The familiarity was inescapable. How could he know these things? How could it be so? But in that instant, he knew the place well.

They ascended the stone steps and entered the theater. He stood quietly under the arched dome rising in Baroque splendor six stories above, stood in awe at the bottom of the impossibly grand staircase as it descended from two directions in a sensual sweep of precious, polished, marbles past gleaming bronze *torchères* to the floor laid with mosaics as intricate as carpets. He imagined elegant ladies of the haut monde with long, white necks in ankle-length gowns of black satin with subdued floral embroidery, silk trim and ruffles at their hems, slightly lifting their dresses, revealing slender ankles, climbing the stairs. The shock of memory took his breath away.

"Remarkable," he said in reverie, "it's the most magnificent place I've ever—"

"Almost didn't happen," Sanja said ascending the staircase still bound in the tight tailored suit having come straight from the office. "Construction halted many times: lack of funding, the Franco-Prussian War, the demise of Napoleon III's empire…during the 1871 siege of Paris, the half-finished shell was used as prison and munitions storage. Nearly a hundred prisoners were chained to the walls, left alone in darkness with only the drip of water and fear of instant death caused by some reckless guard smoking around stores of gunpowder. You can still see initials carved into the walls next to rusted manacles. Back then, people wanted it demolished. Represented a fallen empire. If you go too far in any of the theater's deep underground passages you may end up in the catacombs, connected to the cellars in several places. They are serpentine, stretching under most of Paris, and filled to the brim with human skeletons."

"What saved it?"

"Love and fire," she said. "The old opera in Rue Le Peletier burned down in 1873. Nobody knows if it was arson or accident. Suddenly, the wealthy had nowhere to go at night. But aristocrats loved their opera, and opera loved their wealth. It's obvious. You cannot have theater without large generosity. It finally opened with a lavish gala in January 1875 to a standing ovation for its creator, Charles Garnier, and the glory he had brought to Paris; but the architect himself had not even been invited.

"Bixby Endicott is a great patron of the opera; an archangel on the board of directors of the Met in New York. A great philanthropist…gives millions out of his own pocket…are you all right?"

"Oh, yea…fine…fine…" steadying himself.

"Look a little distant."

"The rich surroundings."

"Don't let them fool you. From prima donna to stagehand opera is governed by intrigue and rumor: everyone jostling for position, defending their territory. Bix has been trying to entice the young diva here to perform at the Met; hasn't met the little vixen's price yet. Everyone has an agenda. It was always that way; the height of fashion was to have your box at the opera where you could receive your mistress and conduct business. But it was the masses that filled the audience. Even the cheapest top-tier seats are covered in red velvet. Trickle-down economics."

"That's one way to see it," he said, pondering how insufferable it all was, thinking of the theater's cost borne by thousands who were not granted access to it. He had never attended an opera because of this instinct: that it was the art of an elite culture, the expression of a tyrannical class made possible by exploitation, built by a small aristocracy on the backs of impoverished subjects. It went against his nature.

She smiled an insider's smile. "For the price of our company box by the stage, we can disappear behind a doorway to our own red-carpeted lobby, into a boudoir swathed in ruby silk damask. On the edge are pull-up panels to ward off curious glances from the mob — to reflect incited passions."

All at once they emerged into the breathless grand foyer. It was gilded and sumptuous, full of intricate detail and majesty with two lines of giant bronze and crystal, double tiered chandeliers, dangling from ornate painted ceilings, rising to over a hundred feet, sheathed in gold, braced by towering columns of Pyrenean marble. Legendary tales hung in the air as a prelude to the spectacle to come in the mythic place of art that held its secrets close.

"It's the magic of it…" Sanja said glancing back, making her way to the box seats beneath a massive fresco by Chagall and a grand chandelier that hung like an elephant by a thread—whose counterweight once fell under mysterious circumstances, killing an audience member, fueling the Phantom's legend.

Soon darkness descended and a faint light appeared on a seemingly insignificant conductor lost in the theater's haunted heart. Devlin felt a chill. Suddenly the dramatic first chords of Mozart's Die Zauberflöte overture lifted everyone on wings to a timeless world just as at its first performance in 1791. The ethereal music swept Devlin with godlike crescendos so deeply moving, so charged with life that he was stunned. Snow-blind and without boundaries he could not resist. The real world faded then disappeared and he drifted free of work and traffic and entanglements astonished at the power. Soon the full cast of characters trickled into the onstage fantasy, bathed in blue violet starlight, and perfect otherworldly voices rose intertwined leaving him enraptured.

Just as he thought nothing could surpass his experience and when he had been drawn into the wonderland completely, a figure appeared: regal and dark and commanding. The Queen of the Night stormed the stage. While all other characters cowed in her radiance, paled beneath her umbra, she began to sing an aria so exquisite, so flawless, so unearthly that Devlin felt an overpowering urge to rise from his seat and take flight never to return. The thundering power and tumultuous force of that fine soprano transformed everything in that moment and he saw a flickering light, had a brief glimpse of an essential truth so elemental and elusive that it could have fulfilled everything he had ever searched for but never found. It was a fleeting glimmer of something missing, an answer to his imperfections, an explanation for the unknowns of existence. But it was fleeting and once passed forgotten. Tears flowed from his eyes despite a struggle to hide them so no one would notice his weakness.

All the while the young diva Revenia, goddess of the spotlights, sang. He felt hope for the first time since he was a child and was witnessing a phenomenon beyond his grasp. Though he tried to believe the feeling was real, struggled to accept the unknown, he couldn't and so was pulled back into the dark whirlpool of his life.

Since before he had arrived in Paris, Bixby Endicott had been in damage control: a tumult of meetings ensued to reassure clients, bolster investment managers' confidence and try to land new business. All of his friends, the East Coast Brahmins, the digerati committed to high speed computer trading, the ones who had thought him such a bon vivant and so charismatic, who had applauded his genius and shared in his success, were now suspects. Sleep eluded him because he never stopped and even when he hit the sheets, usually past 2 AM, he made calls to New York and then spent the rest of the night fitfully trying to figure it all out. The attacks not only threatened his intellectual property, but by proxy his mental stability, which he could never allow anyone to discover if he was to maintain any political ambitions. The meeting at his compound in North Harbor had gone well, American Voices was generating dark money campaign funds at an ever increasing rate and most of the party's heavyweights saw him as marketable, but someone was trying to stop him and worse, trying to deplete his resources. It all sort of validated his supreme belief that money was the root of everything and without it he would be dust, just one of the faceless billons that subsisted in droll anonymity. The thought incited panic; fear that left him shaken. Something would have to be done, but he didn't know just what yet.

"I want you to come to New York and make history," he said. "I have reassurance from the management at the Met nothing will be held back to stage a truly legendary production—" The incessant buzzing of his cell phone drove him to distraction as he fumbled for it in his coat pocket. "Excuse me…I have to take this…" Moments later, after brief but heated discussion with his office, "I apologize. My life has become a labyrinth of anxiety; caught between crisis and ambition I guess," he smiled unconvincingly.

"… between faith in yourself and doubt," Revenia said showing strong interest. "Sometimes it's difficult to tell light from dark."

He just looked at her for a minute letting an overwhelming wave of grief pass, and then rebounded. "I am such an admirer; your art is truly a gift. It's just that I want a wider audience to experience it, now, when you are just on the cusp of a great career."

"You flatter me…but I can never leave Paris'" she said. "My agent has told you the same."

"I never rely on a third party when negotiating a deal. Would be something for you to remember the rest of your life, a touchstone, and I wanted to appeal to your artistic nature. It's really all about art, isn't it?"

"Life is long, so you never can tell," she said blithely, then furling her brow uttering, "…much longer than you might think."

A waiter came by with white shirt, black vest and a bow tie and filled the glasses with San Pellegrino. The young diva picked up the flute with long thin fingers and drank while Bixby pondered the profanity of her sweet lips out of which such glorious refrains issued and through which she consumed food like an animal. Her face was young and smooth and exquisite.

"It just may be that someone else knows better; that you should trust us for the greater good. For art. Opera is on fragile ground these days."

His words seemed to darken her. "I have a difficult time trusting anyone…" The thought trailed off as if it was too close, too private.

"To me," he said perplexed, perceiving some unfathomable contradiction that made her unwilling to open up, "I just can't imagine what it must be like being you; boggles the mind. You see, I live in sort of a rude, callus world where everything is based on statistics; how many, how often and how much? The main emphasis being on 'how much.' People just can't get enough. All comes down to what someone had, what they have now and what they want in the future and the whole damned scrambling game is focused on one thing; getting more…the sooner the better! Everybody wants more."

"How do they carry the weight of all that greed?"

"Were all stuck in the scheme…like politics, the greasy pole, it's possible to make it to the top, but staying there…that's another matter. It's a drug, makes people nervous, makes them feel stress all the time— you can get so used to it that after a while becomes part of you. Until a reminder comes along, a reminder of who you are, what life really is… that's valuable, can't buy that, it's really priceless. Your talent, your gift… you're that reminder. You must know that."

Stunned, her eyes became a translucent veil between worlds and glistened in the most vivid electric blue he had ever seen, as if a terrible secret was about to be uncovered. "I know," she said. "If I couldn't sing; I would be lost. But it's a very fragile thing, this body, youth is fleeting, it's all so easily broken. Music itself is…I like to think of it as what spirits sound like. The theatre is where I come to life, all the rest of the time…I'm a shadow passing. There it is…I can't explain any more why I must remain in Paris—everything in life hinges on something else, like a house of cards—this is where I am sheltered, where I am guarded— "

"You'll have the best security— "

"It's not enough, I'm a woman who must have everything," she said. "I must have everything..."

Later that night, after the premiere performance of a reimagined Die Zauberflöte, just yards from paparazzi lurking like land sharks, across from a throng of fans hoping for autographs, just off the traffic circle where the blur of vehicles melded greater Paris with the frenzied stream of people leaving the Palais Garnier, Bixby waited by his rented limo. He had been left breathless by the opening night performance despite her refusal, and it redoubled his resolve to seduce the young diva away to New York. So, he had arranged a late night celebration for her with select luminaries including the Ambassador to France, some celebrities and expatriate American financiers that owed him. This was his last chance; he could not endure failure.

The paparazzi boiled, piranha at the smell of blood. Revenia descended the steps like a Catholic saint on the arm of director Jean-Luc Vigo, buoyant at his resurrection from near obscurity. Bixby waved to her, camera flashes popped off like fireworks, voices cried out, arms reaching, hands grasping as she made a mad dash toward his car. Everything seemed so happy, everyone so joyous that the specter of anything other than a fairy tale ending to a perfect night was unimaginable. So when the shots rang out with that unmistakable, finite, realism which rose far above the din of the crowd, over the cries of autograph seekers, unbelievably shattering the afterglow of the night, which the crush were carrying to their cars as keepsakes, the emotional impact was devastating. Bixby's bodyguard shoved him down hard to the ground and crouched in front leveling his 9mm automatic with deadly aim trying to sort through the chaos. The red dot from his laser sight streaking across the crowd seeking a man fleeing the scene. Three more shot rang out in rapid succession. The running man fell. From behind his hired gun, Bixby could see the mass of people parting like wheat in the wind while two bodies lie still as a centerpiece: that of the young diva Revenia and triumphant director Jean-Luc.

With a crazed frenzy Bixby broke free of his bodyguard, who yelled helplessly after him, and bounded across the distance until he was on his knees at the side of the bloodied pair desperate with grief, reaching down for life, praying to a God he didn't believe existed. Suddenly, she looked up at him startled; in her eyes was the determined glare of a soldier who had seen many skirmishes, endured many hardships and suffered many broken hammers not at all the pale fire he had imagined of a frightened artist. She arose, but the director Jean-Luc did not. He lay still in a widening pool of crimson with a blank stare that showed no pain nor sorrow of a life incomplete, or anything as he soared, suddenly released from the body, above the commotion and looked down with remarkably few regrets. He had failed, but had regained his self-respect and was again at the pinnacle; he had taken what he could from this life and now must move on. Photographers descended like locusts, elbowing their way through the crowd, trying to capture the fresh carnage, relishing how much each shot would bring on the world market. Sirens screamed. Police appeared from nowhere, calling for back up, corralling the crowd while the camera flashes continued in a never ending stream like lightening on a summer's night.

"Come on!" Bixby said grabbing Revenia's arm, dragging her unseen from the mob, shoving way behind his bodyguard back to the waiting limo. And then they were gone, fleeing from the real, seeking refuge in the road. Only one thought remained, one that he would not forget; how much she had wanted to be sheltered, to be guarded. If she didn't want money, he could offer that.

Only moments before Revenia had appeared on the steps, from the edge of the crowd just leaving the theater, Sanja Singhal had waved saying to Devlin, "That's Bixby Endecott, over there, by the limo, see him? I thought he'd be here…"

Devlin saw a stocky, well dressed, sandy haired man looking as if he belonged in a sports bar watching football. Behind him a long black car waited, and another larger man was menacing at his left elbow. Then there were cries, applause and cheers, the crowd stirred, and he spotted the radiant diva descending stone steps next to a jubilant young man with jet-black hair. Camera flashes struck like shots painting everyone with harsh, dark, fleeting shadows from the blue white light, shadows that define all in this life as real, substantial, genuine; everyone except Revenia because she had no shadow. For some inexplicable reason it caught his attention, and perhaps it was the incongruity of it that riveted him as if an omen. He squinted up his eyes in disbelief trying to focus, but no matter how much he strived to refuse the reality, she cast no shadow and he was electrified with the unwillingness to see what he was seeing. His mind raced for explanations trying to fit the anomaly into some explainable phenomena; like the refraction of light, atmospheric conditions, cross fires from opposing flashes, too many glasses of Beaujolais the night before—but wherever she moved, it was the same. So bewitched the horrific scene unfolded before him while he stood in utter disbelief along with all the others as the assassin's bullets tore into flesh, bullets from a killer who seconds later was shot dead by Bixby Endicott's bodyguard. And as Revenia fled, being dragged along through the storm of Paparazzi flashes, all he noticed was that no shadow followed.

For days he couldn't shake the feeling that all these things were connected: the mysterious death of the French analyst; the secretive investment firm's founder; the enigmatic opera singer without a shadow and the grisly murder in front of the theater. But how he didn't know.

VII | Chapter 7

He rode the elevator up to the sanctum sanctorum of the commanding heights all the while looking at his reflection in the polished metal between slabs of bubinga wood from a remote rainforest in Cameroon. He pushed back his hair, straightened his collar and buttoned his jacket. He watched a small flat screen above the floor buttons that was broadcasting the morning business report until finally the doors slid open revealing a cavernous office teeming with activity. Long tables stretched out cafeteria style with workstations set up at intervals around which people, young people, were crowded all exhibiting the unbridled enthusiasm unpaid interns are prized for by big business and politicians. He felt a flood of alienation, as if still on campus where the patina of grass and brick and open courtyards filled with gleaming youth blended together as an ideal environment, the kind which the intelligentsia could expect as a fundamental human right throughout their lives — if they did what was expected of them. He was of that tribe of super people; ultra-high achieving, elite, Ivy League graduates, scions of wealth or those aspiring to it, but was not a kid who always had his priorities straight like the ones he stood before now in front of the closed elevator doors unsure if he should proceed. Fortunately, he didn't have to make up his mind; an efficient, bubbly, young woman with fluorescent white teeth escorted him into a glass walled office.

It had all come together in one cathartic instant. A thunderous collision of stars that resulted in something similar to the old, but new like the next stage in evolution. For months, senior party officials had been weighing the asset of donations pouring into their campaign coffers from American Voices against the liability of nominating a politically unknown candidate and risk the election. A generation was dying off. A certain desperation hung in the air. The upcoming contest was for blood. For over a decade, the party had been out of office and in the minority, now they were fighting for relevance, struggling for a voice, reaching out to the rising nexus of youth that had humanism and technology boiling in their veins like some witch's brew that incomprehensibly made them more savvy and more rapacious than any other generation before. Then mysteriously, it had come to them all at once, and was so simple and obvious that old idée fixes peeled away like the layers of an onion: it was still all about money. Hiding behind the veil of technological sorcery and human ascendance was filthy lucre itself; the news of its demise being greatly exaggerated. *"For there are many rebellious men, empty talkers and deceivers…"* To his great satisfaction, Bixby Endicott was immediately notified that the party was backing him for Governor of New York. Everyone associated him with overnight wealth believing as if by sorcery he had found the "Alpha" key to riches of The Street. The PR people swooned over the fact that he was already the geek-chic darling of the press—had even been in Vanity Fair. Hope spread like a gasoline fire and no one was spared.

A man in a white shirt with the sleeves rolled up to his elbows, tanned from too many hours alone on his small sailboat, sinewy forearm muscles rippling as he turned the pages, hair shaved off as a preemptory strike against premature baldness, solid straightforward glare that he learned in the Marines, a worried look he had leaned after his first child died and his wife sank into chronic depression and he realized bad things happen for no reason, poured over his resume.

"I've already seen this of course or you wouldn't be here," glowering at the young man. "We've had over eleven hundred responses, most from top graduates of top schools, some recommended by senators for Christ's sake. What's so fucking special about you?"

"I...uh, my thesis at MIT was..."

"You're an engineer, right?"

"Sort of."

"Whad'ya mean 'sort of...'"

"Well, that's almost considered an obsolete term at this point, it doesn't really describe what we do anymore. It's an old paradigm."

"So, what do you do?"

"I teach computers to make moral choices."

"You specialize in artificial intelligence it says here."

"Yes, in a leading-edge way. Like I said, it really doesn't describe what we do anymore."

"Shouldn't we be very careful about that? I mean, isn't it more of a threat than a benefit? With artificial intelligence we're summoning the demon. You know those stories where there's the guy with the pentagram, and the holy water, and he's like —"

"Artificial intelligence started with the machine age really. Think about it, machines supplanting human functions. Even your email is artificial intelligence, it's just a matter of degree."

"You mean, how intelligent?"

"Sort of...it's not time saving or less work we're interested in anymore. It's game theory; like what role do you want a machine to play, and what role do you want? We're ultimately in control, but a moral machine takes less supervision. It's an artificial intelligence able to autonomously assess a difficult situation and then make complex ethical decisions that can override the rigid instructions it was given."

"...guiding the moral compass. How do you do that?"

"It's a very difficult problem. First, I try to break down human moral competence into its basic components, develop a framework for human moral reasoning, then model this framework in an algorithm that can be embedded in an artificial intelligence. The infrastructure should allow the robot to override its instructions in the face of new evidence and justify its actions to the humans who control it."

"How about influencing the moral choices of others?"

"I don't get—"

"This is a political campaign. What we're concerned with here is perception and response, motivating thought and action, hearts and minds. For the most part, people don't consider political issues in depth except during election cycles, and then the numbers are pathetic— just plot voter turnout. They just want someone to reassure them that everything is being taken care of so they can go about their business. So, the game is how do you reach people, change their minds and get them to cast ballots? We know that politics can influence ideas and moral principles—a common enemy for instance can give political currency and support—but that's infinitely harder for an untested candidate to do than an incumbent who has policymaking and the press to lean on."

"How do I fit in to all this?"

"One idea that has been offered up by Endicott Technologies is to build a candidate model based on all the successful political winners in the past collected into a database as a sort of an avatar. Then, working with a platform based on community organizing…only on a national scale—everything will be based on computer models driven by analytic information we already have, that can contact, take data and remember it, analyze and evaluate it, restrategize further messages and media contacts such as whether it will be social or otherwise…essentially tailor messages and the grand design of the campaign according to popular response. In real time. And all this seamlessly integrated into our infrastructure so that anyone can use it from a campaign worker canvassing the field to an intern somewhere in the organization to our campaign manager and the candidate himself."

"You want to automate the national campaign process…"

"Yea, you could say that. We want a fucking robot that can win an election for our candidate. Can you do it?"

"It will be very expensive."

"Money is no object."

Winter flowed up from the two rivers, down to the sea. Children awoke to crystalline windows and pulled on three pair of wool socks to make their journey to schools around Manhattan. Rich or poor they were all thankful when the temperature rose above zero by the time they had to leave. Breath froze in the air. Skaters played hockey on the sidewalks. Icebreakers trolled the Hudson keeping the shipping lanes open; lumbering tugs followed seeking day wages from stranded freight haulers. Old timers grumbled. Lovers rolled their seed beneath warm blankets, the cold being an excuse to stay a little longer. A generation was being conceived; dreams imagined. It was the coldest season since the Children's Blizzard of 1888 when an unexpected Siberian Express careened out of the Arctic, raced down across Canada and froze the Great Lakes solid before hitting the Eastern Seaboard hard, just as now, stranding many. Technology is mute against nature's grand strategy; humans are only pawns in the game.

Perhaps that was why no one noticed, because it was like the imperceptible shift of light between the summer solstice and the next day when winter begins to approach, when shadows drift a bit longer and colors mingle with darkness making everything appear different without a clear reason why. High above, nearly touching the stratosphere, a thin white layer of cirrus cloud spread over the city like a veil: on the one side was everything people agreed was real and on the other was the unseen truth—the clouds and blue sky obscuring a cosmos filled with interstellar bodies and vast, impenetrable distances. It was like the invisible cloak that hid the difference between the way things were and how people wished them to be. The future was always summed up as…unknown. But something had shifted and people became more thoughtful, some more regretful, others felt longing or a sense of foreboding—all were affected in some way. Those who had never dreamed began to have visions and premonitions. It was an inexplicable phenomenon like the one that triggers great, immutable migrations and it gave the clergy and medical professionals apoplexy. Psychiatrists though, who were at best confused anyway, blamed it on the weather and categorized it as CWS: cold weather syndrome.

"She's coming," the raspy voice whispered in Mirella Elderia's ear.

The cavernous space behind the stage dwarfed the flaming haired singer, hovering in the wings, watching sweaty stagehands in t-shirts change a set, flying the new one in from a sixty-foot elevator, flying the old one off to a slipstage beyond the proscenium arch past the custom woven, gold damask, curtains. She did not flinch nor turn to see who had spoken or even ask who was coming, she revealed none of the emotion that rose up from the complexity of her psyche where things were always smoldering, the well of unruly passion out of which her performances were ignited. There was no way of telling that anything registered at all. During the long walk back to the dressing rooms she did not look at anyone, but with each step petty grievances festered, overrunning her sense of balance until, like a spring tide when both sun and moon are closest to Earth and pull in opposite directions, she was inundated with a sense of lost security and diminished pride.

Bursting into dressing room number one she clawed at the costumes, tore at the clothing and little, personal items, grasped bags, makeup kits and wigs tossing them violently into the hallway, kicking things that didn't move fast enough, clobbering items that lie strewn across the floor with her foot until finally she slammed the door shut and ordered the two closest stagehands to move all her belongings into "that room," the "star's dressing room—where they belonged—right away!" Her mind seethed with hidden conflicts, justified by the loss of artistic vision; first it was bringing in self-absorbed film directors who have never done opera, and as if that wasn't contempt enough for artistic values and blatant adulation of mass entertainment it then became sub rosa policy to cast "star singers" in all performances. "The public is not interested in just someone singing," she remembered Analetta pronouncing at a donor event, "they want to hear 'stars.'" Fuming. What did they think she was?! Then she vanished to one of her mysterious lunches from which she sometimes did not return.

The first stagehand looked at the other. "She needs a good—"

"Yea," came the reply, "and I'm just the man to give it to her."

The social intricacies and behavior patterns of the species opera had evolved out of the struggle for existence through hundreds of years, the force of the real branding learned responses indelibly on artists' souls. It was this hidden influence that evoked misunderstandings, and sometimes inspired dark designs.

Analetta was languishing in a stolen moment when she got the call: just before rehearsals were scheduled and the cast had not yet arrived, after the stagehands had set up and retreated to the back of the house, prior to the musicians taking their places in the pit at the edge of the apron, walking through the massive backdrops for Verdi's "Aida"—in the vacuum between fits of heroic energy and dead calm; in a breathless, evocative Valley of the Kings—searching for the fascination that always kept her going, through chaos, in darkness, the glimmer that had lured her to the theater in the beginning. She glanced at the phone. Mirella's agent. A singer who made "Diva" truly a four-letter-word.

"What complications…?"

"Mirella asked me to speak for her. She was promised the role of 'Aida'"…now it seems—"

"Promised? Promised? There were no promises…far as I know, but the artistic director—"

"It's impossible! Just impossible—"

"What's that?"

"She can't go on with this new French soprano. Impossible."

"French soprano?"

"I'm really trying my best…don't be coy."

"…not sure I like your tone. We have no French soprano."

"She warned me…the unions will hear about this. I'd think you'd be more careful after just narrowly avoiding a lockout."

"Now look. It's the company—"

"That director…he's pacing it too quick for her, she can't caress the notes, she can't give her best performance…it's all about her audience, but that director…some personal vision…it goes against the essence! Has he ever directed opera?"

"I told them…they have to work it out…they're professionals. They have to work it out."

"Remember her 'Carmen!' Mirella's boffo for you. You have to talk to that director. And about the lead role–"

"I don't *have* to do anything, but this is what I will do," giving the silence between them a moment. "We'll compromise. Does that seem all right? I'll give Mirella one more chance to show up when she's supposed to, behave herself and quit wasting everybody's time with frivolous accusations. And if she does these things, if she's diligent about them, then I won't fire her. How does that sound? Does that sound fair?"

Afterwards, she felt deflated. Under siege. Everyone with their hands held out for more. The day had started promising enough, bright with anticipation, as if a spirit had arrived from the other side and awakened the dancing animal, but she burned out right there on the phone in the middle of the magnificent Egyptian set.

Like porcelain, like a priceless piece of art from tombs sealed airless for centuries: with the light of day, one glimpse, one careless move—dust and a million tiny fragments. Like a ceaseless river, she was always rushing; like an ancient torrent cutting granite. Beauty teased and she in turn had chased down its shimmering promise not realizing it was like trying to catch lightening in a bottle until it was too late. Art is long; life is short. To all others, she was an opera maven, elegant, aloof, yet a demanding businesswoman who had garnered curses and respect from the unions for being a tough and pragmatic negotiator. During heated talks on renovations between the city and the directors she had asked the hard questions nobody else would, was the only one who challenged unsound plans, and consequently was panned by the Times as an irascible, trenchant critic against the whole idea when in fact she was simply a realist who could not suffer fools. Asking a colleague why no one else disputed these obvious concerns, he answered that she was the only one who did her homework, and everyone expected she would, so they wouldn't have to. All of these things simmered beneath the glass and no one would have guessed how fragile it all was. As she left the stage and walked up the empty center aisle, looking back, giving the set furtive glances, itemizing the flaws, the imperfections in the aesthetic balance, she made detailed mental notes that would all be taken care of by the end of the night. Aneletta ran the house for blood and had put it in the black for the first time in a decade. She depended on the fact that nobody argues with money as defense for her other faults.

Francotti Benedetto collapsed into a chair, his long black hair slicked back like a Ferrari roadster, unbuttoned sleeves hanging out of his jacket and crumpled up shirttails strewn across his lap. He had been flown in from Rome where he was discovered by one of the scouts making an art film at La Scalla about a ruthless, aging prostitute trying to help her daughter make it as a prima donna. He had never directed opera before but had achieved some acclaim; she wanted him for his aura and the millennials that tumbled in his wake as if he was a rock star.

Analetta hovered in a black silk, crepe suit next to a man with a meticulous goatee. "I'd like to introduce our designer—"

"No...no...I do all my own designs," Francotti blustered in a thick Italian brogue. "Here are some thoughts I had on the plane," producing several cocktail napkins with rough sketches in blue ballpoint and tossing them on the desk, "and a few more I did at the airport bar."

"I'm sure they're very nice, but—"

"Tell me I didn't make the trip for nothing..." he threw up his hands.

"We haven't had the time to bring you up to speed on the resources at your disposal here. At the Met everything is manufactured in-house: sets, costumes—"

He clasped his heart with both hands. "I have a vision! It's the only way I can work. This emotion—"

All day long the line of flat-screen monitors lit up her office above the polished concrete floor and the huge gray carpet centered on it and beside the art on the walls. They peered into every corner of the massive complex and told the story of life in the theater: its heartbeat at any given moment, when the stage was blazing with dreams and when some of them were realized, when voices cracked on the money notes, when sets failed and singers tumbled into the orchestra pit like rag dolls, when audiences rose as one in ecstatic rapture and when others booed and hissed and fell from slaps and bloodied noses. Like shifting tides, like waves upon the shore, the ceaseless roar of creation filled the house at all hours—but she was even more mercurial.

A dozen calls were handled before 8 AM. No breakfast and lots of coffee. Followed by back-to-back meetings with one or the other of the opera's sixteen unions; temperamental artist's agents; city officials threatening a major slice of endowment; donors of all varieties; marketing and PR people pushing obtuse campaigns; fund-raisers; affiliate and network lackeys bickering over broadcast rights; condescending board members and the few all important angels—many of whom lived out of state and had to be wedged in on the fly—who vied to underwrite important productions. Lunch was reserved for meeting with talent: singers, directors, designers, composers—usually with creative managers, agents, scouts and sometimes with the company's music director when he wasn't guest conducting somewhere else.

Afternoons found her on the floor making everything about the opera her business, talking to people in every department just to get the feel of what was happening from those who made it happen—not from the high-tech, video surveillance system that fed into her office where she was expected to absorb the pulse in isolation. She preferred the hot breath.

"Directors..." a seamstress in the costume shop grumbled sardonically, "the new divas!" She spoke with a healthy disdain, "... they're coming into these productions thinking they're making movies. They want real clothes, not costumes! Like...we can't leave as much seam allowance...it's just...too stressful."

Sweeping behind the scenes into the enchanted workshops where sleight of hand was a fine art, where bedazzling audiences was routine, where the present was transformed into other centuries. "We can make plastic look like marble, steel look like wood, and wood look like steel," quipped an artist in the scenic shop, "but it's taking much longer. All the props have to be more realistic...they're shooting it like television, everyone's sitting in the front row!"

"Jobs have changed more in the past decade than in the past hundred years," the master carpenter pined with vague regret. "We have departments that seven or eight years ago didn't exist...nobody could've predicted...hell, nobody would've known what they were!"

Inside a rehearsal studio all the dancers stopped like a flock of pink flamingos in perfect unison, looked at her and said hello, then just as quickly were back in character following the music as if there had been no interruption.

But it was later that night under muted lamplight in her office alone nursing a whiskey beneath the high windows looking out over a New York City flash frozen by the long running cold snap, windows whose corners were blurred with ice crystals, after the singers had reluctantly broken away from their obsession and along with the dancers and musicians fled homeward to see their families and only the craftsmen who expected an all-nighter were left, it was then she thought that grand opera was dying along with its increasingly ancient audience.

"I knew I'd find you here!" Bixby came in for a landing at full tilt red faced and sweaty behind his Ivy League grin.

"I've just been considering mortality" she said startled from her reverie. "The edge of the precipice."

"Yea, yea, it's an existential battle that has to be won…but listen —"

"I've just contracted a film director with a following, but now…I'm having second thoughts. Millennials were brought up to be technological wizards…and to have the attention spans of mice. How do you educate them to like opera, which takes three or four hours and is in a foreign language?"

"She's coming!"

Analetta looked at him unmoved. "Well, I hope *she's* bringing money to help with the deficit I just found out about," tossing down the rest of the whiskey in one quick gulp.

"Wanted to tell you personally. Ran all the way up the stairs… couldn't even wait for the elevator!"

"How was Paris? At least New Yorkers don't shoot the director if they don't like the show."

"Forget Paris…hey, you're buzzed aren't you?"

"Drunk's more like it…first time in ten-years."

"Yea, well fasten your seat belt! I have sobering news. Revenia's agreed to the run of a production."

"What'd you—"

"She's here now! In New York!"

"Here? Now?" Analetta stood up and calmly placed her glass on the desk. "That changes everything doesn't it...how'd you—"

"I think she's scared...Christ's sake someone took a shot at her!"

"I thought the target was the director."

"That's what they wanted people to go for."

"You mean–"

"Police think the guy was just a bad shot."

"I can't believe..." she replied while in her mind's eye a spectacle of light and shadow began to play out against the massive Egyptian sets and though despairing just moments earlier she arose from the ashes at the first glister of hope—even if a fool's hope. All her life it had been the same, inexorably bound to the belief that something will happen; it was the unappeasable law, the ever present judgment of moon and stars that gave her grit and a tenacious drive. Then when something she had postulated actually appeared, infinite space opened up where before there had only been solid ground. It was a rollercoaster between the real and the visionary. Blackness and light and nothing in between gave her a reputation for eccentricity. But she could count on the fingers of one hand the people who had contributed to her; had lost count of all those who had tried to stop her; was a woman of the future who toiled for art up against a world of indifference, but it only took the faintest glimmer—the young French diva arriving—out of thin air—to bring her back from the precipice where all dreamers end up cynical and drunk, inevitable for those who live on thin ice, whose expectations are overdrawn.

"I'm full of bright ideas," she said, "wild ideas. Let's have another drink…Francotti Benedetto and our young diva will mount a phantasmagorical 'Aida' for the emerging world. We will reach new audiences! New artistic heights! New bank balances! Donors will clamor to fund this production; the press alone will make it a success — 'A prodigal singer fleeing violence performing for the first time in America!' She will be our Paderewski; her triumphs will create a furor. I drink to them; they will be our saviors tonight!" The amber whisky sparkled in the cut crystal as they raised their glasses together, drinking it down an elixir to the ever lurking darkness, forcing deeper concerns out of their minds, wishing it would make them vanish, knowing it was only a reprieve.

But there was one nagging thought that refused be relegated to the backwaters, and though she could not understand its relative importance in the scheme of things, it seemed to portend events beyond her powers to control. Mirella had known the young French diva was coming, knew she would take the leading soprano role in "Aida" before Bixby had announced it. Knew it all before she had ever even imagined it.

Chapter 8

Like a figure walking in dreamtime, far on an isolated beach with waves and mist intermingling under a low sky, making recognition almost possible, within grasp—yet just a shade too far away to be sure. There was something in the papers, something in the damned digital files he had been staring at until his vision blurred and he burned with frustration—yet just a shade too far away to be sure.

Devlin still had his hand wrapped around a tall, now lukewarm, cardboard cup of Sumatra on his ride to the office in a taxi he took expressly so he could swing by Brownie's Deli and pick up the one onion bagel in New York he prized—even if Manhattan was the center of the universe for the boiled, baked, bread rings. The Russian scowled at him in the rear view mirror, hair bristling on the back of his neck, thick muscular arms grasping the fragile steering wheel, threatening to pulverize it with his bare hands, parking in the street just so the lawyer could run inside for coffee and rolls. *"If I git a fuking tiket you're paying!"* Later, after Devlin tipped him, he held his hand out for more. More was never enough.

He stared down on a massive vessel moored at the North Cove

Yacht Harbor, looking out the window of his office just south of Tribeca along the Hudson waterfront in Lower Manhattan thankful he had the river to look at despite the extravagances of the rich below that rubbed him the wrong way. It reminded him he had to travel all the way past 165th Street to reach Sherman Creek Park where he launched his scull to row the Harlem River. That was real. With every stroke he connected to the cauldron of humanity seething outside the borders of privilege; he did not want to lose that covenant, it was his blood. The fact that much of the world's population lived on less than five dollars a day and most didn't have fresh water to drink was his cross, it burned into him as if a stigma; looking down he felt like one of the anonymous ants in a glass enclosed farm with the bulk of humanity looking curiously in rather than the other way around. Outside the pockets of culture barbarians still bled: far more outside than inside. There had to be something else to it than ruthlessly carving out a niche, defending it against the mob until one was overwhelmed by sheer numbers; or stupefied by the realization that life is symbiotic and greed violated natural law; or managed to isolate oneself from all things human in a hermetically sealed enclave of wealth desperately pretending that stuff fulfilled every need. Every path lead to death, so how he lived made all the difference. It gave him a reason.

Within spitting distance were many of the great social institutions. Global banks, too-big-to-fail investment firms, the Federal Reserve, the New York Stock Exchange, City Hall...the Irish Hunger Memorial. Inside the fiery beast homeless roamed the streets at night; luxury cars roamed them by day. The incongruity of it drove him wild until he finally realized he wasn't supposed to look at it, at least not all at once, remembering the lessons in public good economics from the University of Chicago, steeling his nerve until he could equate life and death and happiness to the irreducible minimum of how much welfare programs saved everyone in the long run, making them a good investment even for staunch conservatives, shuffling off to their walled compounds where they were free to practice their laissez-faire philosophy. He felt heat from the borders of the world burning to the ground, floods of refugees trampling the glowing embers with their bare feet desperate for opportunity. He heard them crying. It was his motivation.

"What the hell is this?" The heavy galumph of musty storage boxes hitting his desk snapped his attention, which had been absorbed by the flat screen computer monitor for the three hours since he had arrived.

"What you asked for. Pertinent data," the smart looking black woman slapped another box down on the blue carpeted floor.

"How come it's not pertinent digital data?"

"Don't keep computer records."

"Who doesn't?"

"Political action committees."

"What do you mean? They have to keep records. It's the law."

"Keep records all right. Just not digital. You're looking at some — makes them harder to investigate," she pushed the dolly out the door smiling.

"Why didn't you get help?" Devlin yelled after her.

"Boss says you don't get any resources," she shot back from down the hall.

He frowned and took a sip of now stone cold coffee and went back to his computer, scrutinizing the figures, forgetting about the boxes. Numbers were the language of truth and even if some were fudged, inflated, made up, falsified: in the end things just wouldn't add up and he would know the story. It was like a symphony whose composer rode an unruly Pegasus wherever the spirit lead him, speaking the language of music to vent emotions people didn't even know they had, illuminating inner places long untouched, so long they had been forgotten until the symphony resolved and clarified all that had gone before. It didn't matter how abstract and postmodern the notes became on their journey, how they soared in epiphany dissonant and chaotic and untamed like the seas of Cape Wrath, they had to make sense at some point, they had to for it all to be real. Numbers were like that, no matter how meticulous the forgery, they yearned in the end to make sense. And he read them like an epic tale of civilization, its balance between brilliance and oblivion, the numbers told the tale in the end: at least he had to believe they did because there was no other way to expose the most ingenious of all human endeavors—financial crimes.

The Zen of data strings kept him at it all day past the point when the sun headed to the west coast, sending temperatures into the sub zones, freezing the water pipes. He was an interstellar voyager devoid of sensation in the vacuum, sailing through a virtual world sifting for clues, seeking evidence, not really certain what he was looking for, sure he would know it when he found it. Modern civilization careened forward on these rails; some making history, others inspecting it for violations of the law. You just couldn't make that much money legally. It defied human logic—yet at the commanding heights many impossible things were true and he knew without question those were the things that motivated the economic engine and fired the greed upon which the market economy relied for its slavish devotion. All an evangelist had to do was point to heaven and as cynical as an unbeliever might be, they would look. But still, somewhere ran the universal doubt: the understanding that no one could make that much money legally. So he kept at it. Past the boredom, the ennui, the tiredness until finally breaking through unconsciousness after hours of scrutinizing reams of data in hard copy print outs. At three AM he was wide awake and could have easily stayed the rest of the night except for the importance of what he had just found: a guidepost where there had been none before. So he went home in celebration. Some of his best work was done while he slept when all the information that had overloaded his circuits in daylight sorted itself out in quiet epiphanies at night.

"There's one thing I just can't get…" Devlin slid into the mauve, silk, damask, booth next to the man. Twilight streamed down from the skylights thirty stories above the street. A piano player was giving smoky renditions of some Harold Arlen tunes across the crowded room. A chill hung the air.

The waiter came by with preternatural white teeth and a jet black necktie. "More wine? Will the gentleman be wanting something?"

"No," the man at the table replied, the man with the finely woven Italian jacket whose shirt collar pulled open as he threw one arm over the back of the booth in disgust, whose receding brown hair had a sheen altogether too artificial, whose throbbing neck veins gave evidence that he worked out too hard to keep up the appearance of vitality as he pushed fifty, "he won't be staying."

"…how they could let you go when you knew so much," he pushed a business card across the white tablecloth.

The man took a cursory look. "I don't work there anymore. Go ask them. Now, I'm waiting for someone—"

"It's about ENTEC, not you."

"Call my office."

"Weekend. Can't wait."

"I don't have anything to say. Left there some time ago. Go away."

"Acrimonious departure?"

"Somewhat. For reasons not unlike this."

"Whistleblower. I read the transcripts."

"How could you…that's not supposed to be public record. How did—"

"Feds," he shot back glibly. "You dropped your accusations."

"I was mistaken."

"Seriously? I've got numbers. Bank accounts. Investment figures. A lot of red flags for the IRS. Like I said, Feds…nothing stays hidden for long."

"Christ, why me?" He sat up and wrung his hands on the table. "Why now?"

"You're the only comptroller I know who is also an ex-Endicott employee."

"What do you want?" The man narrowed his eyes, winnowing his dart like stare to separate the tree from the forest.

"Where the money went."

"What money?"

"Look," he sighed as if to let the man know he was on thin ice, but also revealing deeper anxieties, "this much I know: that the greatest proportion of ENDEC's income—at least by investor records—is foreign. The Paris office seems to be the hub, correct me if I'm wrong here…as comptroller your claim and your accounting show it to be foreign and parked in the Caymans under an umbrella corporation. OK thus far? Common variety tax haven. I don't really have a problem with that, but then, somehow later it winds up repatriated, tax-free using those offshore profits as collateral for rollover U.S. investments in the form of donations to social welfare organizations—this is where the trail gets cloudy. Thing is, I can't find which ones. There are no records; least I don't have them. I want to know where the money went and who's got it—especially since it was designated as foreign revenue so never taxed then rolled over to donations within the United States—then used as a write-off on what little taxes you did pay."

"They paid, not me. Nothing illegal. It was simply used as collateral for capital. Shareholder responsibility prevents unused assets. Social welfare organizations don't have to divulge their donors. It's the law."

"I know. Just thought you'd want to give me a little insight into this shell game. I'm only following the money—like the IRS would if, for instance, they were auditing someone—though as I said, it's not about you—"

"What's this about?" A woman quietly appeared in a thin black dress.

"Blackmail."

Diamonds sparkled in her ears. A silver belt that looked like a snake wrapped once around her waist its jaws clamped where the buckle should be. Polished lips glistened. Her skin was smooth and youthful, but had too much makeup. She slid in next to the man glaring at Devlin. "That's illegal isn't it?"

"It is," he replied, "like that dress you're wearing—"

"Terrance Roark."

"Who is—"

"Roark & Moisell. A law firm in Greenwich, Connecticut."

"What should I tell him?"

"That you're following the money."

*   *   *   *

Sometimes the only thing left to hang onto is the blade of a knife. From Bixby's rarefied Manhattan high-rise, with its concentric layers of translucent metal reflecting light like pearls in faint rainbow hues, Revenia gazed out across the glittering metropolis. Her escape from Paris had a price: remembrances of being in Gotham before, of the lost faces, of dreams shattered, of friends remembered, of vanished love, but most of all of her terrible purpose and the forces dedicated to stop her.

"You're safe here," Bixby had said as he escorted her into the only vacant apartment on his private floor. It was all done in antiseptic white with Italian leather couches, postmodern art on the walls and Kazak rugs on faux rosewood floors. "The building has the most advanced security in the city—I've put two men on this floor 'round the clock." Like a precious bird in a golden cage whose beauty was so delicate it could not endure the duress of modern life, he pandered to her. She mustered a sad smile. Far below steam rose from manhole covers and subway gratings under which the rumbling trains ran, over which taxis rattled horns blaring into the night: buyers and sellers forever bickering, pimps and their customers under neon, emigrants looking for something, and the upwardly mobile who had found it escaping something. Nobody was satisfied. The social veneer gave it all a civilized gloss and hid the incipient brutality that sought out the slightest weakness until the strong collapsed to their knees and the weak just faded away. "It's the safest place you could be," flashing that collegiate smile confident in the infallibility of his charm, but he neglected to mention that the guards had already been posted for over a month owing to his own fears in the aftermath of the cyber-attacks.

That night she paced like a cat in heat silhouetted by huge windows far above the street—fragile protection from freezing winds. Though weary from jet lag, sleep eluded her and even with the promise of safety she was chaffing for escape. Confinement in the apartment was smothering all clarity. So she slipped quietly into the shadows by the door, cast her gaze on the two burly security men as if an incantation, waited for their eyes to droop, and then slipped by. At last on the ground where the rush of cold air slapped her cheeks Revenia felt truly safe under the cloak of anonymity. She passed the conflux of faces hurtling to their own destinations, breathing in the spice of life, letting the clattering, deafening, cacophony of the streets in because here, at the brink of chaos, she was filled with inspiration. The history of cities and that of opera were inexorably intertwined. It was why people came to the theater. Art harbored many mysteries. She reveled in the invisible brilliance from which men had fallen eons ago.

Later, perched on a stool in a dingy Vietnamese restaurant she sucked up the spicy pho on which fresh basil, chilies and mint were piled. It burned her mouth. She watched people crowded in together as a medley of languages wafted over her like the aromas of fish fried in hot oil, cardamom and lime, perspiration and cigarettes; their meanings obscured but their faces told tales of people who had spilled over borders following paths of their own, interlopers on a new land seeking the next step in their evolution. She was intoxicated by the symphony.

"I know who you are…" a hoarse whisper intruded.

Startled out of her wits, she jerked her head round to see a man peering from under hooded brows. He brushed long, gray-streaked hair from his cold, blue eyes, the collar of a once expensive jacket turned up against the weather, a burgundy scarf wrapped around his neck hiding the ratty black sweater underneath. Tinny oriental music played in the background

"…you're the Queen of the Night!"

Sucking in her breath, her eyes darted into the surrounding shadows electrified. "How do you know?"

"Fantastic! A fantastic thing…can't you see? I recognized you at once. Just like riding a bike—"

"Don't mind him," the swarthy Vietnamese behind the bar rasped, "really crazy! What d'ya want mister? What d'ya want? If you not buy, get out!"

"We're talking!" The man sternly patronized the cook with a glance that froze until he slunk to the end of the counter to tend his steaming rice noodles.

"How do you know?"

"Seems so far away now doesn't it…don't you think? But once—"

"Once? Where? What do you mean?"

"Where?" He paused incredulous, "Vienna of course. The opera. Your opera. You can't have forgotten…"

"Impossible," memories he could not possibly know flooded her. "Who are you anyway?"

"Keikobad…I recognized you at once. Like all the time that's passed never existed…in crowds I always see people I've known before, they stand out more real than the rest like moonlight's shining on them. You though…you're easy."

"Why?"

"No shadow…you have no shadow—"

"Shhhhh…" she hushed guiding him to a small table in the outdoor café, away from earshot against the wall. "Who are you…" imploring in utter confidence, "really?"

The night swept up around them. Darkness bristled. Breaths of wind rustled leaves and brown paper, lifting them off the sidewalk, spinning them into the air, twirling them around and setting them back down before moving on. Traffic noises echoed. She inspected the man across the table. A refugee caught between two worlds: one that would not let him go and another that wouldn't accept him. Or was it something else, a carefully devised mask to hide some hidden intention. She felt an eerie willingness to face the unconfrontable, to keep vigilant; she knew they were out there.

"Your chances are getting slim," he said with lucid blue eyes. "Who I really am? I gave up on that long ago. Too existential, I don't like to think about it…gives me a headache…my name is Keikobad and somewhere I lost my powers…" adding with a touch of sorrow, "and a daughter. I remember you though, and the opera written for you with the Emperor and the falcon and the crossing over into this world. In our minds is no time—have you noticed? You see things too…I can tell."

"Yes," she replied, "that's true. But I see things differently. All I observe has a past and a future intertwined as one—they are inseparable." But she didn't tell the man the sweeping, multi-lifetime mandala of life and death and death and birth was the endless cycle it was. Surprised, but something about his unstable mental state made it okay to speak of things that mattered. A man on the edge, like a poet, cut closer to the truth. "There are things we cannot speak about with words."

"Oh yes…I know exactly what you mean. Sometimes the only thing left to hang onto is the blade of a knife. Absolutely. It's as if people are asleep, unaware of anything even though it exists all around—we are prisoners in disguise. All of us. What if dreams of the future were really dreams of the past? What if we've missed our opportunity?"

"You haven't…don't worry. Something's coming…but, how do you know my name?"

"How can I explain? I just do. You're the Queen of the Night… looking for a shadow, but time is running out."

He gazed at her with sudden weary eyes, dark circles, devoid of expectation and she could see he had retreated back into a world where no one could touch him and though she longed to bring him back—this ragged, scruffy man once somebody's friend, a husband, a person of value now disregarded as human refuse—she could not. It broke her heart. How many lie scattered waiting for help that may never come fodder for police and psychiatrists.

"I'm sorry," she could endure no more, "I have to leave."

"Watch out," he implored grabbing her sleeve, "take care! They know you're here!

"What do you mean?"

"The one with the red hair. She knows the answer. She knows the answer…"

The next night a line of scintillating limos rolled into the Met's underground garage as illuminati gathered for a private soiree; Revenia was guest of honor at a gala reception celebrating her arrival. Analetta had spared nothing to make it the most envied gathering in town hoping to attract a whole new cadre of generous patrons. Bixby, who underwrote the whole fête, was overflowing with excitement now he had finally arrived in the world's toughest city in which to breakout socially—thanks to the coup he had pulled off with the same blazing detail and power of intellect that had propelled his meteoric rise in the financial world. For tonight he let go his insecurities, forgot about the vicious cyber-attacks and anonymous enemies who were trying to destroy him and was more the way everyone loved him: charming, friendly, full of largess, the perfect political candidate.

The idea for the event had been conceived as soon as she got news Revenia had arrived from out of nowhere. Like snow falling on a pristine sea, where pure white ran down the pebbled beach to the water's edge, where waves were muffled at the hearth of winter. Like all imagined things it had started with silence. In the heart of the theater lay a rehearsal stage that offered a blank canvas ready for her creative vision. It was here Analetta had staged her campaigns for new patrons; the logistics and strategies of which were usually devised over lunch at the Plaza Hotel. Now, she had the ceiling painted dark midnight and the chief electrician strung tangles of miniature white lights high in the air like billowing constellations. One of the company's designers brought in baroque set pieces from the wings and with them a faux imperial ballroom was fashioned. The resident lighting expert pulled an all-nighter to create the perfect ambiance, so that when guests finally arrived they left the real world behind to weave in and out of otherworldly shadows. A Bösendorfer grand sat center stage, which was purchased following a legendary tenor's endorsement, "...I try to sound like a Bösendorfer," but tonight a fragile soprano was performing a selection from Mahler's song cycle to its accompaniment .She filled the hall with unrequited emotion, as she had once done on the main stage in her prime, before the messy divorce and alcohol muddied the clarity of her upper register, before her face reflected life's disappointments as she approached fifty-five alone, before she dreaded getting up some mornings.

"Where is she?" Analetta was rapidly giving way to anxiety just one step from panic.

"I don't know." Bixby agonized. "Christ, she wasn't in her apartments...out late last night."

"After Paris? Where was your damned security—"

Then, as if a glow from an open door in the dark, she appeared. Revenia walked out alone into the crowd; all eyes drawn to her. A smattering of applause followed like rain on a roof. Excitement rippled across the sea of black suits and evening dresses and Analetta swooned with relief.

In a corner, backlight streaming through the wild tangle of reddish curls, Mirella also watched. "Who do they think she is, a fucking princess?"

Her partner, a tall dancer with perfect posture and the lean body of a Saluki, dressed in a tuxedo jacket over a black t-shirt and blue jeans, turned his Nordic face toward the object of desire, long blonde hair moving sensuously. He posed effortlessly as if standing on the prow of a ship descending into battle while observing everything with complete aplomb, but could offer up no opinion because to him it was all kinetic and everything was in its place giving closure before any thoughts could form. Mirella had accidently come across him in this same rehearsal room after hours one night and secretly watched the danseur noble practice in front of the floor to ceiling mirrors. She was fascinated by how the exquisite creature leapt across the space seemingly suspended in air, followed by a series of deft pirouettes, culminating in an impossible stance on one leg with the other turned out and extended behind — both held perfectly straight. Then with bended knees and a rigid back he launched into a frantic whirlwind of turns starting with his foot flat on the floor, extending a leg and then whipping it around to the side, retracting his foot to the supporting knee, continually gaining speed until he was turning so fast he was only a blur. Then with several long, horizontal jumps, starting from one leg and landing on the other, he crossed the room and was suddenly face to face with her. She gasped.

"That was the grand jeté. Did I do it right?" He panted with a big smile.

A sea smoke descended numbing her higher faculties and Mirella stood mesmerized, lips slightly parted, breathless, without words, at once wanting to flee but compelled to experience this unexpected windfall of a man. The silence was brittle. She could hear his breathing as if magnified. The air aflame with motion and the static of creative energy, but most of all it was the intoxicating smell of him that captured her, the inescapable animal musk that made her dizzy. In her mind she scrambled for witty repartee, but all her energy was drawn into the whirlpool at the center of her body, into the primal boiling pot seething with desire. Her skin felt raw with sensation. An overpowering impulse gripped her, a dance so ancient its origins had vanished before memory along with any hope of controlling it. In a moment, she was lost.

"They say it's going to rain," she said raising a delicate hand, hypnotically placing it flat against his heaving chest slick with perspiration, letting the heat of his body burn down through the extended arm to her groin almost convulsing with forbidden pleasure. The dangerous space of the rehearsal hall closed in around them luring with the knowledge that anyone could walk in, that she shouldn't be there, shouldn't be touching him—circumstances which conspired to make her want it all the more. The inner turmoil blazed like a kerosene fire: moral codes battling for right and wrong, survival and desire, submission and resistance. The inferno precluded any logic and the finer wavelengths of rationality were smothered by a palpable sexual sweetness dripping like honey over the two stranded figures.

As he watched transfixed, in awe of the company's principal singer, she licked the salty sweat from his breast, looking up at him sweetly, inching her hand down over his stomach, across a muscular abdomen to the hot swelling in his tights where she cradled his sex as it grew in hardness—despite embarrassed efforts to control it—then pressed it lightly but firmly, just once, and held it as their eyes connected. And they burned like a high voltage wire.

No denial was her creed, her mantra and her banner; it was the characteristic that defined her more than anything else and revealed who she was beyond the erudite mezzo-soprano where she possessed the capability to elevate emotions to ecstatic heights. Once she had the scent, no power of gods or men could keep her from possessing forbidden fruit.

It was her flaw, even above the concealed dark purposes that ultimately drove her. It was her sweet and secret vice. Now Mirella surrendered completely and fell to the floor with the dancer like a mindless animal in heat, ripping and tearing until clothing lay tossed around them, bare skin sliding on the birchwood floor, turbulent arms and legs flailing, thrashing, pounding as she abandoned herself to the muscular young man who rammed her demonically in front of the floor to ceiling mirrors afraid his heart might burst, compelled by a power greater than his own into sexual acts that hurt like the cut of a knife — just where she wanted him. The sounds of their lovemaking filled the space and the danger of discovery brought them to an excruciating climax.

From that moment on she owned him, but ignored the dancer only bringing him out when her carnal needs demanded release or for social events, like tonight, where everything was show business and all that was glamorous. She wallowed in the illicit aura around them knowing it titillated those who denied themselves.

Beneath the miniature constellations sophisticates threaded in and out of the dappled light making everyone seem bigger-than-life romantic, like faded film stars in the shadows. Most admired from a distance, but a few fawned over the enigmatic diva, queuing up to bathe in her umbra, hoping some magic would rub off and change their droll existences simply by association. The murmur of conversations droned, the heat of the shoulder to shoulder crowd pressed, the smell of cologne and perspiration imbued everything with the paradox of the human condition. Revenia fathomed all of this. She could read their faces, divine emotional states from their eyes, so accepted patronizing kindness gracefully as Analetta waltzed her around to key players making an effort to ingratiate herself with the big money, letting slip that the role of patron for the upcoming "Aida," in which she would star, was a high water mark on anyone's social resume. Trolling for donors, she had no pride at all.

Meanwhile cool champagne flute in his hand, gazing intently across the room as he engaged in a series of conversations, each more gregarious than the last, struggling to portray a conservative attitude, even buttoning his coat so as not to betray his condition, Bixby was quietly getting hammered. That was not his initial plan. The alcohol had accidently crept up on him as he let down from the constant pressure he had been under. He was determined to enjoy his accomplishment of securing the most sought after singer of the decade for his opera—the house he owned in the same way he owned all the companies he invested in.

"Are you one of them or one of us?" Even her speaking voice was musical as Mirella sashayed up beside him during an interval between chats. It was bell like, seductive and charming, as if from a disembodied spirit: intimate, but not so near that the words didn't resonate with a slight echo.

"Hmmm…that's the question isn't it?" He tossed down the last of the sparkling wine then grabbed another off a passing waiter's tray acutely aware of her and feeling a sudden sensual confusion from the intoxicating femininity. "I try to be democratic—"

"The people yes!" She raised her glass then touched it to glistening lips without drinking, watching him with dark mischievous eyes.

"I never thanked you for performing at our fundraiser—"

"American Voices…I was interrupted…a man nearly fell from the gallery."

"So I understand. Unfortunate. I wasn't there."

God! I couldn't tell if my singing drove him to jump or—"

"How can I make it up to you?" He soothed.

"Well…one man tries suicide; another doesn't even show…what's a girl to think?"

"Yes…trouble at the office I'm afraid. Computer glitches. Have to pay the bills."

"You have those too? Thankfully, my business manager handles all that."

"I know! Great idea! You may not be interested in politics, but… you must come to the next dinner. Very hush hush. It's ten thousand a plate— a sum that gets you something like an al fresco meal of tomato and mozzarella salad, lobster, strawberry shortcake and an intimate conversation with the possible next governor of New York—you'll be my guest; I hear the President might even be there—hobnob with the power brokers! What do you think? I'm inviting you. It's official, and besides… you can't deny the next Governor."

"Really…you? The next Governor? I am fascinated by politics," she shimmered all of a sudden, a mysterious European accent hinting at her origins while keeping all secrets. "Does that surprise you? Not all little birds we singers—some of us are even galvanized by public events. Opera comes from a long line of street performers," she bowed mockingly, "and we always needed patrons—gentlemen such as yourself, men of power; art was such a sordid undertaking and simply left to the mob it would have been filled with seamy tales of greed and lust, war and death."

"I can't say I ever thought of you as a street performer," Bixby smiled while sipping his wine, "but isn't that what opera is?"

"Of course. But the greed of kings, the lust of the star-crossed and the war of ideals! That's something else isn't it? It's the difference between art and mere entertainment. Deep pockets helped safeguard all that—even if only for status—it would not have happened otherwise. Money and power are the catalyst; politics the driving force. Revolutionaries? My disgust—just the mob. I imagine there is nothing to compare with the feeling of true dominant influence in this world," her eyes blazed, "true power. Don't you find that so?"

"You look scintillating tonight."

"I thrive on the admiration of strangers," she smiled while placing her hand on his arm to patronize and dominate like she did with other men, but was suddenly startled by a backflash of energy that hit her, an uninvited vision revealing enough of the future that she became anxious and had to struggle to calm herself. The source of power she'd always wanted was right there. She glittered as if before battle.

"Have you two met?" Analetta appeared next to Bixby with the radiant young diva at her side like Venus on the half shell and just stood with a sly grin.

The sopranos looked across at one another and the air went ozone. "We know each other," Mirella said chilling all present.

"Yes, "Revenia replied emotionless, "we met in Paris—seems like centuries ago, doesn't it? Centuries…"

A haloed moon rose to its apogee above Gotham. Scientists claimed it was caused by light refracting off ice crystals from the extreme cold wave that gripped the Atlantic Seaboard, but to others it was a sign. Far below in the streets where life was hard and unbreakable as cold steel, without sympathy, where everything was a paid for experience, where hope for many was just a four letter word, where the vast resources of the world were owned by two percent leaving the rest with nothing to show after a life of doing the right thing, a sign went a long way. It was down there bathed in moonglow where people needed a lift from victory; where they had gone underground fleeing the glitz and celebrity, the bullshit and the hyperbole, the betrayals and the promises, where who you were was not defined by what you had. It was there signs were sought after for their deeper meanings and the halo around the moon was an auspicious one because it was evidence that two worlds still existed; the one of men and the other of spirits. Everyone talked about it; no one can live without hope.

By the massive loading docks behind the theater where worn doors marked the egress point for those whose life was spent creating opera, a light rain had begun to fall that soon turned to fine white crystals and patches of snow started to cover the frozen puddles where city lights reflected ivory in the night. Below, on the valet level, the Rolls Royce Drophead coupe sat waiting, its exquisitely engineered motor rumbling to keep heat rolling out its ducts. Revenia emerged followed by Bixby who had assigned himself the mission of seeing her safely home mortified that she had slipped out earlier by herself and left him holding the bag.

A shadow fell over them just as the pair stepped into the clear; like a cloud passing before the moon they were caught. Out of nowhere the silhouette of a figure rapidly approached with coat and scarf flying in the wind like evergreens dancing on a ridge at midnight.

Bixby almost went into cardiac arrest, expecting no one, reeling from too much drink, but then he recognized her through the alcohol haze and reached out, "Oh…it's you…c'mon with us, we'll give you a ride…it's too damn cold for anything *human* to be out tonight!"

The figure of Mirella furiously pulled away from him and seemingly rose in the air to face Revenia as a gust flailed at them all. "*Go scriosa an diabhal do chroí,*" she spat out, tossing the wild red mane back from her face, burning hostility flaming in her eyes, turning on her heel, storming off into the night.

"Jeeeze…what the hell was that?" Slurred Bixby, "I was just trying to be polite."

"It's Gaelic…a *mallacht*…a curse."

"A curse…meaning?"

"May the devil destroy your heart."

Chapter 9

The drive up to Greenwich was a welcome respite from the
city. Nothing had been quite the same since Paris and he needed
space. Overhead, great gray cumulonimbus towered into the heavens,
dwarfing the sprawl of urban landscape that spewed all the way up
the highway from Midtown. Though soon enough it was lined with
flaming trees: yellow, ochre, and red beneath the ice and snow
weighing down their branches—save the barren ones that had shed
their leaves at first freeze—passing beneath the stone bridges arched
like Roman aqueducts, heading north.

For more than a century, the hamlet attracted some of the biggest,
newest, glitziest fortunes in America. Devlin knew that money now
came from the trillion-dollar hedge-fund business—or as he thought
of it, mutual funds for the super rich—taking up much of the town's
office space and whose managers were responsible for the flurry of
over-the-top real-estate deals, teardowns, and mega-mansions. It was
like going behind enemy lines, but he couldn't dispute the cachet
about Greenwich; when you get there, you've arrived.

Among lawyers Terrance Roark was considered a brilliant and

highly disciplined renegade. Devlin had looked him up, in fact had vetted his background, studied him, read his profiles in the Wall Street Journal and Vanity Fair and even researched his tax records. Once, ten years earlier, he had been a celebrated hedge-fund manager who had nerve that made others sweat and near clairvoyant instinct that amassed a fortune so huge he was still considered a mythical figure on The Street. Then he walked. Just like that. Settled with his money in one of Greenwich's sprawling 1920's manor houses: one designed by Elsie de Wolfe—a prominent figure in New York, Paris, and London who scandalized French diplomatic society by attending a fancy-dress ball dressed as a Moulin Rouge dancer making her entrance turning handsprings—with hand-painted chinoiserie wallpaper, black marble floors with inlaid copper, and a study paneled with cedar that had been stripped from a venerable mansion in London. The main house had six maid's rooms, there was a stable for horses, two greenhouses, a six-car garage, and a guesthouse with its own courtyard and several cottages to house the butler, the chauffeur, the head gardener, and an estate superintendent who oversaw the 184 waterfront acres.

If **Roark** was known outside of financial circles at all, it was because of his kidnapping: dragged from a parking garage, blindfolded and handcuffed, he was held captive for a week until he convinced his abductors that the police were closing in and gave them a check so they could get away. He was unceremoniously dumped bloodied and nude on the highway. After the kidnapping he became obsessively secretive and never returned to his office in Manhattan. Up to that point he had lived modestly, but then let loose and purchased the mansion, installed an elaborate security system, thanks to his connections with military contractors, and modernized from the ground up—even those unfazed by luxury were startled by the excess. Now he practiced law for a select group of fund managers just to keep his intellect from atrophying, as a sort of a hobby. They trusted him implicitly; true believers.

These days Roark traveled with a bodyguard and slept most nights with the TV on. His offices, situated in an eighteenth century colonial on an Old Greenwich backstreet overlooking the sound, were anonymous: the firm's name did not appear on the front door and Devlin drove past twice trying to find it. As he walked up shafts of sunlight hit the water through breaks in the clouds. It seemed to grow colder.

Terrance Roark's fine dark suit draped elegantly like a second skin; soft shoulders Savile Row style, unvented in the Italian manner. The tightly woven fabric barely wrinkled when he moved, shooting his crisp white cuffs, adjusting one of the six flat screens assembled on a multi monitor rack beside him to compensate for glare from the windows. He made the same gesture whenever he had to shift position: holding perfect posture as if officiating at a formal dinner, focusing on the task at hand even if trivial, hiding any vestiges of imperfection, deficiency or weakness. The polished wood floor glowed amber having born two hundred years of household traffic from scurrying children chasing their pet cats to the town's petite bourgeoisie and more recently to the hyper wired, quantum speed network of hedge fund managers and other caretakers of high net worth individual and institutional assets who had taken over most of the town's office space. A huge, Turkish rug of hand knotted silk and wool shimmered color and contrasted with the hard edge, postmodern furniture seemingly from an exclusive Milan showroom. The massive Louis XIV table behind which he sat radiated with a lustrous French polish that had not diminished through the ages.

"Looks like a trading desk to me."

"Habit," he said, "just habit. The only investments I manage now are my own."

"But I understand you have a number of clients from Wall Street—"

"My client list is no secret, but out of curiosity; how did you get it?"

"Most of my time is spent researching. Think of me as a virtual gumshoe sitting in his car outside drinking coffee waiting for something to happen. Due diligence."

With a sudden implacable look he asked, "Which client?"

"We have many ongoing investigations: including complaints against brokers, firms, advisers, agents, funds, and other market participants—"

Let's cut to the chase here Mister…" looking again at the business card on the desk, "Wolfe."

"You specialize in securities law, so I'm sure you're familiar with the Foreign Corrupt Practices Act."

"And…?"

"This isn't about you, it's not about you…"

"You're here; it's about me."

"It's about the anti-bribery, internal accounting controls, books and false records provisions of the Securities Exchange Act of 1934."

"See my accountant."

"It's not about you, but it appears you have been acting as a transfer agent for Endecott Technologies."

Silence overwhelmed them as if drifting through interstellar space. "So…what is it you really want?"

"I'm following the money."

"Has there been a formal order of investigation?"

"I'm here aren't I?" He lied without any expression at all. "But look... this is voluntary; you don't have to answer my questions. Of course you could be indicted if you falsify statements or mislead the investigation..." lying again.

He just looked at Devlin for a long moment. "When I moved here permanently, I discovered a well-designed sailing yacht is a thing of pure beauty. My boat's been locked in ice for a month," Roark walked to the colonial bay window facing the cove and Great Island beyond the banks. "Never thought I'd like sailing; didn't get the point of pleasure boats—don't produce anything—especially on Long Island Sound—can you imagine lobstermen, oystermen, striped bass or cod fishers going sailing on their day off? I was still too stuck into the business where it all has to mean something. When she was launched in 1933, the *'Eidolon'* represented the cutting edge of technology and sophistication. The boat was only used for three seasons, then after World War 2 she never sailed again. Spent 60-years deteriorating as a houseboat moored up a river and when I first heard of her was about to be cut up for scrap. I restored it to near original specifications—except for modern electronics and the tallest, one-piece carbon fiber mast in the world—took two years. Felt like I'd been waiting my entire life for that moment. She' a J-Class."

"J-Class?"

"That's right. Started in 1851. The yacht "America" was built that year. An innovative new design. Then sailed to the Isle of Wright from New York searching for a race. Can you imagine it? Blustering, arrogant, New Englanders sailing that boat all the way across the Atlantic just itching for trouble. At first excluded from racing against British yachts by the Royal Yacht Squadron, she was finally allowed to

enter the 'Round the Island Race' for the '100 Guinea Cup.' Well…
she won and the cup became known as the 'America's Cup' and taken
back to the states where it stayed waiting for a challenger. Before the
J-Class, yachts were designed to be bigger and bigger. The towering
rigs of the Big Boat Class such as 'Lulworth' and 'Britannia' dwarfed
all other yachts. Then, in the late 1920s, came the 'Universal Rule.'
This new formula controlled the size and displacement of new yachts,
so they could be raced as evenly as possible. That's when the J-Class
was born, to win back the America's Cup. Pretty arcane stuff, huh?
I didn't know what they were either until I just happened on an old
man down by the water one day. Told me about when he was a kid
staying here. On the last day of racing he was sitting down on the
waterfront—just about where I met him… 'Suddenly out of the fog,'
the old man wheezed, 'a huge shape loomed up… aye, it was a 'J'
sailing back to her mooring!' Of course I didn't know what the hell he
was talking about, but he was so emotional…I just had to find out."

"Quite a tale."

"Yes. She's 120 feet with a beam of 21 and raced with crews of 35,
of course mine is much smaller."

"Of course…it would be," He muttered, half under his breath,
as if paying homage to the inconceivable wealth this man possessed,
suppressing a primal rage churning up from where it could not even
be articulated. It was the kind of feeling that nurtured revolutions,
that needed no outside agitators, no intellectual complications to stifle
the roar against inequality. The same feelings had been behind his
big schism with the University of Chicago economics department that
had exiled him into the profession of law where at least the semblance
of justice could be worked for. When he had discovered that one of the
first individuals to formalize the study of economics was a Protestant

minister who saw it all as a moral question, the same as right and wrong, sin and virtue, his purpose became greater than he was. From that moment until now it had been a struggle of minds in which the public good battled individual desire and out of the resulting tension the capitalist system reared and bucked like a wild stallion. The question he was left with was: how can someone carry the weight of all that greed?

"The golden years of the J-Class yachts lasted just eight summers," Roark continued, "only 10 yachts built between 1930 and 1937—I have one of them. Are you a sailor mister Wolfe?"

"I'm a rower," he answered as if the assumption he had deep pockets filled with enough lucre for the gentleman's sport confirmed his disdain for the man. "Single man scull—mostly on the Harlem when I can't get up to Poughkeepsie to row the Hudson."

His face darkened, "I left Manhattan to get away from all this."

"I know," Devlin empathized as the cage closed. "I know."

All he had to go on was an address given to him by the reclusive Terrence Roark. It was where he sent checks made out to the conservative Super PAC "American Voices," checks initially drawn against Endecott's umbrella corporate accounts in the Caymans, then rolled over into their Delaware corporation accounts to repatriate it before being donated to a tax exempt social welfare group euphemistically known as a "401c." Revealing the information was ostensibly a violation of client attorney privilege, but the lawyer justified it as soon as he realized it would save him further SEC scrutiny and likely an IRS audit, which was always costly even if nothing was wrong—after all, he was just a transfer agent. Devlin understood strategy. It was like war. Using the European funds as collateral was key to skirting a fine line between the legal and the illegal. Foreigners can't back U.S.

political issues; overseas funds laundered through a U.S. corporation legitimized the donations to a political action committee; no taxes were paid and if the candidate wins...the money returns to the right hands with interest; and if there's enough money, the candidate will win.

In his mind he imagined an old storefront with activist posters on the windows like the Black Panther headquarters on Bleaker Street he remembered as a kid, or a subdued office looking like some milquetoast accountant with beige walls, beige carpet and department store art looming over everything like a curse, so he was unprepared for what he found—driving right past it, not even seeing the address even though it matched the one he was looking for. Entering the *PayDay Loans* store he had asked the small, dark, Pakistani behind the counter where he might find the address, shoving it under his nose for good measure.

"Here!" He said. "Here. You come to the right place, can't you see? Back there. There! There!" He thrust his finger toward the bank of PO boxes lining one entire wall in official gleaming silver not even trying to hide his annoyance. "Why don't you look next time!"

He had found the office for "American Voices." It was an insignificant PO box: top row, third from left with a small dent in it and scratches around the lock making it appear as if it had been the target of a botched burglary at some long forgotten point.

The next day he arrived before dawn when the garbage trucks gingerly lumbered over the ice patches on the street that had not melted despite the salt laid down the night before. It was freezing. Through fogged windows he managed to find a parking spot giving him clear view of the PO boxes lined up against the far wall in the *PayDay Loans* store, especially the one top row third from the left. The motor was running for the longest time while he nursed his coffee, watching the city awaken, stretching its brawny arms, opening its giant maw to belch out exhaust and steam as the traffic picked up, listening to the taxis racing by—even at daybreak the manic drivers rushed to get their first fares for the morning—each one rattling a loose manhole cover as it passed. He pushed himself back down into the driver's seat for the duration and began to shiver after shutting off the ignition for the sake of anonymity and with it the heat. Normally he would have hired an investigator, but he was denied that luxury, so attacked the stakeout with aplomb wearing his warmest black leather jacket and a dark, cable knit turtleneck for the role that he thought would keep him warm. It didn't.

For nine hours he sat in the car watching an eclectic assortment enter and exit *PayDay Loans*. A few times someone had accessed a cubicle close to the suspect one, but they were just false alarms. Then at last a well-dressed, young, woman who clearly didn't belong in that neighborhood opened the box. Like an efficient secretary she took out some envelopes, locked the compartment again and briskly walked off, hurrying as if she had a train to catch, trotting as women do when their heels are too high, skipping across the ice and snow undeterred. Devlin was not prepared for this. Bursting from the car he rushed across the street before he realized he hadn't locked it, turning to click the remote he saw a cop roll up, remembering he hadn't put money in the meter he raced on.

He chased the woman for six blocks, trying not to look like he was following her in case he was spotted, but she never once looked back. Then she vanished inside a building. Devlin ducked into the glass enclosed, marble veneered lobby and watched helplessly as his prey waltzed through the turnstile flashing her magnetic employee pass card. By the time he had gone through security, concocting a story on the fly about a surprise audit of an accounting firm he had just happened to see on the building directory, flashing his Federal ID, the woman had already disappeared into an elevator. Frustrated, he watched the floor numbers to see where it would stop and then took the next car, hitting each of the five floors the previous riders had, hoping for a clue, furious at the prospect of losing her after waiting so long in his cold car like some cheap detective.

On the fifty-second floor he got out of the empty elevator. Peering down a long hallway where marble floors butted against the dark sapele wood veneer and polished granite that ran up two stories into skylights tinged with copper oxide that gave the light a slight aqua glow he saw the object of his desire. She had stopped to chat with another secretarial type; the envelopes still in her hand. There, above the reception desk, in small, refined, matte titanium letters was the firm's name: Endecott Technologies.

Mirella swept into the room like an illuminated cloud of sheet lightening, the shock of auburn curls spilling down across her silk taffeta gown, shimmering between deep cobalt and midnight blues with an overtone of red amber glowing when the light hit it just right. The dress rustled when she walked and not a man who heard could keep from imagining what pleasures lie beneath as she left a trail of pheromones mingling with perfume in her wake. She was not unaware of the effect she had on men, it was one of her closely guarded powers and unlike the mysterious ones of a higher nature, which even she could not fully comprehend yet, it was the most ephemeral and so she used it freely hoping to avoid regret later in life when it had passed.

The ten thousand a plate fundraiser was being held in a brownstone at Madison and 72nd, once the most architecturally ambitious cross town block in Manhattan. It was a beautiful, Romanesque style house designed by Stanford White in 1905: just months before he was murdered by millionaire Harry Thaw who shouted, "You've ruined my wife!" as he fired three shots point blank—referring to the beautiful Evelyn Nesbitt who White had seduced at fourteen. In the resulting "Trial of the Century," Stanford White, once New York's most sought after architect, was demonized by the yellow press as "a sybarite of debauchery, a man who abandoned lofty enterprises for vicious revels," and after testimony revealed the girl frolicked nude for him in a red velvet swing, the price for all his buildings skyrocketed. The one on Madison and 72nd now owned by an aging industrialist and staunch Republican fundraiser who normally lived in a huge stone manse on Lake Superior and only used it on rare visits to the city and to fill party coffers at exclusive events. A string quartet in the corner played Bartók while secret service men lurked, canvassing the place for security breaches.

It was a small gathering of fifty-six key players from the commanding heights: lots of gray hair, expensive suits and trophy wives, their fleet of luxury cars had been whisked away to who knows where on the crammed Upper East Side streets by swarthy valets hired for the occasion. Bixby had spotted her from the other side of the room; she pretended not to see and basked for the moment under the heat of other men's attention coquettish and free.

"I'm so glad you made it," he said smiling effusively in the endearing boyish way he had that made everyone like him, but with an unexpected pang of jealousy. "I hope my driver was polite...he was hired as a bodyguard, but likes the Rolls so much I can't get him out of it,"

"He's coming, isn't he?"

"Who?" Bixby replied, looking around the crowded brownstone's great room; dark oak trim framing the richly ornate, embossed, wall covering; pre-Raphaelite paintings strung from the molding; queen palms in the corner; low yellow lights like candles glowing, a fire flickering in the dining room behind the long formal table where waiters scurried readying fifty-six place settings.

"Sunglasses inside...at night...it's a dead giveaway."

"Oh, you noticed. Secret Service..." he confessed, "they do that so you never know who they're looking at...the President said he was coming, don't be disappointed if he doesn't...he's busy...very busy you know...so don't be disappointed," he suppressed the high anxiety that had been building all day, trying to mollify himself more than she, knowing that if the top executive showed it would be a signal, almost a guarantee he would be elected Governor, fearing party politics if he didn't, hating himself for losing his independence and caring what anyone thought.

Mirella smiled a coy secret smile her eyes gleaming in the warm radiance that flowed through the room intoxicated that she was rising above the slights suffered that afternoon in Analetta's office. She cursed the General Manager revivifying the incident in flashes of memory:

Analetta's face had flushed red. "You have to suffer to be a soprano."

"Not indignities!" Mirella replied querulous, moody and petulant, slouching as much as a prima donna could without harming her image.

"Oh come on…I've already discussed this with your agent."

"I have no agent. I fired her."

"Really. You are too much —

"I was promised —"

"Nothing! You were promised nothing. Look, Mirella," she patronized, sending her through the roof, "you're a valued talent; we've given you the role of *Amneris*, one of the greatest mezzo characters in all opera, a classic romantic triangle — Radamés, Aida, and Amneris — why are you complaining?"

"Why that French tart?"

"She can sing over a full orchestra and command the attention of the audience. She has an imposing, electrifying presence. Her voice is full, rich, powerful, and her dark timbre can arise feelings of awe… and besides, she's good box office…it's the first time she's performed in America. A cause célèbre after the incident in Paris."

"Don't quibble over details. Should I have someone take a shot at me?"

"Don't ask…many aspire to become dramatic sopranos; only a few actually make it… only after they have matured both as singers and as women. You have to suffer to be a soprano."

Mirella took hold of Bixby's arm and squeezed tight, feeling a sense of security as if she could orbit around him like a planet around the sun without fear. It was the first time she sensed a power outside of art that was of comparable magnitude to her desires, and she liked it, she liked it very much.

He wore her hand on his arm like a badge as they circulated and he introduced her to people, some he knew and, as the evening wore on and he had a few more drinks, some he didn't, revealing to them she was a principal singer at the Met as if it was in confidence not to be divulged to the general public, a diva who had escaped the rarified atmosphere of the theater to schmooze with the politically elite, a visitor from another world mesmerizing all she met with her intensity and voluptuous presence. Mirella, he knew, was an aesthete. He longed for her acceptance because above all things it was the art of the opera he revered and would go to any lengths to ingratiate himself into their inner circle, the clique denied just a patron—the piñata full of money.

A sudden scurrying activity caught their attention, a rise in the energy level as if doors had been flung open and gusts of chilled wind blew in, billowing autumn leaves in summersaults of red and gold. Men with sunglasses stood on the periphery. Mirella thrilled in anticipation, feeling childlike, vulnerable, not at all the way it was on boards where the lights and fourth wall blocked out all thoughts of the audience as she stood emotionally naked for her hour upon the stage. This was real, the brokerage of power at the commanding heights and a surge of energy coursed through her as the man everyone assumed to be the President and his small entourage arrived amid a flurry of activity. Making their way through the room while everyone crowded in to shake hands or at the very least brush his shoulder as a sign of solidarity; her eyes glazed over as he came their way and grasped Bixby's hand with a baby-kissing grin.

"We have every confidence you'll be the next Governor for the state of New York," the President's chief of staff declared. "Every confidence!"

"I appreciate that, sir, but…isn't the President coming? h…let me introduce you to Mirella Elderia, principal singer at the Met."

"Madame Butterfly," he said gracefully kissing her hand. "Charmed, I'm charmed," as he was pulled away by grasping, groping hands to the next donor where he could be heard saying to their wives, "Charmed, I'm charmed…"

But she was dazed by thunder and paid no attention. The tumultuous rush of power was feeding her needs, which up to that point had been confined to the carnal and remained unfulfilled, and lifted her vision beyond the petty bickering in the art world where everyone was obsessed with being eclipsed, with becoming extinct, and above the management hierarchy and agents who had performers under their thumbs, and the vagaries of audiences here today, gone tomorrow. It gave insight into what one could really accomplish with the right connections. Now the force behind it all was made clear as if by divine revelation, the arbiters of the haves and the have-nots, the owners of the system that takes the pursuit of self-interest and profit as its guiding light, and even though it did not satisfy the yearning for some meaning beyond, she liked it, she liked it very much. Few people would die with the words "free market" on their lips, but to someone who knew what to do with it…she could use that power, give it meaning where it had none, give it a face and make it relevant and useful to the wickedness she sometimes felt. The thought was tremendously sensual, it excited her and made her realize how unsatisfied she had been all her life and she nudged closer. Bixby sensed the electricity when she touched him.

Then the President's surrogate was gone. All who remained shuffled into the dining room before the great fire where they indulged in Maryland crab and chorizo pozole, peptia crusted bison, poblano whipped potatoes and chanterelle ragout with gold and red tomatoes. In the early hours of morning they drove towards home on the frozen, hollow streets of Manhattan huddled together in the back seat. Bixby watched as the city fled by in chilly scenes of winter consumed with thoughts of victory and how, despite adversity and the moments where he was certain he could not continue, everything eventually came out all right. It gave him great comfort after the vicious attacks that had left him stunned, it gave him faith and hope—at least for a night where he was sated with good food, reeling from good wine and blessed with this sensuous creature of the opera close enough beside him where he could feel her heat and hear the rustle of skin against silk taffeta. He breathed her in.

Mirella absently trailed her fingers on the inside of his thigh knowingly bringing him to fever pitch. She too looked out the windows, feeling a rebirth as if having emerged from a cocoon, feeling a new sense of destiny and now moving toward a future in which she was confident of domination. Because she had to dominate to survive, it was the only way and there could only be one, all others had to be eliminated. She, the French diva, who was so sweet and pure and clean; people like that made her ill. Her intentions spiraled into the night sky as a fuming cyclone of wrath, the power of the commanding elite and her own fury welded by greed, a witch's marriage in common cause that put everything in a whole new light. The boiling purposes inside imbued her with an overwhelming sexual energy that dripped from moist lips as Bixby gently kissed her goodnight, not expecting to be burned, as her fingertips touched his face, as she breathed her fire into him. But somewhere in this mingling of souls, in the deep where only lovers go, Mirella suddenly sensed a weakness within herself, a flaw where there had been none before: a reason for hesitation. She shuddered, having never felt that way, never feeling the human touch like tonight and was shocked by the impulse to reach out to this earthly man—to care for him and to be him instead of just use him—so she did something out of character.

"Not now," she said, laying a finger to his lips, "now is not the right time."

* * * *

Florescent light flowed through the office like Tupelo honey covering every surface and crevice with a thick, sticky layer of baleful photons. The young man hunched over a desk with three monitors suspended before him by a grid attached to the wall. His hands moved on the keys as he stared intently at the screens, slack-jawed and hungry for sensation cramming a handful of cheesy corn chips into his mouth. A pizza box and aluminum soft drink cans overflowed the wastebasket. He knew what it was like to be alone. That was the way of it on the fringes of Camelot.

The winsome young man from MIT hadn't talked to anyone in ten days. He sat in front of the computer screens in the depths of the offices at the committee to elect Bixby Endecott; letting the blue light seep in until his consciousness merged with that of the operating system and the programs and the protocols and the binary digits written as strings of logic that created addictive universes. He had not invented these languages: they were not communications from the other side about hidden barriers in his mind that kept him from being who he really was and finding true happiness, they were not secret pleas for help encrypted in the thousands of lines of code that he wrote, they were not an escape from the alienation he'd felt at school, but they were a mirror of humans descending the dark ladder into complexity violating the natural law that all great truths were simple. He was not merely automating the national campaign process with a "fucking robot that would win an election," but creating an artificial intelligence that could reflect back the aspirations of each person who came in contact with it…on the fly, in real time with infinite variations never once going out of character. Unlike a salesman might blow the big deal at the final moment by letting down and revealing his true self behind the bullshit, revealing smoke in the wind. His avatar had no true self, its sole purpose was creating the perception of whoever someone wanted it to be, like the perfect politician. Once socially connected online, this was public relations at an entirely new level, advertising in its perfect form free from all the weak characteristics that plague humanity. The young man thrilled at the prospect of having created something relevant, something beyond the soulless pursuit of profit, something that would capture hearts and minds and influence them. *It's too good for them*, he gloated just as the phone rang.

"Yes," his voice echoing in the empty office.

"I haven't heard anything," a man at the other end exclaimed in muted hostility. "We're on a deadline here—I think I explained that to you."

"I've been distracted."

"Distracted…Christ sakes, tell me something good!"

"Avatar."

There was a long silence. "That's it? What the hell does that mean?"

"A fucking robot that can win the election for your candidate."

"You can deliver that that?"

"Possibly…I have the design of an artificial intelligence able to autonomously assess moral, ethical and emotional situations and then make complex political decisions. It operates as an avatar: an artificial, autonomous web presence that can infiltrate social networks, analyze and evaluate big data and transform its personality into precisely what is needed and wanted—then deliver that in the media. Instant analytics. I call it 'Surrogate' because it allows your candidate to be in more than one place at the same time…a social network phenomena…a holographic world of many realities…but it's a prototype; not the real thing yet, still an incredible simulation…there's a lot of work left before we can expect full capability."

"What do you need?"

"Help. A crew of very advanced programmers."

"You got it. What else?"

"Money," he said oozing the word from his lips. "Lots of money." *It's too good for them*, he thought as he hung up the phone.

Chapter 10

The tin tiles on the ceiling were painted gloss black over Victorian designs. They had been put up in the nineteen twenties when the place first opened to cover cracks in the plaster, but now gave it an elegant, postindustrial, humanistic look. A row of round, white glass light fixtures hung suspended in a straight line over the booths up against the wall in the long, narrow café. The Formica counter still had swivel stools in front of it bolted to the floor with corrugated chrome wrapping the seats and padded, maroon vinyl on the top. A certificate hung on the wall from the New York City Landmarks Preservation Commission next to some black and white photos of longshoremen and stevedores eating there when the harbor was a kaleidoscope of working piers and sweating men at the crossroads of America and the rest of the world. Behind the bar a fry cook shot an angry scowl at Thierry Reynard as he pushed his way in the front door, fighting to close it against a blast of Arctic wind that rushed inside cooling plates under the heat lamps.

"It's like fuckin' Chicago!" He shot back at the surly hash slinger, having been on a crime scene most of the night, looking for any excuse. "Gimme some orange juice, two poached eggs with sausage, pancakes, coffee with sugar and *cream*—so leave room!"

"Squeeze one, Adam and Eve on a log, short stack, hot blonde in the sand…"

Devlin waited with a tall cardboard cup sitting next to a half eaten plate of griddlecakes smothered in the thick, amber colored, goo passed off as genuine Vermont maple. They tasted stale and institutional, but were hot and reminded him of kitchens and families and times when security didn't hang in the air like a passing breeze.

"Someone at Endecott's funneling money from their European subsidiaries into U.S. political campaigns—under the table—didn't even try very hard to hide it."

"That's bad…right?" The detective replied warming his two hands wrapped around the thick, beige, porcelain mug at his lips.

"You could say…it's sort of open for debate…" he wrinkled his brow, "multinationals have taken the place of foreign military as threats to stability…it could be a national security issue, depending on which congressman you talk to…"

"So…they're acting illegally…why don't you burn them down?"

"It's not that simple. Law says that any foreign national is prohibited from 'directly or indirectly' contributing money to influence US elections—and since their foreign offices are technically employee owned investment firms…that means no campaign donations, no donations to super-PACs, and no funding of political ads."

"Yea…fine, they're not supposed to do it—how do they pull it off then?"

"Via dark pool markets: sophisticated algorithms—software designed to be stealth and escape detection. That's where the law gets murky. Profits get sent electronically to an offshore account in the Caymans registered to a Delaware corporation, then used as collateral for capital loans from U.S. banks and are subsequently rolled over, tax free, into a 501c."

"Ok, I get it… you're a lawyer, but what the fuck's a 501c?"

"A tax exempt social welfare organization. A Political Action Committee, super-PAC to you; campaign financing without actually funding a candidate—if your guy wants to cut taxes, you can pour all the money you want into a committee to cut taxes supporting him by proxy without being subject to campaign finance laws."

"You sure about this?"

"I followed the money—after all that technology it was moved by check, snail mailed to a post box in a *PayDay Loans* store then taken by hand to…guess where?"

"Endecott's offices."

"You got it. Violates Federal Election Commission laws, IRS tax laws and Title Two of the Patriot Act designed to prevent money laundering for a start. They could go to jail, but more important; they could forfeit all their funds and have offshore assets frozen."

"I'd murder someone for that."

"Exactly."

"You did good my friend!" Thierry Reynard nodded. "Maybe that French quant threatened the setup somehow…?"

"Maybe the French quant was the setup."

"Meaning…"

"…we don't know who the fuck would kill him—" Devlin said.

"…right."

"…but now we know there's a powerful incentive any way you look at it."

"The wife; a blackmailer who got too greedy maybe; someone at Endecott—"

"Someone out to destroy—a competitor, or an investor who wants to short the market when they fail—"

"There you go again talking like a member of the bar..."

"It's like this: when you short sell a stock, your broker will lend it to you. The stock comes from the brokerage's own inventory, from another one of the firm's customers, or from another brokerage firm. The shares are sold and the money credited to your account. Sooner or later, you have to cover the short by buying back the same number of shares and returning them to your broker. If the price drops, you can buy back the stock at the lower price and make a profit on the difference. If the price of the stock rises, you have to buy it back at the higher price, and you lose...but nobody wants to lose."

"Is that how they get all that money? That's it? What a great con...I can't fuckin' believe it! Where've I been all my life! So maybe someone wants the big money and the quant found out. That helps. Now I only have about twenty-five thousand suspects."

"Pandora's box all right—"

"Told you I needed your help."

"You were right—I just didn't want to admit it."

"He was one of you guys. Too much money for any of this to be coincidence. I knew something was dirty."

"War with the Ethiopians is inevitable," Francotti Benedetto intoned under the spell of relentless muses, pausing to sweep a shock of shiny black hair from his eyes, pacing with the creative energy of the dammed, pulling the jacket close over his shoulders, adjusting the muslin scarf wrapped twice around his neck, peering from a well of soul behind darkened eyes his face painted with the terror of impending battle, "we may all die before this is over."

Looming above him as if from mists a vision of the Old Kingdom dazzled: an enchanted Egypt of his fertile imagination. From the reign of the Pharaohs when war raged across the Two-Lands and the palace boiled with illicit passions, treachery and deceit. It was an opera that was too grand a spectacle for most companies. Knowing this, the Italian director had taken the old sets for "Aida" that had been marched out every year for over a decade and reconstructed them from the ground up: in the process terrorizing scenic shop carpenters, prop builders, and costumers for weeks with an inner vision so gigantic yet so private nobody else could see the whole of it, just the pieces they were working on. Tantalizing speculation gripped the company as costs escalated and still no set appeared. Everybody thought Analetta would fire him in a fit of fiscal responsibility. It was only later, when the puzzle came together that the magic happened. At some hidden moment in the making of it the great halls, the temples, the massive columns, the gigantic bas-relief warriors all took their first breath were no longer just sets, they had come to life.

Once completed, he assembled the entire cast and orchestra to absorb the full spectacle demanding the wingmen fly in the set pieces on lines and battens, roll them in on scenery wagons, swing them in on the turntable then assemble ancient Egypt—every nut and bolt. Francotti Benedetto wanted to immerse the company into the tragic universe of captive Ethiopian princess Aida and her impossible love for an enemy warrior who must do battle against her father...all destined to tragic ends. Opera noir at its finest.

"This story is as essential to life as breathing," he paraphrased Nietzsche: "Unrequited love is indispensable to the lover, which at no price would they relinquish for a state of indifference."

Weeks were spent in rehearsal while record cold raged outside. The director even required members of the orchestra be shunted in while only blocking out scenes, using live music just to keep the performers frosty, racking up huge overtime costs, increasing Analetta's persistent funding problems, bringing her to near breakdown on the subject. Nevertheless, she let it all continue as part of the master plan convinced that in the end the production would be a triumph and place the company at the pinnacle of the opera world. In a culture gone mad with electronics, she fought for pure, live art out of the belief it was the highest form of human endeavor, but never imagined the escalating costs that gave her constant nightmares of financial ruin. Francotti Benedetto, however, cared nothing for money and drove the cast and crew like an invading army, pushing them to their physical and emotional limits to get the raw edge he was seeking on stage, enough to fill the huge theater with palpable emotion. For him, there was no alternative to triumph.

The young diva attacked her role with inhuman dedication. It was as if Revenia was channeling the captive princess while spellbound all the while guarding against the unknown. As long days passed and they began full orchestra rehearsals, the relationships of the characters flamed into a life of their own, none more vivid than the enmity between the French diva's Aida, and Mirella's daughter of the Phaoah, Amneris—who would have her revenge in this world or the next. But she was even more troubled when memories were awakened. Rumors went, the story for the opera had originally come from French Egyptologist Auguste Mariette, based on an actual incident in the ancient history of Egypt or one so closely paralleling earlier lives that Revenia was swept into in their umbra. She noticeably changed, became cat like, mysterious, even her eyes were more almond shaped. A hunted creature

It was night; they had been bullied beyond limits, the director reaching for that elusive state of grace that only exists in the artist's mind, and only seen on earth in rare, unpredictable fits of genius. Blood ran high. Fuses were short. Tempers flared. At last Mirella appeared on the high parapet, beaming iridescent, sliding under the blue-ivory glow of the faux moon as a light came up revealing someone other than the sulking, petulant young woman with a rancor against all those she felt were keeping her from the acclaim she deserved. Now with a look, a mere glance, she unleashed a sea of emotion simply by lowering her head and gazing out across the blacked theater, commanding all with her prescience. In her eyes burned another world: the domain of art and endless wishes that beckoned to everyone who had come this far saying: all was not lost. Her voice resonated from deep within as if it had been trapped there forever yearning and then, as the rich mezzo soprano began soaring ever higher with the full orchestra lush and overflowing, everyone in the theater soared with her remembering what had drawn them to opera in the first place. She was no longer Mirella, the Euro-gypsy too quick to anger, the flaming red insect inciting outrage with her stinging grievances and hidden conflicts; she was Amneris, daughter of the Pharoah princess of Egypt.

Even Francotti Benedetto—who had no experience with opera, or classical music for that matter, who was a film director whose ideas unfolded in visual scenarios, always keeping in mind camera angles, lighting, cinematic technique and the impact all that has upon audiences—was staggered. The scenario, as he thought of it, was laid out in scene cards pinned up on a corkboard. Scripts were always debatable, so he had blocked scenes with the cast until the whole production was a clockwork masterpiece of lights and darks, color and timing, parallax motion and the sweep of costume against lavish backdrop in his mind. That was where he could create undisturbed. It was a visual tour de force. Of the music: up until that moment he had considered it almost secondary to the tale, an archaic embellishment to an art form that had seen its day over a century ago. But now the Italian was stunned and could only watch unmoving as the great duet of act two unfolded never before realizing that the fire of high art could burn with such intensity.

In that fleeting moment of brilliance, watching Mirella perform, listening to her exquisite voice, experiencing the sweep of emotions that rendered all material things insignificant next to the living art they were witnessing, the stage hands and the dressers and the wingmen peered past the fourth wall into the blazing heart of creation. There, with arms raised in triumph, in full flight, she shuddered in ecstasy with the realization that nothing could surpass her artistic accomplishment secure in her complete and utter domination—there could be only one.

Then out of the shadows Revenia appeared. She moved with the music like an apparition under starlight, descending across the stage feline and gossamer, the orchestra ebbing and flowing in lush refrains when suddenly all hearts beat as one and the young diva flashed her eyes up at Mirella. Inexplicably the theater was electrified. *"How can I be happy far from my native land…"* she sang in a high, lyric soprano that cut to the core of even the most cynical, laying waste with emotions few knew they could experience and at levels where glass shattered, where diamonds exploded into dust, where spirits dwelled between this life and the next.

After that, everything changed, and a dark, unnatural aura descended on the production. Things began to happen that were ignored at first, but soon identified by the superstitious in the company—a trait performers and career stage workers embraced—as mystical events. One morning just before rehearsal, cast and crew arrived to find all the inside doors locked; locksmiths were called, but by the time they arrived all locks mysteriously had opened. Then there was the apparition, spotted at various places and reported by different people—even Analetta saw what she thought were specters fleeting across the video screens in her office causing enough alarm that she hired extra security and charged them with investigating the rumors and catching any intruders, unwilling to believe they were supernatural. For the initiated that was all nonsense, of course they were beings from the other side and would never be caught and people's disbelief was their best disguise; perhaps it was the real Phantom following the French diva from Palais Garnier, or the souls of Aida and her lover Radamès seeking revenge for being entombed alive violating sacred ritual in the "Book of the Dead," or any one of many explanations being tossed around. It wasn't long before rumor had spread in the subterranean world of the theater that this *"Aida"* was possessed; ostensibly haunted by the souls that had been so unjustly wronged some twenty centuries before Christ upon which the story was based. Speculation ran crazy that magical qualities infused the hyperreal Egyptian sets and might have disturbed ancient curses guarding the tombs and the secrets they buried; that the alignment of the moon and stars were mathematically identical with the actual events causing a psychic parallax; that malevolent forces were bent upon disrupting the production to avoid retribution for their crimes in the next world; that the spirits had returned so they could at last overcome the dangers encountered after death and emerge safely in full spiritualized form — or even that union agitators were trying to sabotage the box office to get concessions. In all the wild imaginings and backstage gossip there was only one thing everybody agreed on; the two principal sopranos were at the center of it.

Revenia had a remarkable run of close calls. In one case a piece of scenery came crashing down followed by a batten from the flyloft in the exact spot she had been standing just seconds earlier; in another superglue was discovered where her eye drops bottle should be — she just happened to drop it feigning surprise when it stuck fast to the floor. Then there was the understudy testing out Revenia's position on stage when the set collapsed underneath her catching a leg in the giant turnstile gears, which froze and she couldn't be extracted for three hours — thankfully requiring only stitches. In all cases the prodigy took it with aplomb, composed and unruffled adding to the speculation. Mirella, on the other hand, went around in a huff demanding the respect she deserved, so much so that some of the backstage workers complained to their union of abuse. She too was plagued with disturbances, whether real or imagined was in dispute. Most of her troubles were personal; missing makeup cases, not receiving message about schedule changes resulting in reprimands from the director, and at one point mid aria with her arms raised on high, a wardrobe malfunction caused her dress to slip exposing both breasts to cast and crew: she retreated in an nonplussed hissy fit to one of her early lunches from which she never returned.

Management took a more refined and subdued view of the matter: until the marketing department caught it on the grape vine and in a cathartic moment realized this was a windfall — a publicity jackpot. They couldn't buy such promotion; it was already all over the social media landscape. Soon stories began to be leaked, a whole PR and advertising campaign was thrown into the works and freelancers brought in to exploit the rumors to the maximum, outside consultants retained to help strategize it, anything to feed the wildfire. The insider leak of "*Aida's Curse*" became the hottest story in the media — advanced ticket sales were out the roof. There was nothing the public loved more than a mystery; there was nothing marketing loved more than giving the public what it loved — true or not.

Walking down the long hall to her office, Analetta was yanked into the ladies' room so hard it nearly gave her whiplash.

"There's someone you have to see!" Her secretary said suppressing unrestrained excitement so hard her cheeks flushed.

"What are you talking about? Calm down!"

She gave her that look. "He's been trying to see you for a couple days."

"So…what does he want?" Rubbing her neck. "Can't you handle it?"

"He said Terrance Roark recommended him to you."

"The Terrance Roark? The financier?"

"That's it. I checked him out with Roark's office…he personally spoke to me like the man was a close friend. This guy's loaded! Told me he's one of Forbes highest earning hedge fund managers—ever!"

"I understand you're in the investment community." Analetta asked casually all sunshine, sensing a windfall, having just been ushered in by her secretary to meet the potential benefactor, rushing from an earlier meeting where she had rallied opera volunteers mid fund raising, after spending all morning on the phones bringing in $1.2 million to make up for a donor who pulled out at the last minute leaving everyone in the lurch, tasting blood.

"That's right," Devlin said, entitled and nonchalant the way he saw the financial elite being. "Institutional fund management."

"Well…" her strong interest concealed, "an investment in culture has many rewards other than money."

"Of course," he smiled, knowing a patronizing, fund raising piranha when he saw one. "That's why I'm here…I just happened to see Revenia in Die Zauberflöte—"

"In Paris."

"Yes."

"Queen of the Night."

"That's right. You understand then…my interest…when I heard she was here, in New York…well, such a prodigy—"

"…the chance of a lifetime."

"Exactly."

"We feel the same," she agreed, as if giving witness to a repentant person with the secret shared between them that nothing erases the past. *"Aida"* will be the grandest production the Met has staged in over a century—and still some coveted donor slots available…lucky you! The set alone is…intricate, grand, magnificent—for lack of better word— they say so realistic…it's quite haunted. Would you like to see it?"

"I…you're busy…"

"Nonsense…" she beamed grabbing his arm, "let's keep the magic going!"

Getting the appointment was easy; getting the money was not. In Manhattan everybody had your number, there was no such thing as a perfect con in the place that invented the game, and he was not the expert being plagued with moral ambiguities that prevented crossing lines—at least crossing them too far. The scheme had come to him on a breathless night, caught between breathing out and breathing in where even snowflakes took their time descending like feathers. He lay awake in rumpled bed sheets trying to rearrange his life and make sense out of all the things that hadn't gone as planned so far, still missing Veronica with pangs of fire and, though past experience had proven it was about as effective as pushing against a brick wall, spent hours trying to figure it all out. By morning nothing had changed except he was even more tired and restless and almost envied those who copped out to barbiturate sleeping pills—something he decided long ago was bad for him. He threw his robe on, made some coffee then made the call.

"What are you getting at anyway? I'm not even in the office yet.

How did you get my number?" Terrance Roark sounded groggy and hoarse as if he had been awakened from a deep sleep.

"The yacht club directory—I was impressed, it's the second oldest in Connecticut."

"Cut to the chase…too early for crank calls! What time is it anyway? Sun's not even—"

"You could be in a lot of trouble."

"You're mistaken," suddenly awake. "I'm a lawyer. I give other people trouble."

"Not when it violates SEC regulations, Federal Election Commission laws, tax laws and Title Two of the Patriot Act not to mention the Bar Association ethics rules."

In the milliseconds it took to reply dozens of scenarios went through his head, in the end he responded like the fund manager who had nerve that made others sweat.

"What do you want?"

"A favor"

"A favor. At this hour?"

"I've given it a lot of thought and all things considered… you're making amends, cooperating with Federal authorities…quid pro quo."

"I won't violate attorney-client privilege if that's what you want. Whatever you need to know about Endicott, you won't get it from me."

"Trust is the hallmark of a relationship with a lawyer. Your notes, observations, thoughts and research are protected from any discovery processes…I'm counting on your ethics."

"This is getting too complex, perhaps if you'd quit being so obscure—"

"Attorney-client privilege only protects the essence of communications actually had by the client and lawyer and only extends to information given for the purpose of obtaining legal representation."

"I'm surprised. Correct me if I'm wrong," he paused, "are you asking me to represent you? Can't afford me—"

"You can't afford not to. Quid pro quo, with consideration you'll see the fees and the penalties cancel each other out. Connecticut state law under the Statute of Frauds allows for oral contracts, so…will you represent me?"

"Awakened at the crack of dawn, called on an unlisted number at my private residence, threatened with jail, disbarment and blackmailed into giving free service—how can I say no to such generous terms."

"Is that an agreement?"

"Yes…as much as it pains me to let you win."

"Our conversation up to this point was recorded as proof of contract; just in case you change your mind."

It was all so very simple. He had remembered those get-rich-quick real estate seminars where young men who looked like models in toothpaste commercials revealed the secrets to buying properties without any money and turning them over, banking profits and investing in another property before anyone was the wiser; now you see it, now you don't. He didn't need any money; it was a confidence game and who better to bolster confidence than the legendary Wall Street trader who was so rich even Forbes couldn't calculate his wealth. It was as good as a letter of credit.

In his mind, the one sin that could not be forgiven was hypocrisy. It had given him a clue. No one would give such massive amounts of money to a non-profit unless he had chronic remorse; yet arrogance laughs at repentance and no one could gain so much wealth without an exaggerated sense of one's self. The conflicting data was a dead giveaway. There was something about the opera that linked everything; Bixby

Endecott and his high frequency trading firm, the murders of the French quant and the director from the Palais Garnier, and the laundering of illegal money into political campaigns. No evil traps us but the evil we love.

The courtship of Devlin Wolf was a delicate affair. He could not show so much interest that his cover would be blown or that he was a sycophant just wanting to get cozy with the inner circle, but could not be so obtuse that his intentions as a serious donor with deep pockets were doubted. He had to do something while still remaining out of reach, and the opportunity presented itself almost immediately. On that first tour of the stage the engineer from supertitles mission control appeared with complaints about the obsolete computer used to monitor the system that translated each opera's lyrics into English displayed across small screens on the back of every seat in the house.

"It's not working! It's just not working!" The engineer was frantic.

Relax..." said the cue caller, "it's working. You just turned it off."

"It turned itself off. Called a crash...Jesus! God! How can you be so stupid? The computer's obsolete...processor's too slow...it's maxed out, can't add more RAM, nobody supports it anymore...!"

"If I can help...?" Devlin offered after witnessing the deadlock, realizing instantly the opportunity to ingratiate himself without a huge investment, allowing him to continue to be romanced like a virgin after putting out just enough to arouse interest on the first date, thinking it would only run a few thousand easily covered with his expense account, wanting to toss it off like lunch money, finding in the end that it cost him over twenty five thousand which he had to siphon out of the division's inquiry float fund, praying his investigation paid off in big indictments before anyone found out or he would be stuck with it. After that, he began to be invited to special events and gatherings for premiere patrons only where he glided among the glitterati and trays of spicy puffed salmon canapés with Pouilly-Fuissé and where he began to meet some of the opera's stars pressed into service for the occasion.

* * * *

The first time he saw Revenia was across a crowded room. Delicate and commanding, cast iron and frail, not at all the way she looked on stage when in full bloom and infused with character. He stood holding a chilled glass trying not to appear he was staring as he wondered how such a typhoon of creative energy could come from this lithe figure, from dead calm to a raging storm, from the sea inside. She was standing by the elusive Bixby Endecott, Grand Poobah of the angels, who always arrived late to the soirées which explained why Devlin had never been able to run into him before. He would not suffer a missed opportunity again now he was swimming with the sharks.

Everything became more complicated out on the borderline between the place where he came from and the one where he was heading, where his perspective became clouded with ghosts always intruding at the worst time. He strove to create a future, but its visions flickered in and out like a faraway television channel where all you could get were indistinct images and snow. That was how it was. He walked the line on the one side of which was moral bankruptcy and on the other ideals. It was the violence of transgressing every fine and righteous dream he had ever had that made him too bitter for his own good. Like people who were so self-assured they were suspected of hiding something utterly degrading that made them just like everyone else: struggling and chasing figments of dreams until their days ran out. He remembered a friend in college: "People are all alike," he had told him disillusioned and stinking of bourbon. *People are all alike.* He prayed he wasn't becoming like that, but that's exactly that way he viewed the rich; too well balanced, always the sated look of a well fed cat. It made him believe firmly and intrinsically that they had something to hide, some crumbling infrastructure that they shored up with all that wealth, hoarding it close in a desperate attempt to keep from being like everyone else: pawns to the wind.

"Devlin Wolfe." He thrust his hand out Boston Brahmin style.

"Bixby," grinning with charm, "Bixby Endicott…just call me Bix. Of course… you recognize Revenia de Havilland…our new prima donna!"

He was surprised at how much more exotic she appeared up close; moving restlessly like waters along the shore, enigmatic, pregnant with life. From under short, dark hair that looked as though she had just come in from a windstorm. The young woman looked at him coolly and shook his hand.

"I couldn't let the opportunity pass of meeting the man behind the high speed trading revolution," Devlin said.

"…in the business?"

"Funds management…institutional…in a way that's why I'm here," he said not taking his eyes off the young diva.

"How so?"

"When I was in Paris I happened to stop by your office and ended up at the Palais Garnier, courtesy of Sanja Singhal…my first opera, and you…Queen of the Night took my breath away…so here I am!"

"You saw then—" Revenia began.

"…our Chief Technology Officer," Bixby interjected anxious to change the subject. "she's a pip! Are you a donor?"

"Well…not like you…but I help out a bit."

"Glad to hear it," slapping Devlin on the back. "Glad to hear it."

Then they were gone, mingling with others neither looking back, leaving him at the cold end of a handshake, spending the rest of the night trying to decipher the frosty reception, reviewing every nuance of their meeting, praying he hadn't blown his cover from the start. Though some comfort came from the fact there was little chance of being traced. Traders in Manhattan were like actors in Hollywood: one day glittering stars, the next shattered glass and sorting out all the pieces in between was impossible.

The second time he saw her everything changed. It was only by chance he happened to be out in the street that late afternoon, having just met with Thierry Reynard to compare notes while double parked off 8th Avenue and 47th Street. A fresh snow had blanketed the city the night before and then in the early hours skies cleared revealing billions of dazzling stars shot gunned against the ether. Without cloud cover the infinite cold of interstellar space descended. Under a pale sky just before twilight his breath frosted as he jumped to the sidewalk, went into a coffee shop and emerged holding a steaming Sumatra. She stood out like a diamond on a black man's ear and he watched her across the street still pouring sugar into the cup. How could eyes not be drawn to her? …the dark, exotic girl with windy hair, scarf wrapped twice around her neck, full length tweed coat, high boots with knit leg warmers pulled up to mid-thigh. He was startled because of the idea that somehow she really didn't exist outside the theater.

He followed her around a corner, anxiety jumping to life in his stomach. She was a crucial link between all things he was interested in, his entire career might depend on her now that he had violated SEC protocol and besides, he was curious where she was going in such a rush. Devlin hurried, jostling pedestrians, enduring their wrath and curses, sloshing hot coffee all over his hand before he reluctantly tossed the fresh cup in the trash. Just ahead over bobbing heads he could see her, struggling to keep track in the fading light, watching as she darted across the street, looking like she was trying to elude someone, hoping he hadn't been spotted. Then he spotted them: two men who had taken the same tack, at exactly the same time, matching her pace step for step, stalking like a couple of coyotes, holding back just enough so they wouldn't be seen.

He was close enough to hear one of the predators just behind her rasp, "Do you believe in déjà vu?"

Ravinia swirled in anger and faced the two young men with a look as wild as the wind whipping up around them.

She did not flinch as Devlin approached from behind. "Couldn't believe it was you," he fingered the pistol in the small holster tucked into the back of his trousers under his coat that he was never without. "Oh, did I interrupt. Can I help you…gentlemen?"

"Fuck off asshole!"

"You should respect your elders," Devlin said stepping forward and bitch-slapping the young man like a rattlesnake, gripping the butt of the concealed gun, leaving cheeks bright red in the cold. It was met with little resistance and much whining. Nobody moved for the longest time. The smell ice and fear was in the air. After a tense moment, the two men slunk off into the crowd and disappeared like smoke.

"What was that all about?"

"Elders? I hope you weren't referring to me!"

"Well, thank you too."

"Thank you," she turned and walked away, "I had it under control."

"I could see that."

Revenia turned and was about to yell, but just sighed through her teeth. "Women are not helpless."

"What did he mean 'Do you believe in déjà vu?' Have you seen them before?"

"How should I know…street people."

"Doesn't seem you're very safe out here…" he caught up, feeling relief that nothing violent had happened, disturbing his dark side—the subterranean part where his *twilights* dwelt along with all the other emotional turmoil he didn't want to deal with. "You don't remember me do you? Devlin Wolfe, we met a few weeks ago at the Met reception… you were with Bixby Endecott."

"Of course," she inspected him, "thanks again," and walked on.

"Wait! You at least owe me a cup of coffee for rescuing you. I spilled mine in the chase!"

"You didn't rescue me!"

Later, on a stool in the dilapidated Vietnamese restaurant she had discovered, the international opera prodigy sat sucking up spicy bún bò huế off chopsticks while he nursed a weak, tasteless brew that the waiter insisted was coffee, but was suspiciously like strong tea. The pungent aromas of garlic, fish sauce and lemon grass were so overpowering even the disinfectant lavished on the kitchen floor every night was disguised. The folding glass doors to the street had been pulled closed against the freezing weather and steam from the inside turned to ice on the outside, camouflaging a blur of passing people into anonymous strangers without features in muted colors that all seemed to run together. Night slowly fell.

"How does it happen?"

"What happen?"

"The rest of us just muddle around down here in traffic, in offices… from my window I can see a harbor where some of the most fabulous superyachts in the world tie up—I suppose while the owners check their interests on Wall Street…can't imagine…I appreciate them, but it will never be my world. I'm on the outside. When I saw you up there that night, under the hot lights getting me to feel like…it was the same."

"It's a mystery," she shrugged.

"If I could just once…but like I said…things look different down here on the ground. How does it happen?"

"Some of us just choose to reach for something unobtainable… very selfish really…the way the world is. I often think I should be out on the front lines helping refugees or some…you for instance, there must be something you care about, something you'd be willing to die for."

"I'd die for a good cup of coffee right now."

"How about spicy food…" she stuck the bowl under his nose as she sucked up another mouthful of rice noodles. "Try some? Vietnamese are not known for their coffee."

Cigarette smoke wafted above them from restaurant staff taking breaks behind the flimsy partition to the kitchen. The sound of chatter filled the room. A clatter of noise from the cooking area hidden behind the screen, and sweating Oriental faces appearing regularly to check that everything was all right out front—unlike at the stoves where everything was chaos. The smell of chili oil hung in the air. She was bright and articulate in English despite a heavy French accent tinged with precise elocution he imagined came from the close attention opera singers paid the many languages they had to learn for their roles, but seemed guarded on certain subjects so steered the conversation to avoid those rocks and shoals. Her beauty was ethereal, now that he had the chance to look up close, for when he concentrated on her features he could see they were rather plain though somewhat exotic, but when she had flights over something he had said she shimmered with an otherworldly grace that transcended the physical giving her an allure that acted like a drug. It was inexplicable.

"It's not a moral question really…" he went on, "I'm just saying that anything can be digitized. In my world for instance, all aspects of the financial markets succumbed almost overnight—the impulse for profit was too enticing—now everything is done faster, more efficiently and without the one thing that no one was ever prepared for: human error."

"Greed you mean. So, you think virtual reality will eclipse the need for any live performance? A frightful thought—"

"That's not what I'm saying…I'm just saying: it's possible. All music can be synthesized, every sound—"

"It's not the sound; it's living communication. Seems to me you've got a religious conflict raging in your head; gods and men, that's all it is." Then she looked at him as if from somewhere else bristling with emotion. "Who is to keep these ideals, this art? A machine? What about future generations?"

Just then a waiter came by and poured two beers. His shiny face beaming a smile. Foam ran over the glasses.

"We didn't order these—"

"No, no, it's OK. On house," he beamed again, "on house," looking down, as if he was privy to some secret all three of them shared. They looked up at him and could not stop smiling, helpless against good intentions.

She made a quick call on her cell then gazed at him from across the table, eyes in a blazing luminance, and he suffered a slight loss because of the chasm between them: aloof yet alluring, delicate yet severe, her sculpted beauty so fragile and untouchable as if an image in the clouds. He struggled for words because it was so different than just overcoming barriers of unfamiliarity between strangers where conversation and the inane questions people first asked one another usually revealed their preferences and peculiarities—What d'you do? Where're you from?

Who're your people?—that gave faint impressions of who one was, how one behaved under pressure, what choices had led one to this point. It went into the mix, assuming there was a common ground that would soon give way under social banter to the emotional realization that one was very much like the other under the skin. Notwithstanding the many times he had been completely hoodwinked by the portrayal of truth and the reality of it; lying was a skill that humans had mastered somewhere back in their primordial state as evolution wrenched changes each time a Darwinian crisis hit on the long road to the present. Adapt and survive, but somehow Devlin didn't believe that was the case. It was as if she was a different species, somewhere further along the evolutionary ladder and he was staring into the future.

"Can I see you again, I mean…on our own…like this?"

"I don't think so Mr. Wolfe."

"What if I won't take no for an answer."

"It's impossible."

"Seems sort of severe."

"Nothing personal. It's involved, very involved. You wouldn't like it here."

"Try me…"

But she was gone. Rushing out into the street where he caught the last glimpse of her climbing into the Rolls Drophead coupe as it rolled away billowing white out its twin exhaust pipes. He had meant to win her over for an inside track to her patron—the elusive financial tycoon with political ambitions—but it had the exact opposite effect; expecting a temperamental young woman with an inflated view of her own talent, finding instead something he didn't quite recognize: gifted and egoless. It gave him vertigo like reaching out anticipating a wall and discovering only the infinite.

Chapter 11

Bixby Endecott heard it on the wind. A cry so plaintive and honest whistling down over ice and snow it penetrated to the bone. Like a chanting impassioned warrior summoning courage from every wild longing; champion of the race. In a dream he saw a lake frozen over, mists rising with first light, yellow sun through frozen reeds, and on the other side where the feral things ran, where men could not go a bird rose powering through the water with a clarion call from deep within racial memory. A signal to all those who had dreamed that now was the time, no one would be left behind, and even though an insurmountable journey lay ahead he cried out: "We will arrive, we will arrive..." the wind had told him so.

It was still and quiet for a very long time after that and then gradually Bixby began to awaken and realize where he was and saw the faint light that was coming in through closed draperies. Moving slightly, he was surprised by warm flesh lying next to him as soft and smooth as anything he had ever felt and smelled the sweet humus of her that filled the air with the lingering scent of sex. A tangled mass of red auburn hair burned across the pillow. Her breathing broke the silence like waves upon the shore. He pulled the blanket up under his chin and considered the events leading up to this moment as they began to come back to him in bits and pieces.

Earlier, cool air had slipped through ducts in the ceiling with an almost imperceptible whistle. If anyone guessed somebody had air conditioning on in the city during the Arctic cold snap they would have labeled him certifiable, but they didn't know. The man sat behind a gray metal desk with his sleeves rolled up over brown, sinewy forearms absorbed in a page of statistical demographics of the voting districts, historical party trends and yearly changes in the makeup of the population. Next to him was a large, white, porcelain mug with a Marine Corps logo on each side and a pack of unfiltered cigarettes: the top ripped open with lacerated cellophane and torn paper that was foil coated on one side jutting out like there had been an explosion from within. An ashtray made from a single piece of billeted aluminum overflowed with butts. White shirt, necktie, close cropped hair: the whole scene was an anachronism, but he didn't care. Everyone else thought he turned on the air conditioning in his cubicle so he could smoke with impunity, but that wasn't it, that wasn't it at all. He was always hot and believed his high metabolism was the reason he didn't sleep well and why he was up punctually at four AM every morning roaming the house looking for some solace that didn't exist, as if walking it off would make him suddenly tired and then he could drift off to meet with the sandman like he did when five years old. When he looked at his wife lying there in bed with the cool light of the moon washing over her like the tide and strings of damp hair clinging to the side of her face like seaweed he remembered what a beautiful young woman and how full of fun she had been and was locked into a hardened sadness by the fact she had given up after their first child died and let herself fall irretrievably into the abyss. He didn't know what to do, he had never known, so he got up at four AM every morning and wandered the house looking for some clue. The air conditioning kept him awake, it braced him as if it was the wind and he was still rushing into a skirmish with the full flush of youth in him commanding a small detachment of men in the winning moments he had been trying to recapture all his life. God and country, duty, that was all he had left now that his wife was lost.

A commotion from the elevator caught his attention. A group of bounders tumbled out, talking loudly, walking so that their heels made the floor vibrate, sloshing coffee from cheap paper cups, causing everyone in the whole office to look up, peeking over their cubicles with sardonic looks, losing the train of thought it had taken hours to achieve, wanting to yell or throw something to show their profound displeasure, but holding back from the temptation knowing they would probably lose their job and then where would their car payments be? The door to his office burst open.

"This is Burt MacGyver, your campaign manager."

Bixby Endecott thrust his hand across the desk smiling broadly, "Glad to meet you... just call me 'Bix.'"

"Lance!" MacGyver yelled before anyone else could speak. "Get your butt in here."

He stood erect, placed both hands on the desk and began a thirty-minute dissertation on every aspect of the campaign he envisioned so far and how it ought to proceed, running through a series of rich snapshot sketches, portraying competing candidates — first within the party for the primary and then all possible contenders in the general election.

"This is how I see it..." he pronounced drawing diagrams on a large, white, plastic board with a broad tipped, erasable felt pen until when he was finished there were scribbles all over and it looked exactly like battle plans unearthed by historians researching key skirmishes in major conflicts.

One of the men who had accompanied Bixby, who had been sitting motionless, listening impatiently, bordering on exasperation, walked over to the chart and pointed to it. "What does all this have to do with public opinion?"

"The purpose is to win," MacGyver said, "losers get nothing. They just go home and grow old. Wining takes strategy. This is what I do— strategy."

"It's a little complex isn't it?

"We are developing something that has everything to do with public opinion," Lance Norcross interrupted looking down, shuffling his notes, uncomfortable speaking to groups just as he had been at MIT where he had learned tricks to keep from being called on in class: but realizing tricks wouldn't work here, not when they were paying good money and this was the moment he had been brought in for. "It's not completed yet, but will be fully functional in the run up before the primary."

"That's why we're here…what is 'it' exactly?"

"It's an…avatar."

"What the hell…?"

Putting up his hands, "I had the same reaction," MacGyver said. "Let him explain."

"An algorithm really, a robotic algorithm—"

"An algobot," Bixby interjected to help clear up some of the profoundly mystified looks. "Think of it as a computer program that can travel over networks autonomously, networks like the Internet for example, that has its own intelligence—a certain freedom of choice to act a certain way in response to certain stimulators—depending on what it's programmed to do. At our firm we create algobots to monitor investment strategies and they work 24/7—without pay."

"OK," Lance continued, "OK, but now think of it as having an infinite freedom of choice based on its ability to learn — in our case, the ability to recognize and remember what people like, what they respond positively to, what they want, their emotional characteristics. Then imagine this 'algobot' having sensors in order to collect and feedback data from each encounter to a central database where it will be crunched and evaluated; then, depending on the results, new programming will be sent back to the 'algobot', which in turn will modify its behavior and responses. In a nutshell: it becomes what the audience wills it to be — almost in real time. The more input, the more it reflects exactly what the people want to hear — it has the ability to learn and most importantly to make moral choices autonomous of its original program. You can actually have a conversation without knowing it's a computer program."

"Sounds like a politician...but it can't just say 'yes' to everything and expect to win elections, it just can't promise — "

"This is artificial intelligence...intelligence being the key word here, but at a whole new level than how you may have thought of it in the past. Your policy platform will be hard programmed so there will never be a mistake: it will never be at a loss for words or unable to explain something persuasively: no more failed interviews, no more lost voters. It doesn't get tired, confused or sick, and makes everyone feel as if they were best friends. There's no question it can't handle perfectly. We have massive databases of information that can be linked into it — including the entire Internet — with instantaneous access, evaluation and response."

"That's not human!"

"Exactly. A human being could never assimilate so much information so fast."

"That's not the half of it...go ahead and show them..."

"The term 'algobot' just doesn't encompass everything anymore.

What if it could develop its own personality? Evolve over time? What if you really couldn't distinguish it from another human being?"

"You mean like…an android?"

He flicked a switch and the flat screen on the wall came to life showing a picture of Bixby Endecott sitting at a table in a navy blue blazer facing the camera smiling. Then the eyes blinked. "Hello," it said.

"I don't remember shooting that," Bixby mused.

"You didn't. It's an avatar. It doesn't sound like you yet because we still need some voice imprints…and the model needs a little work, but it's pretty good I think. It can do interviews, answer phones, be on social media…anything that's over a network… be in multiple places at once and nobody will know the difference. Nobody"

"Think of the possibilities…" MacGyver said.

After a moment of silence. "Gotta be kidding. You paid the kid how much for…a video game? Gimme a break. We've got a lot of money riding on this campaign."

"Good work kid," Bixby said as he left the office leaning close. "Don't listen to him—death cries from the old world."

Racing through the morning they touched base with all the key constituents and opinion leaders that could be crammed into four brief hours. Party managers had set up meetings with military precision and they blurred together in an onslaught of faces, leaving only slight leeway for the unexpected, as the campaign to launch Bixby Endecott's political career shifted from bickering caucuses into overdrive. First came the top contributors dutifully queued up to be sacrificed from whom the lion's share of cash was simply expected as tribute to the party: they were willing victims. Then, like preaching to the converted, he glad handed his way through a high-dollar-per-plate luncheon with representatives from the financial, pharma, real estate and tech sectors who all came with hidden agendas expecting hefty paybacks of one kind or another—believing some of the magic would rub off from touching the evangelical futurist of high speed financial markets. Guerrilla fundraisers worked the room, clamping onto the crème de la crème like pit bulls eliciting mega corporate donations. But to most present the investment was a no brainer, like the sequel to a hit movie they blindly threw money at it expecting huge returns, and though this was his first time running for political office, the aura of wealth and the fact he was a Boston Brahmin entitled him to start at the top.

By midafternoon his feet were sore. He'd had cocktails and wine at lunch and the buzz was fading into a realization that he might have to start explaining his position on some of the less stratospheric concerns; things that didn't have anything to do with investment strategies, business incentives, capital gains tax and the fodder that ate at the well-heeled. It made him nervous to rub shoulders with the real after he had ascended to the commanding heights in the virtual world of financial markets; it was all so much like a video game, juggling the assets of millions of wage earners: there was no impact, no looking into someone's eyes, and like holding the joystick of an attack drone bombing villages thousands of miles away there was no pain when the explosions hit blowing limbs in all directions, only the elation at a confirmed kill. However, in the back of his mind lurked the precept that in war and business it was essential to engage *mano a mano* in order to see the pain inflicted, to be splattered with blood and hear the screams; it was part of nature's checks and balance system.

"It may shock you to think that you're supporting the unions," the man smiled grimly, "but you're working for a lot of us already—so you might as well give in right now."

"Really, I didn't know you were making demands," Bixby grinned back, squeezing natural charm out of weariness, wondering if somehow he was violating natural law with his success. "How so?"

"Retirement funds: all that capital is how you guys make money. Well, we produce the capital."

"I never quite looked at it that way, but you're right—benefits trickle down don't they?"

"More like they trickle up..." another growled. "Eighty percent owned by the top ten percent. Wages remain stagnant. Upward mobility has lost its meaning. What the fuck can you possibly bring to the table?"

He watched beads of perspiration form on the man's face. He was sweating too, but not from the warm room. His understanding of economics had been inculcated from the study of sophisticated theory starting at the point where mathematical models were created of real world economic ecosystems using calculus and game theory and culminating in privately owned algobots that roamed the investment networks seeking rent on the sly: a consequence of leaping from university to Wall Street missing all the struggle in between. Somehow in his rarified world, the human side had been completely missed; the fact that the subject of economics spawned from the misery of the human condition that had been festering unchanged for thousands of years until some religious and social activists began to try to figure it all out. People like the men who sat across from him now. Before that, poverty and wretchedness were thought to be an unalterable part of life to be endured by some and shouldered by others as the white man's burden. Now he panicked at how glibly he had accepted the meeting with union officials when first rattled off to him couched in the long list of other constituents on his "must-see" schedule: because he really didn't know anything about their struggles.

"Unions make up over twenty-five percent of voters," his campaign manager had said, "probably thirty or forty…odds are greater they'll cast a ballot than the affluent…got more at stake. They're essential to your election."

He began to sweat more. Bixby Endecott's political philosophy was made up of an abridged version of the conservative agenda: believing that the "mob" should not be allowed self-rule, that a free market creates a free society and that inequality is a natural state of man; he believed in less regulation, smaller government, incentives for business developers and in the holy of holies: trickledown economics—what's good for business and the markets is good for everybody. It was all self-correcting if you didn't fuck with it. He also believed that unions were an anachronism—that they belonged to an era where eight year olds were working twelve hour days in coal mines and could only expect to live until forty—and the idea of collective bargaining and workers having the power to disrupt profits in the digital age was sinful, a moral crime much in the American tradition that a failure to amass wealth was a moral failure. If it weren't for entrepreneurs and the owners of capital, there would be no jobs and no need for unions. But he still sweated across from the uncompromising men unsure that he was enough of a political thinker on the fly to capture their endorsement—and the twenty-five percent of the vote he needed to win.

"If unions vanish people lose their rights. No more collective bargaining. Shrinking wages and benefits—if they can't purchase, your stocks lose value," one complained. "We're all in this together."

"Businesses now produce more with fewer employees," said another, "and offshore workers also cut companies' bottom line—but even those who've kept their jobs haven't seen their wages rise despite being better educated and more productive."

"Right! What they lack is power. That's where we come in. Unions aren't going anywhere in New York!"

"It's really about the future," Bixby found himself compelled to apologize. "I don't have any vendettas—"

"Not yet…not now, but all politics is local; you walk in and all we see is the Republican agenda to erode labor standards, undercut wages, and undermine unions—"

"That's it. In a nutshell, local politics has become nationalized; state legislation written by the staffs of national lobbies, funded in a coordinated effort by national and multinational corporations—"

"Gentlemen…my concern is the public interest. My job is to get to 'yes,'" Bixby said. "If I don't make a deal, I get nothing done. If I get nothing done, I am a failure. So, what can I do to open a dialog—this isn't the era of steel workers and coal miners and other nineteenth century industrial holdovers. It's the era of disruptive innovation, high-speed digital business, offshore workers; whole classes of employment are becoming obsolete; whole segments of labor are being displaced—"

"Consequences of a campaign at the national level to castrate labor! Right to work laws, anti-collective bargaining laws—"

"You guys have an image problem," Bixby shot back.

"As far as unions go, so do you!"

"But I'm part of the new world. You're not…as much as you want to be. Unions are losing relevance. Those in the new economy associate you with their grandfather's generation and me…with the future. Don't you think it's about time we start working together…like you say: labor produces capital, we invest it, everyone benefits. We're all in this together."

That evening, suspended high above the tangle of traffic snarling in icy streets below, overlooking Central Park where only a pale reflection of the starry sky shone off the lake, rumbling clouds obscuring most of the heavens, snow flurries coming and going, frosting the terrace where potted trees had been covered with plastic to protect them from the cold, where many summer get-togethers had been recorded in liberal elite memory, cocktail glasses were clinking amidst the rise and fall of voices and laughter and a lone pianist was playing Cole Porter in the background as the party of high net worth political patrons neared its apogee around midnight. Bixby Endecott had left the union meeting feeling deflated, despite his last minute bravado, and started drinking single malt scotch in the rented limousine on the way to a champagne dinner with some hedge fund managers and their wives at the St. Regis—where after a few more drinks he finally forgot all about it. It was ten o'clock by the time he reached the soirée where alcohol and being on the stump for eighteen hours straight had obliterated any personal thoughts and he couldn't get the song "Night and Day" out of his head.

The place was crowded. People came and went seemingly on the periphery; shaking hands, patting him on the back, wishing him luck as he began to let down, but after they had gone he remembered none of their names: just ships passing. The evening had taken on a dreamlike flavor making him unsure if he'd had too many or was just punch drunk and overflowing with nameless faces reaching out for more. He viewed it all from a distance tinged with unreality—until he felt a warm hand on his arm.

"You looked so enigmatic standing there," she said simmering, "so fragile…"

He turned to see Mirella, hovering like a fully blooming spirit in a jet black dress that clung to her like wet ink poured over her breasts, then flowing into a scalloped skirt undulating when she moved like the arms of a sea anemone luring prey. Her ripe beauty was poisonous with a clarity that obscured everything else.

"I didn't expect to see you here!"

"What kind of a woman would I be if I did what was expected?"

Bixby Endecott breathed her in and was filled with an inexplicable urge to escape. He was confused about the tempestuous singer; drawn to her warmth like fire he feared the burn and hadn't yet decided which way to go. "There's something about you," he said smiling apprehensively, wagging his finger, watching her eyes dance, sensing a danger zone, "something very..."

"I've changed my mind."

"About...?"

She leaned over brushing her lips against his, her perfumed breath an unendurable sweetness, and then with amusement at his nonplussed look turned the corners of her mouth up in a delicate simper and replied, "Get me a drink will you?"

Later they rode together in the back of the Rolls on opposite sides of the car; she staring out her window at the frozen tableau passing, saying nothing; he feeling the presence of a woman and the magnetic attraction that was not under his control: like predestination sweeping him into a vortex as he helplessly watched his own demise. But he didn't believe in omens—and that was his first mistake.

Bixby had very little faith in anything outside of what could be sensed, measured and seen—except for the complex algorithms he wrote in an outpouring of academic brilliance, but then that was all part of the material world, just cause and effect like concentric circles in a pond. It was when he had learned how to morph intellectual ideas into marketable products that his life really began and he woke up to how easily money could be made, now he had to continually straddle the fence between the real and the virtual in order to make it socially because...who could understand his idiomatic logic? So he smiled boyishly and cultivated friends with his engaging personality and put people at ease with his charm. But Mirella rattled him; she seized on a more primal and essential part that had thankfully lain dormant like something inhuman and wicked sleeping—until now.

"No, don't turn on the lights," she whispered entering his apartment. "I like the darkness."

He first thrilled at her touch when she fumbled with the buttons of his shirt, watching the elegant figure bathed in an ultramarine glow, seeing her eyes flash in the dark as delicate fingers did their work, smelling the scent of her hair as if just come in from a storm, hearing her steamy whispers in the night betraying sexual longings, feeling like he had been lonely all his life. Her hands were hot when they touched his flesh and once more he felt like he should run, just bolt from the door and never look back, but it passed as clouds before the moon and like a wild seed he let the wind carry him.

As he lay in the aftermath, breathing silently with the dangerous creature sleeping at his side, feeling violated, nursing spiritual bruises, fighting the pervasive sense of degradation left from their lovemaking, wondering at the unexpected animal like intensity with which this woman had taken her satisfaction from him. How someone who created such exquisite art became so sexually voracious, so whorish and shameless was beyond him. His lips were swollen. There were scratches on his arms and back. He was sore. Everything was spinning. When he first lay down searing flesh against flesh, it all seemed so gentle, so controlled, so deeply human, but when her first savage kiss drew blood he became confused. Then she devoured him, smothered him with emotions he couldn't handle, invading his body, violating and provoking him to physical acts he never knew he could do as if driven by a malevolent force. He had thrust and thrashed against her like a feral dog; she had become ferocious and feline tossing her wild hair back and grinding skin to skin until it hurt, slick with perspiration, bringing him to painful climaxes, one after another, draining the life from him, devouring his spirit like a dybbuk until exhausted he had retreated. It all came to him now as memories skimming over the ocean. He watched her sleep not knowing what he could ever say to her after what they had done and the places they had gone, and then he closed his eyes and drifted away convinced he had been bewitched.

At the same time, uptown in the small hours were others who had business that dark cold night. They had been trickling in since late afternoon: knocking snow off their shoes, hanging up parkas, scarves and sweaters, settling into their seats, unpacking their instruments, putting up music stands and laying out the charts they had been practicing for the last two months in their spare time when the Met was dark. Some had walked, others had taken busses or the subway and a few rode in on the train as usual—none were chauffeured or free from worry: they had debts, bad marriages, crushing defeats and unrealized dreams, but somehow their art happened anyway. The conductor had arrived earlier to meet a grizzled stagehand he had hired to be there and help with the lights and the heat so hands wouldn't freeze up when he wanted his musicians to play *allegro, energeico, expresivo*. He paid the man out of his own pocket because it was essential; there was nothing he would not do to transform his operatic players into one of the world's great orchestras and he longed for the triumph of recognition by his peers and so drove his players mercilessly, which somehow earned their respect.

The mammoth auditorium lay empty. It was cold all the way up to the gallery; every seat was folded in the blackness just the way it had been left after the last performance two days ago. The enormity of the space dwarfed the members of the orchestra huddled in the pit beneath the apron far below as lights came up on just them like an island in the cosmos.

The harsh, discordant sound of instruments tuning up was the prelude that lured Revenia out of the practice room where she had been rehearsing alone. In the dim light, as she made her way backstage through the labyrinthine hallways, the first strains of Mahler's Ninth Symphony came echoing on cat feet as if heralding the arrival of Gods with a haunting, graceful beauty that disguised the vengeance and ascending power to come. As it wafted through the passageways she thrilled to the sounds and so ran breathless until silently arriving in the half-light behind the proscenium arch back of the gold damask curtains where she stood alone on the empty stage listening. Out front the conductor danced to impassioned sounds in his head, he swayed and rose and fell waving his baton and obsessed over every note rallying the musicians to his impossible standard. Soon the music arose and Mahler's dramatic darkness passed over all of them searing souls with his demons in the swirling, rhapsodic, rollercoaster of emotions that the symphony became.

Suddenly Revenia was lost. She forgot all sense of where she was and became one with the most famous, death-haunted place in orchestral music; swooning to apocalyptically slow movements as they bridged the gap between sound and silence; rejoicing when the brassy, stunning, breathtaking crescendos threatened to bring down the whirlwind. Without choice she journeyed to glimpse another realm beyond worldly experience; it made her remember who she really was, feel truly alive, it was a hymn to end all hymns, it was a dance-whirl-struggle to an elusive joyfulness. The conductor and his players wrung a feverish intensity from every note striving to reach ever increasing heights in the empty theater where there was no one to hear except she, and to her it was a revelation, a transformative experience that cut deep.

Enchanted in the faint light as she stood alone with arms outstretched and eyes closed, feeling the symphony's rapture inside, a faint gossamer glow began to surround her. An arc of energy that grew as she listened, a halo that cast dim and subtle shadows within shadows as slowly she began to rise up from the boards, aching her back, reaching to the heavens until at last she was clearly thirty feet above the stage floating in a crucible of light.

Unseen another presence had also been lured by the music. He was dark and brooding and stood transfixed as well in the shadows of the wings. But it wasn't the music that held him so rapt; it was the soaring angel he never would have expected to find—he who had been the harbinger of her arrival and had warned of her influence now felt exonerated by this sign. He saw the omens plainly and resented the way he had been dismissed, certain now the threat was all too real and vowed he would rid the world of this saccharine faerie and possess the fiery Mirella as well for good measure after the rebuff: feeling nothing but disdain at her hunger for humans.

Wind tore the sea white. The race of raging water beneath him roared and icy spray hit his face like buckshot. Devlin leaned backward past the edge of the great sailing yacht as it heeled far over from the near gale force tumult, filling its massive spinnaker with sonic boom like cracks as all sails snapped taut, running three sheets to the wind making the halyards and shrouds whistle and shriek, struggling to tame the twin forces of air and water with sail and keel to do just one thing; go faster. He stared incredulously across the broad teak deck as the giant ship heeled more and more against the huge forces, riding the thin line between windward and leeward until the churning sea was foaming over the far edge, looking behind at the twenty foot drop into Long Island Sound; everything creaked and moaned as carbon fiber rubbed against wood and metal pushed to its limits by sixteen testosterone imbued maniacs who only an hour earlier had seemed like nice college boys. Above the sky was ripped with cirrus clouds streaking white against deep cerulean blue and the heady adrenaline mix of excitement and fear made him wonder where he'd been all his life.

He had driven up to Greenwich on impulse. Snug in the worn leather seat of his late model Volvo wagon he concocted a plan out of the nebulous thoughts from the night before and somewhere along the road determined it might even work. Things were pressing too tight in the city, he was beginning to feel wild and anxious that his charade at the Met was wearing thin, had been fragile at best from the start, and the risk of discovery now and the prospect of having to begin from scratch with his investigation compelled him to attempt something extremely foolish. It wasn't exactly illegal, but not entirely straight up either and if found out would provide just right amount of fodder Deputy Director Arthur J. Biggs and Associate Director Patterson needed to have him sacked, and probably indicted as well—which somehow made him want to do it all the more.

He found Terrance Roark on the quay at the oldest yacht club in Connecticut. It was a cold, bright day and the wind whipped his hair biting into him as he jumped from the car and walked the long mooring down to where the big boats tied up: where a group of men feverously prepped a yacht to cast off. Close heeled to the dock was a huge, sleek, black leviathan of a sailing ship, straining at her lines with a restless rolling from the angry sea beyond the breakwater, chomping at the gate for the challenge of the open ocean. Both needle like bow and stern swept out as if expecting to escape earth's atmosphere, extending twenty feet or more from the water line where the red of the lower hull peeked from beneath the waves, a thin line of white separating it from the obsidian gloss above. "*Eidolon*" was painted across the transom in windswept, serif, italics. Narrow teak planks of the broad deck wrapped sinuously around the low mahogany cabin, set slightly aft, following the streamlined contour of the hull. The mainmast soared infinitely into flawless deep blue; sails yet to be set. Like etchings in bankers' offices imagining the towering rigs of the *Big Boat Class*—such as King Edward VII's legendary "*Britannia*," built in 1893, that won thirty-three firsts of thirty-nine starts in her maiden season—the enormous beauty of it took his breath away. Something about the fact that despite terror and war, poverty and insanity; despite the brawling masses bleak with nihilistic visions, where any forward progress was like dust and ashes blowing; where dreams of freedom and spiritual enlightenment were routinely crushed under the burden of economic slavery; where love festered and died; this grand illusion was spawned of men's minds for no other reason than it was possible, for no other purpose than to sail across the strong back of the sea cutting a ribbon of whitewater through the chop racing before the wind. It took his breath away.

"A bit cold for sailing isn't it?"

Roark shot a look over his shoulder, holding a rope in his hands with an unfinished bowline knot, yanking it tight, scowling in the sun, drawing his lips tight, "Not for real men."

"No ice in the sails or anything like that?" Brushing wind whipped hair from his face. "Seems like you'll freeze your nuts off."

"It's a challenge. Were getting ready to sail, not much time…what do you want?"

"Can we sit down and talk? It's important."

"You kidding?" He gestured to the others feverishly readying gear. "Takes sixteen people to race this yacht!"

"Really…God, it's a great boat," looking down the quay. "You didn't tell me it was so beautiful."

"You just weren't listening."

"I hate you guys, you know…? I just…my office looks down on the North Cove Marina—smack in the financial district…don't know how the city missed destroying it. Across the river it's Jersey—built by child labor and the industrial revolution—the last state to abolish slavery; south is the Statue of Liberty—you know '…tired, hungry masses,' but below are these mega yachts of the pornographically wealthy like it's the meeting place for the Fraternal Order of Billionaires. But…she is beautiful isn't she."

"No dream can possess her…I'm just taking my turn at the wheel," standing straight, gazing at the huge sailing yacht. "You couldn't possibly understand—I don't feel entitled, it's an anomaly of nature, I'm blessed by it…simply a custodian."

"My dreams…well, let's just say they're not so grand…but I do love the boat!"

"It's not a 'boat.' So, what do you want anyway? You didn't drive all this way for the scenery."

For a moment, all that could be heard was the wind. "I want you to make an investment."

"What do you mean 'investment?' What do you mean '…you want me to?' Invest in what?"

"Freedom," he deadpanned.

Roark paused. "Oh God, a cause…a handout? Why didn't you

just call…isn't the whole tax system a charity? You already get too damn much of my money! I don't have time—shit, you guys are incessant… what 'freedom?'"

"Yours."

"Hmmm…" trying not to roll his eyes, "I thought we went over all that! Quid pro quo, remember? Unless I'm losing my memory…and believe me I wonder…or is this more extortion?"

"It's supporting the arts."

"Hush fucking money you mean!"

"It's going to be a hit. Haven't you read about it? '*Aida's Curse*,' the haunted production…it's all over the news, social media—"

"I'm antisocial."

"You could be an angel."

"I doubt it. Isn't this illegal?"

"Jail…there's the crime"

"What do you really want?"

Devlin drew his mouth into a wry smile staring down the quay at the "Eidolon" shimmering in the winter sun with a shiver of excitement, "I want to go sailing."

He wrapped himself in the bright saffron storm parka retrieved from the clubhouse—a huge, multistoried, Victorian octagon with slate gray gables and a covered portico encircling the entire structure— slipped into borrowed deck shoes and rope knit sweater then tied a scarf around his neck as the final barrier to the cold. Roark barked terse orders: "…sit there, do what everybody else does and don't get in the fucking way—especially when we get going—and hang on; can't turn this thing fast enough to fish you out…even America's Cup boats have lost men." After the lines were cast off and the giddiness at being free of the dock hit him, he watched the former Wall Street wunderkind at the wheel close hauling the great yacht masterfully out of the harbor without any offshore wind at all, feeling the beast slice through the waves beneath his feet as a prelude to the rash of open water running uninterrupted to the horizon: water beginning to feather in the chop. Not another sail was visible, giving him more reason to have second thoughts at putting his life in the hands of strangers, gripping the guardrail cable until his hand ached. All was quiet as they slid past the breakwater out of the harbor; each man poised at his station, each with that euphoric look of someone about to slip free of mortal bonds straining to hold fast to the lifeline yet straining to break away at the same time. Their eyes were set like men going into battle; addicts to the terror and the glory.

The sleek leviathan lurched into the open ocean unleashed from the harbor's heart. Suntanned young men scurried across its deck wheeling sheet winches so fast their hands blurred, trimming sails, pulling the maze of lines taut, untying and tying them down again, ducking the boom swing without looking as they sought the elusive path where all forces conspired for speed. Shot spray exploded as they cut the waves and all danced as one, like insects all knowing the right moves as if spawned from the same gene pool. It was a mystery where that sweet spot was, but Devlin felt its power. The hand of nature thrust them forward into the roiling sea, its fist slamming the sails, its sinews straining against the keel, forcing the bow to part whitewater, using stillness versus chaos to conjure energy out of nothing. Devlin ran with the wind. With every tack he followed the scramble and sat teetering on the edge of the deck as the yacht heeled over each time more radical than the last: the great boat rolling up with such power they were all flung skyward like ragdolls. The halyards shrieked as they plowed through the water riding the thin edge of capsizing where losing one's grip meant sliding across the deck into the churning froth or tumbling backwards into cold oblivion. He braced up against the weather listening to the creaks and shouts, the slap of the giant hull against the sea, the whistling in the wires, the thrashing whitewater and above all, the hammer of the north, the polar vortex they were trying to bridle on the edge of chaos as storm clouds rapidly approached from the north.

It all slammed his senses as he grappled to follow the lead without falling overboard, unsure how serious Roark had been when he said even experienced men had been lost. There was no incentive in returning him to shore if it looked accidental; there was every motive not to. He considered human nature as he struggled around topside becoming wet from the spray seeping down into his jacket, soaking his pants and deck shoes and numbing his face with cold, wondering if it had been a mistake indulging his impulse to see how the superrich played. Off in the near distance the wall of black cloud suddenly towered out of the clear blue and he could see the telltale blur of faraway rain. For the next three hours as the magnificent yacht pursued a perfect run with the wind, pounding through the waves became incessant yet still Roark drove the boat to its limits and the crew was relentless keeping it there, hanging over the lip of the massive hull as it breached the water under whip and spur goading it ever faster. Devlin began to realize it was not just sailing, that it was not just a yacht, that the old renovated J-Class was a composite of a ten-thousand year jihad men had with the sea and all the experience of those seasoned warriors' had been endowed in this ship to make vessel and men a single moving part. He, like others, became caught up in the struggle and saw the purpose that drove her was not the wind and the waves, but the same drive that propelled Roark to conquer markets when others floundered hapless and broken. It came to him in a flash so contrary to his every belief that it almost hurt; this was the secret of the rich, the "Alpha" everyone longed to discover, but he let the thought pass—its creation and destruction occurring in the same instant—subconsciously unwilling to have been so wrong all his life. But it reaffirmed his hate of the rich; now seeing the drive as an obsession to possess, to hoard, just as Roark's obsession now led them into an approaching storm chasing some elusive performance goal as if he could be freed of guilt by unlocking its magic in the wind. He feared now it was a warship and the soldier crew was in it to the bloody end driving the great sailing yacht to beyond its limits, crashing through wild seas.

Devlin muscled his way hand over fist aft along the lifeline to where Roark was planted at the wheel his lips drawn into a tight line. The huge stiletto hull heeling over to its event horizon, one more degree and they would have torn the keel from the water and rolled into the wailing ocean to freeze. He grabbed the metal rail of the pushpit and shouted out, but at the same time wave spray crashed over the cabin knocking him silly and he would have slipped away unnoticed into the boiling brine but he grabbed onto a stanchion with one gloved hand and held, straining every sinew from head to foot, praying his fingers wouldn't give way. Then, with inhuman effort he pulled himself up first hugging then bracing against the metal rail where navigation lights were hung, wedging his foot where the post was bolted to the deck to keep from sliding off the yacht again as it leaned further pounding through the breakers like a juggernaut. A peal of thunder cracked the sky from the black nimbus looming up ahead announcing the apocalypse.

"Can't you see there's a storm coming?" He shouted. "Can't you see it?"

Young men swarmed the foredeck in clockwork precision responding to the rising sea. Roark, unmoved, was intent watching sail and angle against the darkening horizon line and said nothing as they raged on.

"Is it safe?" Devlin yelled. "Are we safe?"

Far aloft at that moment, while racing on the edge, unseen at the tip of the masthead, a wild flickering blue flame appeared radiating against the backdrop of the approaching storm. Its beauty scintillated translucent in a gale that would have snuffed out any normal fire, and danced with a flourish down the main halyard as if bridging two worlds: that of men and that of spirits where interplay between earth and sky had more than one interpretation. Quietly it spread down the lines its hissing buzz obliterated by the wailing sails, the sounding sea and the shouts below; reaching out then withdrawing and reaching again until it flared in different places all at once when suddenly those up forward saw the spirit candles and stopped their struggle to stare. The eerie lights ran down the guard wire ringing the boat and set the pushpit rails aflame as if from an inner fuel, appearing then disappearing, darting and vanishing, jumping gaps from line to rail and back, its elusive sparks leaping like glowing sea spray. Some in the crew were yelling, their voices lost in the gale, pointing and waving at Roark, who yelled back, unheard, trying to get them to man their stations, unaware of what the commotion was about as the great yacht bounded forward. But as he pointed a flicker across his hand shocked him, the arms of his parka also becoming luminous and a wandering flame traveled up his back like hackles. He jumped back holding his arms out to see, turning the boat windward so it settled down in its race, staring up the halyards at the glowing spectacle with the brightest flame, undaunted, still at the mainmast's peak.

"*About, about, in reel and rout, the death fires danced at night; the water, like a witch's oils, burnt green and blue and white.*" Roark recited in amazement.

In moments the winds eased up and snow flurries fluttered down from dark clouds putting the lights out, but it was all anyone could talk about as they made their way back to the harbor, as if they had broken the barrier between this world and the next and received a sign they had reached the limits of the possible.

Later, as Devlin nonchalantly unsheathed his fountain pen, having cornered Analetta at one of the Met's donor events, he felt guilty for flaunting morality: writing out a check for one hundred and seventy-five thousand dollars that wasn't his, almost forgetting to put in the all the zeros it was so over the top. Secure in the belief there was more where that came from, Analetta gushed and kissed him right on the lips, proving only that both of them had knocked back too many glasses of overpriced pinot noir some caterer had donated for the tax deduction. Devlin ruminated on the mysterious appearance of St. Elmo's Fire, which he took as a sign heaven's gate had opened and shamed the rich man into giving back some of his filthy lucre — praying the IRS wouldn't find out before he could show some results of his off-the-books investigation. He hated the rich and didn't want to take the fall for any one of them.

* * * *

The phone rang. Bixby Endecott lurched up from a profound sleep, fighting a deathful premonition centered in the pit of his stomach, barely able to open his eyes, reaching out blindly for his cell lying on the stand by the bed.

"We're bleeding again," the voice said as the device display cast a soft, blue light across his face. "They hit us in afterhours trading." He hung up and turned to where Mirella should have been, but she was gone.

Somewhere his boyish charm had fled; he felt raw and damaged as he rode the dark streets to his office in the hour just before dawn. Yellow lights streamed from shop windows as they readied to open, homeless huddled around blazing trashcans, moving restlessly to keep warm or still asleep under newspapers on the grates where steam rising from subways kept them from freezing. Now things seemed different, he felt violated by an invisible hand adjusting the scales against him and was losing the one commodity that had buoyed him through everything up until now: hope.

The frozen city was a wayward island in the storm. From space however, it appeared as a great vortex of light whose radiance branded it as one of the priceless jewels of earth, an epitome of humanity where millions of parallel stories played out against the collision of poverty and riches. In this place it was possible to live well on the economic flux alone, which like spontaneous combustion generated an ecosystem made up entirely of surplus from commerce that lumbered through the streets like a monstrous, relentless army: in the path of which devotees threw themselves as burnt offerings to the Lord of Wealth. Despite his private jet, his luxury cars and his enclave at Northeast Harbor, Bixby Endecott was no exception. He spent three straight days chained to his computer, tearing his hair out, trying to unravel the latest cyber-attack paralyzing their systems while millions slipped away, struggling between fury and the Zen like state of grace he had to be in for exceptional work, fueling himself with coffee, soft drinks and takeout until at last they ferreted out the Trojan Horse and got all trading on the upswing. Afterwards he slept a full night and all the following day dreaming of the subterranean seas of Ganymede.

Chapter 12

Once again MacGyver had risen while his wife was sleeping. He always waited and watched her as if some miracle would happen: looking always, looking anxiously for some sign, that while it was expected was already gone, passed unseen in the night, as if time would turn if he took long enough and it would be the way it used to be. But she seemed to sleep later as years passed and even when she was awake the sleep remained. They once had impassioned sex in the early mornings while the still mist hung in the air and the smell of plant life from their garden permeated everything and the light poured in like honey: before either of them connected with the day and could be anyone they wanted, soaring out of dreamscapes into each other's arms, exploring the limits of the possible in ways denied them in real life, spirits safe beneath the harbor lights. They would always make love in the morning, always. He remembered her cool skin like delicate flower petals encircling him in a steamy embrace, like beauty's imprint it was the only truly spiritual thing he had ever experienced in his violent life. His love for this woman and she waiting at sunrise had given him reason to go straight through till morning; otherwise it would never have happened because of the darkness in his soul, the darkness in his mind and the darkness in his past that haunted. He only held out with the faintest hope, but could feel that fading and the old self rising to the surface now that he lacked restraint, lacked the civilizing influence that she used to be when they were really man and wife, now that they just shared a common space.

He looked up at the huge stained glass windows a hundred and fifty feet above the chancel: The Rose, they called it, by a Boston artist "...*one of his major works*," looming as if a tattoo in heaven. His eyes caressed the landscape of ionic columns supporting clouds of crisscrossing arches that separated the nave from the world he knew was living outside, but was somehow distant when he visited the cathedral. He breathed in the stillness. The smell of ancient oak benches hovered in the pristine dawn before anyone showed up for the first mass when even the beast of the city was still sleeping and everything was hushed awaiting what madness might come. He ran his hand across the reddish brown surface burnished smooth by generations of the faithful, bringing who knows what burdens to this place. Sanctuary. It was the time of wanderers, of sojourners, misfits and fringe dwellers when the disenfranchised owned the streets in the interval between when those of the day arose and after those of the night had retired. One didn't choose to belong to that fraternity; it was a cruel judgment fated by the gods.

With a great bundle of grief he arrived seeking nothing other than refuge because he didn't believe in redemption, but at the same time was drawn there, as he had been to similar places by some half remembered promise. Once while meditating alone in a huge, dimly lit mosque redolent of the atrocities committed in the name of Islam, aching for salvation, tethered to the whirlpool and reaching for a lifeline, an imam approached as a brother of mercy. But all the man said to complete his disillusionment was: "...*please remove your shoes.*" Other times he had sought out churches and cathedrals and haunts of the spirit as a sacrificial gesture; to atone for the sins of his life or to seek shelter from the storm or just as solace for his lost love that lie sleeping never to wake again. The bitterness would have overwhelmed him if it were not for these interludes in the off hours, these safe harbors, even though he determined help was myth along with all the other metaphors written in holy books—only reminders that he was just not good enough. A priest appeared and walked toward him; he looked wise as if overflowing with human kindness and divine purpose and MacGyver's heart raced as he drew near. But the cleric passed without even looking down, soon his footsteps faded and he was alone again. Then he left, looking at his watch so he wouldn't be late for his appointment, his belief reconfirmed that strength of character was the only virtue and everything else was a fool's holiday.

The man in the olive drab M65 field jacket and jeans looked out of place in the exquisitely designed, palatial lobby of the luxury, residential high rise that had won many prestigious awards for its severe use of minimalist, postmodern motifs. Midcentury lighting hung cantilevered from the high ceilings throwing random shadows across the Italian parquet marble floors as he sauntered apprehensively to the security desk.

"MacGyver, Burt MacGyver to see Mr. Endecott."

"Yes," the swarthy man said looking at the computer screen for a minute, running his hand over a three day growth of beard that matched the stubble of hair on his nut brown head, flexing the muscles in his jaw as if a sign, his white shirt open at the neck with the top three buttons undone under the tight fitting black blazer finishing off the intimidating package. MacGyver had seen it many times before. "He's expecting you. Penthouse elevator to the left."

"Thanks."

He watched ice cubes melt in the glass of orange juice and discussed minor issues that could have been easily dispatched with a phone call, still in the dark as to why he had been summoned so early in the morning. There had been another man in the hallway outside the apartment as he emerged from the elevator and he had expected a pat down, but the man just looked at him through glazed eyes—the way Bixby Endecott was looking now, as if he hadn't slept well in weeks.

"I believe the image a candidate projects is…well, obviously image is everything. It's a PR world isn't it?" He said in an effort to muster his trademark enthusiasm.

"Central to our campaign strategy."

"What do you think? How do I look?"

"Like hell."

"Exactly." He leaned forward, set down his glass and in the most confidential tone imaginable said, "I need to know if I can trust you."

Bixby Endecott knew he could, knew it before he ever invited his campaign manager up for a private talk. He had been vetted by the best that money could buy; there was nothing he didn't know about him. He knew MacGyver was former military: a veteran of the Special Operations Regiment, and a Marine Raider trained in leadership, close combat, languages, weapons deployment and autonomous mission execution in spartan environments. He had read every word in the man's classified records: of his forays behind enemy lines, of clandestine domestic operations as well as the rationale for every decoration awarded for achievement—all sub rosa so as to not breach national security. Driven by duty verging on a religious fervor, he knew he could trust the man and only asked the question to bridge into why he really had invited him up for a talk.

Weeks on the campaign trail while directing damage control after each abrupt cyber-attack left him taut and near the breaking point; so fragile he couldn't sleep and was forced to take huge quantities of minerals, in lieu of pharmaceuticals, just to counteract his chain-drinking coffee. All night long he sallied out to face whatever demons were taunting him at the moment, a restless prisoner of thought: except when Mirella stayed over—on those nights, reminiscent of intoxicating perfume, she wore him out with insatiable sexual demands, for which he always seemed to have energy…far more than enough as it turned out, the desire originating from somewhere outside himself beyond his control. But in the aftermath when she lay sleeping lightly, perspiring gently, breathing sweetly, sheets thrown haphazard across her small, voluptuous body, he thought about the rumors that had surfaced about him and his company. Accusations of collusion with government agencies that allowed faster market access over high speed optical cable routes nobody else could afford—a nanosecond made the difference between success and failure in the market. After sex he didn't sleep either, but it cleared the air and brought a kind of clarity—charges of political corruption before he even held public office. That's when the catharsis happened: a steaming consequence of their lovemaking, in the void that remained where all moral codes became insignificant and he could easily have swung one way or the other without concern. It came to him that it all might be political—a thought that had never occurred to him before. Everything had always been about business, accumulating wealth, the search for the utterly impossible: the Alpha. It had been hard for him to even think seriously of anything else. But politics, this was a new animal; the destinies of men were at stake. That's when he decided to call in his campaign manager.

The smell of newness permeated everything and as MacGyver had entered the lavish townhouse it had been like entering an elite department store or an exclusive furniture showroom where everything was so precious nobody touched anything for fear of soiling it. Out the window, past the asymmetrical layers of translucent metal that reflected light like pearls with a faint rainbow hue, he felt like he was in an airplane passing over Central Park having only ever seen it this way in pictures: the broad green stripe surrounded by the ritziest of Manhattan's architecture, the lake and planned forests now all frosted in white making it appear unreal like a fairyland amidst the garbage and the flowers. He rubbed his hand over the porous leather of the couch, hoping the oil in his skin wouldn't stain it, feeling uneasy with all the artwork on the walls, the way he felt in museums where all that creative beauty was relegated long ago when it had become inaccessible to normal human beings still locked in the workforce. Art and architecture were like religion to him: ideals meant to lure the mob forward with the promise of possibilities, without the slightest chance of ever attaining them. It was all about the rich and even though he never thought of it in those terms, his entire life had been spent in catering to their whims: God and country, duty, sacrificing his desires for the common good. Empires were built of that mortar; power depended on rent seeking from people like him and he never once realized he was the pillar on which their ability to influence the course of events relied, too satisfied with the marrowbones he was tossed.

"Of course you can. With your life."

"I'm not doing that great," he tried to focus, struggling to make it through the fragile wall on the one side of which everything would always be all right and on the other chaos—leaning forward with his brow set, pressing his lips together as if watching something from a long way off where details became indistinct.

"I thought it would be easier than this, but I don't know where to start," Bixby said.

"Best if I know everything," he replied callously master to tyro, confident with skills in which others only saw the mystery; through which he could see behavior so unpredictable as to appear random.

"Somebody's out to get me," he whispered hoarsely. "And I'm not the paranoid type, I'm really not. You believe that don't you?" Outside his penthouse the weather buffeted the floor to ceiling windows and rushed past with such ferocity it sounded like branches of huge eucalyptus trees swaying in the wind. "Just not used to dealing with threats…I manage investments for Christ's sake, economics, virtual intelligence! I'm a code warrior not a god dammed…" stopping himself suddenly aware of who he was talking to. "What do I know about—"

"You'd better start from the beginning."

Bixby Endecott, ruler of a thousand hedge funds, so wealthy he couldn't even spend it in one lifetime without help, target of every nonprofit fundraising scrounger, sat hunched over with his elbows on his knees pouring his guts out as if to a confessor. He spilled it all: the ultra sophisticated algobots that nearly brought down his firm the first time, and this last attack breaching firewalls and cyber security so advanced the military would be years catching up with them. Sweat poured down his face.

"Whoever it was is a fucking genius," he exclaimed, "up until they killed my French quant and that man in Paris…that was a mistake. Too random. Defied chaos theory. Somehow they knew I wanted that young diva in New York. Only an insider would know that—"

"The overawe factor."

"What do you mean?"

"Someone wanted to impress you so much you'd become careless. Make mistakes. Fold up. That's why terrorism works."

"Nobody wants to die!"

"They count on it, but if you choose death to begin with then there's no more fear."

"You'll have a hard time making that popular—but I like the sound of it."

"'…one's intentions should be to grasp the long and the short swords and to die.' It's the way of the warrior, the etiquette of self-immolation."

"All right then," he nodded thoughtfully. "OK. I'm glad we understand each other, because I want to ask you to do something that falls outside your job description."

"How far outside?"

"Find the son of a bitch that's doing it for a start!"

"Then what?"

For the rest of the day Bert MacGyver stood a little taller. It was part of an axiom that when wars are over and amnesia sweeps the battlefields, a tide of normalcy settles everyone back down through the cordite haze into the way it should be, behaving the way they're supposed to, forgetting the bloodlust of lives frittered away through acts inhuman or simply incompetent; but the living warriors…nobody was supposed to make it through, conflicts were a zero sum game and the only reminders anyone wanted were pricey memorials to the honorable dead. The past is only a shovel full of ashes. He was a highly trained embarrassment; a symbol of the violence lurking just beneath the surface. The hidden influence. The inexplicable: like the sudden rampaging murderer who slaughters a schoolyard full of children, who a day before had been a meek and perfect neighbor…"*he always seemed like such nice man, always a kind word to say, kept to himself…we were all so shocked, it wasn't like him.*" It's not like anybody: and that was the terror of it, and the fact that men like MacGyver existed in peacetime, was a symbol that something was slipping through the cracks, something that couldn't be rationalized for long before it reared up again to cleanse the race of its weakest members. Consequently, let the dead be dead was the credo of citizens. Even so, he thrived at being recognized and now longed to exhibit his hellish competence.

"Lance!" MacGyver yelled. "Get your butt in here." He explained the scenario bare bones to the whiz kid; mission ops to him. What else did he need to know? The young had everything to lose, but were willing to risk it all on a whim; the old had nothing to lose and were so cautious it hurt. "Here," he placed a couple of gleaming hard disks on the desk between himself and the young MIT graduate. "Someone broke into this system—twice. Millions of dollars were lost. Two men are dead. I want you to find out everything you can about these people, where the money went and who's got it. If you get it right, there's a bonus in it."

"And if I don't?" But it was a moot question; Lance Norcross was already fully engaged in solving the problem with postulated sequences of events reeling away in his hyperwired head.

MacGyver understood perfectly. Nothing secured loyalty like an impossible goal, and he'd just thrown the kid a Gordian Knot: the stuff hackers dreams are made of.

In the vortex of opera swirls a classic, tragic theme. Acolytes have flocked to it since the beginning seeking a strange and exotic life separated from the mainstream by its profound, almost unobtainable beauty. Hopeful converts dipped their toe into the vitriolic brew just to find out if they would be consumed body and soul or released back into the world destined to such mundane fates as secretaries or real estate salesmen confined to cubicles for decades. It was an act of courage. Many are called; few are chosen.

"Why does he keep stopping everything?"

"To fuss. He's a film director," as if that explained it all, quickly adding, "with a *huge* millennial following."

"Any more perfect and something will break."

"She has such lyric musicality…don't you think?" Analetta swooned during one of the director's fits, "…and can sing mezzo too. Once in a lifetime…she'll be one of the greats. This production will put her on the world stage."

"I saw her in Paris—"

"That's right, you told me? Introduced you to opera…now you've paid her back."

"It's…opulent. I didn't expect it to be so grand."

"It's Italian. Took our old sets and rebuilt them…from sketches on cocktail napkins…Neapolitan style—I nearly died when he first pulled them out of his pocket all wrinkled. The old ones were a top draw for almost twenty years. Now it's like a film set ready for a close up."

"Is he an opera director?"

"I found him making a film in Rome. Hates to speak English…had to have him…did I mention he has a *huge* millennial following?"

On a cold, crisp afternoon with the smell of frozen oak leaves in the air Devlin had yanked the now familiar stage door at the back of the theater open, pushing against crusted snow that had piled up, consumed by the minutiae of other cases he was handling, worried he was wasting time among other things, ignoring the career consequences if he came up empty handed. He was left with a gnawing in the pit of his stomach. But the moment he crossed the threshold all those concerns faded and he plunged headlong into an alternative reality that had bewitched him since his first breathtaking experience at the Palais Garnier. He had come to witness a full dress rehearsal at the invitation of Analetta—who sent him a cryptic text message one of the twenty-somethings at the office helped decipher—a perk for special friends of the opera, especially those with deep pockets. He tried not to think about the underlying crass commercialism—even infiltrating high art and confirming rumors that everything was for sale—because it was all role playing at the core: just as he was not the philanthropist he pretended, Analetta was not the guardian spirit of the house she so skillfully portrayed, but more hardboiled.

A rush of energy swept over him. Everywhere people were in motion going about their business, feverishly working to fit intricate logistics into the union's time clock and avoid profit killing overtime. He passed the carpenter shop and the cavernous rooms where up to five productions worth of scenery could be stored for quick staging—swinging the flats in from an expansive fylfot that hovered above the entire back of the house—winding past others who scurried through the labyrinthine hallways too, making his way toward the main auditorium, feeling the excitement swell around him as everything ramped up for the crescendo of a fully staged rehearsal. Out of the stillness "Aida" rose newly with each performance, as if from the sands thirty centuries before Christ a colossus of artistic achievement materialized defying the material world and all its zealots. The event shook the firmament. Fragile artists came together against all forces allied against them, somehow making it to their mark, giving it their best; despite the specter waiting in the wings of a heartless universe where just when you thought it couldn't get worse, it does; just when you needed mercy, there was none. Despite the overwhelming odds, out of an idea in the mind, still and pure, unmoved against the cataclysmic forces surrounding everyone came this art: echoes of spirits.

The air bristled. Everyone was breathless with anticipation.

The first notes of violins and oboes could be heard tuning up. Devlin stopped dead, cursing and lost down some backstage hallway, anxious to take his place out front in the roll of fledgling angel beside Analetta—whom he intended to grill with veiled questions hoping for some hot dope now that he was in her confidence. Suddenly, a young woman dressed in a pale green smock with a makeup bag slung over her shoulder rushed out a door leaving it ajar. He called after her for the way to his seat. "Follow me," she said without looking back. But he had caught sight of something and stood transfixed and as much as his mind commanded him to move, he could not. For through the crack in the door he saw a young woman pulling her costume on over mocha brown skin, mysterious and erotic in her sublime privacy. There were silver beads and the fine linin kalasiris of a captive Egyptian princess and blood red roses sitting in heavy glass vase in the corner, but the shock was what reflected in the mirror where he saw the angelic face of Revenia unaware a voyeur was present. Dressing rooms, his mind screamed, he was by the dressing rooms, but the scene was so intimate he had to look. Then to his horror she looked up seemingly into his eyes and he fled unable to explain himself, heart racing, flushed with regret at his weakness for the sudden beauty, wondering if she had recognized him.

The brilliant moments turned the air ozone during the rehearsal. Arias were performed flawlessly, dancers came and went on wings with fluid elegance all the while the Italian director, Francotti Benedetto, paced and constantly barked out directions, adjusting set pieces, giving orders to the resident lighting designer over a handheld two-way and micro directed every nuance on stage: driving everyone to the edge, holding his hands up to his face, contorting his fingers into a viewfinder so he could look at the scene as if through a camera. Paying no attention at all to the music or the singing and simply expecting it all to be perfect, his concern was the telling of the story, the immersive experience that was his mantra: filmmaker as a brand. The conductor of one of the world's great performing orchestras remained stoic and aloof, wrangling his over one hundred, high strung musicians—who were only mid stride in their two hundred performances a year plus rehearsals such as this one—so there would be no unseemly outbursts justified though they may be, but personally he'd had it…to the moon…and would have given anything for a stiff drink. The whole scenario was volcanic; it could go either way from brilliance to oblivion depending on how far the Italian pushed things, and Francotti Benedetto was out for blood.

Whenever Revenia looked out over the audience he felt she was looking right at him, but knew that was improbable, having heard it's nearly impossible to see past the lights when on stage and they were all the way up in the twentieth row. But he couldn't take his eyes off her.

"There's something different about Revenia…how did she come to the Met?"

"Oh her…our little Parisian diva? A gift from another donor."

"Really…"

"Unfortunately…yes."

"Unfortunately?"

I know that sounds terrible…but we prefer our benefactors simply to fulfill their roles and let the professionals fulfill theirs. With a global reputation to maintain, a very fragile thing these days—the institution is over a century old and there are hundreds of companies all vying for talent, so we're very competitive—we have to watch it."

"But, they're opera lovers…I understand Bixby Endecott has been extremely generous. Papers say he approves everything."

"We can't let some sybarite ruin us!" Her eyes flashed momentarily, grasping the arms of her seat to keep her hands from shaking, then getting a grip purred through self restraint: "We are the best; the pinnacle of the art world. Donors come and go—no offense—but opera is forever. However, I am pleased."

"It worked out then?" Devlin was surprised.

"As you see—overjoyed," she responded matter-of-factly.

"Interesting…excuse me I'm so new to all this, but I never thought of it that way. How do you handle that? …and let's be upfront; I'll never put you on the spot by making artistic recommendations. I'm a financial guy—in it strictly for the ride."

"Of course—" she smiled for the first time.

"So, tell me. Really, I'm interested. What about Bixby Endecott, how much sway has he got here? Is the New York Times right?"

Squinting her eyes at the stage, "A newspaper is a device for making the ignorant more ignorant."

"H.L. Mencken…right?"

"Does an education possibly lurk behind all those dollar signs?"

"Blame it on some anonymous English professor—"

"Art is no democracy."

"I can see that."

"Can you imagine? If it was we'd get the lowest common denominator…we'd get Hollywood…we have to keep higher ideals alive."

"Must be a lot of pressure, after all…this doesn't come cheap."

"Someone has to be the arbiter."

"They say he funds up to seventy percent of your endowment. What's in it for him?"

"As much as he can get…apparently," then hissed under her breath, "like any misogynist dinosaur. If you must know, I hear he's screwing one of our principal singers, the one who gives new meaning to the word bitch. Perhaps he feels empowered to make artistic decisions because a soprano gives him an erection."

"Don't hold back," he laughed. "I guess my next question is: why?"

"It's a takeover bid. He wants to add the Met to his portfolio of companies, just another conquest like his little tart—I don't think she'll perform better after all those late night political rendezvous—but we've always depended on the generosity of strangers."

"Seems pretty generous—"

"May think he's buying influence, but it's just a tax write off. And we thrive on tax write offs. Look, this is mine! I won't let it be bought! Artistic integrity is why we get donations in the first place; unfortunately, egos come along with no-strings contributions. Part of the game."

"How much influence does he have?"

"I make all decisions…consulting with the board—of which he's a member—but no one dictates the art, no one makes artistic decisions but me. It's blood simple."

Theater people were different. They seemed to live on an exotic wavelength imperceptible to normal humans. For the next eight weeks he felt like a primatologist inching his way into the good graces of a foraging mountain gorilla troop, nursing a constant fear the simians would see through his thinly disguised intentions, pick him up by the ankles and flail the life out of him. Despite this constant guilt, he became a familiar face backstage and at the frequent impromptu gatherings, usually in some restaurant or another, overflowing with hugs and kisses on the cheek, neither of which were native to his particular species and both of which he tried unsuccessfully to avoid—especially from the excessively effusive whom he guessed were over compensating for genetic deficiencies. He tried hard to loosen up even though his grounding in market based economics and securities law acted like heavy chains preventing him from ever soaring and often from entering into the spirit of things at all.

Devlin was serious by nature. Not in the morose sense, but in the way that he believed anything of value was closer to fundamental truth than human conversation could ever hope to approach and so he had a hard time making it socially; talk had to have pith, chitchat needed to cut to the chase or he simply lost interest. It was the secret behind his *twilights*: intervals where his purpose evaporated into the meaninglessness of normality and only a basic thrust to survive carried him through. The same driving force had fueled a rapaciousness for learning that had dogged him since school to the point that many weighty tomes always sat by his bed as late night reading material. Treatises that would put anyone to sleep enlivened him. Women in his life saw these things and imagined the strong-yet-sensitive-type carped about in romantic pulp glad to have something to talk about after sex, but soon realizing he actually understood the books lost all interest branding him too unemotional. Everyone except Veronica, she was the only one who could match his intellectual Pegasus—and then some. But now that she was gone perhaps loneliness explained his infatuation with the young French diva. The whole idea of it was counterintuitive to his investigation, like an event horizon, the crossing of which violated every thread of common sense, but from the moment he first saw her in Paris she had haunted his dreams and the erotic image of her in the dressing room lingered.

He had only spoken with her in passing a few times since they shared a coffee at the Vietnamese restaurant. Then one night he was invited to a post rehearsal get together down in the Village and he went straight from the theater to the 7th Avenue subway alone, hoping some of the pretentious glitz would rub off shoulder to shoulder with simple humans. Sitting on the train bench, inspecting the graffiti carved with delicately filigreed detail, breathing the stale air full of humus and exhaust, hearing the roar of voices and the murmur of the clattering wheels, watching stations roll by in a blur of lights and faces as in every city on earth with people racing to destinations, trying to outrun the fear of death, the light of longing in their eyes. It was like bathing in cool water and the experience left him refreshed, reminded him of who he was, climbing the stairs at the Christopher Street Station, making his way down streets frozen and streaming with life.

Nobody still owned a private house in Manhattan, at least nobody Devlin knew, nonetheless he entered the narrow brownstone townhouse midway down one of those nineteenth century streets lined with American Elms and resplendent with red brick and stoops with black iron railings. Home to a successful infomercial director—think "Amazing Ginsu Knife"— whose wife was a costume designer for the opera, and who never tired of telling the story of how he discovered it completely in shambles and renovated the structure utilizing all original materials and vintage techniques cost be damned. Led across the golden oak hallway he caught glimpses of sequestered rooms—behind the massive outer walls covered with creeping vines, looking like a fortress of red brick on a street of anonymous doorways—behind which mysterious lives transpired. He emerged into a brick courtyard with high walls beyond which other buildings soared, in the shadow of a sweeping pine tree where the carriage house stood: a shining jewel of the 1870's now filled with theater people each holding a glass. The warm interior was overshadowed by a mezzanine loft with a wrought iron railing, the walls sandblasted to the original masonry, raw oak beams supporting a gabled roof with huge glass skylights that he could see the night sky through. As he mingled with the crowd, half inside and half spilling out into the frigid air, the thought of astronomical renovation costs for this landmark property stunned him like hitting a glass ceiling at full speed and though able to see the stratosphere beyond, being unable to ever reach it. Some of the pretentious glitz began to form about him again: crustaceans on the soul. He channeled his disdain for the rich into his purpose for being there, smiled and put on his most charming face.

"The stars are there," Revenia said appearing at his side, "just hidden beyond the veil."

He was startled. "Thought I might see you here," smiling self-consciously, wondering if she had recognized him outside her dressing room.

"I saw you looking for them. Weren't you...from memories? Ever wonder why?"

"Why I have memories or why no stars? Don't know. Haven't seen them since I was a kid in the Adirondacks. Been in Manhattan too long. Clouds I guess. The city...light pollution—don't know...why do I have a feeling you're going to tell me?"

"They're only hidden from people who have forgotten."

"Forgotten what?"

"How to see of course."

"It's sort of murky isn't it? The price of cities. Darker in some parts than others; little, faint, glowing, pinpoints of light—shrouded, as if... what do you see?"

"I can see it all."

"What? Stars?"

"Certainly. I never forgot."

"Guess I have complete memory loss...I don't see a thing, just some hints something might be up there. Looks like industrial soup reflecting the city's glow."

"The sky is an open window. Look into the universe and you can see

forever, in the night, if it's dark enough—if you know how. Come here…
stand by me." She put one arm around his waist, another on his shoulder
and held him steady, looking up into the ether. Moments passed.

"I don't know what I'm—"

"Shhhh…" she said, "hush. There's some kind of truth in you; I
can feel it. It's just…you need to know how to know. Look up silly, can
you see them now? Can you?"

I dunno…something…" Perhaps it was the night whirling past, or
the fact of her breathing so close as flesh and blood after performing
where she was soprano as goddess, or the warmth of her luminous voice
in his ear as she spoke of celestial lights, but for a split second he thought
he saw brilliant pinpoints blazing and the distant Milky Way spilling
like a shot spray of diamonds for light years across a cosmos where
unknown galaxies, Magellanic Clouds and untold nebulas roamed. He
was astonished.

"Whooh…! What's that! Wow! Wait…wait, now it's gone…I
thought I saw, I thought…it's gone now…"

"Yes."

"I saw stars, like when I was a kid! Like a glimpse beyond the veil.
They're gone now. How did you do that?"

"The stars are always there…just hidden. You can see them if you
know how, if you haven't forgotten."

"Must have been a break in the clouds. Fantastic! I love that! Such
an incredible thing…looking into the universe. Makes you remember—"

"—who you really are."

"Exactly…how did you know?"

"Oh…well…we all love a beautiful night," she said suddenly
reticent, pulling back. "Forget it…just forget it. Everyone feels that way.
Everyone."

All the way home he thought about it feeling like a stranger exterior to everything as if viewing it all from a dream yet with a vibrant immediacy more real than real. He kept looking out the rear window, conscious of sounds following them, but it was only the rolling wheels of his taxi winding through frozen streets in the dark. The image of Revenia lingered in his mind, her untouchable grace, her subtle eroticism and he couldn't stop thinking about her, fighting the desire, not wanting the distraction—too much was at stake. It was almost like being in love.

His cell phone rang. It was Veronica. "We have to talk," she said. "I'm missing you."

*　*　*　*

The man sitting in his study never suspected anything until he felt the cold blue steel against his temple. No noise, no footsteps, only the sound of the quiet voice telling him not to move.

The business end of a pistol pressed against your head is an inscrutable thing. Nothing seems to mitigate the threat. The matrix of violent images that incessant entertainment and constant news supply are no comfort because the human species has not yet become desensitized to real terror: it has evolved into one of the most effective technologies known to man despite being subjected to state suppression and popular condemnation. But a person never knows how he will react to it when it really happens, as the man was now forced to realize, sweating alone, cold from the pit of his stomach spreading to his extremities like frost, listening to the measured breathing behind him, waiting as he heard a trigger being cocked by the unseen intruder, thinking this was the end.

"Who is it?" An emotionless, rasping voice asked.

"Who is what?" The crack of the gun barrel across the side of his forehead nearly knocked him unconscious.

"Who is it?"

"I dunno! I dunno!" Tasting salty blood. "Please, what do you want?"

"Who is it?"

Thierry Reynard carried a list of names in his pocket. Some of them had a check mark next to them in pencil, as if an old forgotten grocery list in a world agog over electronic devices—where failure to use them was considered a moral deficiency. Friends had asked him; "Why the fuck don't you use a computer for that?" He didn't know what to say. Until he touched it, it wasn't real. So he made lists, kept little notes stuffed into his pockets whenever he found a piece of data. He looked at the list right now and checked the number on the door to ensure he was at the right place, then knocked loudly. Suddenly electrified. There was a muffled cry from inside, then a barely audible thud as something heavy hit the floor.

He threw his full weight against the door and when it gave way stumbled inside the darkened room, but as he straightened up was hit with an excruciating pain in his right shoulder and neck. Agony shot through his body like a fifty-amp current causing him to cry out as his knees buckled and he collapsed helplessly in a heap covered by the whirlpool of blackness that swallowed everything. A moment later he came to, rubbing his arm, seeing the door open, feeling a numbness that kept him from moving. Then, pulling a Sig Sauer 9mm, he leapt up and tore down the hallway to the elevator, which was already showing two floors down.

"Officer assault! Need assistance! 72nd and Madison—unit 632!" He shouted with his cell in one hand, barreling down the stairs with his gun in the other, trying to head off his assailant in the lobby, breathing hard unstable legs still wobbly, bursting through the door on the first floor into the empty lobby except for a hapless concierge, running to the sidewalk there was no one, swinging his pistol wildly in all directions, scanning for his assailant when all of a sudden a car started out from the curb and he lurched into the street to head it off, holding his gun up with two outstretched arms, screaming at the top of his lungs to stop, yelling "I'm a cop! I'm a cop!" The middle aged woman behind the wheel froze in terror, panicked and hit the gas instead of the brakes, slamming into a parked car at the same time Thierry fired off two rounds, shattering the windshield and missing her by millimeters.

"No forced entry," the uniformed officer said as he walked back into the apartment, "except yours."

"Next time I'll use the key. Is he all right? Did the guy let him in? No other entrance except windows six floors up."

"Says so, but don't look too good. Says not, didn't hear a sound,"

A man sat straight backed in a chair with heavy eyes, one of them bruised and swollen shut, as a paramedic wrapped his head in gauze.

Walking over to him. "What the hell happened here?"

"I got slugged."

"I can see that. Why would someone want to hurt you?"

"We have to take him to the hospital…" a paramedic said lifting him on the gurney, "severe concussion. You can talk later."

"Cummon buddy," grabbing the man's arm as he was being led away, "gimmeee something?"

"It's not safe…"

Gray water swirled in eddies where the current was strongest, reflecting dappled sun like shining mercury. There was bluish ice along the shoreline. Against the ominous sky an unidentified flock of birds hightailed it south in a last desperate effort to flee the cold that would not release its grip. They formed a strung out "V" shape with the weak and the old trailing behind where soon they would fall to earth exhausted. It was the way of it, basic truth for all living creatures subjected to the relentless forces of nature, and even the social nets so deftly strung by the humanists intelligentsia grew tattered after a while letting all but the fat cats fall through—testimony to the adage: one law for the rich, another for the poor.

The tips of carbon fiber oars dipped into the water without any splash. Devlin pulled against them his body springing to life, sliding in the seat, as his scull thrust forward like a bird in flight. It looked like rain and he almost had not come, but with too much trouble in mind to be useful at anything else he needed to wash himself clean. With three mighty strokes he was midstream on the Harlem heading down toward Mill Rock where the current met the East River, straining to feel the burn in his muscles and not easing up for almost five miles. Only a few weeks ago it had all seemed so simple as he rummaged through the random thoughts obscuring the answer to whether it was all worth it or not. Life would always be out of balance; that was inherent in the system. Capitalism depended on someone winning and everyone else paying rent. There was only so much room at the top. No one could determine who that someone would be, it was a toss of the dice—one man sane the next not, one man moral the next not—no better than hereditary monarchs who begat nothing better than indigenous poverty and thousands of years of blood and revenge as a legacy. Though agnostic, he knew it was a religious question, knew that cutting off the head didn't kill the snake, it was cutting off the body that did it. Without soldiers there is no power, reconfirming his reasoning: it was the arrogance he hated most, the entitlement that oozed from the pores of the wealthy like a God given right, and if he could bring justice one indictment at a time perhaps that was enough. He gripped the oars until his knuckles turned white.

Two days earlier he had driven north of the city to the site where the house had burned down at Larchmont Harbor. As he drove up Thierry Reynard and another man stood shivering in the cold each holding a steaming coffee. Snow covered everything. Wind swept in off Long Island Sound smelling of ice and fishes.

"Look, I just want to feel safe again," said the man with the bandage on his head.

"So did this guy!" Thierry shot back.

"What guy?"

"Know where you're standing?"

"Why the hell did you bring me here? I'm freezing. For the view?"

"It's where the French quant's house was burned down."

"Guillaume Marchand?"

"He wanted to be safe too, look what it got him."

"I used to work with him."

"He brought me here too," said Devlin. "Christ's sake, what is it with this place Thierry?

"It's real. Nothing else in this god damned case is! One body floating in the river and a lot of 'rythms, lot of fucking 'rythms, virtual nonsense if you ask me!"

"'Algorithms,' think of them as tiny computer programs —"

"Oh, shit—that helps. They don't talk. What I need is some cooperation, that's why I brought you here. Someone murdered Marchand, someone burned down this house. You said you had information…now, what the fuck what is it?"

"You're with the SEC, right?" Looking at Devlin.

"Yes."

"I think the guy that attacked me works for them…"

"For who?"

"…used to work for Endecott Technologies, with Guillaume Marchand. Fired me two weeks before he was killed—ungrateful bastards! Think the same people are after me."

"Why? You know something?"

"Better believe it. Plenty. And I want you to promise me he'll burn!"

"Who?"

"Bixby Endecott."

"So…what have you got?"

"He's fighting a war.."

"What do you mean?"

"A turf war. It's like this: for the first time in financial history, machines can find, analyze and execute trades far faster than humans ever can. Emerging technologies have changed Wall Street beyond recognition. Markets are wilder, less transparent, and so lightning fast a trade is now measured in microseconds. Algobots can execute one in less than a half a millionth of a second—more than a million times faster than a person can even make a decision—and they battle for fractions of a cent. A huge percent of all trades are done without any human intervention."

"That's all very interesting," Thierry seethed in frustration, "but what the fuck—"

"Designed by quants, like Guillaume Marchand—"

"The dead guy?"

"Right. The dead guy."

"Just want to make sure I'm not getting a fucking science lesson for nothing!"

"Point is these algobots—little computer programs to you," shooting a condescending glance at Thierry, "exploit minute movements and long-term patterns in the markets. Buying and selling at a thousandth of a cent profit, for example. Insignificant as it sounds, do it 10,000 times a second and the proceeds add up. Constantly moving into and out of securities for tiny slivers of profit—that's what Endecott does. Twenty-four hours a day. Seven days a week."

"OK," said Devlin, "so what is your point?"

"These programs send and cancel orders in a never-ending campaign to deceive each other, sometimes just to slow each other down. They can flood the market with bogus trade orders to fake out competitors. It all comes down to how fast you can buy and sell. The fastest trader can sell higher, buy lower. A connection that's just one millisecond faster than the competition's could boost a company's profits by as much as $100 million per year. These buy and sell orders are all transmitted over optical cables regulated by laws over how close a trader's equipment can physically be to the stock exchange data center. It's a physical place, located on a piece of real estate, in a building. We had ten people researching, buying and managing real estate just to get better cable routes. Like I said, it's a turf war. Fortunes are at stake."

"Physical…" Thierry grumbled, "now I can understand that."

"Immoral maybe, but not illegal," said Devlin.

"It is when it's rigged. A close cousin to insider trading. Too fast to fail. Seventy percent of all trading activity is high-speed and Endecott is paying off someone inside the New York Stock Exchange data center in New Jersey where all trades are processed. First they buy real estate as close as possible, then someone gives them a speed advantage once their transaction hits the inside. They can trade faster than the competition."

"You got proof?"

"Routing logs. Signed documents."

"How did you come by these items?"

"You forget, I was an insider, trusted with the most sensitive information—then the son of a bitches fired me once it was set up. More for them…the American way!"

"This information, damming as it sounds, would take a long time to substantiate. It's only circumstantial evidence unless you've got visible proof. I can see teams of prosecutors tied up for years—"

"I'll get it. Call it leverage. Guillame was my friend. He wanted to stop the practice and threatened to blow the whistle."

"…so they killed him."

"That's why I was fired. I overheard them arguing."

"Have you been to these places? Did you see them kill him?" Thierry asked.

"Of course not."

"That's not evidence. It's bullshit."

"Maybe not…but they killed him! Now they're after me!"

"Then you better watch you're back. Lie down with dogs—"

"What do you want from me!"

"More. I want more."

The scull rode the strong current of the river as Devlin hit his stride. Cold air bit into his lungs. Beads of sweat streamed down his face in the wind and he felt the burn in his abdomen run up into his shoulders and halfway down his arms as he pounded out a ferocious rhythm. All he could hear were the sounds of oarlocks straining against the force of the oars and a din coming from the omnipresent city. The water was just slightly disturbed as he passed, moving so quickly, leaving a thin wake, trailing off into the murky, polluted swirls that sliced Manhattan in half.

Convinced Bixby Endecott's operation was dirty, he yet nursed the knowledge like something precious he wasn't willing to give up just yet.

There was enough circumstantial evidence to obtain warrants, and if he went to the Director it would almost certainly be designated a "National Priority Matter," assigned to an Associate Director who in turn would assemble a team including Bob, from Cornell, who was on everybody's Christmas list. But that wasn't what he wanted. He wanted more. He wanted blood. Politics and dark money held the indelible fingerprints of all who touched them; both the guilty and the innocent were branded. If Endecott was using foreign money to fund a campaign all to avoid taxes, more than one person had to be involved and there would be a trail.

Almost dead certain he was behind the murders of at least two people and of using his firm to structure a complex illegal scheme to amass inconceivable personal wealth...they just needed the smoking gun. But one question dogged him: why? What else does he need to buy? How much money does a billionaire need to be rich? And as Devlin glided down the Harlem under low ominous skies, sucking in the cold air, sweating as he passed the icy shoreline an answer came to him. To purchase the one thing he doesn't yet have: political power.

That night it rained. He had heard the drops patter against the window as he dressed, getting ready to go out, wrapping a scarf around his neck and turning his collar up against the cold, but it had frozen before he locked the door and the showers turned to sleet that flittered down in the night lights of the city and streamed across the headlamps of rushing cars. He was meeting Veronica at an Italian restaurant that still had black and white photographs of Frank Sinatra hanging in the shadows. It was the first time they would sit face to face since she had left him. But his thoughts were consumed by how the murdered quant fit in to everything, fear that the extorted money funneled into his off-the-record investigation would be found out before hard evidence could exonerate him, and a hopeless infatuation for Revenia — made even more confusing by the return of Veronica. An inner turmoil bled into the evening full of strangers and taxis and falling snow and colored everything.

Chapter 13

She saw the saturnine man by accident, looking over her shoulder, fixing her hair in wind that was whipping up the trees, peering surreptitiously in his direction, pretending she had not and continued walking. Malevolent footsteps followed. So close that Mirella could almost feel the sweat on his brow, hear his breath, like running a finger lightly down the edge of a razor blade and trying not to draw blood—the danger of it thrilled her.

Sundown tore the sky when she first emerged from the theater after a day of rehearsals. All emotion had been spent, lost pouring her soul out for the Italian film director who fiddled with blocking the performers and played with the set no end, seeing only the illusion of opera while she held its beating heart in her hands. There was no explaining why he couldn't understand, but she had nothing but disdain for him so walked out to regenerate in the park only two blocks away. The fine tessitura of her mezzo soprano had seared the air; its mystery of infinite fire emerging from a static nothingness at her core like magic. Lesser singers cowed before her talent—all except one: Revenia the innocent. It drove her into a fury and gave her a kind of energy that suns had or tsunamis or stars going nova, but of grace and beauty she had nothing left to give. Mirella needed the darkness to fuel the light.

Hundred-year-old street lamps mysteriously turned on just before dusk throwing out yellow glows in all directions. Pausing, she smiled in a slightly twisted way and turned up a side path into a grove where icicles from the trees sounded like wind chimes as they were blown shattering to the ground.

Over a low rise and then down through a stone pedestrian tunnel, echoing footprints followed, looking back only once, knowing he was there, feeling a sudden nervousness with the game she was now committed to. Above the trees the high rise of buildings loomed silhouetted against the dusk with their lights twinkling, and sounds of the city filtering through the bushes with the constant ebbing and flowing of traffic. Walking faster he suddenly rushed by, brushing the bag slung on her shoulder, turning back just up ahead where the lamplight fell off. Shadows were thrown low across his face, but what alarmed her was that he cast no shadow from the light above, no shadow at all.

Mirella swirled to face him. "What do you want?"

"We're concerned." he lifted his swarthy face, twilight rustled the trees, shiny black hair was buffeted by wind.

"What do you mean?"

"We think," he hissed, "you're getting sidetracked."

"Do you? Well…what makes it your business?" Hackles raised like a cornered cat. "Besides, I'm not—"

"Can't afford to lose sight—"

"There you go again…don't think you know who you're talking to!"

"Look at yourself. For your good, as well as ours. Common cause here…we feel you're seeing too much of 'that man,' neglecting other things…more important things. This isn't about personal appetites."

"It's under control."

"We don't think so."

"Deep complaints!" She mocked. "You're so…" fuming with frustration, "there's more to it—if you could only see…more to be gained than you understand."

"We're listening. Enlighten us…if you can."

"Power."

"Power? What are you thinking? You have power."

"Not like this."

"Nonsense. What more…" anger flared, then silence and the man sighed, "perhaps if you explained—"

"I don't need permission to survive!"

"What is it you don't already have?"

"I want everything! Domination. Influence at the commanding heights…beyond these petty arts with their insipid, shallow audiences. I possess a leader of men. I intend to absorb his life. I will advise him," eyes shining steel like, hypnotic, brilliant. "his mentor."

"What…? Incredible! No…! Not so proud, not so proud. Don't fool yourself—"

"You think so? I have him already. He's mine. I possess him!"

"He's human! He's mortal! You have everything to lose; he can only lose his life!"

"Don't give me that! I have a shadow…in case you haven't noticed. I fit in to his world. You? You're an apparition. Like smoke. A waif. Some of us long for the human touch…that's all. Living fire. Some of us have more appetite for life."

"We never lost our memory; you never remembered. Lifetimes endless tell the story."

"Well, it's too late. I've moved on. It's about more than a few that need to be put in their place...nobody cares about their dammed keepsakes. It's a bigger game now, far bigger...about influence, domination. The affairs of men...easy...these petty humans with their hates and prejudices, they're so suggestible, hypnotic, subject to hidden influences, compulsive—"

"No! We think you're mistaken. There're too many. You can't possibly...there are too many. They'll find you out. They'll organize. You'll be destroyed. It's too big a chance...could expose us all!"

"Know what your problem is? Stuck in the middle ages. This world runs on information, data and access in case you haven't noticed...you need to be a player, an insider, hidden and influential. Well dressed, well heeled, I can make him think any way I want. It will be I who is the agent of change; he's just my instrument and I have him wrapped around my finger already—he's addicted. One taste of honey and he was hooked... humans are such incurable hedonists; they'll give up any cause just for sex."

"We think you're endangering all of us. We think—"

"Don't care what you think! I'm the future. Beyond your command. It's a new world, get out of my way if you can."

"You're wrong! Only illusions change. You violate natural law and there will be blood!"

"Watch me!" She stepped forward violently waving both her hands, wiping away the phantasm, and the man vanished into the wind.

Fuming all the way back to the theater, ruminating why everything she had done was right, feeling more compelled than ever to prevail, realizing at once she had made a pact with the devil by spilling her guts when she should have kept her emotions to herself—been more diplomatic—now there was no way back. She hated that. Succeed or face extinction; where the lost will finally cease to exist—the second death.

Mirella felt more imperiled and more alone than ever, but it fueled her grit to protect herself at any cost, to dominate to survive.

As she approached the back entrance of the theater the sky was nearing full twilight. In between sporadic clouds that tumbled in darkness, illuminated by the eternal Gotham from below, stars could be glimpsed through clear patches. There at the curb ahead, Devlin was talking to Revenia and she stopped to watch them. A yellow taxi pulled up, fumbling in his wallet she saw him drop something to the street unnoticed. Then they got in and sped away. Moments later, standing in the exact spot the automobile had been she looked down and picked up a small white card from the ground, reading with utter shock what was written on it: *"Devlin Wolfe, Senior Investigative Attorney, Federal Securities and Exchange Commission."* Instantly, surprise turned to foreboding. She didn't know why it was significant, just that it was. Anxiety overwhelmed her other concerns like blood across the moon now believing the terrible purpose on which she had staked everything was threatened.

Like a locomotive screaming down upon them with brakes complaining, opening night was approaching. Everyone prayed nothing world derail it, as sometimes happens in theater, almost everyone that is. But all were committed because for the first time in years every performance was sold out in advance—even standing room was being scalped. Though in a state of high anxiety, Analetta oversaw the furious activity as if from Olympus, assuming complete ownership of the production that the papers were already alluding to as "...brilliant, a mesmerizing tour de force from the acclaimed director of..." thankfully squeezing in the name of his obscure last movie, a hit to the millennial audience she wanted so badly. The opera critics chattered comparing the exotic French diva's first American appearance to the triumph of Paderewski's debut in New York over a century earlier—an association she had specifically plotted with publicists and fertilized with some well placed bribes to stir collective memories. After all, she reasoned, the director was an iffy proposition at best, one she nearly threw out of her office on their first meeting, so felt entitled to big rewards. The fact of Bixby's coup at contracting Revenia after all her efforts had failed never entered her mind. Now it was hers completely. He...only a necessary evil, just a piñata full of cash.

As the day before the first public performance arrived the heightened atmosphere backstage was a brittle mixture of excitement and fear. Only the most self-absorbed were suffused with confidence, for the majority it was a period of vacillation and introspection, wondering if it they were good enough, if they could make the grade compared to the brilliance that had preceded them—the mob was a harsh mistress—or was it actually as they thought, each in their worst moments alone and drunk with self-pity, that they were delusional and hopelessly longing for something that could never be. The saying went: you can't beat a woman into being beautiful...but that was the magic of it, when out of sheer will one could transcend mortal bonds and take their place amongst the immortals. Many had been there, seen those moments before, legendary performances that became the fodder of backstage lore, religion of those condemned to a short life in the theater where flames that burned twice as bright lasted half as long.

Devlin missed many rehearsals. He still had a full caseload in addition to his sub rosa investigation, burdened by the synthetic persona he had to keep up, concealed from everyone except his cop friend, Thierry. It caused extreme personal distress because he was basically an honest man, a good person, and pretense pushed the boundaries of his moral code. The theater, though, was his one link to Endecott, and he hoped his growing relationship with Revenia would be his ticket into the luminous circle where some revelatory slip-up would make his case. He knew it was there, but like the meaning of a lover's dispassionate sigh not what it was.

He appeared as a work in progress, a partial transformation into his alter ego: insouciant and nonchalant with more money than good sense. He could never make it all the way, but he did feel the danger, the magnetism, the allure of a world he had stood on the peripheral of all his life not just as a mere critic, but as an enemy. It was a sense that he could be sucked into the vortex at any moment while playing the role and become permanently lost. People viewed him as a "fat cat," their treatment of him different than of others, he was elevated, allowed more leeway, elbow room, forgiving and even expecting moral lapses as if a sovereign right of the wealthy, debauchery bought and paid for as the answer to the ageless question: what is the purpose of life? Within this spiritual buffer zone accompanied by the absolute best of everything was where the turbulence lay, where the risk of treason waited, shoals for those to betray themselves upon. The ease with which one could slide from the light into the dark muddied the truth.

Only the night before he'd had dinner with Veronica, not expecting the sudden waves; the emotional hangover lingered still, a quiet hunger. She had come through the door of the restaurant in a burst of energy at the same instant a lick of wind tossed her blonde mane and car lights converged in the street silhouetting her with a backlight like a grand halo. They embraced, but the conversation began to edge him into one of his *twilights*.

"I can't speak about it," Devlin frowned, hoping the subject would dissipate.

"Ahhh! The magic words," Veronica touched the vodka martini to her lips, "now I'm really interested!"

"You're a compulsive trial lawyer."

"Don't like settlements…someone's got to pay, don't they?"

"Sue the bastards!"

"Should be our national anthem," setting the glass down, now branded with lipstick.

"Isn't it?"

He loved the way she smelled. Like barley drying in the hot sun after a warm summer rain. Never a hint of perfume, like some women who left vapor trails for three hundred feet.

"So…?"

"What?"

"Are you going to tell me about it or not?"

"I dunno…hear you're up for Assistant Director…not really one of us anymore."

"Never was. I've got breeding…blue blood if you must know."

"Yea…seen the shots of you and Skipper out on the Chesapeake in your sloop rigged daysailer—"

"Held its own in a brouhaha…very stable, all wood, genius in design—"

"I wouldn't know. I'm not a Brahmin."

"You're changing the subject…come on, we have no secrets," she chided.

"Well…" frowning for a moment, "it all started after that fundraiser for 'American Voices…'" he finally confessed, thinking of all his secrets, feeling a tinge of sadness. The story he reluctantly unfolded was peppered with legalese only another hired gun could appreciate, the obsession with moral equity being indigenous to any counselor whether they admitted it or not, so she listened never taking her eyes off him.

"Maybe he's not guilty."

"Impossible."

"Circumstantial…so far, unless there's something you haven't told me. Is there?"

"Of course not…except he's an opera lover."

"Boy…now were getting someplace, that's really criminal—"

"OK, OK, I didn't tell you about the French director."

"French director?"

"The one who was gunned down outside the Palais Garnier. You must have seen it in the news. Next I hear the Met announces Paris Opera's enigmatic young prodigy is booked for a production of "Aida" —all knew she had refused every overture, in fact flatly refused fabulous offers and had vowed never to perform outside Europe."

"So you think…wait a minute, is this Thierry's idea?"

"I don't know what I think. But there are two corpses. Both of them connected to Endecott…and a whole lot of financial irregularity that points to 'American Voices' laundering foreign money into campaign financing…his firm is behind that Super PAC."

"You're stepping on a lot of toes…"

"So I've been told—"

"…if it's true."

"He's dirty!" she just looked at him bursting to say something. "Trust me. I know he's dirty! He's got these thugs around him. Afraid of something! His own bodyguard shot that assassin in Paris…! He was there…right there!"

"I know, I know…read it in the Times."

"Don't look at me like that."

"Like what?"

"You know…"

"Should turn over your evidence to the Federal Prosecutor's office. Most of this isn't even in your jurisdiction."

"I want him."

"It's circumstantial."

"He's dirty."

"Why? Because he's rich?"

"No. Because he's so…fucking entitled."

"I understand you. I really do. But…this obsession with the rich—"

"What…?"

"You know."

"Maybe I'm flawed. It's different for you, from that culture, innocent—like a Catholic saint."

"That's pretty simplistic. I think you're confusing wealth with hedonism—let's face it, a poor person ends up in the gutter with a bottle of muscatel; a rich person ends up on a mega yacht with a bottle of Chateau Margaux: both are drunks."

"That may be true, but I'm still going to burn him down. How can anyone be allowed to squander resources like that? You should see the lobby of their offices! The rich are trying to make it through life buying happiness, the rest of us are just trying to make it through the day—"

"It's called a free society. Didn't law school sink in? The top ten percent funds most social betterment groups; the wealthy invest in philanthropy. What about that?"

"Right. Makes me wonder about all the university degree programs in non-profit fundraising, that's where the money comes from. It's not philanthropy; it's a market. Tax write offs. Increased profit margins. You know what it takes to get hired by the United Nations to help with the poorest of the poor, the world's refugees? An MBA from a top Ivy League school. Know what that costs? The wealthy are socially incestual, they only invest in things that produce their kind; inbreeding that weakens the social DNA until it becomes extinct—like the Hapsburg line."

"I think you're romanticizing some pain in your head. It's what works that's important, find what's right and make it better. You've got pixels in your eyes, but I think you're still dreaming."

"Come on, you're just like me, you love bagging big game."

"Difference is I have no vendetta."

The subdued din of the restaurant suddenly intruded: the tinkling of glasses, low murmurs, muted kitchen noises, a cacophony of aromas and the scent of wine in the air.

"Yea...so where've we been?" Devlin said. "Can't talk to anyone like I can to you."

"Dunno. It's all so fragile isn't it?"

"Crystal," he said. "Just like crystal."

"I miss you at night..." she replied suddenly intimate.

"Where does all the time go?"

"...roll over sometimes and can't believe you're not there."

"I know."

"It's like another life..." Veronica said, "don't know what happened."

"Got tired of the bullshit, I guess."

"When you called from Paris...I just wanted you to call me back."

"I couldn't."

"You never did."

"I know."

"I think there are things that are just...so personal, so private, so close to who we are…I can't explain…can't even name them…words fail…like they shouldn't be spoken."

"The river's like that for me…primordial."

"You have to wonder: is there is a whole other world hiding just behind what we see? We try, but can't seem to reach it. The damnedest thing."

"Maybe the difference between what is and what could be…"

"I know. I know. Or what should be…" she said, "we cling to these rituals as if they're the only touchstones that keep us from being flung out…" searching for words, "into the stars. Now I'm supposed to this… now I'm supposed to that…how many times do you end up where you wanted to go?"

"Life is a river. You reach for something out in the distance and by the time you get there…it's gone. Everything's moving, all at once, nothing stays the same. Try to deal with life in flux and get with the program, but each change is a vector that flows on out into the universe and we're bound to it by our own decisions. I've seen rivers, ancient rivers…guess that's why I love them…they're permanent in this upheaval…constantly moving, yet cutting through mountains they flow so long in one place. The Harlem's just a short canal. Thank God it's not the Mississippi, otherwise I don't think I'd stop until I hit the Gulf of Mexico. You just want to run sometimes…you just got to run…"

"I suppose that's what it was. I was just running for the hell of it."

"Drink to that," Devlin clinked his glass against hers and looked deep into her eyes now that the words ran dry.

She would never speak when they were having sex, as if they were in church and any sounds would disturb the comingling of body and soul. When they reached her apartment, Devlin entered as if for the first time feeling like everything that had come before was gone and whatever may come was a new creation. In the dim light she emerged as an enigmatic and distant woman, a phantom of desire he couldn't quite recognize, letting her hair down, kicking off her shoes, dropping her dress to the ground, turning on one dim lamp whose yellow light suffused the room with a gossamer glow and imbued her naked figure with warm emotion. There was nothing familiar left as he tentatively reached out and touched her hand, pulling close this strange new woman, kissing her with the slightest touch of his lips. Her breath was like rosemary wine as he gradually embraced her, feeling the hesitation as if balancing on the edge of a dark precipice beyond which passions lie, seething in heat, waiting for the precise moment to attack, feral and unruly. Both trembled at something beyond their bodies as they melted into each other.

Clothing lie crumpled on the floor as he penetrated her; she sucked in breath and abandoned herself. The tangle of limbs, the caress of hands, the kisses and unconscious whimpers as they pulsed together in jazz like rhythms, ebbing and flowing, struggling against the longing of flesh where every slight movement was like a knife cutting deep until they at last surrendered, unable to resist human nature. Veronica cried out silently, straining against him glistening with a sheen of perspiration down her breasts, damp strands of flaming blonde hair sticking to her forehead, muscles rippling across her abdomen running into the fur where she convulsed in unison with him as he rolled his seed to her for a long, seemingly endless moment.

They lay upon the snow white bed while light glimmered through the open window frosting them with stardust and dreams. Neither moved for the longest time, content just to lie in each other's arms, shelter from the storm one is not supposed to feel, suffering triumphs and defeats in silence, achievements and setbacks, where the most cherished purposes may not be important to anyone else, where dry land is a long time coming.

But he still could not shake the image of Revenia from his mind.

When he had arrived at the theater the security guards greeted him by name, stage hands clapped him on the back as he passed, dancers hugged him, singers smiled, and Analetta took him in arm as if royalty and led him to a special seat to watch the first opening night performance. Everyone was drunk with excitement; "Aida's Curse," the haunted production was causing a sensation in the media. No self-respecting critic in the city was absent. Expectation and fear ran high. Devlin did the best he could in his half-formed persona to exude an aura of magnanimity and wealth, portraying a confidence such that even with a collapse of global markets, he had so much nothing could touch him. But inside flared insecurity and mixed emotions and he was filled with trepidation, wanting to run just for the hell of it—not knowing why he was really there anymore: if for his investigation or for the enigmatic young diva luring him toward the rocks.

Act one was flawless. From the moment the orchestra struck the first note weeks of pent up emotion found voice and wretched the audience from the mundane world of routine and rushing buses, of bills and failing marriages elevating them to lives greater, feelings deeper and purposes seemingly truer than their own: existences so diluted with compromise through the years as to become indistinguishable from when they were new. Here in this wonderland of light and illusion they could immerse themselves in a spirit world on brief hiatus from normal life without fear of losing their way back. Singers pranced in their time on stage with each magnificent voice a direct connection between one world and the other, as all material barriers fell away and disbelief was suspended for the precious moments that were the essence of theater. No one would have suspected danger, but once the door was opened it was out of their hands.

"Gimme the wrench! Gimme the wrench!" The man rasped in the semi darkness that light streaming over the edge of the set gave, struggling to keep his voice down backstage, reaching up expectantly, half frantic.

Unaware of this hidden drama, a storm was unfolding in front of the audience. Pride clashed in wild collision, unleashing passions as swirls of voices rose and fell like smoke from a forest fire: flaring then receding to embers then unexpectedly ablaze again in soaring arias, threatening to bring down the house. Grand symphonic movements swept it all along capturing everyone within earshot, wringing the last essence of emotion from them. The painted moon hung over a darkened Egyptian palace awash in deep blues and clouds seemingly gathered from out of nowhere like magic.

"Cumon, put your goddam back into it, give it all ya got!" The other man stood over him. "Shoot the works." He was taller and leaner, vest hanging loose over a denim shirt, and was scowling now with frustration. "What the fuck you doin' down there. Set's gotta move on cue!"

"Turnstile's jammed again," spitting in disgust, "just like before. I'll get it though…just…almost got it, don't pop your pantyhose!"

The stage manager ran up to them, "What's goin' on here? Sets gotta move. Didn't you hear the cue?"

"Turnstile's busted." The tall man pronounced.

"Not busted…jammed! It's stuck!" Cried the stocky stagehand down in the well between the edge of the turnstile and the floor of the stage. "Like before," there was a swipe of grease across his right cheek and his biceps rippled beneath a clinging t-shirt, arms glistening with sweat as he struggled, "…cept there's no soprano caught in the gears this time."

"Well, just move it will ya? Got a show here…ain't gonna give 'em their money back!"

"Forgeta'bout it!"

"Get outta here!"

"I got it! I got it"

Just then the whole stage jerked to the right almost a foot accompanied by a huge metallic clunk, the gnashing of gears and the creaking of wood as everything moved. Sounds of loose set pieces toppling over out front could be heard above the din of performance as if someone was dropping shoes. Then came the scream. The slightly overweight contralto had just ascended the highest level of the palace and was beginning to belt out the deep requiem for the fallen slaughtered by Pharoah's army when, reaching a long sustained note, she disappeared over the precipice and her voice faded into a terrified, muffled cry causing the audience to rise to their feet in a standing ovation for the powerful emotions delivered by the singer—heightened by the histrionic sleight of hand, which everyone thought was part of the show.

The soprano landed on the tall man with a sickening thud as the astonished stagehand yanked himself up out of the dark well in which he was working, mouth agape, refusing to believe what had just happened. Nobody moved for the longest time as if it would all go away if they waited. Then the woman whimpered, slowly rolling off the crumpled figure of the man, rising to her feet and began crying in disbelief that she was still alive.

"I broke my arm," the tall man said calmly, pushing himself up on one elbow, looking at his right forearm that lay sprawled out in an L-shape on the floor beneath him. "I broke my fuckin' arm! God that hurts!!"

"Don't move him, don't move him!" Someone yelled as a small

crowd gathered. "Jesus, don't move him!"

"Lie still."

"Don't touch him."

"Is the bone protruding?"

"Is he breathing?"

"There's blood isn't there, I see blood…shit, I hate the sight of blood!"

Ignorant of events backstage, the orchestra blithely played on, unwilling to let go now that they had captured the audience. But the night had just begun for "*Aida's Curse*," a fact that would later go down in theatrical lore as testified to by a select cadre of witnesses to the miracle of raindrops appearing on stage. Theories differed on where they brewed, somewhere high above the catwalk was the consensus, where vapor clouds miraculously formed in the flyloft, oozing down behind the proscenium arch, hanging ominously dark like miniature cumulonimbus just before a tornado. Sudden drops appeared, enough to make the flo`or glisten and mascara run. At first the performers all thought it was the misting system gone haywire, the one installed between the dressing rooms and the stage—after some long forgotten diva complained that her vocal cords dried out while walking from the green room—but few looked up. If they had the sight of unholy clouds churning in the flyloft would have brought act two to an abrupt end since actors, especially stage actors, are stricken with superstitious mumbo-jumbo in which they revel, poking fun at themselves in self parody, but in which they deeply believe.

Two or three of the dancers slipped on stage, but managed to recover, the audience hardly noticing, though the same could not be said of several chorus members who went up on their lines in the confusion. Meanwhile backstage, dressers frantically tried to revivify damp costumes with jury-rigged hairdryers as a row of performers stood by nonplussed, grumbling in their underwear.

Like a holy woman, in a dark svelte dress accented by burnished silver jewelry, Analetta hovered coolly in the half-light of the wings, witness to everything. Though trembling with suppressed fury, she betrayed no emotion as the one around which confusion aligned, doling out detailed instructions to her three excited, young assistants, all daughters of wealthy patrons, sending them into the chaos like little airplanes with her orders to defuse each burgeoning disaster before the audience caught on. It was her way of crisis management. Because in her mind any flaw allowed to pass threatened the holistic balance, so she was obsessed with details that presaged the unwinding of all that she had sweated blood for.

But it was not the earlier specters that had flitted across her video monitors prompting an investigation, nor the plump soprano teetering over the precipice or even the inexplicable raindrops all adding to the haunting rumors that bothered her: it was the fierce battle onstage between two divas that imperiled everything. There was something unholy about it, unnatural, and though what it was eluded her, she couldn't shake the feeling of apprehension. It could fall either way with these two: success or infamy. Because at its heart the theater was a spiritual cauldron out of which illusions boiled and fantasies emerged: tragic, funny and profound they held uneasy audiences, always shifting with the wind, always seeking the next big thing. Theater was ephemeral, like fog vanishing in sunlight.

On stage for the final act, entombed within soft blue illumination, the young French diva as Aida had hidden in the vault to share Radamès's fate. Suddenly, the irresistible power of their voices filled the space as a golden glow encircled the lovers. In a stunning duet, she shattered an electrified house with her otherworldly lament of desire and loss while at the same time from the temple above, Mirella as Amneris, with cold blue fire, strived to possess Radamès's soul as well with an equally exquisite incantation. Two spirits tore his heart with forces of good and evil. At the final note, the audience hanging suspended between this world and the next, snow blind with beauty no human could bear, sat silent. Not a sound was heard. Analetta held her breath fearing the worst for the long moments the crowd took to return to earth, to comprehend that something magnificent had happened, to recover from breathlessness. They sat quiet. Then, as if by spontaneous combustion, the pandemonium of applause thundered into legend for an hour and fifteen minutes and a hundred and sixty-six curtain calls—five more for Revenia alone.

The achievement justified everything, Analetta thought, everything she was doing and it steeled her resolve to carry through with her plan despite serious reservations.

Earlier, on a cold, crisp, blue morning, when the wind chirped around corners smelling of ice, she had met with the man in the huge, bright, conference room overlooking the frozen Hudson through a wall of glass. She ran her hands across the smooth surface of a massive table, over the seamless juncture of titanium and rosewood buried beneath resin that looked like foot thick liquid. Two dozen black leather chairs stood at attention. The aroma of coffee hung in the air. Prune Danish beckoned on a white platter. Small bottles of water sat glistening with moisture. A helicopter droned in the distance.

"Larry," she said, lifting the bone china cup with long, elegant fingers, "I didn't think it would go this far."

"Oh yes...." the man replied, round faced and healthy, slightly overweight with cheeks like fleshy ham and the beginnings of bags under intelligent eyes. Sand colored hair bushed out of his head like a Welsh Terrier, clipped neatly but for an unruly cowlick in the back, and his chubby neck was cinched by a pale blue shirt with a pale salmon necktie contrasted by a slate gray suit whose material reflected a sheen of light each time he moved. His thin lips were struck between a smile and a grimace making it impossible to read his hand. "When we first began our discussions, admittedly I was skeptical. We took a chance as a philanthropic gesture—for the Met. But now…it's blossomed into a genuine business opportunity. Frankly, we're excited."

"If nobody finds out."

"Law does not regulate high frequency trading…yet. There are no traditional red flags. We're simply taking a bearish, short-side position."

"Betting on falling prices?"

"It's a little more complicated…but that's the gist of it."

She pursed her lips, narrowing her eyes. "Who gets hurt…?"

"Well…" he looked down at the table, "investors accept risks. Capitalism is essentially an amoral game. No matter how altruistic the objectives, it's war: there are winners and losers. Only room for a select few at the top." After a moment, when she didn't respond, he chided gently, "You approached us, I assume to win no matter what. That's all we do. You must consider everything—"

"I understand there was a death, a murder…"

"Unfortunate…and shocking. You don't think…?"

"I am quite committed, Larry," she replied in measured tones.

"Good. We're not turning back…as I said, we see opportunity that goes beyond initial profits. It's a half-full proposition—"

"Bixby Enecott has been very generous to us—can't help feeling we're eroding his empire. No, that's not accurate…'destroying' is the right word—"

"...but not generous enough. I understand perfectly...we're alike, you and I, we want control. There's something about power that's very sticky, something beyond money."

"It's more than that. It's the dilettante board members. They're incompetent! Just don't know how to raise money. You knew, of course, they must be patrons to get on the board to begin with...and guarantee certain contributions? Well, it's painfully obvious we just can't rely on donations anymore; there've been fundraising shortfalls—now such a huge percent from one person? His heart may be in the right place, but it's too dangerous. You must understand we're a world class arts institution, a very important one. I simply can't allow an amateur to meddle! Oh... well...there's always give and take, patrons will always be pampered...it's the nature of the race, playing it hot and cold. But no one can take down our artistic integrity! I won't allow it; we're the finest; have a reputation to uphold; there's a line—"

"Exactly," he took a sip of coffee, "there's a line," lowering his voice, taking her into his confidence. "Endecott is our primary competitor in the high speed market. Nobody else comes close. We compete for talent, for infrastructure, for trades...but there can really be only one. Everybody knows that. We feel the government has lost control of the currency and somebody has to take up the slack. He's just another profiteer; no moral responsibility. This is a pivotal moment in history; it will never come again. Of vital importance. For the first time ever assets can be controlled by pure intellect rather than knee jerks. Like the fall of the aristocracy, it's for the common good."

"Maybe true," she festered, "but we need the money. It will secure our artistic independence. Nothing's more important."

"Everyone benefits from trickledown economics. It's an arms race. What with all firms building increasingly sophisticated systems...the more competition, the lower the profits. Someone has to seize the day. This is a fleeting opportunity and will only happen once. You brought it to us. You're the beneficiary."

"I still don't get how you're accomplishing all this, or the cost. Who else is on the inside other than me?"

"The less you know the better. Your account balance is all you need to look at. During the last five years we made a profit every single day, losing money just once. It's unprecedented."

"That's not enough. I'm on the inside. I'm risking everything."

"We are experts at managing risk."

"Humor me, in layman's terms: just how are you doing it?"

"We," he corrected, "we're doing it. In a word: confidence."

"...I said layman's terms."

"Look at it this way: all investments are based on an idea backed by confidence. We are simply eroding that confidence in Endecott Technologies."

"And...?"

"Look, billions change hands every day. More money that you can easily imagine. It doesn't take much to change the balance of power... especially with a little inside information. Devaluate a few key securities, undermine system effectiveness, leak some information...and you influence the market dynamics."

"You have that power?"

"High frequency trading accounts for over eighty percent of all global trades, especially considering dark pools."

"What's that?"

Dark pools? Think alternative electronic stock exchanges where trading takes place anonymously; most orders are hidden or 'iceberged.' Gamers or 'sharks' sniff out large orders by 'pinging' small market orders to buy and sell. When several small orders are filled the sharks may have discovered the presence of a large 'iceberged' order and can get there first. It's all about speed."

"You're losing me…how can a person do all that?"

"We call it 'cyborg finance.'"

"That doesn't answer my question."

"They can't. It's not done by people. Computers make elaborate decisions based on information received electronically, before human traders are capable of even processing the data. This is the age of the algobot; it all depends on who wins the computer wars. Our future depends on programs and algorithmic trading—and the quants, those who make it possible"

"Like the one that was murdered?"

He frowned for the first time. "Computers running complex algorithms have replaced humans in the financial industry. Finance has become a business where machines and humans share equal roles— there's bound to be collateral damage as they battle for dominance," nodding his head slightly, gloating over having the last word. "But, as I said, we had nothing to do with it."

After shadowing the target for a full day, Lance, the winsome young man from MIT, sat in the muted, palatial reception of Endicott's top competitor filling out employment forms, just as MacGyver had ordered him to do, watching the receptionist strike poses: as if for an audience, as if she was Norma Shearer in pre-code Hollywood beguiling men with her smoldering sensuality and silky smooth legs.

"That it?" Standing before the reception desk, handing the completed forms to her.

"Yes," she replied leafing through the papers to ensure all the signatures were in the right place. "Human resources will call you if they're interested. Oh…" she turned to a smiling man emerging from the inner sanctum accompanied by a tall, elegant woman dressed like a piece of modern art in a black, silk suit. "Larry, here's an important message…said they're waiting for your call."

Lance looked up. The man he recognized as the target he was assigned to tail. The woman…strangely familiar, but he couldn't place her. Not just then. Not at that moment, but the image of her face festered. It was later when the memory intruded, that night at four AM when he awoke from a sound sleep with the realization he had seen her often in the Arts section of the Times. She was the Executive Director of the Metropolitan Opera. Bixby Endecott's opera. All of a sudden he was wide awake with the significance of her appearance. Picking up the phone lying next to his bed, the display bathed his face with light in the dark room as he dialed MacGyver's number.

*　*　*　*

Moonlight shone through the picture window. Outside cars streamed by their wheels muffled by snow, ivory lights cutting the darkness, blurred figures behind steamy windshields, heading to mysterious destinations. Above them soared the trees of the park; dark silhouettes dancing languidly in winter's breeze. Only a few, braving the cold, passed by on the sidewalk: most had just a short distance to go, others had no choice. A man wearing two pair of knit gloves with no fingers and a pea coat with the collar turned up around his ears and a hoodie pulled over his head peered inside the bar, pressing his nose to the glass, steaming up the window, showing no expression, none at all, as if it had vanished eons ago.

Bixby was staring at the expansive murals of Central Park, painted by Everett Shinn over a hundred years ago, listening to another man talk, and didn't see the street person as he walked off into the night.

"Quid pro quo," tilting his head the man across from him tossed down a shot of tequila, licked salt off his hand and bit into a lime wedge. "Scratch my back, I'll scratch yours."

"Can't do that," Bixby replied. "It's illegal."

"What…? It's business. Just business."

"Violates the Supreme Court's definition of corruption."

"I'll just pretend we didn't have this conversation…Christ's sake Bix! It's one of the top ten pension funds in the world. Almost two hundred billion—Endecott's had a good run, but this…? Nobody's going to trust something this size to your damn quants with laptops, not completely, not high speed strategies with all that money."

"They're not laptops. Server farms…think lots of computing power."

"What would you do?" Looking across into Mirella's eyes.

"You're just teasing," she smiled seductively, her hand tightening on Bixby's thigh under the table, digging her nails in, reeling at the proximity of power.

"Frankly Bix," giving a show of letting his hair down, "I'd rather do business with you than the other guy, but if it comes to shove…we can do a lot for each other."

"You know, dreamed about this for a long time. Now there's a real shot, I've been chosen by the party—I'm their candidate."

"Of course, I know you had communications problems with labor before…" continuing the pitch as if he had heard nothing. "I can deliver the public employee sector, and let's face it: they're not going to vote for you without the unions' endorsement."

"Just a momentary misunderstanding."

"Not what I heard."

"I'll win without labor."

"You need us. No one's ever been elected governor without labor, not in New York."

"It's a new world."

"That's what I'm saying. We've made terrific progress over time. Hell, there's garbage men making in the high six figures! Teachers' wages rising—can't fire 'em, they got tenure! Water and power retirement after twenty years: full salaries, full benefits for life...you can help us grow, vote for progress with the right legislation, stop this mindless attack on unions, it's the common good."

"I appreciate your faith in the firm, but they're two different things."

"Like 'American Voices?'"

"I just help them get donations...it's entirely legal."

"That's what I'm saying...politics is business. Giving your firm the funds to manage, that's business too, just business, but it sweetens everything doesn't it? I wouldn't gamble if I didn't know you guys had a consistent track record. Due diligence. Did our research to come up with this offer. Think about it, I know you'll make the right decision—if you want to sit in that mansion up in Albany."

The thick sweetness in the air was suffocating as they returned to his apartments, soaring above Manhattan, glimmering lights shooting across the frozen Hudson visible out the windows, discovering he needed her like a fix, and if even a week lapsed between Mirella's all night visits he became someone else: moody and snapping at people for no reason. She seemed to float in an embryonic fluid of sexual sensation that trickled off her fingertips languorously like nectar.

"Bixby," Mirella said running her hand sinuously up the inside of his leg, "he can make you governor!" Her lips crushed against his and there was no will to resist. Before this, he had not known the moral conflict of unbridled passion, never met it face to face. Even when his uncle had his troubles.

Bixby Endicott Crowninshield was his given name—of the East Coast Crowninshields. One of the Boston Brahmins—many of which families trace their ancestry back to the original 17th and 18th century colonial ruling class: Massachusetts Governors and magistrates, Harvard Presidents, distinguished clergy and fellows of the Royal Society of London. He dropped the "Crowninshield" because of the bad association with his uncle, defrocked priest Bishop Crowninshield, long in prison for molesting young boys…and so went by "Endicott." Though he was only a teenager when the trial made headlines even in the New York papers, he rode the family crisis with blissful ignorance not letting the import of it sink in. If he had, everything would have been different; the optimism with which he grew up, dated blue blooded blondes, attended Ivy League schools and worked with scions of the "Old Boy's Club" in government would never have happened. He would have slithered off to where the rats and the addicts lived, where perverts quiver in dark places and deviants rant for social change to justify their crimes against nature. But now he wasn't so sure of things anymore. The stress of anonymous attacks on his business and some of the borderline financial dealings he had done to get the party nomination weighed heavily on him taking the edge off that healthy confidence that everyone loved. He could still charm them to bits, but his heart wasn't in it.

Then, out of the chaos she was there, this unruly artist falling into his arms, a libertine taking him places he should never go, but the worst was that he could not resist things bad for him. The addiction consumed all. Every time they made love it was like the first, and as if it would be the last: a clinging, sweating, aching, gasping struggle that drew him down into dark pools of sensation where he swam the electric sea. He became lost within the tangle of her hair, and like mist singing down high voltage wires it burned to the core. A beast was hiding in him; so primal it overwhelmed all intellect and any cultivated senses remaining with the dull, throbbing, pulsating, moist tropics of sex without moral restraint. Heavy and thick, it scrambled his thoughts. Always mortified in the aftermath, always broken and contrite he yet longed for more and then more after that. Mirella, she of the wild red hair and hot breath, was waiting with pent up desire so compulsive he believed it was depraved, but always succumbed anyway to the demon who mesmerized him body and soul.

Imprisoned out in the star swept ether, where spirits lingered on the borderline, between the trap of being human bound by rituals and the freedom of irrepressible creation where everything was beautiful and fine and pure was where he roamed. Unsure how to escape yet unwilling to try. A perfect balance. A dichotomy. An equilibrium that kept all his devils alive.

Now he lie in damp sheets. The room smelled musky. His head was swirling from alcohol. A pale light drifted in and washed across their naked bodies: lying side by side, she sleeping finally sated, breathing that slow, measured rhythm like dragon's breath giving notice of danger. His eyes traveled greedily across radiant flesh, absorbing the flower exposed, now cocooned in tangled bedclothes still glistening with sweat. Everything was saturated with sex: the chair, the bed, the lampshade — Bixby struggled to get a perspective as his body even now trembled, making his stomach ache with longing, wondering what had happened to his life, the one before everything went out of control, wanting to wake her up and lose himself again.

The phone rang.

"It's MacGyver," a voice on the other end said. "I've found out something you need to know."

"It's three-thirty in the fucking morning! Better be really important."

"Depends on what you call important," he deadpanned, "but if it's life and death, this is it."

Chapter 14

The fjord at Somes Sound froze the sea beyond Mount Desert Island. Even the profligate wealth that held sway here couldn't break through. Lonely ice fishermen had looked with envy at the splendid manses dotting the shore. Everyone thought the Great Depression and a World War would mark the end of such extravagance, but it was only the harbinger of a postmodern invasion bringing fund managers and middle-aged movie stars seeking refuge when they could no longer get good parts. With affluence on a scale without precedent, this select group of rusticators transformed the landscape of the island with elegant estates they called "cottages;" luxury, refinement, and ostentatious soirées replaced picnics and daylong hikes of an earlier era—especially at Northeast Harbor, a place so rich it was known as "Philadelphia on the rocks."

Devlin said his goodbyes, made his apologies for leaving before election returns were confirmed—probably late the next morning—and slammed the car door dislodging ice from the roof. Daylong snow had turned to sleet freezing in place where it fell. He was glad to hear the engine purr and see the huge estate looming in his rear view mirror, ablaze with yellow light streaming from windows where silhouettes of the party faithful and deep pocket donors from the Met cavorted. The drive to the airport was slow going through dark, wet snow and the roads were eerie and treacherous, but he had a plane to catch and miles to go before he could rest.

Like indigo, he felt tainted by the stain of opulence and extreme, unobtainable wealth he had just emerged from and breathed deep draughts of cold air, stinging his lungs, slapping his face, thrusting him wide awake into real life. It had been something his alter ego, the spendthrift donor, demanded he do for illusion sake, but attendance at Bixby Endecott's victory party in his Northeast Harbor mansion turned out to be more of a trial than the trifle he imagined when flying up earlier. From his first footfall into the foyer he recalled the entitlement reeking like some aromatic cheese left out on a hot day and the assault on his sensibilities left him at a loss for words—at least civil words.

He had roamed the room an invisible man. Sophisticated women in skimpy black dresses reclined on silk damask couches sipping martinis laced with holy basil and anise seeds—created by some celebrity bartender who was an adherent of the haute cuisine school of booze—their older male companions rutted in an intellectual ritual. Flesh softened by overindulgence; the spirit still in the game. Devlin, despite his philanthropist disguise, could not help but view it through a muckraking haze that made everything slightly unreal, out of reach, when the information he really wanted lie just beyond that veil taunting him for still being in the workforce. He did not even notice whether he was happy or not, satisfied with the quality of his life or hopeful for the future; the endgame of all his efforts was rarely in mind; none of the many hungers that plague other men such as desire for the exotic, lust for command, need for stimulation was present; he had no other dreams to pursue, no greater aims, nothing that he could call on when adversity struck, only the drive for justice fueled by a hate of the rich verging on obsession that reduced him to its pawn.

A huge flat screen droned the Gubernatorial Primary returns minute by excruciating minute peppered with low budget commercials, but only a few diehards endured the tedium because Bixby Endecott was expected to win by a huge margin. It had been the lowest turnout in the modern era with less than twenty percent of registered voters even bothering. Most guests ignored it completely.

He finally found refuge leaning up against the eggshell trim of a wide doorway that demarked the living room from the reception room and through which people ebbed and flowed in a never ending stream of restlessness and by staring out across the Chippendale that nobody was sitting in. There, holding center court, mesmerizing a flock of admirers and sycophants, Mirella stood at her darkest and most lovely, radiant like a black pearl. Bixby Endecott hovered nearby in oblivious conversation. Their eyes met awkwardly.

"I guess where Bixby goes, opera goes—"

"I…" freezing the air with a smile, "am opera. I follow no one."

"Of course," he said nonplussed under the skin. "I didn't—"

"Just looking…or are you a political patron as well?" She relented only after an uncomfortable moment during which Devlin realized he was staring at her décolletage.

"Could say that…" eyes averted across the room, "I wanted to lend my support."

"Well…he's won already in case you didn't know. Guess he didn't need your support, but I suppose you had some other motive in mind?"

"Not really…didn't think the returns would all be counted until morning."

"That doesn't matter," shaking her head and pointing to the crowd as witnesses, "as you can see, we're not worried."

"Officially the candidate then?"

"That's right," she smiled, "it's official. Are you disturbed by that?"

As he was trying to figure out her frosty responses, a man shouldered his way in on the conversation.

"It was the union endorsement…"

"Really…that important?" Devlin demurred, scrambling to mask a sudden hostility.

"Nobody wins in New York without union support—public and municipal employees all back him. Perfect timing, announced it two days before the election. Quite a coup actually, we all thought he was having trouble—"

"Sounds like a meeting of the castes; something must have happened."

"I happened." Mirella purred. "It was I made him win."

"Really," the man was amused, ruddy cheeks displaying his blood-alcohol level, eyes blue against the bleary haze. "I'd like to know that secret!"

"Wouldn't everyone—"

"Simple really. Put a spell on him," she said from under wild, red auburn tangles with an impish look as she took a sip of sparkling Prosecco from a chilled glass giddy in the knowledge that no one would believe her anyway. "He's bewitched that's all,"

"Knew there was something I was missing," the man patronized. "We'll never tell." He liked nothing more than tossing down a few drinks and socializing.

She looked directly into Devlin's eyes as if to plumb some unrealized depths. "Then I won't talk either…we'll all just keep our secrets and pretend. Let's drink to that."

"Ah…my rallying cry!" Bixby intruded with raised glass. "What are we drinking to?"

"Secrets," Devlin said.

Mirella flashed her eyes at him and Bixby paused, but grinned in that way he had of making everyone feel at ease, lifting his glass higher. "Secrets it is!"

Despite the good natured hellos and defusing the troublesome moments with Mirella, he found it even more difficult to connect with anyone afterward because he felt violated, timid, not at all like himself, as if there was a wreath around him. Something in her demeanor he decided, the way she had cut him with a few choice words; did she know or not? Wishing she would just come out with it—making him furious.

He couldn't hide his bristling hostility toward the rich, there was an essentially amoral element about having that much money, carrying the weight of all that greed and besides…everyone seemed so protective, scrutinizing him, prompting him to drink more than he planned just to keep paranoia at bay, awakening feelings of inadequacy, realizing that anyone in the room had his purchase price as pocket change and in the end all that really mattered was one's financial worth not one's value at all, as it had once seemed at university where things were black and white unlike in the real world where things are infinite shades of gray. It was the angst of the moment that brought on his *twilight* this evening. The utter nihilism of it. After that, he didn't care what anyone thought and consequently became somewhat belligerent, fitting right in with the political dilettantes and wall street refugees, striking up conversations easily with the like minded.

The dark pearl roamed amongst the invited beguiling them all with her black, taffeta dress featuring the jaw dropping décolletage, her stormy auburn hair and the aura of diva that preceded her. She blithely charmed her way through the guest list as if playing the heroine in a tortuous opera of manners in which the immorality of the plot pivoted on Bixby Endecott as both effete icon and struggling man of the people — particularly of the unions who were key to his first success at the polls. But inside a labyrinthine brew of emotions festered causing her worry to the point of hysteria as she felt her plans threatened by one Devlin Wolf: SEC investigator disguised as "Arts Angel." Mirella did not know what he was up to, but his appearance tonight was not coincidence. Unwilling to be a pawn in his game, she composed a spell while flitting around the room as the urbane sophisticate, which took the form of an intention: a powerful, dark, malicious purpose that dribbled off her tongue like hemlock as she silently spoke it in ancient Gaelic behind a deceptive smile while sipping sparkling wine.

Headlights bore into the night. Bare oaks and frozen sumacs fled by behind snow flurries. The clarity that had been eluding Devlin earlier was found on the road. He mulled over the blur of faces and compromising situations that had inhibited him at the victory party, sorting them out in the perspective of distance on his way to the airport. But just as he was beginning to feel better, the phone rang.

"Got his statement," he recognized Thierry's excited voice. "Wrote it all down and he signed it. Got it on fucking video."

"Thought he'd come around. Wants revenge," gripping the wheel. "Strongest intention there is...nothing stands in the way of making someone wrong."

"Yea. Guy's out for blood all right."

The padded silence of tires against fresh snow filled the air. It muffled the sound of the wind and the motor. Visibility was poor. "Any revelations?"

"Looks like it's all about the money trail," he spat out the obvious. "Both him and the French quant were key players…like god dammed glorified accountants…just because they got some fucking computer juggling the books they think they're too hip, couple of intellectuals in fancy houses…to me, just a couple of sweaty embezzlers—"

"So…?"

"So…plain to me someone doesn't want any witnesses. Someone with a motive. Someone who would be ruined if—"

"Someone running for office."

"You got it!"

"Did he name him?" A beat. "What else?"

"What the fuck else do you need?"

"No murder weapon. No eyewitness. Circumstantial—so what else?"

"Enough right now to indict him for SEC violations, not to mention illegal campaign funding—he'll break after that."

"Not enough!"

"Christ's sake! What do you want?"

"You brought me into this, remember. Dead body in the river…you wanted help, I want Endecott!" He barreled headlong into the blackness streaked by snowfall caught up in the high beams. "Want to burn him down!"

There was a long quiet on the other end. "The quant's wife. Think she was shtupping him."

"Why, think maybe the quant wanted revenge?"

"Most murderers are people one knows."

"He'd just hire someone. Why risk it?"

"Bigger risk having him alive—"

"No…I mean, the quant's wife?"

"No man's made of asbestos."

"Except the rich aren't like us, they're like cancer!"

"Don't hold back...hey, what am I missing here? What do you really want?"

The dark fury he felt while considering the question could not be named. It rose out of the well of souls where spirits could be heard awaiting the last day, it was so black the night was obscured, so overpowering heartbeats were stilled, so insidious it hung breathless like the eye of a storm. It had been with him since his mother was hamstrung by the system she had fed her entire life until the last ounce of blood had been drained leaving him alone with promises and longings and sticky expectations still unfulfilled. Like skin he couldn't remember any moments without it. But because of it he was able to make at least one thing right in this world and it gave him membership in the human race. It also gave rise to the constant disdain he felt for common hedonists—the upwardly mobile who when hitting the inevitable ceiling on their dreams strove to experience as much pleasure as they could by playing the everything-for-me-nothing-for-you game. Greed gave structure to economic life. Rewarded the few. Lured the many. Scattered the broken pieces as society's morally bankrupt.

To Devlin Wolf the invisible hand was a myth. It belonged with immaculate birth, resurrection from the dead and messages from God and all other superstitions that have engendered extremists and enslaved with belief for millennia. So as his car hurtled down the icy roads it never entered his mind that he was racing along the edge of good and evil and above all else, that things were not what they appeared to be.

But the firmament was alive. Stars shown unseen above low clouds. Spirits lingered. Voices intertwined. The feeling of being watched was all pervasive. It was as if the barrier between common life and that which exists beyond nature had become translucent and visions could be experienced between worlds—some events occurring according to natural law and others according to a separate set of principles unknown yet undeniable — like his earlier memories of past lives in Paris. And so it was as he sped over a rise on the busy eight-lane highway, glistening with ice and sleet, his tires suddenly broke free of their grip on the road and he became a wild card in the cosmic game straddling the wire between this world and the next. At first he didn't notice, still elsewhere talking with Thierry on his cell, but gradually perceived his car wasn't plumbed right and though travelling forward was slightly askew beginning a long, uncontrolled slide. It was precisely then a shadowy image of Mirella's face flashed by leaving a malevolent sinking in his stomach then a light headed, weightlessness as the car began to skate sideways while rushing downstream in traffic — unaware that he, agnostic disbeliever, was caught between shadow and light.

Five hundred miles away, in a darkened room, Revenia bolted upright. An image of Devlin had appeared while she slept. In her mind's eye she trembled at the danger, so with fear racing composed a spell which took the form of an intention: a powerful, luminous, miraculous purpose that flowed off her tongue like fireweed honey as she silently spoke it in ancient Gaelic behind a troubled brow.

He dropped the phone and grasped the wheel heart thundering; the car sliding as if floating on air. Panic hit, his mind rushing to remember what he was supposed to do when this happened, but nothing came to him, it was blank. For a breathless instant he flirted with the idea of plunging into the abyss and even lifted his hands slightly just to see what would happen flushed with a brief euphoria at the prospect of never having to face the bullshit again. But the river memories caught him up in their mighty current, the ancient, dusty current, and he was filled with longing for all the things he loved: chilly mornings on the Hudson, dawn light filtering through mists above glassine water, the cry of a distant loon;

the moral victory of true justice realized; the smell of Veronica's hair. He touched the brakes; they locked up. Then, remembering, he lightly began pumping the pedal; still the heavy car continued its inexorable sideways drift. He turned the wheel into the direction of the slide. When nothing happened, he began sounding the horn, tooting frantically as he caromed toward other vehicles. He forgot to breathe. Even as the car twisted into the awkward angle that looked so out of place it took eons before he realized it would inevitably crash. He thought of when he was a kid one summer day at the beach and spotted a small plane nose diving toward the shore. It was so incongruous, so inescapable he just watched in disbelief as it crashed and burned its occupants alive leaving two charred silhouettes visible in the wreckage. The car hurtled across the lanes of traffic like that nose diving plane with a sickeningly slow sideways spin that always signaled the utter loss of control followed by inexorable tragedy.

Devlin watched helplessly as the surreal landscape turned askew around the endless slide, struggling with the wheel, pumping the brakes, shouting out profanities, missing cars by millimeters, bracing for impact. It was only in the last instant that he saw the black chop of the sound roiling against the rocks as he spun across eight lanes into a low embankment of snow beyond which was oblivion. He died in that moment of impact, that instantaneous moment when the car slammed so hard it tilted up on two wheels and teetered at the brink of overturning into the dark, churning white waters below, but in the last second came crashing down, bouncing twice, cracking the side window against his head before it came to rest in total silence without a scratch. He shut off the engine and squinted at the stream of facing headlights impatiently making their way around him realizing traffic had not even slowed down, as if his whole life was invisible, as if he was inconsequential to all those others whose own personal concerns were so much more important, whose lives were of such greater value and that he was just collateral damage in their wake sitting there on the frozen shoulder like road kill. Breathing heavily now, sweat streaming into his eyes, he at last came up against it face to face and realized he had become just like those he pursued, a hollow man, a vacuum with nothing but hatred of the rich to propel him into the future. Just like them. It was the bleakest moment of his life so far.

Later, after the tow truck had pulled him out of the gutter, after he had caught a midnight flight back to the city and after the long limo ride from La Guardia he showed up outside Veronica's door with a gaunt and hollow look.

"What are you doing here?" She said, rubbing her eyes, clasping her sheer robe at the neck, blonde hair windblown like it once looked long ago after day sailing the Chesapeake with friends.

The hawk came out of nowhere. In the night after sleep had captured most everyone and they all dreamt wistfully that the Siberian Express had finally passed and they could go out into the morning without wearing two pair of gloves, layered sweaters and wool scarves wrapped twice around their necks. But it came again just like a giant razorblade blowing down the street and all the clothes in the world couldn't help: architects not predicting that the gale is sucked down onto the sidewalks by ungodly skyscrapers piercing nature's skin. When it comes there is nowhere to hide. The icy wind that growls: "Beware of tempting me; I am Mister Hawkins. I am the howling-ass wind that kills, the cruel wind lashing down on workers huddling at bus stops, making their bones ache."

In the brittle evening footsteps rang out. Smooth leather heels pounded tattoos on polished concrete at the theater's heart. Doors sealed out the cold. Windows steamed over. A cacophony of voices filled the air and anxious people hurried everywhere. The art of suspending disbelief was a hard, sweaty business, a demanding master.

But everything was hushed behind the half-inch plate glass, in the dark where LEDs flickered and the slight smell of burning ozone lingered, where hands flew across digital broadcasting keyboards like earlier hands drew music from multitiered keyboards of pipe organs so gigantic cathedrals were built around them. The atmosphere was electric as past and future met in collision.

"We're sitting here in the media booth with the director of the Met: the enigmatic...you don't mind if I call you that?" The fleshy woman at the microphone fawned hardly pausing, "Analetta. She's relentlessly picked up the pace since beginning her tenure and hasn't let up yet—more new productions, more aggressive marketing—rumor has it everyone from chorus members to major donors have felt the strain. But now this exciting new production has once again set New York clamoring at her feet. Are you presiding over a leap into the next century, or the slow decline of the world's most extravagant opera house?"

"No one can live without art; we're definitely reaching new audiences. Francotti Benedetto is a gifted director with a following—a millennial following," she added in the off chance that one or two of the little aliens were not wholly absorbed online, chatting with friends on social media or otherwise usurped by some virtual void, "...simply gifted, and he's introducing a whole new generation to opera. Our box office tells the story—we've been sold out for weeks."

"There's no denying the excitement surrounding this production of 'Aida' ...it's polarized the critics. But how does an Italian film director who hasn't even made a movie in English fit in?"

"Well...he speaks Italian."

"Of course..." she twittered self consciously, "of course, I get it...'Italian opera,' but is that enough?"

"I'm making fun...no it's not, he's descended on us like a virgin, without preconceptions," she said, "it's Goddard, Antonioni, Charbrol, it's the new wave...only now—truly a creation for the present. The great mystery of art as you know is where these people come from? These disruptors creating new paradigms."

"More importantly, why do they appear?"

"Personally, I try not to put it under a microscope; all great mysteries are fleeting, we should allow them to suspend our disbelief while we have the chance."

"Now, the Khedive of Egypt commissioned Verdi to write this opera for the opening of the Egyptian Opera House in 1871, isn't that right?"

"Yes, but didn't realize its great triumph until the European debut at La Scala in Milan a year later—"

"...and isn't our attention still riveted on the Middle East? Do you feel that has something to do with its success?"

"Yes, the story is more timely than ever, but I'm surprised you haven't mentioned our biggest attraction—people have come to hear our great young Diva: Revenia. This is her American debut. And like Paderewski she has simply captured Manhattan."

"Yes, certainly, but you have two diva's now don't you? You know what they say, 'too many cooks...'" she sang liltingly, twisting her thin lips into that smirk signaling one is in the know. "Give us the inside story, didn't you bring her in to mix things up a bit? Artistic rivalry... great audience draw...I hear the fireworks on stage are not to be missed, devilish...if the stories in the press are to be believed—"

"Indeed, they say it's haunted don't they?"

"What do you say?"

"Who am I to argue with the public?"

"Or the press for that matter...you're keeping secrets aren't you? But what of your other diva? Isn't that chemistry on stage worth everything?"

"Yes..." Analetta deadpanned without a hint of emotion, "isn't it."

"Found her! Found her..." the carpenter blurted out breathless and perspiring, pushing his way through the door as the announcer tried to shield the microphone.

"Where the hell is she?" Analetta barked like a fishwife while the announcer frantically tried to shield the microphone.

"Down in the dressing room. She's here — in the building!"

Within seconds he and the announcer were left in the dust watching Analetta and her small entourage, bearing clipboards and coffee cups, rushing down the hallway.

"Royalty," the woman holding the microphone intoned religiously, "theatrical royalty."

"She's the queen bee alright," the carpenter replied squinting his eyes after her.

The young woman sat before a dressing table mirror ringed by clear twenty-watt bulbs franticly putting on makeup. A plump Puerto Rican dresser was arranging costumes.

"I hope they fit," she said, "you look fatter than her."

"Takes one to know one," annoyed, wrecking the straight line of her mascara. "Shit," she muttered.

Analetta exploded into the room, a quiet storm, all business. Everything stood still: the dresser looked up expectantly, the entourage was motionless, even coffee in the cups stopped sloshing. All except the understudy applying makeup, hands shaking in near hysteria. Nothing worse could happen. She had just slid her famous lasagna into the preheated oven of a vintage O'Keefe and Merritt, pasta meant to impress a certain disheveled writer she had taken a liking to, a bottle of Tuscan red stood waiting on the tile countertop when the call came, demanding to know what she thought she was doing, where the hell she was, requiring her to cancel everything, overriding all objections, even death would not be tolerated, and ordering her to get to the theater immediately via the car soon to be waiting at the entrance of her building — barring the gridlock Manhattan is known for. She called her tousled young man, but there was no answer.

"We have faith in you," Analetta said placing her hand on the young woman's trembling shoulder. "This is a great opportunity."

"Oh God! I could just cry!"

"I know. I know. But it would ruin your makeup."

"Why is it like this? I'm here for every performance, rested, ready, now this! No time! No preparation! What if I run up on my lines? Forced creation; a career in flames!"

"You won't."

"What do you mean I won't? Can't you see I'm having a breakdown! A fucking breakdown!"

"I don't know. It's a mystery, but you won't. Everything will be fine. You'll see. We have faith in you. Everything will be fine. This is a great opportunity."

Later, lifetimes later, Analetta sat in her office shoes off, legs curled under on a severe midcentury couch, watching the third act on her monitors, holding a glass of bourbon with two slowly melting ice cubes staring up at her. Anxiety had miraculously lifted when she saw the understudy perform, accepting standing ovations, keeping the wheels turning, under the spell of the haunted "Aida." Art was everything. There was nothing else: no love, no one to roll over in the night and hold onto, no sounding board, no wound licking, no crutch, only the onslaught of stars: the molten atomic storm of life raining havoc on dreams. She was an orientation point, a stable datum in the chaos, the art maven and art was everything. The stress was hard, but her face had the serene look of a trapeze artist midflight. Somewhere she had found the Zen of balancing forces always seemingly in opposition to one another and it was a great relief when she could just reach out when she felt like it without experiencing repercussions either by law or morality or personal integrity. It gave her a freedom she had never known and she regretted not realizing it earlier in her life, before she became old and cursed with the vanishing, which loomed in the near future. It was because of this she drove herself mercilessly. Time was running out.

So she couldn't imagine anyone cancelling a performance at the Met as Mirella had done, at the last moment, without an apology, without conscience. A performer's life is short enough without flaunting the devil. The little slut, she thought, to be seen at Bixby Endecott's political soirée—in fact only calling in to announce she wouldn't be there, leaving a message, making her frantic after all the feverish work of the past several months just to keep the show alive let alone successful. Fearful the understudy, having to perform without notice, would ruin a flawless run—but it was another triumph for Revenia, who carried the night. Another triumph for the haunted "Aida."

Taking a sip of bourbon, letting its fire remind her of events that forced her decisions, relieved her scheme with Bixby's competitor had taken the next step at end of trading Friday, even though she didn't understand all of it, the betting on Endecott's losses, short selling, reaping obscene profits. Art was everything; all else existed on a different plane—and the worlds would never meet so that what happened in one was separated by natural law to that which happened in the other. Now, in the waning of the night she could refocus on the problem that had overshadowed almost everything else in recent days and had thus far eluded solution: how to implicate Bixby Endecott for the murder of the French quant. It was the only way to erase all the bothersome, unpleasant guilt feelings she had no use for.

It wasn't that she didn't like him; who could not feel for the convivial, vulnerable Boston Brahmin. He had the knack; no doubt about that. Women clung to him and his success made men green, but something in the mix disgusted her, something in his attitude of entitlement delegated him to the category of prey unlike the other donors who she only toyed with draining their wealth with small vampire like seductions: she didn't just want major contributions from him, she wanted it all. Those simpering, wealthy, useless people—who will miss them? But art, it is eternal and all that money destined to fulfill self-indulgent whims can be changed by alchemy into the stuff of dreams.

Though it seemed like a distant memory, as if the mind was playing tricks, it was not so long ago. Cold she remembered, it had been so cold that morning, the city so fragile with translucent frost she had to walk carefully out into the mist so as not to shatter the behemoth's infrastructure. And she walked a very long way over its labyrinthine sidewalks, taking long deliberate strides like someone on a mission, swallowing whole blocks in minutes, passing the stone and concrete and glass monuments to lives vanished like candles in the wind; struggling, searching, toiling masses all living shoulder to shoulder whose spilt blood was soon forgotten—except by the stone and concrete and glass she now consumed in passing. Analetta turned down one way streets where traffic rushed, she walked past brownstones just coming to life, in front of steamy café windows where burly men swilled black coffee, and over three bridges just to cover her tracks in case anyone was watching. But she never looked back, it was far too late for that.

He had appeared like an apparition in the fog three hundred yards away across High Bridge, whose steel arch soared a hundred and forty feet over the Harlem River steaming far below in the bitter cold. For fifty years it had sat dormant shuttered to human traffic by a man lost in time named Robert Moses, but in his day the most feared power broker of all who had built modern Gotham. Now, its construction seemingly never done, high chain link barriers behind the railings lay like open wounds as if Moses's ghost was at work wrapping up loose ends death had not allowed him to finish, leaving available invitations for the disenfranchised to end it all with one courageous leap. Indeed, it was the reason she had chosen this spot for the meeting—the imperfection of the city as a work in progress. Even at this great distance she could see the sheen of his fine suit beneath the long camelhair coat dancing behind as he walked toward her.

"It's bracing! In-vig-orating!" He said breath steaming, French accent thick as maple syrup. "I never knew it was so cold in New York."

"No. Nobody did," smiling cheerfully, drawing her coat tight around her neck. "It's an anomaly! Only happens every century or two."

"Happy I didn't miss it," he replied in a certain distingué manner that put her off.

"Me too." She had snared him on the way into his office, at the crack of dawn because he had to be on the Europe desk finding out what happened in the markets while others slept; she told him to meet her on High Bridge, take in a bit of history she had said, though it had only been here since 1848 unlike the ancient phantoms of Paris, but it was the oldest bridge in Manhattan.

Guillaume Marchand was fastidious. His close cropped hair was neat and freshly trimmed, his clean shaven cheeks, ruddy from the cold, but blemish free; the way he shot his cuffs standing there in the pale dawn light, rocking on his heels like a paper General Pétain just before Paris capitulated to the Nazis, contemplating the invincibility of the Maginot Line. He was barrel chested with a peasant's face, she mused—having been immersed in the French way since college with every other person she met back then an intrusive Francophile anxious, almost evangelic to convert her—but in her eyes they were a rude obnoxious people who didn't bathe enough and always smelled either of perspiration or Gauloises cigarettes. He beamed a big, gregarious smile like a Labrador who had just dropped a bone at her feet covered with saliva.

"Well," he said, "here we are."

"We have a new production of 'Aida' in the works with your name on it."

"I hope it is not indelible," nodding his head with lips drawn tight.

"I have an Italian, a young Italian flying in from Rome—we found him making a low budget movie," throwing up her hands, ignoring his attitude, "who ever heard of him before? Art films. He makes art films. Huge millennial following—mentioned it to one of my girls and she swooned so I almost had to put her on the fainting couch—"

"Female hysteria no doubt."

"…worthless the rest of the day. I'm going to give him the production. It's some secret underground language he speaks that's unintelligible to anyone over thirty, but will bring in whole new audiences. I can see the future, and you can get in on the ground floor."

"That may be," shaking his head, "but as I told you I'm not really a philanthropist…tried to explain on the phone…not like Endecott, he's the one you should talk to. Not even a music lover. After all, I'm just a sojourner, just passing through…we still have our house in Paris for God's sake."

"Consider the Palias Garnier, the Opéra National de Paris, they are much older, and subsidized by the state for over three centuries… but we…The Met is the finest opera house in the world. The pinnacle. We have the greatest talent, the grandest productions… legendary performances that happened on our stage have become classics, like paintings in the Louvre…we keep the art alive in this cesspool culture with hip-hop moguls and suicide bombers. And it was done by businessmen just like you, entrepreneurs—our angels from the beginning. Surely you want to be a part of that!" She looked him directly in the eye, making contact, fishing for some kind of emotional response that she could feel, finding only an abyss looking back. "I thought if you could stand out here and feel Manhattan in the raw, breathe in its energy…it's a global city—truly global. That is why it would mean so much…" stopping short of patronizing, tears forming in the corner of one eye while her internal demons fumed at the resources slipping through her fingers like quicksilver as day by day the man squandered them to quench pedestrian desires. What deceit! She knew for instance that he had just purchased an extravagant estate in Larchmont Harbor overlooking Long Island Sound—why would he need that with a house still in Paris? She had made it her business to know these things and even had a map stuffed in her pocket, part of the mini dossier she had compiled as due diligence before the close, which now looked doubtful.

"Personally, I'm not a music fan. Little jazz now and then in the clubs…but at home, only my wife plays music. I don't have time. Too much news to catch up on. Too much to read. Just don't have the time."

"It's a matter of priorities," she entreated. "You can enrich other's lives—"

"But I do…trickledown economics. I create economy. The market: that's the only music I'm interested in. Sorry," he said flatly, "I can't help you," then turned and walked off sensing the futility of a formal au revoir.

"That's too sad!" She called after him, "Art is everything."

"Not for me…" over his shoulder, "gotta run. Like I said, talk to Endecott…he's the philanthropist."

"Why not come to a rehearsal? Do yourself a favor—"

"Thanks," he turned walking backwards arms outstretched. "I'm sorry, really…I get a lot of pitches…can't support everything can I?"

"It's not a pitch," she replied under her breath watching him cross the bridge, "you fucking social parasite!"

It was only moments later, after turning to go, that she heard the voices shouting: moments long enough to have formed a complete alternative strategy for funding her new production, in the time it took for two strangers to fall in love, or long enough for a comet to steak across the sky and come crashing down on some remote Russian industrial town as a monstrous fireball annihilating five square miles, or as long as it took for an old man's epiphany that he couldn't stop the wind from blowing. She whirled to see a young man in a sweatshirt, hood thrown up over his head, accosting Guillaume Marchand at the far end of the Bridge. An eerie filigreed moon hung suspended in the morning sky. The Frenchman seemed to be handing over something, but he was distraught and began yelling—even she knew you didn't do that when someone was mugging you, not in New York City, not if you wanted to come out of it alive. Exasperated at his foolish entitlement, she ran towards him mouthing warnings that had no sound, clip clopping over the icy cement in her high heels, wanting to instruct him in the etiquette of the streets, but she was too late. The young black man saw her and punched the French quant in the stomach at the same time snatching an object from his hand. Then he ran, took off like a greyhound as fast as he could from the end of the bridge down along Harlem River Drive the hood from his sweats covering his face.

By the time she got to the Frenchman he was breathing hard and just beginning to realize what had happened, speaking incoherently in shock, staggering up against the railing, bracing himself with one hand. An odd patch of blood spreading out over his crisp white shirt like ink on a blotter and the silver hilt of a knife stuck out from its center. Disbelief filled him.

As he teetered there unsteady at the railing by a huge gap in the chain link—where anonymous city workers had rolled it back months before and left it while they, feckless with fully funded city pensions, moved on to another project—she curled her hand around the cold silver hilt of the knife sticking out of his stomach. It was on impulse. She meant to yank it like pulling a tooth, so fast it wouldn't hurt, return everything to normal, like it was minutes before. But there were second thoughts; what were you supposed to do with something puncturing a person? Some sharp object half in half out? So certain when she ran up to him, confident she could take care of everything like she did at the theater, just will it right by force of personality, but all of a sudden she wasn't so sure. Would blood come spurting out like extracting a nail from a tire, would it cause more damage internally? She froze with indecision holding the hilt of the knife with Guillaume Marchand wriggling in agony on the receiving end, like a fish on a line, like a worm on a hook, she could feel his life force on the edge—and sometimes there is nothing to hold onto except the blade of a knife. It sent a jolt through her in a supreme burst of energy.

Analetta looked intently into his eyes, a water color blue, seeking that emotional connection, but finding only the abyss looking back and impulsively instead of pulling it out she gave the knife a slight push, a little jab to test the waters, enough so that she felt the warmth of his flesh on her hand, but not enough that he lost his balance. His face ignited in terror. She was unmoved. Then with a shudder of excitement she gave the knife another shove, this time a good solid shove so that she felt the weight of him and he tumbled backward over the railing and through the hole in the chain link left by the city workers falling a hundred and forty feet into the Harlem racing by below with a muted splash. Swallowed by the river she watched with strong interest as he surfaced, struggling manically to strip off his waterlogged camelhair overcoat and then floundering frantically for a few moments before he rolled over and was still on the strong back of the freezing current. In the distance she could see the runner who had never looked back and now suddenly a bright red rowing scull sliced underneath the bridge where she was standing and powered downstream as if trying to catch him. It was all so surreal like one of Francotti Benedetto's movies, choreographed with layers of disrelated motion all contributing to the whole. Later she would look back on it as an empowering moment where she took action unrestrained by any other morality than her own. Wealthy, useless people—who will miss them? It was a personal decision, God like in its ramifications, except for those unpleasant guilt feelings she had no use for.

The knife was warm in the palm of her hand. She calmly wrapped it in a handkerchief and placed it in her coat pocket without knowing why, but somehow feeling it might be useful. And then just walked away.

Later, much later, when Bixby was pacing the floor of her office offering his irritating suggestions for future productions, she realized the wisdom of keeping it.

"Hand me that letter opener will you?" Sitting at her desk, opening correspondence, seemingly unconcerned.

Bixby picked up the silver knife and handed it across the desk. "Jeeez…what's that? Looks like blood."

"Don't be silly…just put it down there. Thanks." And went back to her reading as if nothing had happened, suppressing the glee she actually felt inside, the incredible lightness. Because now he was hers, inexorably trapped, and there was nothing he could do. She had let the blood dry on the murder weapon and carefully wiped it clean of all fingerprints, except those Bixby Endecott had just put there.

At the same time Analetta was leaving High Bridge, Lieke Marchand was leaving her husband unaware he was floating face down in the Harlem. Perhaps it was the strain of the preceding months, the incessant quarreling, the move from Paris, something had driven her to distraction. She had put on a pot of oatmeal with currents and pecans after Guillaume left and mysteriously while it was cooking the decision formed in her consciousness that she just couldn't take anymore. She felt battered. Raw. Used. The whole situation damaged her artistic temperament and she resolved to withdraw and create her art alone; to salvage her sanity rather than spend another day at that dank Larchmont Harbor house overlooking Long Island Sound waiting for her husband to return from the city long after the terns and gulls had disappeared. So she hurriedly stuffed two bags, tossed them in the back of her car and drove away down the tree lined street with no sidewalks where foliage hid most of the grand manses to passersby and vanished. She was so distraught that the oatmeal cooking on the stove was forgotten. It began to burn even before she had navigated the long driveway and just as she hit the Boston Post Road it burst into flames, first igniting the faux antique wallpaper behind the stove, then racing up the side of the wall, creeping behind the lathe-and-plaster, torching the peg-and-beam frame and like kindling the hundred-year-old oak two-by-fours exploded in a fire storm. It burned hot in the cold wind for two hours straight. By the time she crossed the George Washington Bridge into Manhattan all that remained were ashes and embers and smoke in the breezes swirling out over Long Island sound where sunburnt water skiers glide in eternal summers.

Chapter 15

"What're you doin' here?" the detective barked fueled by too much coffee. "Someone die?" He was one of those men with a huge upper torso, short spindly legs and no waist. The physics of how he kept his pants up was a mystery best solved with complex mathematical modeling, algorithms of the same type that fueled the financial markets in sleek, hidden, hyperwired freeways. His jacket just barely buttoned over a protruding belly, the result of unrestrained indulgence.

"Just a hunch." Thierry Reynard said one hand in his pocket, shoulders arched, flipping his ID at the sergeant charged with keeping order over the crime scene, sauntering across the floor with surreptitious glances here and there. "Mind if I look around?"

"Won't find anything."

"You got the log huh?"

"Just about to go home and I got shanked—now I'm chasin' ghosts."

"What happened?"

"They tell me someone broke in at 2:37 AM. Got an exact time because they compromised the computer system. It's all in the log."

"What'd they get?"

"Fucked if I know. All in the log. Greek to me."

"How'd they get in?

"Nobody knows."

"What do you think?"

"Someone hired a real professional. Everything's clean, not even any prints—so far. No forced entry. Didn't trip the alarm. Security downstairs didn't see anything, didn't hear anything….just waltzed in and…it's a brokerage right? A brokerage. Ought to have the SEC here not me! Get some fucking computer expert, not me! Not even any clues. What do they need me for?"

"Feeling obsolete this morning are we?"

"Mind reading I can do, but gotta be a fucking computer scientist to catch criminals these days."

"Yea…I gotta friend like that."

"…don't need a fuckin' shoulder to cry on."

"Who's the well dressed Buddha head?"

"The vic."

"He let you in?"

"Keep it buttoned, this isn't homicide—it's uptown. You know: stock brokers, political donors—people who are real sensitive. Is this connected to that floater you found?"

"I'll just look around a little."

"You do that."

Thierry Reynard tread lightly through the brittle morning because something was wrong. It wasn't that offices didn't get broken into, it wasn't that at all, but this wasn't just an office. It was an HFT firm: "H" as in high turnover rates, and high order-to-trade ratios that leverage high-frequency financial data utilizing edgy, high tech, computer tools to rapidly trade high risk securities. Trades that take place in microseconds.

And they happen up to 800 million times a day for each firm. Anything that technically sophisticated would have leading edge, impenetrable security. Anyone with that much to lose would not take chances. Places like that didn't get broken into.

He put his phone to his ear and punched in a number.

Devlin had been awake for some time, he just couldn't open his eyes yet, everything was so delicate: the balance of day and darkness, shadow and light, no color, no contrast, and he wanted to savor the calm in between. Because there was always a crisis edging the horizon else lying bruised and weary in one's aftermath with scarce interludes where he could embrace qualities that convinced him he was still alive. That other thing, the work thing, illusions crumbling like icebergs that had traveled too close to the equator, like Icarus, like fleeting wild egrets, like wisps of desire you can never put your finger on, like melting snow, like brittle newspapers scuffling down the street in the last breeze of summer. It was so fragile. If he moved there was a danger. He couldn't bear to go back. At first he smelled her, the scent of humus and the indelible perfume of sex lingering in cool sheets, evidence of a comingling left behind by careless strangers, but then he saw an interloper fleeting down the hall. It was she of the soft round belly, the clinging arms and mouth, the jungle of blonde hair. Shades of sunburnt youth. He wanted to be anonymous, but knew it was impossible.

"Croissants and fresh squeezed orange juice," she chimed from the kitchen — though he pretended he didn't hear her for the longest time.

"I crave nectar de los Dios," he finally spoke.

"Well…I don't have any Sumatra, you'll have to settle for Jamaica Blue Mountain."

He hadn't gone into the office for three days, but had rowed the Hudson in his bright red scull with fourteen-foot carbon fiber oars feathering the hatchet blades so they barely disturbed the water. Fighting current and dodging ice flows on the way out, riding its back victorious on his return, each day going further pushing himself until his heart shuddered inside like some floundering bird.

"What are you trying to prove?" Veronica scolded, handing him a coffee as he lay still snow burned from the day before.

"Nothing," he replied.

Like a Turner landscape brushed with pale cirrus clouds the eggshell blue sky went on forever, and everyone waited breathlessly to see what was next. Because a palatable sense of something coming infected people, something out of the ordinary; whether it was true or just some premonition inspired by the primordial landscape its promise fueled rituals that held life together. Devlin watched Veronica. Her delicate hands poured coffee and flitted around the kitchen doing a million different things by instinct, the way it had always been done, but it was new to him. He was a refugee from a disintegrated family and had forgotten the way of it, so watched every breath and step of her feeling strangely satisfied—happiness being a fleeting thing, coming and going capriciously, but she had given him a harbor if even for a brief moment, a fact that had not eluded him.

"When I was a kid," he said, "heard a tale about something that *'happened.'*"

"What do you mean...*happened?*"

"Out on the plains beyond where I grew up...you know—there was always something to speculate about out there, like crop-circles and alien abductions—out where you could drive through cornfields for days without seeing anything except grain silos looming up against a huge blue sky, where phantom cattle roamed bleak endless grasslands and towns so small they were just crossroads you'd miss if you blinked twice. Out where prairie winds festered. Seems some young guy had set off one winter day to see his girl just as snow flurries started. Like always. No second thoughts. No big deal. But with no warning the flurries turned into a storm, which devolved into a furious blizzard that wouldn't let up, the way it does in a cold snap, like a mad dog, and soon enormous drifts had piled up twenty feet in some places. Thing is, he was never seen again. At first everyone just thought he must've taken shelter somewhere, thought he'd turn up—this tough, square-jawed, farm kid with calloused hands, strong back, corn husk hair and a cowlick who was used to being outdoors, used to working in the weather. Even when the snow began to melt and no one had seen him there was not too much concern. Figured he must have taken off somewhere. It was, however, a great mystery providing fodder for hearsay at all the morning coffee shops for miles around. But the drifts, the twenty-foot drifts, took a long time to thaw and it wasn't until late spring they began to fade completely. Soon cattle started showing up like the mummies of Pompeii. That's when they found him. Hung up on a barbed wire fence still frozen. There's a famous magazine picture of him dangling there: denim jacket and jeans, red bandana around his neck looking like he was going to see his girlfriend. This strong young man frozen in time."

"Jeeze…"

"I'll never forget that picture."

"I guess not!"

"That's how I feel, like that farm boy hung up on a barbed wire fence."

"That first night you were in a thousand pieces; you just needed to find out who you really were."

"Yea, that's right." Devlin said, rushing somewhere in the future; self-inspection being a luxury he couldn't afford. "It's all part of the conspiracy."

"I'm serious. You're just running to nowhere—"

"—don't think that's true…so what if I am?"

"—no place to ever arrive."

"Maybe not…don't think so. Just tired. Need a rest. That's all."

"C'mon, what've you got? Nothing. Getting older…can't live on the streets like a kid. No family, no roots—what's it all about?"

"I've got the river."

"Be serious—it's got you. If you don't change, you'll run till you die."

"Maybe I was born to live on the wing."

"Nonsense! You're nothing without roots."

"You for instance?"

"Pshaw…why would I try and catch the wind?"

"I thought women always wanted what they couldn't have."

Regarding him coldly. "That makes you sound foolish," she snapped, "just foolish!"

He went quiet. "You're right," his eyes bore into morning looking for something more honest, "it's just a saying isn't it. No relation to truth at all. I throw myself on the mercy of the court," realizing he had not even come close to who he really was yet, as if he was listening to himself from a distance.

"I'd rather you threw yourself on these eggs I just made for you," she said sliding a plate clattering across the kitchen bar. "Homemade chipotle and fried green tomatillo salsa with queso fresco and black beans on the side."

They ate breakfast silently across from each other. Sun glinted through the shades and branded the wall. The Hudson looked like a river of gold in the early morning, out the bay window, through the maze of buildings, under endless winter skies. The city had not slept but ebbed and flowed between light and dark as the cast of characters changed drifting in and out of slumber; a nocturne. Later they ended up making love again very sweetly, barely touching, like liquid flowing into liquid she reaching for and retreating from the impossible lightness, while he struggled with the irresolvable contradictions that consumed his life. In the afterglow all was still, as if they lay between where the world had stopped spinning one way before it had started spinning the other. She wanted to say she loved him, but did not.

"To me," he broke the silence, "it's still a battle between faith and reason."

"What...?"

"You know...?"

A long sigh. "Not what I was hoping to hear—"

"The French called it Siècle des Lumières, century of enlightenment," he sat straight up while she pulled the sheets around her, "you probably don't realize, but it just never ended..."

"I confess...never entered my mind—"

"That's right...still fighting the abuses of social and religious orthodoxy—only now it's inbred, in the genes—politics, religion, the culture of want and the ruling class: all the inequalities of fundamentalism whether religious, social or economic. Know what I mean...?"

"Of course. I always drive men to wild political philosophy after sex."

"You remember—they first thought poverty would always be a part of human existence, until suddenly it wasn't. Then they invented capitalism; the game where only a few can win. But now there's the top two percent...in neon lights like a gigantic theater marquee...just makes me insane that's all! Can't help it. I'm a rationalist. That's the problem.

A rationalist in an irrational world."

"That is a problem."

"Can't stand bone heads—don't think people can change their minds. That's the problem. Now you see it; now you don't. You can convince them, but then they get beaten down in life again and all bets are off. Back to their Neanderthal ways.

"What about you?" She mocked. "You haven't really changed. You're not a rationalist—you're a romantic. You want the same things Rousseau wanted. Natural man, uncorrupted by progress. Just listen: even the music you like is dreaming. I think you're rationalizing some pain, something that keeps you from being intimate, keeps you from being you."

"You do? Really?"

"We just made love…and you're talking political economy? Explain that to me."

"I had a moment…that's all…just a moment."

The phone rang; reluctantly Veronica answered. "For you…" as if pronouncing a verdict.

"Who is it?"

"That cop," she scowled, handing him the receiver with a look that made it clear there are some places you can never, ever return from.

As he listened, the look on his face changed like sundown being dragged across a burning landscape.

"We've got him." Thierry said.

"What do you mean?"

"There was a break in last night. One of his competitors. Very ritzy. Looks like they're real touchy about such things because I just received some pretty incriminating evidence—at least if it's what they say it is."

"Who's they?"

"Dunno. Sent by messenger. Anonymously."

"How do you know it came from the competitor."

"You kidding? Retribution!"

"What is it?"

"Documents on campaign finance violations. Account numbers, names, dates…might never get another chance like this. Once we have him, he'll break. The rich always break. It's now or never!" Thierry didn't tell him he had also received another mysterious package, one containing a silver knife—and if it came back from the lab with the DNA and fingerprints he expected, they wouldn't need the documents. Under the Federal Rules of Evidence, he had the smoking gun.

Devlin just looked at Veronica igniting fires he thought had been extinguished. But like a tempest, he was dressed and gone wearing that distingué suit he always wore to the office and Veronica just watched, speechless, as if gold dust were running through her fingers and she was helpless to stop it.

A whisper of chiffon and the glimpse of a well formed ankle disappearing around the corner met Terrance Roark as he entered the foyer. The air was tinged with a perfume so married to the scent of the woman it was like a gossamer fingerprint. An austere oriental man took his wraps and escorted him into the sunken living room where he sat down on a hard edged, Roche Bobios couch; the aggregate polished stone floor was littered with intensely colored Kazak rugs. He glanced out past the overhang of translucent metal layers reflecting last light with a faint rainbow hue, through a wall of glass, across the effervescent glimmer of Gotham and relaxed, satisfied that decadence was confined to the streets far below. Then, just when he felt the distance between him and the mob, he saw McGyver sitting in a chair across from him like a sad, surly mercenary awaiting the next opportunity of social unrest and became unsettled again.

"Thanks for coming," Bixby bounded into the room grinning, busting with charm, clasping hands.

"Burt McGyver," the mercenary, stood, but offered nothing else to Roark. He had been mulling over events that had brought him here, conversing with men he would never have met in normal circumstances, hovering above the city in the dark, like riding a spaceship, but as he sat down and ran his hands across the exquisite Roche Bobois upholstery he suddenly placed them in his lap feeling guilty that he might soil the fabric somehow; the look of the lawyer had made him feel unclean, stirring up the ribbon of guilt that ran through his life for inconsolable acts real and imagined. Like those against his wife, clearly a victim, though he couldn't remember what he'd done, the boundary between fact and fiction having become obscured; it was the cost of standing in the line of fire. Courage, valor and violence were an anathema for people bent on self-indulgence. In fear they had called him to duty playing on patriotic and religious themes, then abandoned him with empty patronizing words, lip service to fools, of little consequence to the needs of those who were compelled to stand watch reasons unknown.

"Don't ask me how I know these things," McGyver said after a few drinks as the conversation began unwinding.

"Cut the details," Roark shot back. "Don't want to perjure ourselves if somebody gets indicted. What we don't know, can't lie about."

The break-in had been McGyver's idea. He had planned it down to the last detail, winnowing the technical data needed to access the virtually impenetrable security out of Lance, the winsome young man from MIT, who had overcome his conscience with the grease of ten thousand dollars and stole confidential information from the corporate computers in the dead of night. The kid was a genius; an asset because his moral compass was broken making Burt wonder what the hell they taught in school these days.

"I just can't believe it…that's all," Bixby struggling with a loss of innocence.

"Obviously there is some kind of hidden financial arrangement between this woman Analetta, the Met and your competitor," Roark intoned shaking his head. "You can't trust anyone…even your mother may be lying."

"Like film noir…where everybody dies in the end?"

"My epiphany after thirty years in business."

"But how legal is this? You're my lawyer, what's your advice?"

"It's relative. Moral law or civil law? Depends on how much you want to survive. Personally, I've gotten used to certain things."

"That's pretty fucking ambiguous isn't it?"

McGyver, simmering under the restraint of the two men who always hired someone else to do what was needed, tried to articulate his philosophy in a simple, unmistakable way.

"You have to grab them by the balls."

"I'd say that was sound policy," Roark concurred turning to Bixby, "if you want to win the election."

"You think…?"

"It was on the disks," McGyver said, "spreadsheets with details about funneling foreign funds into the campaign. Why would they have that if not to use it?"

"Why indeed."

"I knew nothing of that! Nothing!"

"You didn't want to know."

"I trusted you to —

"There's nothing illegal about it," Roark exclaimed. "All offshore. Converting funds from income to investment capital. Just stick to your mantra. You hired me to manage your money —"

"Somebody's setting you up," McGyver deadpanned cutting through the crap. "It all adds up: the attacks on your business, which could only come from the inside, and the death of the quant, who must have found out. Someone really doesn't want you to be Governor."

At that moment Mirella descended like a night fog, knowing, as if by some spirit messenger, that her interests were endangered. Her scent caused Roark's eyes to go dreamy and pierce the shadows seeking the well shaped ankle even before it appeared. She had heard everything from the wings and it fired her reckless nature so that she could no longer keep still: she with dreams, she who did whatever was needed to reach them.

"I believe the French director was killed to intimidate," she purred, sashaying into the room, secretly knowing it was an attempt on Revenia's life by others, "but still…how can you assume Analetta is just a pawn? I don't think so…" remembering the imagined insults she had endured at the hands of the Met's general manager and then spoke with a low growl, "I don't think so." The room became hushed with dark overtones.

"You're saying these murders are connected with me?"

"Makes sense," McGyver said sitting on the edge of the couch, elbows on his knees, touching the ends of his fingers together to the beat of a silent drum, knowing it always got worse before it got better.

"But…why?"

"Money," Roark said.

Mirella sucked in her breath, narrowed her eyes and decreed, "…or power!" Alternatives had never occurred to her, didn't jive with a reality where all that mattered was desire and blind faith.

"Or a struggle on behalf of God!" McGyver said, "Political extremists with nothing to gain from moderation. Radicals."

"I hate fanatics...but not likely," Roark replied.

"Don't be so sure. Cicero said 'duty' is a result of being human, a moral obligation—"

"—it's greed that's a result of being human. The engine of the economy. Fuels everything...out of our hands since we've endowed machines with our worst qualities. Computers and algorithms do it all now. People..." pausing, "we just clear their path and collect profits."

"So...?" Bixby said consumed with anxiety.

"Basic economics. Someone's clearing you out of the path—don't you get it? Less competition; more profit. When Endecott goes under, your competitors inherit the huge volume of trades your firm makes. How many rent seeking algobots will be unleashed after yours have fallen?"

"No..." he said in a cathartic moment chilling the air, "no, not the trades—someone wants our cable routes into the exchange."

"What's that...?"

"It's all about being first to market. That's the secret. All these MBAs and PhDs and we're paying off some trade school technician in the New York Stock Exchange data center in Jersey where all trades are processed. Basic science. With our servers nearby, it gives us a speed advantage once the transaction hits the inside. We can trade faster than the competition—faster than anyone. Trades that happen in a millionth of a second. Hundreds of thousands of times a day. No one else has a chance."

As the men spoke in low resolute tones, oblivious to nature swirling around them, the polar vortex shifted in the night, allowing wild arctic air to escape the cyclone and flee from Canada down across the Northeast shattering cold records from Maine to Mobile. Temperatures plunged to staggering lows, the wind chill drove them even further cracking subway rails, bursting water mains, stopping mass transit in its tracks and icing the homeless in their frosty beds as the jet stream shot the bone chilling freeze south. But it paled before the cold hearts of those fleeing their own acts never asking who let the greedy in, who left the needy out.

In the heat of the moment plans were laid. Words were said. Agreements made. Bixby shook on it. And smiled in that charismatic way that seemingly eased other men's consciences and made him one of them, a partner, secure that even if nobody else understood, at least he did. But in the days that followed he somehow wished he could turn back time and return to the essence he no longer could put his finger on, the simplicity with which he once approached life that gave him the reputation as a bon vivant. Now he couldn't remember who he was and struggled with a search for the meaning he once took for granted.

"I should just give it up," he grumbled to Mirella dark and late, feeling like an alien, "don't give a damn about getting elected anymore! It's gotten too complex, too much risk. Need to take care of my business, that's what's really important...my legacy, what I've created. Nobody cares if I get elected governor." Then he plunged into self pity like a man bent on consuming a whole box of chocolates in one sitting.

"I do," she said, brushing her lips against his, basking in the midnight sun now that she was so close to power, feeling the heat of victory, fearing the cold umbra of defeat. "Snap out of it! We'll spread your light like a blaze across the sky. Nobody can deny you this moment, nobody!"

It was then Bixby realized the event horizon had been crossed; but it had happened earlier, at some indistinct instant slipping by unnoticed and now he could never, ever return.

The ephemeral city glowed with light like an ice palace, cars crisscrossing fresh white snow like the tracks of tears, people bundled up like Eskimos, everyone rushing somewhere, prodigals returning home. High above stratocumulus clouds streaked across the sky and TV weather girls argued whether they were at the front end or tail end of worse weather and if the atmosphere indicated storms to come and even deeper cold or relief. Despite it all the heat of life burst up through the frostbitten concrete. The wealthy whose every desire was satisfied struggled to overcome ennui; the poor whose every effort seemed to vanish like smoke trudged ahead toward uncertain victory. The paradox was they all seemed to thrive under the challenge of winter's hand.

At its center beat the luminous heart of the Met. The run of "Aida" had entered legend, bringing both acclaim and tabloid headlines to Manhattan—the city of extremes. It really found its legs in the press after an enterprising inkslinger had coined the sobriquet "Haunted Aida" spawning story after story of strange preternatural happenings. Everyone knew it was just gonzo journalism, but lingering in the collective consciousness was the idea it must have some truth for there to be so many tales.

Tonight, a command performance in the works incited feverish activity everywhere. It was called to commemorate the success of the production and the weeks of sold out shows that had inched the company into the black for the first time in years. New York's illuminati were expected and the Met's directors had arranged a special celebratory dinner to mark the event—many board members known only for their donations up to that point found themselves flying in on short notice from such exotic locations as Houston, Tulsa and Orange County. One of the rehearsal halls upstairs had been abandoned to the caterers, lined with banquet tables and equipped with huge flat screen monitors so the board members could watch the performance while they dined. Fans had been running day and night to eliminate the smell of perspiration and rosin leftover from the dance company who had sweated out their daily classes there for years.

In the park, only a block away, wind rattled the trees flinging icicles helter-skelter and the landscape had returned to a more primal state. Now it belonged to the ground squirrels, ravens, feral cats and any remaining waterfowl that had not frozen to death. Only the heartiest visited and even they barely disturbed the unfolding natural drama: cross country skiing over the greens nestled beneath a frozen snowpack, telemarking into the distances where once exhilarated dogs chased brightly colored Frisbees. There seemed to be a feeling of impermanence to the asphalt meadows and concrete canyons surrounding the park as if some living breath more ancient and wild than man waited patiently, watching for all the edifices to crumble, knowing these changes were predestined. The cities of gold and the epithets of greatness, the songs and the monuments, the hoarding and the pillage, the hunt and the extinction, the father and son, the wisdom and waste all going with the wind as civilization's fragile shell shattered in careless hands. Somewhere a higher power simply waited for the inevitable opportunity to take back lost ground when the cities, the greatest that ever were, became fields of weeds again.

Francotti Benedetto was riding high on the saccharin of public acclaim. He had become insufferable in his new role as prima-donna-auteur of the opera and ran the company like a puppet master through alternate bouts of narcissism and megalomania—during which he could make or break a serious operatic career in minutes. It was for this reason the artists patronized him. Everything for Francotti Benedetto was as if through a camera obscura and he habitually framed his view in the rectangle made with his thumbs and forefingers, sometimes even in face to face conversations, which drove people crazy with frustrated urges to do harm. Management, however, indulged his every eccentricity thinking only of the bottom line and not wanting to inspect success too closely: in uncertain times nobody was willing to mess with Mother Nature.

Except for Analetta. For some time now she felt quite on par with nature. So she suffered the Italian film director, but like a martial artist knew how to use his careless disregard and unbearable arrogance to her advantage so when he burst into her office with his usual hubris brandishing a bottle of champagne pilfered from the caterers with two flutes dangling from his other hand she just sighed, smiling slightly, and sat back in her chair to scrutinize him.

"Well…!" He grunted, shooting his unbuttoned cuffs, "It's time we toast each other!"

"Why," in disbelief, "is that?"

"You had the good sense to make me come here…" giving him the silent treatment, "OK, I admit, I didn't want to, but you saw something… now look what I created…we're all winning! Aren't we?"

"I'm busy right now—" she mumbled.

"Indulge me. You were right, but I'm a *yenius*! Besides…you've been looking too sad, entirely too sad…fucking gloomy actually! Not haunted by "Aida" I hope…you haven't been reading the newspapers?"

"Haunted by bills is more like it…" tossing some papers aside on her desk.

"You know what they say: money-talk is more important than talk-talk…except for maybe right now. A time for everything…here…" he sloshed some wine in her glass, "tell me you don't enjoy leading the greatest opera house in the country—"

"…the world!"

"That's right…let's not be tightwads…especially after *my*

production!"

"Glad I could play a minor part…" taking the glass, feigning disgust, gazing into the bubbles, "you know of course this institution has been here over a hundred years?"

"Yes I know," he drawled in his best Italian brogue, "but I am new blood."

"True…but the tide is coming, wave after wave of relentless youth… there is always 'new blood.'" She regarded him, "I am curious though; is it pride with you or just old fashioned conceit?"

"Why—"

"Listen…the arts devour new blood, they are insatiable. We're as good as our last performance, you and I, and memories are short in this business while careers are long."

"That's the danger of creative work isn't it. Not like money in the bank. I hear what you say…really, I do. I'm aware of how precarious it all is. A fragile dazzle above the 'mob,'" holding his hands up in mock defense eyes dancing playfully for a moment then sobering. "This is it for you isn't it? Me…I would never have thought of directing opera if I hadn't been accosted by someone in Rome—I mean…confidentially it's a dying art form isn't it…and I'm all about the future, right?"

"You? Just new blood," she said, "ripe with life…maybe, but still… we theater people know how to make it real don't we? Admit it…we bring it to life. Pry visions out of that 'only-one' universe you creative geniuses live in. Think about it: where would you be without the stage? Lying in some flat boring some fleshy ingénue with your dim thoughts—just secret wishes, not real. People like me wrench them out of you and give them bone and sinew, sweat and emotion, sound and fury! You need us and I guess we need you; yet there is a price that must be paid for our hour on the stage. A steep price indeed."

"Yes…it's fantastic. Sometimes I stop cold, look around and can't believe it's all happening. Every night coming to life again—out of nothing. How do you keep this place going? How do you do it?"

"You're right. I'm a creature of the theater; there isn't another place on earth I belong. This is it for me. But what happens? We get bored when it's done. Accomplished, but no more game. A year from now, ten years—who'll remember. It's all happening right now in the present. If you don't pay attention it'll be gone."

"But we're artists…" he said incredulously, "nothing is better than that!"

Ohh…artists are important; we've always attracted the finest…like moths…there will always be someone in the crowd yearning to be up in the lights. My job is to keep the cathedral here…keep it world-class for new blood…and I think I've found a way to do just that!" She lit up, "So, my Italian charmer, let's toast the future!"

Crystal glasses clinked together chiming into the uncertain night. Though everything at that instant aligned to convince her she should feel heady with success, there was a pall above that could not be broken. It was the cost of standing in the line of fire and the burden of things she didn't want known. The feeling took the edge off any joy there may have been.

But in her mind everything was explained by one tidy narrative; the overriding importance of art institutions in society that justified any sacrifice, any measure. Where else can higher ideals be preserved? Not by the mob; nor by the intelligentsia. Even religion had failed. Too many people dead in the name of God for anyone to heed the call. Analetta believed she was a keeper of the silent graces, an angel on mission. It was this story that had justified the coup de grace of the dying man on the bridge—because the rich had no place if they were not true to their purpose—like the sailor who falls from grace with the sea. This same story supported the impulse to destroy Bixby Endecott—to her, the paradigm of greed and self-satisfaction—and was why she had sent off the knife with Bixby Endecott's fingerprints on it to the police. He was worth more dead than alive, and in the long run it was all about money, and that was the ultimate solution to keeping the art institution going in a world where taste and sensitivity were dictated by sampled sound bites and entertainment requiring ever-shorter attention spans on an ever growing list of electronic devices. She was repulsed by the idea that people could even watch movies on their phones now, a fact that took her several years to come to grips with. Even elevators and gas pumps had video screens—to stave off boredom while topping up the tank she surmised. People didn't ever really speak to each other anymore, they didn't have any need for rhetoric or penmanship or oratory, those subjects that once consumed half the years spent in education; it was all email, text messages, social media and worst of all, video clips. Infinite numbers of video clips watched mind numbingly by young and old from birth till death like a passing wall of virtual reality living for them. All is fair against these enemies.

But still as fine as she should have felt, something was wrong and it seemed entirely illogical because everything was working out perfectly.

Chapter 16

He didn't believe in omens, which was why it got missed. The unmarked police car that had expired somewhere around Greenwich and 7th just north of the Vanguard—once a homey little place now jazz cathedral. An unknown component buried deep in the vehicle's computer failed and it just died quietly, no smoke or sputtering, no backfires like gunshots making everyone nervous, no mechanical whining, just silence as it rolled to a stop. The frozen night fell around them. Thierry and Devlin waited for the patrol car to pick them up trying not to let the inconvenience blunt the fury with which their flame burned. Because it all depended on that: fire and ice, truth and retribution. Other cars flowed by in endless rivers each one unique carrying anonymous people to their destinations—every once in a while someone looked out a window and their eyes met Devlin's in an electric, fleeting, intimate, instant that said everything. He looked up at the buildings towering into the darkening sky, yellow lights flickering with signs of life, and he felt it once again: the human yearning that was the underpinning, that gave him purpose and motivated his being. There was something in the conflict, the endless struggle, in the covenant he had with faceless people whose confluence built these great cities seething with unfulfilled aspiration. He longed to help, but didn't know exactly how. This was his best shot.

Under neon the patrol car jostled past lit up shops and fast food joints of every nationality thick with the racket of voices; it sailed through buyers and sellers and palm readers and haute restaurants rationing out nouvelle cuisine as if it was the last food on earth; it passed hotels that lurked on every block deepening the mystery of who filled all those rooms; it crossed moon shadows of office buildings where no one ever seemed to arrive or leave—with no-vacancy signs stuck up to ward off inquiries; flared its blue and red lights at the stubborn and barked its siren at the oblivious. Devlin sat in the middle of the back seat bracing himself with every turn and couldn't help but think one thing: all cities are the same. He could be driving through any of them and it would be the same. If he went up three flights to that loft there would be an immigrant family sitting down to supper full of hard luck tales tinged with angst over all they left behind and it would be the same. Limousines cruising below in sublime vanity. A million people in the streets, a melting pot of faces, all the same, all wondering where to, what next?

"You're pretty fucking quiet back there," Thierry said without looking back.

"I'm thinking."

"Thinking! What about?"

"Stuff."

"About that rich mother-fucker we're gonna burn down tonight I bet."

"Something like that." But in his mind he was back at the night the man from the bank came. He was just ten. It was the week after the company his mother had worked at for 25 years went under, but it was the knock at the door that drove her down the dark ladder. Devlin stood in the shadows at the bottom of the staircase in the heart of the two-story wood frame house they had called home much of his life, so much he knew little else at the time. All he heard were voices filled with emotion: brutal, adult, primitive. It unnerved him since up to that point almost all grow ups had sounded assured and confident—except those in the movies. Most of it he couldn't make out, except that his mother was pleading, incessant, unwilling to let it go until the man stood up in frustration and walked out the front door leaving it open to the still of the night where fireflies and moths buzzed the porch light. Then he heard her sobbing. It was a deep earthy sound like an earthquake shaking everything he knew, a whirlwind ripping through town exploding buildings, lifting whole roofs off and carrying them away and leaving cars parked on the tops of trees. It didn't make any sense, didn't compute. That was when he entered the stream of the river, the ancient dusty river, and it had carried him ever since. In two weeks they were gone. Everything they could pack in suitcases went with them and the rest left behind for scavengers. Tokens of a lifetime. Wind tossed their lives exploded like clapboard houses in the tornado and all he could remember were the dry tracks of tears down his mother's cheeks that remained with her the rest of her life.

He hated the rich. It gave him reason, filled him with nuances and dynamics far beyond normal human beings whose social awareness had been dulled by instant gratification. He envisioned the fall of Bixby Endecott: humiliated at the height of his ambition, aspiring governor, self-made billionaire, social icon that everybody wanted to get close to, brought down by a dogged bureaucrat in his distingué suit. He took a certain, simmering, hateful pride in that.

Except now something else was intruding, subtle and profound, as if a tear in the fabric of reality was being born and he could just make out something on the other side though he didn't know exactly what it was yet, something wonderful. He had never been spellbound before until that night at the Palais Garnier in Paris, never knew love before until now, never felt its warm embrace until Veronica—freckled and flawed with lipstick that was too red. It didn't make any sense, as if some prescient power from the outside was making him see that the course of action he chose had everything to do with love and happiness, like breathing out and breathing in. He tried to keep the animosity flaming, but it was burning out right there before him.

The black and white pulled up in front of the Met and parked in the red—much to the consternation of limo drivers vying for position, dropping off paying customers, hoping for big tips and repeat business. "Wait for us," Thierry said as they piled out taking long determined strides across the concrete through throngs of people there for the gala: a command performance of the haunted "Aida." Devlin had left as an angel but was returning as a warrior. Their breath turned to mist in the air and trailed behind them like battle standards.

* * * *

Rarified instruments stood at attention in the orchestra pit: violins from Cremona hand crafted before the execution of Louis XVI by guillotine at the Place de la Concorde—where 1119 people were beheaded—created with varnish formulas so coveted blood was spilt to keep them secret; bassoons hewn from Yugoslavian red maple; oboes of granadilla from east African savannas; brass worn to a mirror finish by anxious fingers reflecting dim lights; and the lustrous, black, Model D concert grand from the old Steinway Hall on 57th Street near the Russian Tea Room. To the untrained eye it was chaos, but everything was placed with care as if by a landscape architect because no musician of any salt was above the music and each summoned the saints as they picked up their instrument with moist hands never knowing if the next performance would be the last. Art is an ethereal thing beyond hope; the artist an addict of the impossible.

Bixby Endecott knocked on the dressing room door.

"Who is it?" Came the impatient response.

"Me," he said brows furled looking down the hall expecting trouble.

The door cracked open. "Ohh…not right now," Mirella said, an otherworldly burning in her eye, "I'm preparing."

"I know…I know…only wanted to see you."

"You alright?"

"Yea…it's just that…well, something may happen…"

"What do you mean 'something'? The campaign? Is anything wrong? You didn't drop out…?

"No, no…it's not politics, it's —

"Well…everything's OK then isn't it? It's OK. Don't scare me like that, but it's all good isn't it…so tell me later…" she kissed him and whispered, "in bed," then closed the door.

That was not what he was looking for: left alone stricken with vertigo, isolated in a sea of people running crazy, ramping up for the performance, uncertain whether he could go through with it, nearly crumbling, like being someone else, not at all the person inside. He wanted consolation, but all was scorn and praise.

C'mon."

A hand grabbed his arm and he turned to see Burt McGyver—suddenly remembering why he came along.

"I don't know."

"Yea, you do."

"She's a friend. Maybe there's still time to make peace."

"Sometimes the only peace is a Carthaginian one."

They pushed their way down the narrow hallway past the carpenters, stagehands, musicians, dressers, electricians, dancers, stand-ins and extra players. Roark stood holding his briefcase at the end silhouetted by light streaming from behind like in the movies. It was a coup d'état and he was hoping it wouldn't get messy because he hated the idea of it, had hated it from the start, but it was a politics, despite what he had told Mirella and if he wanted a leadership position, if he really wanted to climb the greasy pole he had to be strong enough.

Stars had aligned for this dark errand and he realized they had only this one slight chance, so he forged ahead on faith alone because like all assassinations stealth and timing were everything. But it stabbed his conscience with regret because she had become a confidante, someone who called him "Bix" and shared his problems. He understood her, Our Lady of the Opera, never married, forever envied, whose life was so intertwined with the theater's that it was impossible to separate them. She had suspended his disbelief along with all the others with the vision of a palace where stories were told through great music, a spiritual covenant that had only one reason for being: true art. It had taken his breath away many times and drawn him to her inner circle, which now he would destroy. There was no denying the gravity of his act. The queen must die if he wanted to survive.

The evidence of her betrayal was overwhelming, though who knew why she was conspiring with his competitor and attacking his trading business—who knew what she was after? Who knew what she was capable of? He still could not believe it, but that didn't mean it wasn't true—Roark was carrying documents proving she had embezzled from the Met's endowment to invest in the market for personal gain. Had in fact depleted eighty percent of the fund's value and hidden the fact with creative bookkeeping. It was a forgone conclusion what the reaction of the board would be when this was revealed at the gala dinner, jaws dropping into the tomato aspect he imagined whatever justifications she might give in defense. It would be as Othello said: *"Tis a shrewd doubt, though it be but a dream."*

His father taught him when he was very small: never do anything you couldn't tell others, even if you're not proud of it, never do anything you have to hide. Out of the depths of his mind, this phrase was resurrected just for this moment and Bixby had been pondering it for three days. But it would not resolve under the test of right and wrong, of good and evil, all so finely balanced in his psyche that they held an equilibrium of forces. No one way stood out; just infinite shades of gray. The faith of his father had prompted him to tell that piece of wisdom to his young son, no doubt spoken to him under similar circumstances, it was that faith he was missing and so consumed his thoughts and denied sleep that he was unable to make his own choices. Politics, he concluded, was compromise and so he opened himself up to the suggestion of others violating yet another bit of wisdom: keep your own counsel and make your own decisions.

*   *   *   *

Mirella listened to the silence for her wisdom. She had learned to recognize its signs and seek out the stillness where restless spirits lingered. And even when distractions intruded—as had Bixby Endecott rudely knocking at the door—she learned to ignore them. Where else could the power of art come from with its transcendent force of hope? For some, with that wisdom came the ability to help and enlighten, but for Mirella, who knew that no one could live without it, came a weapon.

All day long a feeling of unease gnawed at her. It was an unknown menace lurking in the wings, watching, waiting for a vulnerable moment, as real as night and day. Anyone seeing her would have thought she was daydreaming with that perilous look, but life as an artist is fragile because evil seeks creativity as a target. Now, alone in her dressing room, the atmosphere bristling with expectation, seared by a dark light she transformed herself from the petulant, troublesome diva to daughter of the Phaoah, Amneris—who will have her revenge. Clouds gathered. Hours passed. Then at last consumed by her character she detached from the mundane that traps us all—the world of agents and contracts and things that bored her to tears—and in her lightness untamed emotions festered until she glimmered with energy waiting only to be unleashed. It was the stillness, the silence in the midst of chaos that branded her an artist. Tonight she would sing in a state of grace and from that height conquer her enemies.

Earlier, she had seen him arrive as he strode through the front entrance trying to hide in the crowd and felt nothing but disdain for the impostor who pretended to be an angel of the theater, but was merely a bureaucrat out for blood. Even though whose blood wasn't certain, it somehow threatened her. There was no hard evidence other than that, she just didn't know exactly what he was after but knew the only trophy worth having was the governor apparent, Bixby Endecott, her Bixby Endecott, founder of high frequency trading firm Endecott Technologies, prime target for some SEC investigator looking to make his mark or one with a petty vendetta. Who else would a government lackey be interested in at the opera? Certainly not a mezzo with an attitude breaking some rules. It was unsettling. She had grown accustom to the idea of gaining influence and was longing for the social assentation that came with it—the power of the commanding heights made her reckless, but like songs of the Lorelei it came with a warning: *"Be vigilant over your will and desires, for these are the corrupt forces that dwell within."*

Mirella's dresser was a pale wraith with eyes of water blue and long blonde hair that glinted strawberry in the light. She slipped through the door with an armful of garments and carefully laid them across a worn velvet couch with short claw legs. She had been on one of the upper floors in a room filled with sewing machines mending slight imperfections and adding Velcro where hooks and eyes once were to facilitate quick changes between acts. She obsessed over details that not even the performers noticed because she had begun her career as a stitcher and could sew anything by hand with stitches so tiny they were invisible to the naked eye.

The diva paid no attention to her whatsoever and stood self-absorbed before a full length mirror ringed with tiny glowing lights. She arched her back and let the crimson kimono slip down her shoulders to reveal the flawless nude form so many opera patrons had imagined then raised both her arms like a Catholic saint crowned by a flaming tangle of auburn hair. Without a word the dresser began wrapping layers of costume, one upon the other, wrapping and lacing with impossibly deft fingers so light that Mirella didn't even feel them, as if a mote of dust were caressing her or a lover's breath was washing across her cool skin in the deep hours. The pale girl flitted around snatching bits and pieces from the clothing piles she had brought in earlier knowing intuitively each part of the ensemble and where it lay until soon out of some rags and feathers an Egyptian princess materialized from a moment lost in time. The dresser paid much closer attention to detail than anyone else. She was a master craftsman. An artist herself. It was all second nature now. She had learned to juggle hot coals, learned when to speak and when not to, what to say when nerves grew so tight that actors ran up on their lines, how to give last minute confidence to middle-age-past-their-prime-stinking-of-alcohol singers hanging on the bitter end, how to bring out their best side, how to hide their flaws, how to help them create the illusion. It was magic.

But Mirella was different. With her it was like lacing up the wind. Dark unknown storms raged in that soul, the girl thought, and was thankful the diva had her art to defuse the simmering disaster that lurked just beneath the surface. Thank god, she thought, knowing from long experience with artists these were the forces that converged in the vortex of performance and transcended everything, lifting all onto a higher plane. It was to a realm of thoughts and emotions, of aesthetics and phenomena that could not be explained away by physical science no matter how hard they tried. It was a place where perfectly reasonable explanations had no meaning and believers were made out of agnostics; it gave even the most hardened materialists faith in love. These metaphysical powers had drawn her to art in the beginning and gave her a deeply religious wisdom where before there was no hope and all seemed lost in a brutal obsessive life. For that she was so grateful she didn't even notice the diva had ignored her completely.

Mirella was approaching full power. Energy radiated from her as she made her way through the dark halls to the stage. She belonged up there in the lights where everything was black and white, flaunting real life in which you had to bend a little more with each passing hour, diluting the purity of self by degrees until at last you ended up affable, nice, chummy, good-natured, a genuine team player—it never seemed to matter that all the fire went out somewhere along the way. On stage, getting them to feel like that was different: reminding the forgetful who they were, that they are still alive and have blood passions, telling stories they longed to live. That was why they came. Needing the fix. Nobody liked emotional people in real life. The theater was different; here they came for the whirlwind.

The diva exotica who rendered men's hearts was hell bent. Her dark eyes an abyss out of which one could rescue sinners forever. She was compelled to guard the world against too much virtue because darkness and light ruled with a delicate equilibrium and someone had to watch over it. Mirella was as close as anyone could come to wicked, and though most of the time she suppressed her inclinations, tonight she fumed with demonic fury. By the time she reached the wings into which the low stage lights seeped she was a startling brilliance that made everyone step back as if cowering before her dazzling strength. Only an enemy could fan the flames this high and tonight there was only one: Devlin Winthrop Wolfe the tin angel.

*　　*　　*　　*

Revinia had arrived when the haloed clouds were swept away by an encroaching night, when the wind was at its highest, tossing her long scarf and coattails, thrashing treetops in the park, and everyone was rushing from where they had been to where they were going as if their lives depended on it. Cold permeated everything. Solitary lives drowned beneath the symphony of the city and nothing else could be heard—except for the sound her boot heels made against concrete and ice, except for the wind that lashed around corners. Slipping through the stage entrance unnoticed, she merged with carpenters and stagehands who were flying in set pieces, sweating in their t-shirts despite an Arctic blast from the open door and took refuge in the depths of the theater.

The piano player was waiting. An enigmatic young man in

wrinkled khakis with baggy knees, boney fingers and thick black hair who had mysteriously shown up one day when she was practicing scales in a rehearsal room. Without a word he had walked over to the baby grand and begun to accompany her. Perhaps it was his confidence, or the sense that he was some lost love from centuries past suddenly returned, but it was the sweetest sound. So she just continued on with her melodic minor and Dorian modes racing up and down the scales with a studied imprecision that defined her singing as if he had always been her accompanist. And since then he had always shown up by some remarkable concurrence of events exactly when she did. He just smiled; they never spoke.

It was the fact that she neither hit notes precisely on key nor was diminished or augmented that confounded the critics; they couldn't figure her out—the young man, on the other hand, understood perfectly. The music that flowed from her was impossible to classify; the notes not precisely on key were somehow perfect. It was indefinable, like a star athlete who did things not physically possible—and even in instant replay no one could see how they did them—except there they were. Fortunately for all the journalists she was French so her otherworldly qualities were attributed to being foreign. Still sensing something beyond them, the critics called her "promising," "mysterious," "ethereal" and everything but the genius she was; unwilling to commit their reputation on things they could not fathom.

She always took the stairs instead of the elevator. Childlike. To most she was simply "that French girl," the enigmatic diva insiders were waiting to see if all was superficial or if there was some deep burn smoldering. Each whispered: would they still love her tomorrow? Eyes everywhere were looking for a flaw, and if one existed they would seek it out; in the hallways and spaces of the theater she had the feeling of being watched. But whoever heard her sing never forgot. It was only that some couldn't stand her sense of freedom, the idea that somehow she didn't have to play by the rules everyone else did and saw in her something wild, something to be controlled, suppressed, extinguished. It was all white noise to her. Life under glass. She on the outside and the others watching, forever watching from within.

Before the mirror ringed by small incandescent lights she painted the dark, elongated eyes of the race of farmers who created a civilization lasting three thousand years. In the blurred background behind her a dresser readied the costume of a princess now captive slave: proud, brave, impossible—and slowly the transformation began.

Memories came racing down as if only a few days had passed: the Sirocco roiling up from the western desert where as far anyone could see was sand, so much sand it turned the sky yellow. Then standing in the hot night wind high on the top of a great pyramid, pennants cracking in the gusts like whips, huge oiled Nubians holding torches flaming into the dark, and primordial stars flooding the horizon—brilliant points of light all across the sky beckoning her home. Silence was only interrupted by sounds of wind racing through the fronds and rushes near the banks of the river far below. The perfume of dry wheat chaff from the harvest hung in the air. And she saw henna mud caked on Nubians heads to protect them from the sun god Ra as he sped across the sky in his golden chariot—Ra who called each of them into existence by speaking their secret names. They were the cattle of Ra. She felt his presence tonight, the way she did then watching for the invading armies that would come out of the darkness somehow knowing it was childhood's end. Good and evil flickered like shadows through the half-light the moon gave. One cannot exist without the other. Everything was balanced just so, and that was how the chaos was controlled. Righteousness was the answer to all things threatening in life; opposing forces were countered with all things good. So she was compelled to keep the noble concepts alive in a world drowning in evil and despair, where even leaders were deranged and their best strategies ended in death and destruction. Someone had to be a keeper of the finer things in a life where fires burned on the sea.

At last the makeup was perfect, the costume set and she stood like a presence in the fog. The young diva looked in the mirror; Aida the princess slave looked back. Four thousand years filled the gulf in between. In those precious moments before the curtain rose when everything was still, during the equilibrium between desire and fulfillment, all things were sensed larger than life. The excitement surrounding her was amplified to near hysteria levels with the frantic preparations for the gala performance: whispers wafted through her, massive clunks shook her bones when the giant turnstile locked into position on stage, hopes and wishes soared like prayer songs, fears and heartbreak swept everyone, only fools and dreamers could escape.

Tonight the spirits were restless. The cathedral of art was under threat. The balance of good and evil was tipping and if it went too far over the edge...well, there was not really any clear answer because it had only come close a few times in history. The idea of good and evil were very clear in Revenia's mind. Indelible. It was an eternal battle she engaged in to maintain the balance. Her terrible purpose. Her obsession. When she emerged from the dressing room she had transmigrated from one incarnation to the next. On the outside a slender young woman that walked with an aesthetic aura leaving the impression of beauty wherever she went, but inside the young diva was a maelstrom of raw force guided by a singular purpose.

The house began to darken. A hush spread over the audience like a zephyr across a field of wildflowers. After long interminable moments orchestral strings began to rise and as the lights came up a chill of excitement flooded the theater followed by an unshakable sense that something tragic was going to happen. A glow revealed Mirella Elderia pacing center stage. Then out of a deep primal sadness her voice began to soar until it filled every corner of the massive hall and drew everyone into her umbra

*   *   *   *

Upstairs far above the fray Analetta was holding court: *Guardian Queen* of the house. She was clad in a tight, wool, dress—the color of a dark plum—with a plunging backline and dripping with ethnic silver jewelry that jangled every time she waved her arms emphasizing this point or that. After only a brioche for breakfast and no other food all day, she had unwisely consumed too much Domaine Leflaive Batard Montrachet Grand Cru: a prized, fine, bubbly drink priced at a staggering $5,923 a bottle—which the caterers had assured her was worth the price. The aromas of wine, garlic, perfume and cooking oil filled the room as the angels of the Met were seated around banquet tables covered with white linen beneath huge flat screens showing the performance of Aida underway down below in the auditorium. Nobody seemed to mind that it wasn't live as surround sound reverberated with every obbligato, but despite the ear splitting volume conversation rose above it. They felt very special indeed to be pampered so with the finest delicacies and to be rubbing elbows with other wealthy patrons where money was not an issue—never an issue for those relieved of the burden of the workforce. It was the crème de la crème of donors, and just seeing them all gathered together, laughing and talking and stuffing their faces made Analetta feel secure, like everything would be alright no matter what darkness had transpired in the past. She regretted betraying her friend, sincerely regretted it, but had it all justified in the Darwinian sense: the fittest survived on the food chain through the sacrifice of others. It was what capitalism was all about; the game where only a few can win. All the wine and the good company made her feel a warm glow of success rooted in the belief she was presiding over her lasting legacy, which would be cemented soon with the inevitable killing about to happen in the market.

Many of the donors she had never even seen in the flesh before, but had only dealt with over the phone. It was a salesman's fantasy: all the best prospects locked in a room together, sated with a blockbuster hit even the critics liked, tipsy with wine. So she worked the tables like Mephistopheles trying to collect the souls of those who were already damned.

"It's triumphant. Breathtaking. Just…dazzling!" The woman said.

"I think so…and I'm so glad you can see it too. At our first meeting, I almost threw that Italian—"

"Isn't he grand! Such a coup! How did you ever manage it?"

"It wasn't—"

"Who would have ever guessed…an obscure art film director! It's so…modern—"

"It's sick! I love it! It's just sick!" The daughter added in a little known hip-hop dialect. "I mean it's bad, you know, just sick! I love it!

The mother intervened to keep from death by humiliation, "She means 'it's… good—'"

"Yes, yes, of course…" Analetta replied in her concerned parent tone, folding her hands prayer-like to her breast for the sake of the woman's endowment—then spoke an incredulous aside to the daughter, "You know Francotti Benedetto's work?"

"'L'Eclisse di luna,' I saw it ten times. He's an existentialist realist. An auteur. It's all so hopeless, really, he just...it's what I want to say but can't—he speaks for all of us."

"Exactly," she replied, smiling serenely, embracing the millennial, "how perceptive...your daughter is very perceptive!" Elated her target marketing had produced this living proof the opera would live on for generations and she hadn't thrown the pompous Italian out on his ear as was her first inclination.

"I never even knew she liked Italian films," said the mother.

Analetta moved on gliding gracefully as if over a glassine sea brushed with mist, floating at the top of the food chain where there was nothing that could get her. She felt the peace of the condemned.

"She's a mezzo, right? Look...I'll take your word for it, even though they're wrong—she sings with such a sweet darkness..."

"It's a metaphor for nice tits. He just wants to get into her dressing room..." the wife said.

"...the French girl, listen..." the man lifted his glass to one of the big screens where Revenia was performing a soaringly emotional aria as Aida, the princess slave, "just listen."

Analetta stood by the table where the bantering bunch had gone suddenly quiet, spellbound and intimidated by the gifted French diva baring her soul on stage. It was grander than just second hand sentiment, it was an irresistible compulsion, incomparable to anything felt in the blasé world where people lived—even people like these for whom instant gratification was a requirement of amassed wealth. Art was promiscuous, nonsectarian and struck blindly without prejudice—music above all other forms because it couldn't be hidden behind barriers like paintings. It rode the ether paying no attention to the ferocity of the class struggle.

The truth of it caused those who had vested everything in the material to hide, and the rest to stake everything on the promise.

"Well technically," Analetta said when the aria had subsided with a slight slur, feeling a bit buzzed and not quite caring what she said, "Revenia is quite a prize. This is her first American appearance…here at *your* Met," pausing for effect. "She can sing any part, mezzo or full soprano. She has the ability to play all the great roles that demand deep emotions. That's why she's so special. Mirella…" she sighed thinking only of the she-devil source of trouble, "is a classic mezzo-soprano. She ranges between the soprano and contralto—you know, roles for witches and bitches," taking another swig of her wine.

"She's beautiful," the man swooned eliciting a flood of affirmations from the table, then the wife kicked him in the shin. "Sounds off key sometimes—" he coughed, "but it's just so perfect, like the music should have been written that way. How do you explain that?"

"Art is inexplicable; that's why we love it," she replied over her shoulder as she moved on table hopping, chatting with each for a few minutes then taking flight: a restless, giddy butterfly impossible to catch because she wouldn't stay in one place long enough to get a net around her—the euphoria going to her head the way it does to all those who have left evidence somewhere leading the hounds straight to them while all along thinking they had gotten away scot free. Blithe spirits with blood on their hands left a scent trail wherever they went, and all the victories could not hide the ugly truth that Analetta was getting careless. She was drinking too much and it dulled her senses just enough, leaving her exposed and vulnerable, forgetting the primary rule: it's not over until it's over.

"Shhhh…!" One of the stagehands scowled from the catwalk above them and frantically gestured to keep quiet. "Shhhh…! What th' fuck's wrong with you guys? There's a performance goin' on."

Devlin and Thierry gave each other their best couldn't-care-less look and pushed on. But every few steps some refrain would pierce Devlin to the heart and he would come alive if for just a moment. He embraced the feeling, but native New Yorker Thierry was a Francophile devotee of *machisme* and liked Gitanes unfiltered cigarettes, beer and *jus d'orange* for breakfast and disapproved of bathing too frequently because it washed away the pheromones—ostensibly his attraction to women— which made him smell of sweat much of the time. Breaking through his stoic misogyny was a testament to mind over matter. He resisted as long as possible, but too was engulfed by beauty's umbra.

Far below under hot lights the Pharaoh's palace burned. The yellow gold of the faux sandstone columns rising up from the faux desert just as if it was four millennia ago. A shiver ran through the grid deck where the flymen crawled like spiders moving battens, lift lines and counterweights. The swell of the orchestra and the haunting beauty of voices intertwining was as if hovering over a well of souls.

They emerged far behind the stage on a deserted strip of polished concrete illuminated only by light through open doors. Further on toward the crossover where dappled light spilled in from the stage were animated silhouettes of the crew working silently behind the scenes to make magic happen. Caught in the riptide between two worlds, they hurried upstairs in search of their quarry: the elusive Endecott.

Devlin was beginning to have regrets. He felt hollow in his troubled relationship with Veronica. Numbness had bled into him since he walked out earlier that evening, knowing he shouldn't have left so suddenly with that look in her eye, feeling self-righteous and blind, but still sensing her disappointment in him. Emotion clouded his judgment and he had not realized the profound sense of peace he found with her and how valuable that was. He rationalized everything. "The right thing to do was the hardest thing to do" was his idée fixe; he couldn't ever remember being without it. As if it was a part of him, a self-created truth he used to stay in control, it made him flee from things that were too easy, where every piece fit too nicely and meanings were clear because it translated as a threat.

Forty-six years old with nothing; still chasing bad guys like he was saving the fucking world. The existential void of Opera had been a revelation watching dedication and beauty taken to extremes. Channeling his inner impresario as a "Met angel" was the catalyst that made him realize he didn't know where his life was going, that nothing meant anything—just ideals and violence. His bosses didn't even care to get what he was all about, most people just wanted him to be a team player, to relax, be copacetic. His purpose irritated everyone. Everyone except Veronica, whom he had walked out on without explanation. Until now he got through it all powered by a vitriolic rage against the wealthy—his vote for the source of most social ills—but it wasn't money that was inherently evil he reconfirmed, it was the irresponsibility of those who had it. Like some long dormant illness needing only the stimulus of wealth to nurture its virulence. A plague to be extinguished.

Then he remembered why he hated the rich. If he had wanted to cave a few minutes earlier, now his fury returned and by some specious logic he blamed Bixby Endecott for the whole damn mess and vowed he was going to pay.

Chapter 17

Outside, as if there was no gala attracting angels from the far reaches, there was a continual stream of traffic sliding on blue ice into nightfall. Wind flurries lowered the temperature by thirty degrees. Snow clung to tires, stuck to buildings, covered trees and icicles falling from skyscrapers were so commonplace that warnings accompanied every weather report in hope of saving some hapless passersby from getting skewered. Through it all people were driven by a need to escape the chaos, the chaos that made New Yorkers restless, that made the streets rivers of life.

The opera was an anomaly even in the city where you could find anything. People seemed to know that. It was unnatural, humans were not supposed to sing that way, their beauty not supposed to be so exquisite, no one was supposed to aspire to such ethereal realms. Inexplicably, even those who could not understand why treasured the fact that someone did reach for the unattainable. Perhaps everyone has a dream that hasn't been extinguished yet. Most remain prisoners though: some rage in the streets at night in a drunken effort to vanquish their torment once and for all; others walk the line their entire lives with no light in between, running on faith their belief stretched to the breaking point; others still are running on empty their expectations having dissipated like a death rattle long ago.

In the lights Mirella could barely see the audience, but sensed they were out there. She could feel their emotion and it filled her with life. Inspired, she hit notes with exquisite power holding them far longer than she should have per the score just for the sheer bliss of doing so—and would have held out for eternity if she could. The musicians in the orchestra, who were inured to whole categories of virtuoso performance, thrilled in the knowledge something extraordinary was happening. But to the uninitiated in the mob, beyond the fourth wall, curious and dangerous though pacified for the moment by witnessing art finer than anything they could imagine, it just raised gooseflesh. Opera was a refuge for the privileged, a prize for the highest bidder appreciative or not. But to her, art was all emotions blazing and she smoldered for those who lived off her flame.

A huge tenor voice rang out clear and powerful commanding the entire space with a glimpse into Radames's tortured soul. A man condemned without hope, vanquished and struggling to see a future half in this life half in the next.

She dug deep to answer him; into the inaccessible depths that roiled beneath her polished veneer. Where a storm hewn landscape glimmered, where there had been a wild collision of nature at some primeval juncture and the fires of earth still raged and the winds still whistled through endless, ancient forests. It had always been that way; no beginning and no end. She saw these things as they were, the rise and fall of people in the great mandala so carefully hidden from the small minded who had their fingerprints on everything determined to bring it all down to the lowest common denominator even if they and everyone else died in the process.

On stage it was different, like a portal between realms where she didn't have to pretend and her spirit voice was free to create realities others only dreamed of. The audience witnessed this phenomenon in hushed silence not knowing whether it was from fear of the unknown or fear of their own hidden potential.

She sang an aria gripped with a passion so compelling grown men cried, their tears falling on silk neckties, and women held their breath wishing to break their earthly bonds and soar into the ether. The whole building shimmered, its walls becoming almost translucent as the humdrum faded into insignificance before a higher truth.

It was a song of forgiveness, an offer of hope, a promise of freedom. It was the haunted Aida people had heard about and they whispered excitedly, "I told you…" to each other while the orchestra played on as if enchanted. Everyone was spellbound by the power of beauty, and no one could imagine anything grander than what they were witnessing. Mirella reveled in her triumph, fairly hovering above the boards as the applause overwhelmed her, certain her performance had placed that French diva and all her saccharine feebleness on the road to obscurity.

It was into this rarified moment Revenia appeared. Spotlights arced down upon her in the darkness and she blazed on the wooden deck as everything fell silent save one lone violin. Gazing out through the wall of light she breathed in all the unfulfilled hopes and forgotten wishes swirling in the void, all the emotional baggage that kept people going long after they should have given up and moved on, and made it live again in her own private world. Everyone waited pensively as she stood like a gathering storm listening to the distant thunder of a billion unborn souls only she could hear.

Bixby Endecott pushed his way into the banquet room that was teeming with laughter and witty conversation. Before him stretched long white linen tables laden with half eaten gourmet food, littered with bottles of fine wine, set with gleaming silver and topped with lavish floral arrangements that would have shamed a state funeral. Apprehension nearly crippled him fearing the loss of everything on this gambit.

He had dreamed of political leadership since he was a child, through university and his first lackluster jobs, through those endless nights writing algorithms and testing his high frequency trading software — it was in his thoughts when he fell asleep and when he awoke the next morning. The idea of it was so ethereal, as if he had reached a higher plane on his own through pure willpower and intellect, and in that ivory tower he formed his worldview of political leadership reasoning he could apply the same brilliant logic to statecraft as he had to the markets. He would become acclaimed. Beloved. He would give of himself as was the white man's burden — after all he didn't need the money — and so envisioned a win-win situation in his mind where there was no opposition, no other viewpoints, no real forces to contend with. Except when his unquenchable hubris faltered and his charm failed him, when he viciously beat his ideas into bloody unconsciousness feeling foolish that anyone would have such delusions of grandeur. Thankfully in the end he always managed to come to grips reasoning that the main prerequisite for leadership was having a vision in the first place — and at least he had one. By nature, Bixby was an optimist, but one continually struggling against pessimism like had happened earlier in the evening.

"I think we ought to step back for a moment." Bixby said.

"Thought we already did that." MacGyver shot back.

"I just don't like it."

"What'd'ya mean?"

"I really don't like it. It's not me—"

"What's going on here?" Terrance Roark said catching up, clutching his briefcase as if handcuffed to it.

"Cold feet."

"Look…I love this place…I came here to help it, not destroy its leadership—"

"Can't have it both ways," MacGyver cringed impatient with cowardice.

"Why not?"

"Come with me," Roark's eyes narrowed as he grabbed Bixby's arm and drug him down a few flights to a private elevator next to the box office, MacGyver following like a shadow. Moments later they entered a near empty private dining room confronted by a surly maî·tre d'hô·tel with whom Roark conferred out of earshot.

"He was concerned because we didn't have tails," the lawyer tossed off an explanation as if they knew what the hell he was talking about, "but I reassured him."

"White tie? What is this place?"

"Emily Post said 'A gentleman must always be in full dress, tail coat, white waistcoat, white tie and white gloves when at the opera.' It's the private dining room of The Metropolitan Opera Club—established 1896. Tails required."

"Private…?"

"I'm a member—"

"I don't believe it. Thought all you cared about was sailing that J-Class yacht of yours…what hidden depths—"

"You're not the only one agog by some diva up in lights."

"I'm just not made for—"

"What? Going after what you want? "

"Finance is different now…not like when you were on top—"

"Welcome to my world…"

"…nobody's a floor trader anymore. The stock market ditched Wall Street years ago. The masters of the universe are all across the Hudson in New Jersey—computers piping algorithmic playbooks into a fortress of servers. You wouldn't like it"

"Unfortunately politics doesn't work that way. It's a sweaty cauldron where anything goes—and the rewards go to the ruthless! You hesitate… you'll always be in somebody else's shadow and all those ideas you have: just smoke and sand. Piss in the wind! Life isn't like finance; it's skin on skin, handshakes, backslapping, kissing babies… There's a value to having humans in place at the point of sale—seeing them there provides a sense of security and accountability. That's what leaders are. People don't believe in computers; they believe in people."

Bixby tossed down a single malt scotch. It burned sweetly. He didn't like being talked to that way. So, feeling about as sorry for himself as anyone could, he stuck out his glass for another. Everyone went silent hoping a stiff drink would sort it all out

He glowered into his whisky avoiding the present and not wanting to think about the past when memories of his long lost summers at Spring Pond, Massachusetts swept over him. It was where he was exiled by his parents every year ostensibly as a retreat from the city, but truthfully to be close the old Crowninshield estate at Salem—his father hoping some *Boston Brahminism* would rub off on his son since he himself had never amounted to anything and even his wife held him in disdain. There Bixby underwent the "cure" by the then wooded pond fed by underground springs where fanatics had once flocked in the nineteenth century to be miraculously healed by the waters, making it a favored destination of spiritual pilgrims, which was why the grand resort that once stood in the trees had been closed down—out of fear. The local populace being a group whose cultural pretensions and social exclusivity was particularly at odds with the democratic ideals of egalitarianism and inclusive citizenship. There was no television, but there were brilliant stars at night and he spent most evenings by the fire listening to the stories of old men about the Long Island Express—the Great Hurricane of 1938 that claimed over 700 lives. He still remembered every chilling detail: that the eye of the storm followed the Connecticut River north into Massachusetts; two-thirds of all the boats in New Bedford harbor sank; a 50-foot wave was recorded at Gloucester; winds of 186 mph were the strongest surface gusts ever recorded in the United States; homes washed away and their foundations could still be seen near the beach today. His father never told him stories like that. Never. But just sat with eyes burrowed into the newspaper behind heavy rimmed glasses.

He remembered disappearing into the forest at daybreak and not emerging until nightfall. It endowed him with a sense of independence, of deliverance that never left him. The cold quiet of his footfall on the spongy damp detritus of the forest floor, dew covered leaves that sparkled in dappled sunlight, the pond under a blue blanket of morning mist where he built a raft of fallen branches and polled out into its center and listened to the silence and contemplated his place in the universe. And the day he stumbled upon the old abandoned mink farm deep in the lost weeds where everything looked as if the owners had been run off in the night leaving it all just as it was—the old Model-T rusting in the drive, newspapers from the 1920's, dishes now broken on a weathered table and all the rusting cages where captive animals were imprisoned awaiting execution for their pelts. He never forgot the macabre fascination with his first glimpse of death and the absolute freedom he felt as he raced home all the way without stopping once like a yearling fleeing Eden.

Then it came to him that the problem with mass society was not in the unparalleled number of people, but that the world between them has lost its power to gather them together. He could be that bridge, and being governor was the first step.

"Let's go," Bixby said, slamming his glass down surprising both men who expected a tough sell.

"You're ready to do what you have to?"

"The rewards go to the ruthless."

Revenia had never been in love. Never experienced the euphoria of throwing herself on the flames just to see what happens; never knew the narcotic of a lover's touch; not the completeness that rolls in like silent fog tempering life's harshness; nor the bitterness of regret when it all goes away and nothing can bring back the sweetness. The charms and the wonder of it threatened to consume her, but it was a world into which she could never, ever enter. Like trying to touch the wild. One look and it vanishes. She knew only the ideal of it unsullied by melodrama, betrayal and loss, only the refined essence of it out of which dreams came. She was a keeper of that fragment, a keeper of the fragment love, but would never once know its warm embrace else it would be gone from the collective memory forever—at least that was her fear standing under the spotlight like a wire pulled taut and close to the breaking point.

She looked into the white noise of the audience as if across an eerie denuded landscape where all things of value had been stripped away to feed a voracious greed. Only the rocks and shoals and loam from the life giving tide that will never come again remained. Some turned to alcohol, some turned to heroin, some turned to violence but a thousand faces all shrouded in darkness wished one way or another they could turn back time to escape regret—because to bear those burdens alone that you could do nothing about was a stoic tradition. If you can't beat it, accept it, and if you can't accept it feign madness hoping someone will have pity and let you be until everything just crumbles inside. It was the fear that haunted most, the one nobody would talk about except those who had already given up and lie broken in pieces. Nobody spoke of these things, but came to the theater to be reminded of all the values they had nearly forgotten in real life.

This was her mission. When she began to sing it was not as if she needed to summon energies buried deep in her consciousness. It more like releasing floodgates to raging emotions battling to get out. Like some otherworldly creature her voice permeated to the far reaches of the theater as she launched into the final aria piercing any remaining indifference, enrapturing the audience, imbuing them with life, baring her soul on the stage under the hot lights. This was what they came for; this was what they needed.

The flat screen monitors in the banquet room flickered at that very moment and mysteriously the lights dimmed then burned full again. Nobody noticed but the Director of Lighting who had been impressed for the night to watch over the electronics against his will, so was determined to ignore it. He was insulted by the assignment, especially after lighting "Aida"…which the critics had called a work of genius that alternated brilliant grand processions with a moody and an atmospheric Nile all the way to the emotional finale in a tomb, which they were watching now, "…whose ever-receding light mirrored the ebbing lives of Aida and Radames." He especially liked that last part, so ignored his indignation for the moment and poured himself another as good wine and good conversation enveloped the crowd under tiny ultraviolet lights twinkling just below the ceiling.

All agreed it was a grand evening they would never forget topped off by a legendary performance—which was beginning to cast its spell on the room as one person after another became enchanted by Revenia's final aria soaring above the conversation.

Devlin and Thierry Reynard had slipped in the service entrance and were trying hard to look nonchalant.

"Button your coat."

"Why?" Devlin replied searching the banquet room carefully.

"There's blood on your shirt."

"A scratch—"

"Some fucking scratch!"

"It's a scratch…I don't see him. Where is he?"

"He'll be here."

"Hope we're not wasting our time."

"Meaning?"

"Just have a bad feeling."

"What the hell's goin' on? We've been working on this for months."

"Just don't know what I believe in anymore…"

"What! C'mon. You're a fucking lawyer. You believe in justice… isn't that what law is all about? Wait…there he is. Look, over there…"

Bixby Endecott was slowly making his way through the crowded room followed by two men who were clearly annoyed that so many recognized him and he had to stop at each table, but it was politics, skin on skin, handshakes, backslapping, kissing babies.

"Who's that with him?"

"That's Terrance Roark—once big time hedge fund manager, now of Roark & Moisell; a law firm in Greenwich, Connecticut."

"Looks pretty intense…what d'ya think they're up to?" Thierry took off across the room making a beeline for Bixby.

"Wait…" Devlin said lurching after him navigating tables with their chairs pushed out and groups of half-drunk men in dark suits standing around talking while their buzzed wives gaily chatted.

Analetta took another sip of wine illuminated by a serene glow. Her cheeks flushed with color as she presided over a group of admirers at the head table next to the podium. She had never once realized what the constant stress of worrying about where the money would come from had done to her over the years—until now. For the first time in recent memory she felt a fundamental inner peace and even a slight euphoria at just being able to be without a crisis looming. And she was sleeping straight on through till morning unlike the fitful rest she usually had. Before, she could never even drink one over the limit, especially in public, for fear of losing control—that's what being under threat was like, economic slavery, obsessed with the next donor. But all that had changed. Money truly was the source, and even though she despised herself for giving in, it bought her time to be who she was and that was worth any cost. A little blood on her hands was nothing in comparison; art was everything.

Then she looked up and Bixby was there—the last person she wanted to see. It was a shock, but there was something curious in his eyes, a broken and contrite expression she had never seen before in the cocksure billionaire. It struck her deeply. "Bixby…?" she said, but just when she was about to ask him about it someone else interrupted.

"We have some papers here…" Roark barged in with an accusative, businesslike manner that lawyers have honed to perfection, and just when he was going to say "…detailing your reckless investment strategy with funds embezzled from the Met endowment," the sudden clatter of a chair slamming down on the floor and the crashing of glasses startled everyone.

They all looked up to see Devlin sprawled out entangled with an elderly woman who had been knocked over as he got caught in a wrap thrown over the back of her seat. Too reckless chasing Thierry. Afraid he'd do something stupid if he reached Endecott alone. Something irreparable.

"Devlin…?" Analetta said.

"I'm so sorry…" gently helping the woman to her feet. "Are you alright?"

At that moment, Revenia was mesmerizing the crowd from the theater two floors below. Her lithe figure poised center stage under a moon like glow against the fading tomb. What had begun as a brilliant, soaring aria, which was all anyone could hope for, had become a huge and spellbinding religious experience — as if she had rent time and space revealing an egress point to another world, to a universe of spirit. Now the gateway stood open beckoning. Each who listened hungered to leave everything behind, abandon caution and enter, so teetered on the threshold of an horizon where the slightest breath either way would push them over the edge. Eyes filled with tears of joy and longing and the incredible sensation of being alive.

Everyone in the banquet hall fell silent, all eyes were drawn to the huge flat monitors hanging near the ceiling. Emblazoned across them the final scene of Aida played out and no one was able to look away. There, radiating in fading blue shadows, dwarfed by a tomb of the Pharaohs into which she had been sealed with her condemned lover, the enigmatic French diva soared on spirit wings so wild and fine that a faint yet distinctly visible light began to glow all around her and she lifted all those who listened into a transcendence: her beautiful haunting voice permeating the entire building as if there were no walls, reaching every person as if they were the only one, speaking to each of memory as if there was no forgetting. Everyone heard her differently, experienced something personal, private whispers only they could hear. Then, in the final moments Revenia spread her arms reaching out to the far ends of the earth and to the shock and disbelief of all slowly rose into the air with the last strains of the orchestra until she was hovering twelve feet above the boards with astonished stagehands shining spotlights up on her as the tomb faded away below.

The audience was breathless. Bewitched. Enchanted. Not a sound could be heard for the longest time. So nobody noticed the first snowflakes that fell on the velvet seats in the grand theater, nor on the white linen in the banquet room. But they were real: huge, light, frozen, crystals that tumbled through the air unconcerned whether anyone believed in them or not. Moments passed before the desperate beauty of it all sunk in, then people slowly began to come around and applaud as if unsure of what else to do. From a few hands clapping the ovation rose out of every cranny in the theater, even the musicians in the orchestra pit were on their feet yelling "Bravo! Bravo!" and the flymen in their soiled T-shirts and the dressers and the stand-ins and dancers and the members of the Metropolitan Opera Club swooning en masse like huddling penguins in their white tie and tails. Suddenly the huge flakes could not be ignored. They drove people into fits of ecstasy—even though many believed that some special effects guy had been hired to lift the singer with piano wires and generate snowflakes with a machine like in the movies, their little brains whirring to land on some scientific explanation, while deep inside they knew it held a more portentous meaning and cheered recklessly in awestruck wonder.

Except for Analetta who was fleeing inside: her heart racing, eyes darting back and forth unable to decide who the executioner was—her calm demeanor masking the willingness to gnaw off her own foot to escape if it came to that. But they all just looked at one another, Devlin and Bixby and her, amidst the murmurs of the still dazzled crowd while snowflakes fell around them and stuck to their noses and eyelashes.

Devlin thought of the river. He felt the unsteady sweep of its current suddenly realizing there were no guarantees in nature. It was a lesson in survival. Hate had been burning inside since he first glimpsed the world out of balance as a boy, and then it became his mission. He had few friends, no family and a life overflowing with suspicion and hostility. He had given up everything for it, and had been cut off at the knees. Truth, he thought, was tied up somewhere with the woman who still had dreams of sunburnt youth…the woman he had left standing in the doorway. That was as close as he was ever going to get. And when Thierry turned for the go-ahead to arrest the elusive Bixby Endecott, fingering the warrant in his pocket, shaking off the strange experience he didn't understand, rekindling the animosity he felt earlier, Devlin was gone.

Roark, a jaded man, had experienced unexplained phenomena many times out on the ocean on his vintage yacht the Eidolon beyond places where humans held sway, where sometimes the horizon line is obscured by mist and cloud and imagination. So he looked into himself to get his bearings, wiped the melting flakes from his face and turned to Bixby while producing the damming evidence against Analetta from his briefcase ready to do his worst. But he was met by the face of contrition. Unexpectedly, a delicate balance within had shifted from darkness to light and the impulse to do harm was no longer there. Bixby had never really experienced want, never had a desire go unfulfilled for very long, had nothing but success his whole life, but now just shook his head at the lawyer and quietly walked away.

"Hey…you're not going anywhere!" Thierry barked maliciously at Bixby halfway to the door. "I have a warrant here…" reaching for the papers in his coat pocket.

"You talking to me?" Bixby replied from across the room suddenly confronted with the vortex of hate he had avoided until now.

Something snapped inside and Thierry whirled. All he saw was red as if blood were rushing everywhere. The winds of space were in his ears. Everything he believed in was slipping away.

He should have yelled "Stop!!" pointing his gun at Bixby Endecott's back, but he didn't. He just held his feet firmly on the ground like he was trained, bending his knees slightly and wanted to scream, "Stop you rich mutherfucker!" but instead stood trembling and quiet. Shots rang out. The sound of gunfire was the last thing anyone expected at that moment. Firing off three rounds before he had even decided what to do. Screams pierced the air. Then Thierry was holding his badge high above his head shouting, "I'm a police officer! I'm a police officer!" but it didn't help. And then there was silence. An inexplicably deathful silence as if everyone had stopped breathing. All Thierry could see was a figure lying on the ground with someone kneeling beside it, but something was wrong, something didn't compute in that thick machismo brain of his because Bixby Endecott was still across the room looking back at him in disbelief.

"My God…you've killed the singer!" someone said.

"Where did she come from…I didn't even…"

It hadn't been planned, was the last thing on her mind. But like her art, Mirella was as close as anyone could come to feral—and who could predict the wild? She had just appeared between Thierry and Bixby Endecott the moment a gun was drawn. "Out of thin air…" as a few astonished witnesses would describe it later to the homicide cops who rolled their eyes and took notes. She had struggled between shadow and light her whole life, and every time she thought she held it in her hand something convinced her she was just not good enough. So, darkness became her solace, helping mask the dark things she felt, covering her eyes, hiding from those things she refused to give in to. She lived in counterpoint to the human experience embracing powers and purposes most have long ago forgotten and no one knew what to say. Everyone agreed though it was a tempestuous act, something to do with the heart, people who didn't know her surmised, perhaps a result of her erratic, artistic nature…they murmured, nonetheless a tragedy beyond one's ability to grasp. But the romantics present knew it was an unexplainable phenomenon of a great love, too impossible in its fury, too vast for this world to hold, too powerful for her to contain. It was taking life to the limits of the possible that compelled her to sacrifice herself, but it hadn't been planned, was only an improvisation on a theme and she let the wind carry her. For a moment in time, she knew who she really was. Now the diva lay in a pool of crimson, her wild auburn hair in tangles on the floor, Bixby Endecott weeping over her as if there was no tomorrow.

Watching all this unfold in front of her much the way the shore watches sea fingers change the landscape with the ebb and flow of the tides, Analetta fell back into the tranquility she had felt earlier sensing the natural order of things had been restored. Certain now nothing could disturb the rituals that are more ancient than us all, she turned to the pale astonished faces of the middle aged donors sitting at her table as they all looked to her for some deeper insight into what had just transpired, and raised her hands blessing them as if a mystic who kept the hidden secrets of the universe at her fingertips. She was, after all, holding court—*Guardian Queen* of the opera.

Across town Devlin stood in a doorway with Veronica and just held onto her imagining the salt spray of the Chesapeake in her hair. The following morning ice began to melt on the Hudson and everyone predicted it was the end of the cold snap that had been with them for so long.

Books by Michael Jeffery Blair

The text of this book is set in Electra, an original face designed for Linotype in 1935 by William. A. Dwiggins, the eminent American artist and illustrator. He also created many other typefaces, designed over 300 book covers for his friend Alfred A. Knopf, was the first to use the term "Graphic Designer," and in 1929 was awarded a gold medal by the American Institute of Graphic Arts. Sixty-nine years later in 1998 Electra received a Certificate for Typographic Excellence in Type Design from the Type Directors Club of New York. The new font, which fell into the 'modern' family of type styles, was not based upon any traditional model and was not an attempt to revive or reconstruct any historic type. Because it avoids the extreme contrast of thick and thin elements that mark most modern faces, Electra provided a new 'texture' in book pages. Linotype's decision to hire Dwiggins marked the first time the company had ever turned to an outside designer.

MICHAEL JEFFERY BLAIR is a novelist and writer of non-fiction. He has been involved in the theater, written several stage plays and a collection of poetry entitled "Fisher In The Abyss." His novels include "Exit Point," "The Architect Of Law," "Sudden Rivers" and "The Labyrinth in Winter." His editorial work has appeared in the New York Times and other publications. As an award-winning designer and media artist, he has created communications for many of the world's great companies and is the principal and creative director of a design firm based in Los Angeles for which he has garnered dozens of national awards. His work has been published extensively in the U.S. and Europe.

Made in the USA
San Bernardino, CA
27 July 2020

75779544R00193